The Savannah Stories

Blood Lust

The Savannah Stories

Blood Lust

J.L. Lemon

ISBN-13: 978-0-9796117-7-3
ISBN-10: 0-9796117-7-6

Published 2010

Printed by Lulu.com in the United States of America

For Mom and Dad

For always being there

For my great friend Betty Bryant

Thank you for your support

And your encouragement

"You feel the last bit of breath
leaving their body.
You're looking into their eyes.
A person in that situation is God."

Ted Bundy

"Crap," Savannah mumbled, pulling up to the crime scene. What started as a good day lost its promise and appeal for two reasons. One, the call of a female body in a ravine signaled the return of a serial killer and two, Savannah caught sight of a person she hoped never to deal with. His name was Cole Jordan and he stood near the ravine with Ennis, her husband and partner.

It was a tossup which one she hated worse – the daily radiation treatments following her breast cancer surgery or dealing with Cole Jordan. She saw Ennis and Captain Josh Hunter standing near the ravine and took heart. At least desk duty was a thing of the past and she could finally return to full duty which also meant spending more time with her husband.

She took great care that morning when choosing her attire – a coral pullover with her beige suit. Bright but not too cheery. Best not to appear *too* eager to return to work. The best part: she felt good enough to return to full duty. Ennis voiced his concern and objections to the decision, saying it was too soon. "Is it too soon to throw me in the nuthouse?" she asked. "Because if I stay in these four walls any longer I'll go crazy."

Ennis turned from the ravine. The instant he saw the detective's car, he frowned. He'd be okay once he saw she was feeling good. At least she hoped he'd be okay...

Before exiting the car, she pulled her dark hair into a ponytail. Even with the slight breeze, the thick, hot air hung heavy, nearly choking a person. Since the TV cameras and reporters staked out their claims around the barricaded perimeter, she donned her suit jacket. First day back, must look professional.

Reporters possessed a peculiar knack. They could sniff out a cop within a mile of a crime scene, even if the cop wasn't in uniform and not driving a detective's car. The second she started toward the yellow crime scene tape, they converged, wanting answers.

"Detective, is this another victim of the Ravine Killer?" one called from two rows back. Reporters were like rats scurrying for the last bit of food. They used gang tactics and converged on people with no regard to safety or sanity. Since the ravine killings started they bullied anyone in law enforcement, demanding answers. When they thrust their microphones in her face, she considered that and their tone a provocation.

"I'm not clairvoyant," she replied in a nicer way than she expected. "I mean, I just got here." Instead of swatting the microphones away, she extended her arms to her sides as a silent demand for room. They barely budged.

"Detective," another called from close by. "Are there any new leads in the case?"

She angled her way through the mass, "In the words of my daddy, 'I don't know nothin'.'"

"But you're obviously working the case," a different voice accused, this one with a distinct sarcastic accent.

She stopped, located the offender and asked, "You're not from here, are you?" "Here" being the South. The all-encompassing question residents used to point out a tourist – or in her case – an asshole.

"I'm with the Boston Globe," he answered proudly.

"Let me explain this situation," Savannah slowly started toward the crime scene tape. "Being a detective is like being in high school. You're a member of the student body but that doesn't automatically mean you're going to the prom."

The Yankee's face contorted with distinct confusion. Savannah took great joy in finishing, "In other words, I haven't been asked to the dance yet. Understand?"

No, judging by his silence, it didn't quite register. It did with the local reporters and a few smiled. Despite her job, she was still "one of them" since her accent proved it. And nothing pleased a genuine Southerner more than getting over on a Yankee.

The way cleared and she ducked under the yellow tape. Before walking away, she turned to the large eager gathering, "Anyone who needs answers can refer to Detective Cole Jordan." Savannah searched him out and found him near a crime scene van. She pointed, "He's the big strappin' fella dressed in jeans. Now, if you'll excuse me, I've got work to do."

Yes, Cole Jordan was a big strappin' fella. Problem was, he knew

it and used it to his benefit. She'd heard the stories through the
grapevine. He made moves on any female within sniffing range. That,
in turn, would multiply Ennis's insecurities by the thousands. He'd get
jittery, clam up and keep a close eye on Cole if the guy even winked at
her. If history dictated, her husband, no slouch in the tall, handsome and
muscular department, would draw an imaginary line between her and
Jordan. Over the last few minutes, her great day threatened to circle the
drain. Nausea swirled in her stomach, no doubt from everything
combined – the treatment, the weather, Cole's presence and her
husband's impending jealousy.

She made her way to the ravine before Cole spotted her. She
greeted Josh Hunter, her captain, then, "Is it him again?" The general
term "him" was used lately to label the killer. Cops refused to say
"Ravine Killer" because giving him a name usually inspired more murder
and mayhem.

Hunter nodded, "The guy's getting bolder with less time between
victims."

Shooing her way through a swarm of flies, she crouched closer to
the edge of the ravine. In it lay the remains of a nude woman, her body
posed with legs apart and her wrists crossed above her head, the latter
bound with duct tape. This was the latest in a series of brutal slayings
that had plagued Atlanta. Each woman was found in a ravine but before
their deaths they were subjected to days of unspeakable pain and torture.
The killer subdued them with a Taser and carried them off to parts
unknown. He beat them, raped them then sliced off their breasts and
mutilated their genitals. In a final act of cruelty, he somehow managed

to keep them alive during their horrific ordeal only to drain their blood while they were, according to the medical examiner, conscious to endure the agony of it.

Beneath the woman's right collarbone were slashes spelling out an unmistakable "7". The smooth skin scored so expertly with a scalpel displayed a flamboyant flair as though he took the utmost pride in the killing. The number taunted police, each one counting the number of women he'd killed without being caught. Now there were seven victims and if it tracked with the previous cases, no one saw anything, knew anything or said anything.

She swatted at one fly in particular then hitched her thumb at Cole, "Do me a favor. Go find a turd to sit on." It didn't of course. She figured Cole's personality repelled even insects.

Visually roaming over the remains of the nude victim cured her desire for any nourishment past Tums. The terror etched into the young woman's face tore at Savannah's heart.

Two gruesome circles stared up at Savannah like two red eyes crying bloody tears. The places where the woman's breasts should be now made the detective flinch and she crossed her arms over her own, hoping to rid herself of the sudden ache.

Savannah winced again as her vision roamed the woman's beaten body. Long thin tears in the skin indicated a ruthless beating from something similar to a cane or tree limb. She drew back from the swollen bluish-black wounds. Judging from the brutality on the woman's front side, she dreaded seeing the victim's back. Nausea churned now. Savannah's father R.J., a mean, abusive drunk, used a hickory limb to discipline his children. The scars on her backside reminded her, even in a remote way, what the woman suffered. Memories of the pain entrenched the sickness so deep she debated whether she could hold it down.

The heat and radiation treatment helped intensify the queasiness. She prayed she could fight it down, especially in front of the public, but it didn't feel promising. The old familiar sensation began percolating deep in her gut and the nausea crawled up her throat. It was coming, she knew, and immediately began walking away.

"Where are you going?" Hunter asked.

She lifted a hand to ward off further questions. He'd find out soon enough. At the moment she focused on not hurling inside the crime scene. She checked Ennis's progress with interviewing witnesses. His back was turned to her. Cole was busy talking up a reporter which only spurred the nausea. What they didn't need was the press making a circus out of the case. He'd done enough from what she'd seen. Flashing his pearly whites, giving women reporters preference over the men and generally strutting in front of the cameras while assuring he was doing everything possible to catch the killer.

The urge to puke caught her unexpectedly and she heaved in front of two forensics techs. She bent further, giving in to the second wave while trying to hide her embarrassment. She'd never hear the end of it and the barrage started almost instantly.

"God sakes, Prince, lose your lunch somewhere else," one griped. "You're trashing the scene."

She fought back another wave while covertly flipping him the bird. The satisfaction was short lived when a solid smack between her shoulders produced a coughing fit so violent, she barely heard the male voice behind her, "There you go, love. That oughta help."

Tabling the urge to spit the remains of her once tasty breakfast onto the black Redwing boots beside her, she aimed for the half-digested heap instead.

Savannah slowly stood, "It should help if you're trying to kill me."

A handkerchief entered her vision as he answered, "Detective Cole Jordan, Zone 3. You need a drink of water, babe? That looked kinda painful."

She'd come from her treatment thirty minutes earlier when her captain called to summon her to the scene. That, accompanied by her late breakfast, the stifling heat, sticky humidity and butchered body, spelled disaster. *But* she wasn't about to tell Cole Jordan that.

She pushed his hand away, annoyance quickly replacing the sickness, "It wasn't exactly pleasant and stop calling me cutesy names." Her vision roamed the detective. Up close, she could see how a female might fall for him. He stood tall with defined muscle underneath his gray button down shirt. It tucked neatly into a pair of snug jeans emphasizing his narrow waist and strong legs. Looking up, she noticed his short dark hair as the sun angled off red highlights but it was his blue eyes that stopped her. Small wrinkles played at the corners as he smiled then winked. Yes, any red-blooded female might swoon over Detective Cole Jordan. But not Savannah. She had her own stud and a very jealous one at that.

Cole pocketed his handkerchief and extended his hand, "Okay, what is your name? Wait, lemme guess." His brow knitted, "Who was that actress from way back? Great dancer, long hair, really gorgeous broad. Hayward? No, Hayworth. Rita Hayworth. You look a lot like her."

She guessed it was supposed to be a compliment. But basically being called a "broad" didn't set well with her. Besides, his flattery – and intent – fell on deaf ears. Rita Hayworth was beautiful. Savannah's sister Georgia bore a striking resemblance to her because their mother Charlene had too. Savannah inherited a few traits from their mother but nothing compared to Georgia. For such a smooth talker, Cole gave her a turbulent feeling – right in her palm that itched to slap him. Instead, she reached forward, shook his hand with a firmness that barely concealed her exasperation, "Savannah Prince."

He hooked his thumbs in his front pockets, "Like the singer, huh?"

Gee, I haven't heard that one before. Moron. When she didn't respond, he let it slide, "Just kidding. Actually, I've actually heard a lot about you."

"Likewise," she said and left it at that.

Unaware or ignoring her insult, he forged on, "I think we'll get along fine together on this case –"

"What?" The perversity of the thought hit her. Working with a womanizer was some bizarre purgatory, she just knew it. "Working together? I thought *you'd* want the case since you're Zone 3. You've demanded it with the others," she reminded.

Cole's expression indicated he would demand it if he could, "See?

Ennis followed Cole's pointing finger to the heap of half-digested breakfast. His eyes bugged and she scrambled to settle him down, "The heat, Ennis. It was the *heat*," she clearly enunciated and hoped he caught the hint.

If he did, he didn't show it, "You came back to work too early, didn't you?"

From the corner of her eye, she watched Cole's attention bounce from her to Ennis and back to her. She stepped closer to Ennis, trying to convey her message. Despite the half dozen inches or so that separated her five nine from his height, she tried for her best imposing frown, "I'm fine." *Don't mother me right now, not on the job, not in front of Cole.* Now she had to whip up an excuse for Jordan, "I caught a bug earlier this week and I'm still wearing it off. Now, I'm going back to the victim. Anyone joining me?"

As she walked away, she heard Ennis sigh, "Women."

"Tell me about it, brother," Cole chimed in.

According to Josh Hunter, Cole Jordan ran the investigation in Zone 3. She worried that he took the murders as seriously as he did her throwing up and worked the case as efficiently as he dressed.

True, the weather was a killer. The heat set in and the humidity drove it to the bone. She and Ennis hated summertime because they still had to dress professionally in the heat. She'd worn her beige suit and Ennis wore a gray suit for work. Cole, on the other hand, looked more like a spectator than a cop in his casual shirt and jeans.

Ennis was beside her now. "He's attractive, I guess," he skewered Cole with a seething glare, "in a prehistoric sort of way."

"I hadn't noticed."

"Really?" he sounded surprised.

Savannah pressed a hand to her stomach to curb the ache in her belly. She took the opportunity to survey her husband's expression. He truly felt threatened, judging by his disdainful scowl at their new partner. "For heaven's sake, Ennis, I just puked in front of the man. I don't care what he looks like."

"He likes you."

"Well, I love another man. When you find *him* again, let me know." The sun bearing down and the stress of the situation caused her breast to itch. She'd developed a rash thanks to the radiation and heat from the hot Atlanta days. She'd decided there was no good time to get breast cancer but getting radiation during a heat wave was an entirely different nightmare unto itself. She rolled her shoulder in an attempt to relieve it. It didn't work. "Stand in front of me," she told Ennis.

"Why?"

"Just do it, please."

Following orders, Ennis turned his back to her and halfway stumbled backwards as she tugged him toward her. "What are you doing back there?" he wanted to know.

"My breast is itching." She gently clawed at it as covertly as possible, all while looking around for prying eyes.

Ennis whispered, "Stop scratching it. You'll make it worse."

"Hey, get this rash on your balls and see how well you function without a clandestine scratch now and again. Be still."

"Savannah," he sing-songed. "You get caught and the whole

city'll see you tonight on the news."

She cursed under her breath but she stopped anyway. He was right. But at least she got a little joy and relief from the brief rubbing. While she relished the results, she noticed his dark hair curling at his collar, "You need a haircut."

He perched his hands on his hips, "Seriously. You're making the six o'clock news with this stunt and you're worried about my hair?"

She took advantage of his wingspan and rubbed a little harder, "Just saying. When you get a chance." She blew out a breath, "That's better. Let's go."

They made their way back to Josh Hunter. Hunter was in his mid-forties and a large man in stature. His physique showed signs of regular workouts and the only sign of his age were his graying temples. Over the years, the gray sifted in with the pressures of the job. Since graduating from the academy, she'd been under his command in some form so after so long they became not only colleagues but friends.

In the time she'd raced off to embarrass herself, he'd received a phone call – or made one – but judging by his expression, it was the former. Like Ennis, he was slow to anger which offset her quick one but he was a fair boss. Today, the phone conversation pushed his limits but in Josh Hunter fashion, he kept his voice even, his obvious irritation to a minimum.

With the cell phone shouldered to his ear, he jotted a note while listening to the other party. "Yes, sir. I've got two detectives on scene plus Jordan from Zone 3. Ennis Rutherford and Savannah Prince... Yes, sir. Full time. I understand... I'll call with updates. Goodbye,

Chief." He clicked off with a healthy sigh and a mumbled expletive. Glancing up, he asked Savannah. "You okay?"

She nodded. Their boss was understanding, thank God, and reluctantly approved her return to full duty. He stressed the instant she felt overwhelmed physically to tell him so he could reassign her to desk duty. Desk duty, to Savannah, equaled yet another purgatory. No one wanted it and tried everything from lying to threats to avoid it.

"Did you come back too soon?" Her boss, without intending to, parroted Ennis. Their concern didn't bother her too much yet but if it continued, it would. Cole Jordan insinuated himself closer to her now, no doubt intent on hearing her answer. "Just a little warm," she assured, fanning herself. "What was that call from the chief?"

Josh answered, "He wants more detectives on the case." Then he waved her over. She did so, noticing the men exchanging curious glances. Hunter lowered his voice, "I know it's your first day back from desk duty so if you foresee a problem, tell me now. I can put Mathis on it and update the chief."

And how would that look? He'd already informed the chief she was on the case so bowing out only validated the chief's personal opinion – and other higher ups – that she wasn't fit for police work. "I'm good as long as Jordan keeps his ego in check."

"Good luck." They broke their impromptu huddle which opened Ennis to move in.

"Boss, can I have a word with you?" he asked.

Savannah gave him a visual warning that it better not involve sending her back to desk duty. Her brain went soft with the job. She wanted her damn job back and he should respect her decision.

As Savannah began surveying the gathering crowd of men, women and reporters, she noticed Cole doing the same thing. She also picked up on her husband's plea not just for her reassignment to a desk job but to kick her from the case.

To his credit, Josh shook his head, reminding Ennis it was her decision. Savannah turned to Ennis, caught his eye. Accompanied with a withering glare, she mouthed, "Stop."

An elbow nudged her, "One of these people gotta be the 911 caller. No one owned up to it when we got here. That kinda kicks my instincts up a notch, you know?"

So did anything with estrogen, she wanted to say but thought better of it. Cole's question drew her attention away from throttling Ennis. For now. She returned to scanning the crowd, "And sometimes the caller is the killer. See any candidates?"

A cameraman across the road swiveled his camera over a reporter's shoulder to zoom in on the action. Behind the cameraman she spied a man about twenty-three staring intently at the scene.

Cole saw him too, "How about G.I. Joe, front row, two females from the left? The one having a smoke?"

As Cole noted, the man's green camouflage attire and burred off hair indicated past or current military service. He took a long drag off his cigarette then ground it into the asphalt with his boot heel.

They made their way across the crime scene toward the young man. The reporters huddled closer upon seeing the two detectives approaching. They, including the Yankee, showed tact by not mentioning her puking fiasco…

Savannah and Cole wound their way through the crowd. When the man noticed them heading toward him, he turned and quickly snaked his way out of the masses. Savannah pushed past four more reporters, "Sir, we just want to ask you a few questions."

The man continued shoving people, growling for them to move. Once free from the throng of people, he took off in a dead run, his boots pounding the pavement at an impressive pace. Savannah sighed, "Just what I don't need today. A workout." She was a fast runner but her episode of sickness drained the energy from her. Plus, the radiation depleted her more each day. She wished the treatments were over but she still had a week to go.

Ennis sprinted behind her, "Let me catch him. You've had a hard day."

Savannah decided to let him, "I'll back you up."

The young man had good speed and a decent head start. If the guy was the killer, he'd do anything to get away, even kill cops.

She channeled all her energy into her legs, willing them to speed up. Ennis tossed a warning over his shoulder, "Relax, I'll get him."

The guy shot a narrow glance back at the pursuing cops. Savannah kept a steady pace despite her husband's caution.

A twelve foot chain-link fence running alongside them created a perfect getaway. She feared he'd veer to the right and climb it. Men could climb like cats whereas she climbed like a St. Bernard.

Ennis and Cole ran at the same pace with Ennis a little faster. Cole shouted over his shoulder at her, "Prince, stand down. We've got him."

His order grated on her. Who was *he* to tell her to stand down? Not her superior, that was for sure. If it weren't for her fatigue, she'd have shown that egotistical jerk who could run...

Instead, she leaned onto her knees to catch her breath. God, she was exhausted.

Ennis grabbed at young man's shirt just as Cole tackled him. Jordan and the suspect rolled across the pavement until Cole straddled the man's back. Savannah wiped the perspiration from her face as her right hand drew her .38 from its holster.

The young man still wrestled with Cole until catching view of the gun pointed at him. Ennis, seeing the suspect well under control, tossed a concerned glance at her. She nodded she was okay.

Cole snapped cuffs on the young man, rolled him to his back. "Allow me to introduce ourselves." He pointed to each in kind, "We are Detectives Prince, Rutherford and Jordan. I believe you've really pissed off Detective Prince. Dude, you should know women enjoy the chase but don't like to do the chasing."

Great. Philosophy from the men's bathroom. Cole probably had the phrase bronzed in the bedroom of his bachelor pad – next to the lava lamp and copious issues of Playboy and Hustler magazines.

He winked at Savannah, "As a thank you, why don't you take me out for a drink later? I promise I'll let you take advantage of me."

Her eyes popped so wide, she expected they'd fall out and roll down the sidewalk any moment. The audacity of the man.

Adding to the comical event was Ennis, once laboring to catch his breath, now swallowed audibly. He looked to Savannah then to Cole then back to his wife again. Fix it, he seemed to say. Please fix it before I do.

But all she could muster was, "What?"

Cole shrugged, "I deserve a reward, right? A thank you for nailing this guy for you."

She holstered her gun, snorted at his silly notion, "Since I'm already involved with a man, it'd be rather rude to two-time him, don't you think?"

Cole glanced at her left hand, "You ain't married to him. You're fair game. In my opinion, the guy's an idiot for not making your 'involvement' permanent. I'll bet that blush is prettier when you're naked. Bet it goes from there," he pointed to her face then aimed lower at her waist, "to there. Maybe further."

Somehow she envisioned Ennis strangling Cole Jordan on the spot. From his expression, she wasn't too far off. He looked close to exploding. She tried to remedy that, "And that's why God gave us imaginations. So we can picture things we'll never see."

2

Like the Mississippi River, Cole Jordan's effects traveled far and wide. When the three detectives marched into the station, heads turned and the whispers began. Unaware of it – or ignoring it – Cole greeted everyone the way immature college buddies might, with high fives and an all too gregarious "how's it goin'?"

The desk sergeant who normally bantered back and forth with Savannah, settled for a shake of his head as they passed by. She gave a half-shrug. Other officers, she noticed, tried to look extra busy while others suddenly took off for corners or disappeared behind doors. Cops had a look they gave each other. It signified a certain distrust, a warning to the other cop to beware, this one's a tricky little bastard. Usually it emerged regarding a suspect. Today, it emerged regarding the Zone 3 detective.

Yes, Cole Jordan's path of narcissism and sexism spread like the plague all across town. She and Ennis veered off to find a forensics tech holding a background check on their military marathon runner. Savannah pointed Cole in the direction of the interview rooms. She and Ennis agreed that Cole should interview the witness/suspect because –

and the intent went without words – they needed a moment's peace.

Bookish Grady Portman, forensics tech extraordinaire, had the background check in his hand before they walked in. His sixth sense raised her brow but not as much as his statement, "So y'all got stuck with Jordan the Jinx."

Savannah heard various nicknames for Jordan – most of them x-rated – but both she and Ennis turned to each other. "Jinx?" they said in unison.

Grady nodded, "According to a friend, any case he works never gets solved. I mean, look at how long he's had this one."

True. Cole spent way too much time posturing for reporters and hitting on women to solve anything. She took the offered background report, "Maybe we can break that jinx for him. We have a few solved cases behind us."

Grady crossed himself, "Just don't let the jinx wear off on you."

They stepped into the hallway, Savannah making sure to close Grady's door behind her. "That was weird," she whispered as her phone rang. It was Georgia. "'I don't know nothin'? You were on TV. What were you thinking?"

"I was thinking 'how can I get these vultures to pick on someone else'. Besides Daddy's always said that, especially when Mama got onto him."

"I remember. So were you asked to the dance?"

Savannah rolled her eyes, "They used that sound bite too? Great. Well, as a matter of fact, I was asked to the dance so the press should get used to my colorful quips."

"Savannah, no one gets used to those. By the way, what were you doing with Ennis? You were standing behind him and he appeared rather miffed." Without giving Savannah time to answer, Georgia accused, "You were scratching that rash, weren't you?"

"I wasn't scratching," Savannah lied and swatted Ennis's hand away. He scraped his fingers together in a "shame on you" motion. She mouthed "shut up" to him.

"You'll make it worse, Savannah," Georgia continued. "Keep your hands off it."

"I was not scratching." At least she prayed the cameras didn't get a clear view of her. If one of the other channels did, she was toast. Georgia would never let it rest.

"I'd ask if you went back to work too soon –"

"Do it at your own risk," Savannah warned.

Georgia paused then, "Ennis leaning on you pretty hard about it?"

"You are the queen of understatement."

The older sister sighed, "Okay. Just take care of yourself. And don't scratch."

"Yes, Mama, I hear you. I gotta go. Love you." She signed off and clipped the phone back to her belt.

"Make a habit of lying and you'll go to hell, you know that, right?" Ennis asked.

"Make a habit of nagging me and I'll turn up in the nuthouse first. What does the background say?"

Ennis wondered if the TV station caught Savannah's scratch in full glory. He could only imagine what it looked like in high definition quality. Then he imagined her mortification at watching the late news expecting to see cameras aimed at the ravine and seeing them aimed at her instead.

Georgia's call started off as bona fide lecture and ebbed to a quieter tone he couldn't hear. Savannah backed her off with the "do it at your own risk" comment. Ennis never doubted she meant that one. He still stung from her lashing at the scene.

Savannah waited for him to open the folder containing Jason Gerhart's background and military record. Before inciting a riot with her, he flipped it open. Incredibly, it rivaled Mr. Clean. He left the army a month prior, and had two commendations to show for it. At the scene he told them he'd been walking to a convenience store for some beer when he noticed something in the ravine. That's when he called police.

Savannah and Ennis made their way to the observation room to behold the Zone 3 Wonder in action. They peered through the one-way mirror, listening to the limp interview Jordan gave the guy. It grated on Ennis and it didn't take a rocket scientist to see it really lathered Savannah's temper. Cole soft-balled his questions, led the man with others and treated the interview more like a nuisance than a necessity. Ennis wondered how Jordan climbed the department ladder – with the help of a relative or by intimidating or sleeping with certain people. 'Cause he sure wasn't any kind of a detective.

Savannah seemed to read his thoughts, "You as impressed as I am?"

"More, probably."

They both looked through the glass at the man dressed in army fatigues. He sat calmly as Cole asked questions. Why did he run, Cole inquired. For one thing, Gerhart replied, he feared the cops would label him the killer. Why was he afraid of that? Because he'd touched her, checked for a pulse – any sign of life. He got blood on him, washed it off at the nearby convenience store.

"Did you see anyone around the body before you found her?" Cole asked.

"I saw someone drive away from the ravine. Looked like a guy."

"Can you describe him?"

"Didn't get a good look at him."

"Was he expecting a different answer?" Savannah sneered at Cole from behind the mirror.

Oblivious, Jordan continued, "We have descriptions of him being about six feet, short dark hair, maybe early to mid-thirties."

Savannah turned to Ennis, "Since when?"

He shrugged, "We read the reports. No one's seen the killer until today. Obviously we can't count him either, vague as he is."

"Why do you think Cole's leading him? Does he have someone in mind?"

Ennis crossed his arms, "Maybe he's trying to shed his nickname Jinx." He'd never seen a cop so lax in his questioning. Not to mention so pointed in directing the conversation away from the interviewee's whereabouts and potential motives.

Savannah shrugged, "Or acquire a new nickname like

'screwball'."

Cole came out of the room shaking his head, "At least we know he's not the killer."

"You call that an interview?" Savannah asked, arms crossed like her husband's. "I'd get more information from my six year-old niece. You barely questioned him, you haven't checked his alibi and you did a nice job of pointing fingers at a six-foot, dark-haired, thirty-five year-old. Have anyone in mind for that profile?"

Cole's smile was a tense one that he made little effort hiding, "All due respect, Detective Prince, I've been working this case longer than you. Yes, I have a guy in mind but getting evidence against him is harder than sculpting Mount Rushmore. It's long, arduous and I'll probably be dead when he's finally caught."

"You ever think of sharing this info with us before now?" Ennis wanted to know.

"Subject never came up."

"What's his name?" Savannah asked.

"Duke Shelton."

Ennis was lost, "Who?"

By Savannah's lifted brow, she recognized the name. He let her fill him in. Shelton was listed as one of the richest people in Atlanta. She didn't personally know Duke Shelton but heard rumors the man was odd. He liked his women and the pictures of him she'd seen seemed harmless enough. The man was a knockout – and please don't get jealous, Ennis, it was just an observation.

Duke was tall, she recalled from a magazine article and had short dark hair. He was voted one of the city's best dressed because he always tweaked his attire to the nines. Since he was filthy rich, it didn't help his image of being eccentric. But a serial killer? She questioned Cole's logic. Duke Shelton would have to be a moron to lure the women then kill them. Then again, she reasoned, the rich had their money to bail them out of legal problems if any should arise. Duke didn't frequent the Atlanta nightlife and to her recollection, he didn't the day life either. But to accuse the man of murder was ridiculous, at least until further investigation. "Why do you think it's Shelton?" She asked.

"For one, did you see the beating she took? It sure wasn't with a fist."

"What do you think made the wounds?"

"A cane or a riding crop, hell I don't know."

Savannah put hands to hips, "Hickory limbs do the same thing and any old Joe can yank one off a nearby tree."

Ennis's jaw dropped and snapped shut just as quick. If she wasn't careful she'd expose herself to unwanted questions from a man she detested. He'd ask how she knew that information – from personal experience perhaps? Then the two would go round for round and Ennis wasn't sure who'd win. Trying to help out, he agreed, "She's right, Jordan. Doesn't mean Shelton's the one."

Cole's eyes narrowed at them, "Fine. You keep telling yourselves that. If the whole city ends up missing all its hickory limbs, I'll believe you. Until then, I'm focusing on Shelton."

She rolled her eyes, "I assume you've done background on Shelton."

His lip curled, "I'm not stupid, Prince. Yeah, I've done a background. He's been arrested before. Take a guess what for."

Savannah didn't. She crossed her arms again, waiting. Ennis suspected she didn't trust herself with her language.

Cole shrugged, "Okay then. Sexual battery and sexual assault. Happy?"

"Back off, Jordan," Ennis warned. He situated himself between Cole and Savannah. The bastard was asking for his own beating and Ennis was more than eager to oblige.

"By the way, he not only loves his women, but he dominates them too."

"What?" They both asked in unison. Ennis sounded more incredulous than she. She probably suspected Ennis hadn't seen much of the alternative lifestyle being from the Bible Belt, at least not until moving to good old Atlanta. She'd have been right.

"He's a dominant," Cole continued, giving them a funny look. "You know, kinky sex, whips, chains, stuff like that. Heard of it? He's a rich bastard getting away with murder."

"You believe this because he participates in the alternative lifestyle?" she asked.

"What's the matter? Did I step on your toes? Do you and your guy dress in leather and spank each other when you're naughty?"

Ennis wanted to strangle him. Savannah put Cole in his place, "Actually, it sounds more like *your* style."

"I'll take care of him," Ennis offered. Actually it was the only civil thing he could think to say.

Savannah put a hand to his chest, "I got it."

Ennis sensed a storm building in her and he wasn't exactly calm either. Besides making overt moves on his wife, Cole Jordan treated Savannah like a brainless idiot instead of a veteran detective. His seedy reputation followed him throughout the area, evidently, and Ennis would knock Cole's jaw loose if he made another wrong move on Savannah — no matter what she said.

"Mind if I have a go at this guy, since I was present for the arrest?" Savannah inquired.

Ennis gritted his teeth. She'd helped in the arrest but to tone down the sexist cop, she'd asked for permission to question the guy just to stroke Cole's ego. She'd just validated Jordan's intent to downplay her competence.

Sure enough, Cole's chest broadened and he waved her in, "Be my guest but he won't know anything."

She slanted a quick look at Ennis, rolled her eyes and as she walked out, said, "Well, it'll keep the little lady busy a while."

Ennis crossed his arms because his fists were too attracted to Cole's grinning mug. He watched his wife enter the room with the suspect. The guy, tracing designs on the tabletop with his finger, stopped, and sat back in his seat, "I told the other cop everything."

"Then tell it to me," she glanced back at the mirror. "I have plenty of time on my hands. Why were you at the scene?"

"Hey," Cole's voice sounded too close, "she ever try to sweeten that temper of hers?"

Ennis intended to ignore the comment but his tongue overrode that plan, "She's pushy at times because she's gotta be, considering who she has to work with sometimes."

"Who's the guy she's dating? Is he a cop? I hope not because he ain't getting it very often, if her mood is any indication."

Ennis turned to him, "That's none of your business."

Cole backed off a step. *Good,* Ennis thought. *Serves you right.* But then Jordan hitched his thumb at her, "Bet she's a wildcat in bed when she does put out. The guy probably has to pin her down just to get some."

Ennis forgot all about the interview taking place in the other room. While Savannah chatted with the suspect, Ennis freed his fists and stalked toward Cole Jordan, "You're out of line, Jordan. Shut up."

Cole lifted his hands as a sign of surrender, "*Sor-ry.* Didn't realize you were so close to your partner."

Ennis turned back to the interview room. Savannah was saying, "Account for last night starting at ten."

Gerhart leaned back, his tone challenging her, "The other cop didn't ask that."

She turned back to the mirror, "The other cop should have. Where were you?"

Jason replied he stayed at a bar until two, went home alone then got up at six. He ate breakfast, showered and watched a Clint Eastwood movie on HBO. He headed out about nine-thirty or so for the beer. "I don't have a car so I walk or take a bus. Today I walked." He looked at the door, "Where's the other cop?"

"Busy. Can anyone confirm your whereabouts from two until

nine-thirty?"

His complexion darkened, "Well, the asshole next door might tell you I'm a loud drunk. I think I made enough noise when I came in. Not like he does with his dumbass trombone, blaring it at eight this morning. I pounded on the wall, told him to tone it down so I could watch my show."

She moved on, "So you go out for beer and see a guy leave the ravine and get into a car?"

He nodded, "That's what it looked like to me. He was parked on the road next to the ravine."

"Are you sure there wasn't something you could pinpoint about him? Any kind of description at all?"

The man sighed, "Not really. What that other cop said, it coulda matched. Six feet, dark hair, something like that."

"Slight build or muscular?"

He stopped as if he hadn't thought about it until now. "Muscular, like he works out. And he was wearing dark clothes – hey, it *did* match his hair. Short, dark hair."

"And the car he drove. Can you describe it? Anything will help. The kind, shape, color..."

"Yeah," he seemed surprised he remembered anything. "The guy drove a," he closed his eyes to think, "dark blue or black something or other. It was small to mid-size, not too new, probably coupla years old."

"Could you identify it if you saw a picture of it?"

"Maybe. I could try."

Savannah rose from the chair, "I'll be back with some books for you to look through. I'd like you to work with a sketch artist to see if you can give us an idea of what the guy looked like."

"I didn't get a good look at him. In fact, that other cop's description sounded right from what I did see."

Savannah shifted a frown at the mirror, "Won't hurt to try. His description matches a large portion of the city's population anyway."

"Wow," Cole said. "She's covering her bases. Too bad she's barking up the wrong tree."

"She got further than you. At least we know we're not looking for a beanpole with long hair." His frustration mounted and Ennis wiped a hand down his face. "Just let her work. She's brighter than you give her credit for."

"I get it, I really do. She's beautiful, spirited and you work together. Just tell me one thing. *Do* you have to pin her down?"

Ennis rounded on him, his hand fisting in Cole's shirt. The door opened and Savannah stopped in mid-stride upon seeing the two, "What's going on?"

Ennis fired a glare at Cole and shoved him away, "Nothing I can't fix later. I noticed you got some info Columbo here couldn't. You setting Gerhart up with the cars or artist first?"

Wary now, Savannah volleyed her vision between the two, "The car. If he can recognize the make and model, we can have something to go on. Plus, it'll give us time to verify his alibi and see if he's as loud a drunk as he claims."

"I'll do it," Cole offered. "That is, if you trust me."

She ignored the comment, looked from Cole to Ennis, "Are you sure everything's okay in here?"

"Peachy," Ennis turned back to Cole who nodded.

She accepted the answer then, "I'm hitting the restroom if you aren't gearing up for Round Two."

Ennis waved her off. She probably needed relief from her rash. Since the radiation treatments began, she'd developed a rash that got worse from heat or stress. Thanks to Cole, he suspected, she was quite miserable right about now. "Got what you need?" he asked, referring to her anti-itch cream.

She nodded, glanced past him to Cole. Her brow lifted. Ennis sighed, shook his head.

Cole pushed past him, "I gotta make a call."

Ennis followed him out, "Not gonna follow my partner and make sure she doesn't end up in a broom closet?"

3

The paper dubbed them the "Ravine Killings". Savannah hated for the press to name anything short of their pets. They always glorified the perverted assholes that enjoyed ending people's lives. By giving him a name, they validated his efforts, inspiring him to continue killing.

Over the past months Savannah basically heard the same about the killer that the public had. The city was angry over the lack of police action on the case and the media continually played the victim's stories and outraged families' statements. As well as airing plenty of questions why police sat on their derrieres instead of getting serious about their dying citizens. Now *their* precinct could join the chorus, Savannah groused, and it wouldn't take long to hear it especially since the newest victim, lawyer Anna Wright, was found in a remote area with large estates nearby. Being newbies to the case hadn't protected her or Ennis from the media or public ire. Her phone rang incessantly all afternoon with reporters asking questions she had no answers to. And the few answers she had they didn't want to hear. After so many calls, she and Ennis gathered the files and headed home to review them in peace.

Once home, they slapped a couple of turkey sandwiches together and changed clothes. She opted for a tank top and shorts and Ennis went with only a pair of jeans. Good food and comfortable clothes. Savannah sighed. Finally – life was good.

Jason Gerhart turned out to be correct. According to his neighbor, the sum total of yelling and swearing Gerhart did while fumbling his front door open was enough to blister the Pope's ears. Savannah figured as much but, she reminded Cole, it paid to be thorough on their leads. Something she figured he'd slacked on ever since being assigned the case.

Papers and crime scene photos littered the coffee table and sofa, most of the files open to the women's backgrounds, with Savannah and Ennis hoping for a connecting thread among them. Their birthdates, their landlords, their doctor's names, anything.

The victims were all single, dark-haired and ranged from early twenties to mid-thirties. Cole assumed the killer – aka Duke Shelton – knew the women personally but reading the files, Savannah couldn't quite make that leap. The victims never had a real thread of commonality that she looked for, at least when she wanted to pin the name "suspect" on someone.

Skimming through each file, Savannah noted the women held powerful positions whether in title or salary. Among the victims were a medical administrator at a local hospital, an attorney, bank executive, a surgeon, and a CFO of a large Atlanta business. It may have been a coincidence but, "Two of the women worked at a hospital."

"Same hospital?"

She nodded, "You reckon the others are connected somehow?

Maybe they were patients there not long ago?"

"Could be. Let's get Eager Beaver on that tomorrow. He needs another activity to keep busy."

"Yes, I'm tired of being his new hobby." Pushing her glasses back on her nose, she returned to the file to keep her mind off Cole. Every moment she wasted on him was a moment lost finding the killer – and ultimately ditching the Zone 3 cop.

The phone records were marked with yellow highlighter across certain numbers. A note paper-clipped to the page had the same number written on it, along with a name – Duke Shelton. She assumed that this was Cole's little gift to sell Duke's guilt to her and Ennis. She held the note for Ennis to see, "Cole's hiding Easter eggs in the files for us. Seems as though the first victim called Shelton several times."

"Nothin' incriminating about that."

"Tell me something I don't know."

"I really look forward to jumping your bones when you feel like it."

Savannah smirked, peered over her glasses, "I said something I don't know."

"Sorry," he winked. "Just thought I'd remind you."

His wink sent a thrill through her. His incredible patience during the treatments amazed her. Before the diagnosis his appetite for sex verged on voracious. Since he saw the fatigue wearing on her and her weight loss, concern replaced it. With the treatments soon coming to an end, he'd begun dropping hints and making an occasional suggestive move. And despite her sickness that morning, she felt pretty decent since they'd arrived home. Perusing his body, his defined muscles and hairy chest and abdomen, she began feeling more than decent. She began feeling frisky.

She thumbed through the victim's credit card charges. The pages looked bathed in yellow highlighter. Cole went nuts with the pen, underscoring several charges to Duke Shelton. Of course the woman hadn't shown any self-restraint either. Savannah's jaw dropped, "Dear God, you wouldn't believe how much she spent with Duke Shelton."

"I don't want to either. I can't understand a person paying another to beat them."

She kept perusing the file until Ennis blew out a breath. She looked up.

"According to her financials, Anna Wright spent over twenty thousand dollars with him," he said. He thumbed through a few other files, "Did they *all* know Shelton?"

During that time, she'd flipped through hers too and she'd discovered the same connection he had – the very one she'd berated Cole for, "Every one of them." She hated to admit it but, "Maybe Cole has a point. Maybe we should check Shelton out more. He does appear to have a strong influence in these women's lives. A few of them complained that he stalked them which is amazing since I've heard he rarely leaves his house."

"If he's that rich, he can hire someone…"

True. The longer she perused the files, the more validity she put into Jordan's paranoia. Shelton had a strong link to each one of the victims. He was worth targeting – for now.

Her phone rang and she flinched. It was probably Cole ready to dog her about the files. After checking Caller ID, she sat the phone in her lap. It wasn't Cole.

Ennis gave her a quizzical look, turned his attention to the phone.

"It's Daddy," she replied. She watched the clock for a full minute before

checking her voicemail. R.J. sounded agitated as usual, "This is your father, not that you care. Only time I ever hear your voice is on this damn machine. Accordin' to my buddies, you look too dang thin. Gain some weight. And for your information, I never said 'I don't know nothin'. If you spent more time with me, you'd know that too." The message mercifully ended. Savannah erased it, sighing, "My father is very concise. He managed to insult, criticize and chew me out all in less than ten seconds." She relayed R.J.'s rant then concluded, "And I look 'too dang thin' to Daddy's friends."

Ennis huffed, "He actually has friends?"

"It's code for drinking companions."

"They probably thought you were triplets as drunk as they were."

"Daddy would've killed himself if he had three of me and Mama would've been in the asylum." She placed the phone on the table, "I thought it was Jordan calling. Glad it wasn't."

Ennis sat the file aside, "What's his problem anyway?"

Re-gearing herself to Cole Jordan's behavior gave her a bad taste so she threw back a healthy swallow of Yoo-Hoo. "Are you talking about his presumptuous nature or some other bizarre chauvinist affliction he exhibits?"

Ennis nearly laughed, "Someone took a diplomacy class between this afternoon and this evening. You were slapping all sorts of names on him earlier."

"That's because he's like the hangover that won't go away. I'm married – though I didn't explain that since I hate being called to Josh's office to explain my screw-ups. I told Cole I was involved with someone and to leave me alone."

Her husband rose from his chair, the muscles on his arms bulging as he stood, "He's still after you?"

Savannah rolled her eyes. Ennis, being well built and intimidating himself, could beat Cole unconscious without breaking a sweat. But there was one thing he really excelled at – jealousy. He ruffled at the slightest wink or suggestive smile another male tossed her way. What he seemed to forget: "It takes two, Ennis, and he's one participant short."

He stalked to the kitchen for a beer, "I shoulda finished him off this afternoon. I'm talking to Josh about getting you reassigned."

"Don't. I'm not letting that sexist pig drive me off. He's under the impression female detectives can't..." her frustration mounted from the whole day and the fact she failed to find the right word. "Can't *detect* and I need replacing. Kinda like the way baseball managers throw in a designated hitter 'cause the pitcher can't hit."

She heard the smile in his voice, "The Braves are National League. No designated hitter."

"I know that, Ennis. I was making a point. If given a chance, I'm good at what I do *and* I'm not a quitter."

"Babe, you're still having treatments. Anyone who knows you will not think you're a quitter."

"I will. Ennis, I'm staying on this case, even if I have to claw through Cole Jordan to do it."

Ennis returned with a fresh, cold Yoo-Hoo for her, bending to kiss her while he sat it on the side table. Savannah smiled, met him halfway, her hand stroking his bare chest then hooked her fingers in the front of his jeans.

He smiled against her lips, "You makin' a play on me?"

"Trying." She pecked his lips again. Her hand settled on his zipper, "You interested?"

According to the growing arousal beneath the jeans, yes, he was very interested. "You minx," he gathered the file from her lap, set it aside then grabbed her reaching hand.

He pulled her to her feet and kissed her. She melted into his embrace and as the kiss deepened, she sighed, clinging to his shoulders. She loved the softness of his skin combined with hardness of muscle. So strong yet so gentle.

Then her cell phone rang. She tried parting from the kiss only for Ennis to draw her closer, preventing it. She didn't want to end the passionate kiss, far from it, but if the phone didn't stop ringing, she'd stomp it into oblivion. It was ruining their first night of romance in weeks and she just wanted it to shut up.

"Leave it," Ennis mumbled against her lips then engaged her mouth again.

She tried. God knew she tried. The day's events and Cole's intrusion stirred the need and desire to connect with Ennis in every way possible. She'd missed making love. She missed the quiet intimacy afterward, curling against his warmth, his arms enfolding her. But that phone was driving her nuts...

With its continued incessant ringing, Savannah tried pulling away once more but Ennis tightened one arm around her, picked up her phone with the other and scooted it out of reach.

The phone finally stopped. "See?" he said. "It's all good." His hand glided down her thigh, caressing her bare leg. The tender touch drew her knee to his waist and he smiled, "Hop on for a ride?"

It seemed like forever since they exchanged such words. The weariness of the job and treatments allowed energy for only so much. With her own beaming smile, she "hopped" into his embrace, wrapping her legs around his hips, "Let's get sinful."

Then the phone rang again. Sighing, she gave it a baleful glare, "Let me answer it right quick. Whoever it is can't take a hint."

Ennis allowed her to slide from his arms, "Just remember, we're otherwise occupied so don't commit to anything past saying adios."

She yanked the phone from the table, flipped it open, "What?" She instantly regretted biting the person's head off. What if it was Josh? Bitching out their captain didn't show a shred of intelligence, even if it was an accident. By quitting time, Captain Hunter teetered on the edge of violence, she'd noticed. Her request to remove them from the case stoked that fire until he stood face to face with her, reminding her of the option he offered earlier, "You said you could handle it, so unless it concerns your health, I'm assuming you can."

It wasn't the case she couldn't handle, she wanted to say. It was Cole Jordan. The voice on the phone belonged to just that irritant. She wanted to pull her hair out, "What is it now, Cole?" She watched Ennis shove a hand through his hair then flinch as his hand went to his crotch to readjust himself.

"Looked at those files yet?" Cole asked.

"Just finished."

"You still think I'm blowing smoke about Shelton?"

She refused to let Jordan under her skin again that day. He was a pest, like a flea or nit that just needed the right treatment to ward him off. She was much more interested in getting laid, "I agree he's a suspect. Let's discuss this tomorrow."

A sly grin spread across her husband's features, giving her pause. Cole kept yammering about the case as Ennis stalked toward her. Savannah restrained her temper with Cole. After all, she had to work with him, like it or not. Closing her eyes to calm down, she added a deep breath for good measure. With it, the scent of Ennis's aftershave wafted past.

Soft lips pressed against the pulse in her neck, nuzzled beneath her ear. He wanted her to wind up the conversation and decided she needed inspiration to do it.

When she opened her eyes, Ennis had bent to one knee. He grabbed the tank top and lifted, exposing her breasts.

His warm hand on her bare back pressed her closer. Wet heat enveloped her right breast, as he sucked the nipple deep in his mouth. Savannah arched into him, biting her bottom lip to trap a moan. She was so close to losing control with Ennis and losing her temper with Cole, she fought to retain both her wits and common decency. But her body betrayed her, begging her to just hang up, throw the thing or stuff it in the couch until later.

Her fingers threaded Ennis's hair, holding him to her. "I've really got to go," she said to Cole, hoping her voice sounded firm, not rough with need.

She descended into the delightful sensations Ennis created with his teeth and tongue. The struggle to retain her decorum unraveled at an alarming rate, "Cole, unless you're paying overtime, I'm waiting until morning for this." She clicked off, finally able to surrender to the feelings and sensations rolling through her.

Savannah scarcely retained enough sense to turn her phone off, preventing further interruption. She dropped it on the couch, glad to be free of it. Then to her disappointment, Ennis pulled away.

"For heaven's sake, why'd you stop?" she pleaded.

His brow bobbed, "I've been meaning to get in some overtime myself." He swept her into his arms and headed straight for the bedroom.

Ennis rested beside her in bed, his body nestled to hers as she slept. He smoothed her hair back, tucked it behind her ear to expose her nape. Ennis had suffered from a powerful surge of lust but not so powerful he overlooked the changes in his wife. The rash still hung on strong and he'd stayed away from her left breast for that reason. She had enough hell keeping the itching under control without him aggravating it.

He'd never say it out loud but R.J.'s "friends" were right. She'd lost considerable weight since the radiation treatments began. Since he'd known her, Savannah maintained a steady weight of one thirty-five and at five nine, she was skinny enough. Now, her clothes fit looser and she took up a notch or two in her belt. When he saw her naked the week before and *really* looked at her as she weighed herself, he was mortified at the number. One hundred twenty pounds. That fact reinforced itself when he picked her up for their romp. Her collarbones protruded a bit more than he liked, and his hands, used to feeling a little padding beneath her breasts, now found the curves and hardness of ribs.

Fatigue plagued her since the treatments began and only rooted deeper the longer they lasted. Some days, she barely found strength to go to work so when her friskiness kicked in, Ennis planned to take full advantage of it. He'd missed making love to her. He missed the way she felt in his arms, the sounds she made when she climaxed and the way the sinews and tendons in her neck came to the surface of her silky skin.

He pressed a kiss to her soft, warm nape. For some reason the image of Cole Jordan entered his mind. He was more than a jinx. He was a plague. The bastard wanted Savannah. It took a fool not to see it. The oversexed, chauvinistic asshole did everything but climb onto her at the crime scene. When she rebuffed him, Jordan leaned on Ennis for answers. Ennis tried to keep his temper under control. The treatments and rash caused enough hardship for her. She didn't need the stress of some Lothario muscling in.

He prayed Cole didn't drive her nuts. He also prayed working her first homicide since the surgery didn't deplete her energy past the point of recovery. Investigating a single homicide wore on a detective anyway but a serial case – Ennis dreaded the long hours and work but he'd spend most of his time worrying about his wife.

Ennis kissed her again, his hand following the line of her back. Savannah stirred but remained asleep. They'd made love twice that night. Sheer need and lust drove him the first time and he feared he'd cheated her, despite her assurances otherwise. Her climax seemed too subdued to him. He rationalized it was the fatigue from the treatments. The second time around told him he'd done everything completely right. After their lovemaking, she lay in his arms until finally drifting to sleep. Ennis wanted to keep her in his arms forever but he'd damn sure keep Cole Jordan's arms – and everything else belonging to the Jinx – away from her.

4

The next morning she arrived early at the hospital and, of course, ended up waiting a sum total of forty minutes just to receive a treatment that would make her miserable the rest of the day.

She spent her time wisely – reliving the night before. Their first lovemaking session proved wild and fast – so fast Ennis apologized for his haste. Savannah realized the last several weeks weren't just hard on her. Ennis watched her suffer the fatigue, rash and other indignities like puking. He'd seen her lose weight and refuse to eat. She suffered insomnia and/or slept too much, depending on how she felt. He'd been with her body and spirit the whole way. So when he jumped her with the ferocity of an alley cat, she hadn't complained, at least out loud. He'd picked up on the fact he sprinted to the finish line without her. But the second round of lovemaking turned out to be a slow, blissful ride to heights not seen in months.

After her treatment finished, Savannah dressed and gathered her contented thoughts, determined to keep them at the ready in case Cole Jordan began pecking at her again. She arrived to work shortly after ten o'clock. She went to her office and the first thing she saw was a note on her desk. It simply read, "See me. J.H."

"What did I do now?" she wondered aloud, knowing that being summoned to Hunter's office never meant good news, especially with her.

"Hey," Ennis leaned in the door, his vision resting on her left breast. "How'd it go?"

It went fine, she said, and ceremoniously checked off another day on a special calendar her niece Lindsey drew for her. A few more days and Savannah would be free of the daily treatments, and hopefully the fatigue and frustrating rash that accompanied them.

Concern crossed his handsome face, "You too tired from last night?"

She smiled. "That's a tired I can handle."

His face relaxed and he winked. She hated changing the subject but she needed a heads up in case her boss intended an ambush for some unforeseen mistake she'd made. She lifted Josh's note as though it dripped slime, "Have any idea why I've been summoned to the principle's office?"

His brow dipped and he shrugged. He was about to speak when Cole Jordan poked his head in the door, "Where've you been? I've been looking for you all morning."

Savannah shifted her incredulity to Ennis then back to Cole, "Sorry, but I had things to do, my liege."

Cole barely flinched from the brusque reply, "The captain wants to see you."

"So it's a public hanging," she assumed. "Everyone received their invitation?"

The comment flew past their cross-town colleague. Savannah decided to get the inquisition over with. Before leaving work yesterday, she'd asked for a background check on Duke Shelton. She figured somehow the move backfired on her. Things like that always did and with Cole hanging over her shoulder at every turn, he probably lit the fuse.

All three marched to Josh's office. The captain waved them in, "I didn't expect the whole gang for this but," he centered on Savannah, "we now know your sister watches the news."

It was Savannah's turn to be confused, "And this is a problem?" Then it occurred to her. Georgia called to plead Savannah off the case. Savannah figured it went as far as a two ton brick.

Josh leaned against his desk, probably wondering what he'd done to deserve the Prince sisters. The heel of his hand returned to an already reddened spot on his temple. The headache undoubtedly the result of a long, in-depth conversation with a pissed off woman.

Josh rubbed his temple harder, "She's breathing fire at me for giving you this case and not so politely asked me to remove you from it. I've never been cursed at so stylishly."

"Writers have a way with words." She watched him angle himself into his chair.   He sighed, "I explained you're one of my best detectives, she said find my best *male* detective instead. She said I'm putting you in danger because you fit the victim profile. I argued another twenty minutes while your sister proceeded to inform me, one, that she'd love to see the case from my point of view but she couldn't get her head that far up her ass and two, she'd try being nicer if I'd try being smarter. I'm exhausted and the work day isn't even four hours old."

Despite herself, Savannah smiled. Once hell-bent on something, Georgia bulled onward until she prevailed. This time she met her match in Josh. The two friends argued before so it wasn't exactly news. He'd helped her with police procedure on her books while she occasionally baby-sat his kids. The friends quarreled liked family, Savannah noticed, and this time wasn't any different. "She'll get over it," she assured. "Don't worry."

He blinked a few times and rubbed his eyes, "Question is, will I get over this damn headache she gave me? You feel like you can handle this case, right?"

He sounded way more confident than she felt. Surveying the other men around her, Ennis assumed she'd bow out, even hoping she would. Cole stared at her in a manner suggesting an infant could handle it better. That alone helped her decide, "I'm fine. Just about over that bug I caught." From the corner of her eye, she saw Ennis's shoulders slump in defeat. Abandoning him to the likes of Cole seemed more than cruel to her. Better two on one, she thought. Plus, she'd be around to separate the two roosters if they tangled again.

"Great," Josh tossed a folder across his desk, "because Shelton's background check came in while I was getting reamed out. Take a look at it after we're done. I'd like you to do the interview with him."

She nearly swallowed her tongue, "What?" She pointed accusingly at Cole, "But he's the one who's convinced Shelton's guilty. Let him do the interview."

Cole began to speak but Josh cut him off, "Savannah, I want you to do it."

Her hands clamped to her hips, "I liked this meeting much better when I thought it was a public hanging. That noose I'll stick my neck in. Not this one. Please, not *this* one…"

Hunter rubbed his head, "Ennis, talk to her before I have a stroke." Reaching in his coat pocket he retrieved an aspirin bottle, popped two into his mouth and chewed.

The detectives cringed at the sight. Hunter stopped mid-chew to explain, "Thanks to you and Georgia, I'm forced to keep at least two bottles on hand. My ulcer is your fault." After swallowing, he tried once more, "Savannah, there's a reason I chose you. Cole suggested you go, and after hearing him out, I agree."

Her eyes narrowed at Cole, "I can't wait to hear this one. By the way, was my partner in the room while you wagered my day away?"

"No, he wasn't," Ennis sounded as sour as she was.

She snatched the file from Josh's desk, "Well, I'd better get busy in case y'all think of something else for me to do." Savannah marched to her office with Ennis and Cole in tow.

Cole sidled up beside her, "I can give you a few pointers about him…"

"By all means, since you volunteered me for the mission. But let me pack my own parachute. I don't trust you that much." She sat at her desk, slid her glasses on. "Why won't you interview him yourself? What is he, manic, phobic, does he smell weird or is he a DLR?" DLR stood for Doesn't Look Right. A little like how she saw Cole.

When Cole started to reply, she lifted one hand, signaling him to stop. He did.

"It was a rhetorical question, Cole," she explained. She knew why he wouldn't interview Duke. First, it took work. Second, she had a feeling Jordan was better at delegating work than actually performing it. "Since you're so knowledgeable about him, does that mean you follow him like a crazed stalker?"

"It's called surveillance, Prince. Yeah, I hang out around his property on occasion."

The background had more than Shelton's arrest record in it. It had significantly detailed personal information as well, the type not found in a typical background report and she was curious where it came from. From the corner of her vision she saw Cole raise his hand.

"What?" she asked.

"That extra stuff is my work. I hope you don't mind but I mentioned your name to get it from some of my connections."

"Why, no, I don't mind. You seem to have commandeered my life completely anyway."

"I only did it because they balked when I said I needed it. I told them you were the lead detective on this case. Made all the difference."

"Glad I could help."

"I was gonna drop that file off at your place last night but noticed you had company." He turned to Ennis, "That your Dodge Ram? Looked like it."

His innuendo grated on her but thoroughly riled Ennis. Partners often spent long, late hours on a case, on and off the clock. Clearly this only occurred in places Cole Jordan claimed employment but doled out *actual* labor to other detectives while he partied.

She diffused Cole's question with logic, "We were reviewing all those files you sent with us, remember?"

Cole winked, "At midnight?"

She sensed Ennis about to pounce and put a hand to his arm, "And you really thought I'd answer my door at midnight?"

Cole shrugged, the corners of his mouth lifting slightly as if she asked him to keep a secret, "You know me."

She forced a smile, "I sure do." If Cole signed up for a pissing match with Ennis, her husband would win any category. Perhaps Cole felt inadequate because of Ennis's massive Dodge since he drove a car straight out of Barnum and Bailey. And if he sniffed around her for another notch on his belt, she'd have to tell him she preferred real men to what he had to offer.

To discourage further ridiculous banter, she finished, "Now let me read." She saw that Duke Shelton lived in a Tuscan inspired mansion in north Atlanta. He designed and financed it with his own money. Her jaw dropped at the sheer size of the estate. Twelve thousand square feet? It practically had its own zip code. "Is there a reason why he needs that much space?"

Curious, Ennis rounded her desk to glance over her shoulder. He whistled long and low.

Cole answered, "Yeah. To house his harem. His family was rich and he got the lion's share. He used it to build the house, his business and keep all those women. Now he's financing his murder spree."

She chose to overlook the last statement while continuing her education on Duke Shelton. "The oldest of five children. Well, that explains his control issues." She peered over her glasses at their colleague, "What this doesn't give me is motive for why he'd kill."

After a half-shrug, Cole said, "Control issues, you said it yourself –"

"Nearly every man I've met has those and they aren't serial killers."

His frustration escalated, "You ever get a gut feeling or is that something else men have that you don't?"

"Jordan," Ennis warned, his hands curling into fists.

Cole patted the air, "I'm sorry, but she's not paying attention. Shelton is the one."

Savannah watched the men square off and decided to peruse the rest of the file, "So he's a black belt in martial arts. Comes in handy if I ever need to subdue him. I'll just use my .38. Let's see him Kung Fu his ass out of that." She flipped the folder closed, removed her glasses. "Cole, I'm paying attention but going into his house knowing his favorite color and shoe size doesn't help me. What does," she lifted the police background check, "is this. He's been in trouble before."

"And got off without a slap on the wrist," Cole growled.

She nodded her agreement, "Let me interview him, see what he says, how he acts. I think I do a fair job of it or my boss would've demoted me to janitor before now."

"Be sure to ask about canes, riding crops and anything that might make those marks," Cole reminded.

She rose from her seat, debating whether to give him a slap or the finger. She wasn't a fool but he treated her like one. She pulled her gun from a desk drawer, stared at it, considered her options. Prison didn't sound all that great. Neither did the trial leading up to it. Only people who dealt with Cole Jordan understood how she felt and there was no way the prosecution would consider a jury of all cops. Avoid a situation, her brain suggested. Just go. Savannah slid the gun into her holster, "I'd best leave before traffic picks up."

"Where do you think you're going?" Cole wanted to know.

She pivoted on her heel, "I aim to interview this guy because you offered me up as a sacrifice."

He rolled his eyes, "Prince, you don't walk up to his front door and sweet talk your way in. You gotta call for an appointment."

She sat down, opened the file and dialed the number listed. "I hope you're wrong about him," she told Cole. "I don't like being bait – Hello?"

"Master Duke Shelton's residence," a male English accent greeted.

"This is Detective Savannah Prince with the Atlanta Police. I understand I need to make an appointment to see Mr. Shelton."

"And this is your first appointment with the master?"

"It would be, yes. I need to speak with him today."

"I'll check his schedule and see if he has an opening. Your private number please."

"You can use the department number." Did the whole world assume she was two sandwiches short of a picnic? How smart would that be, giving a potential killer her private number?

"What is your private number, madam? The master requires it."

Great. The master requires it. Rolling her eyes, she rattled off her cell number while questioning her common sense. Evidently there was no threat of Mensa accepting her application.

The man proceeded in the same light English accent, "You understand there's no guarantee he's available today. He stays very busy."

"Tell him I'm with the police."

The voice developed a condescending quality, "Madam, despite what you may think, the master sees ladies of many professions, not just yours. You will wait your turn."

What started as an innocent request for an interview with the eccentric turned so backward, she struggled to find balance again – or at least the emergency brake, "Wait. You think I want to see him for lessons of some sort?"

Cole snickered and Ennis looked like he swallowed a bug. He frantically shook his head so fast she feared it might spin off his neck. As for Cole, Savannah shot a white-hot glare at him.

"That's normally why ladies call the master. They feel awkward at the first appointment and the master works hard to ease their concerns so it necessitates extra time."

For heaven's sake... "Then allow me to ease *your* concern." The nausea flooded back and brought a little friend called a headache. She rubbed her forehead much like her boss had earlier, "I want an official interview with him for a case I'm investigating. That's all."

"No training?"

"No training." *I'd rather be boiled in oil...* She tried to keep her voice calm instead of sounding like he offered her a dead mouse.

Ennis, on the verge of a conniption, repeated the word "training" as if she threatened to get a sex change operation. Then he squared off with Cole who still found humor in the situation.

Englishman's tone didn't waver, "I'll get back with you shortly. Goodbye, Detective."

The line went dead, the only sound in the room was Cole's chuckling. Curbing the urge to bark the words "shut up", Savannah casually placed the receiver in its cradle, "He's calling me back." In anticipation of the call, she sat her cell phone on the desk for quick access.

"Who wants lunch?" Cole asked.

Over the course of the past minutes, Ennis's complexion developed a green tinge. Compared to her anger, his sickness rated about as intense.

Cole's smile evaporated, "Don't look like either of you are hungry."

Savannah replied, "Picked up on that, did you?" Served him right, she thought. He put her in this jackpot, he should suffer too.

Twenty minutes passed. Just long enough for her to get good and angry, "It doesn't take this long to get approved or denied for a damn credit card. What's he doing anyway?"

Cole and Ennis took up residence in the two chairs in front of her desk. Ennis's Kermit the Frog hue faded and his natural color slowly crept in again. In that time, Cole found another way to annoy them. He repeatedly flipped a quarter, caught it then flipped it again. "Chances are he's running a background on you."

Savannah did a mental eye roll. Now she knew why Cole passed on the interview. He had skeletons in his closet. Well, who didn't, she wanted to say. Only hers was now in the hands of a potential killer. She frowned at Cole, hoping he caught the significance of it.

Amused at her expression, Cole said, "He's a picky bastard. He's not letting anyone inside the sacred walls without checking 'em out first."

"And you know this how?" She leaned onto her desk, "Oh, and if he's the killer, you've just set me up for death. Thanks."

Cole flipped his quarter, caught it in midair, "According to you, I'm jumping the gun so you oughta be fine. And I've studied this bastard long enough I know how he operates his business. He wants everything he can get on you, personal, professional, financial, everything."

A glut of expletives flooded her brain, all filtering down to her tongue. Wisely, she clamped her lips tight, swallowed them whole like bad medicine.

Her phone rang and she answered it without breaking eye contact with Cole. It was the English accent again, still rigid and semi-rude, "The master formally declined at first then unexpectedly changed his mind. You will be here at two o'clock, alone and unarmed."

"I'm a police officer. My gun comes with me."

Cole smirked and Savannah slid her hand in her pocket before flipping him the bird. In the meantime, Englishman pronounced, "The master has stated his terms. Take them or leave them, madam."

"Take it or leave it?" Did he really just tell a cop to stick it? Her brain tried to wrap itself around that concept. She didn't give a shit who Shelton was, she was bringing her gun. "I'll be there." Savannah heard the click in her ear before Cole chuckled. She snapped the phone closed, debating about slamming it on the desk or chucking it at him.

5

Interviewing Duke Shelton wasn't her cup of tea. His lifestyle promoted abuse and belittlement of women, not to mention a supposed voluntary loss of control for the female. Oh, she hated doing this. She really hated men who took advantage of women.

Passing a grove of old oaks, she counted the estates leading to his address. An expanse of large, mature trees along with a tall iron and brick fence framed the Shelton estate on each side, nestling the enormous twelve thousand square foot mansion in secrecy of oaks, maples and pines.

The Ford Taurus turned the corner. The fence finally crowned into a pair of large twelve foot gates and an intercom for visitors announcing their arrival. What the rich didn't do to keep the "commoners" out never surprised her. Leaning out the window to press the intercom button, she noticed a security camera. Savannah stopped short of sneering into the lens. Instead she displayed her badge.

A second later a woman's voice rattled through the tin box, "Yes?"

"Detective Prince, Atlanta Police. I called earlier for an

interview." She made sure to clear up that bit first. No training, no whips, no chains. Just an interview and she'd be in charge of it, thank you very much.

The gates began to swing open, "Welcome, Detective. Please drive through."

Savannah started through. In the rearview mirror, she caught sight of two other security cameras pointed directly at the trunk to catch people arriving and when they left. A shiver crawled up her spine. Now she asked herself what she'd been volunteered for. Background checks, appointments, intercoms and security cameras. Paranoia was paranoia but such drastic measures usually were used by people who were hiding something or were up to no good. And the rich criminal was worst of all.

The Taurus followed the road sheltered by overhanging trees. Flecks of sunlight occasionally flitted across the windshield like fireflies. Again, she saw more cameras, these pointed at the driver's and passenger's sides. At last the mansion came into view. The sheer size rivaled the Governor's mansion. As the file stated, the house was built in Tuscan style long before it became popular. The house, highlighted by red and brown tile roof, sat perfectly against the lush green background of oak trees. The three story mansion had windows everywhere. Then Savannah thought about women held against their will somewhere in the giant house, sedated so no one could hear their screams. It was a perfect place for such activity – remote and private. She shook the image from her mind, condemning Cole's suspicious attitude.

Slowing to a stop, she parked the car in the circle drive near the sidewalk. Shrubs lined the stone walk leading to a giant wooden door with wrought iron accents. She spied another camera, this one above the door pointed directly at the visitor.

Before having a chance to knock, the door swung open and a tall, slim brunette motioned for her to enter, "Detective, please come in."

She thanked her, taking note of the woman's sheer orange gown. From shoulders to ankles the transparent fabric concealed nothing, making Savannah's throat constrict. The female inside Savannah shrieked for her to turn tail and run. The cop inside, however, wanted answers to the murders. If Shelton was the key, she wanted to turn him and good.

Stepping in the Shelton house was like stepping into the Louvre. Paintings and sculptures adorned the huge entry. Expensive and classy, she thought. She'd expected a dungeon-like atmosphere. She got elegance instead. The mystique surrounding Duke Shelton puzzled her now. What exactly was he? A classy perv? A misunderstood hermit?

A touch on her shoulders startled her. She wheeled to face a svelte, blond Amazon that, unlike the brunette, did not smile. And unlike the brunette, she wore a completely concealing beige pantsuit, "May I take your jacket, Detective?"

The deeper, nearly manly voice startled her as well. She shook her head, "I'm fine, thanks."

"As you wish," she stepped to Savannah's front, reinforcing the fact she miniaturized the detective's five nine frame. Savannah tilted her head upward to make eye contact. The woman's blue eyes revealed only one emotion – animosity, "Master Shelton requires all visitors remove their shoes before leaving this area."

Savannah stared down the broad-shouldered Amazon while removing both loafers. The woman's large hands extended and tamping down her inner reservations, Savannah handed over the shoes. From another doorway a second woman, this one a brunette with hair flowing past her waist appeared with a metal detector. Waving the wand across Savannah's torso and waist, she jumped slightly when it beeped. Her vision rose to Savannah's, "May I tend to your weapon, Detective?"

"No, you may not," she answered firmly. "Mr. Shelton knew I was a police officer before I arrived. The shoes are one thing, the gun is another."

Concern wrinkled the girl's pretty features, "But Master Shelton requires –"

"The Atlanta Police Department requires me to carry a weapon and I will." *So there.* Another woman appeared now, this one as attractive as the others only she had long, wavy red hair. Savannah guessed her age to be around mid-thirties. Her gait indicated a certain amount of influence in the house. Her attire consisted of a flowing auburn dress to match her hair and a pair of high heels that narrowed to pinpoints. A pleasant smile curved her lips and she touched the brunette's arm, her voice soft and rich, "I'll handle this, Aurora."

Savannah's irritated scowl stayed concrete. Who were these women swarming her like bees? Red retained her bright, congenial smile, "I apologize, Detective Prince. Master Shelton's girls only desire to please him in any way possible. He requires the removal of shoes and weapons of all visitors, if the visitor has a weapon, of course. And I believe you were instructed to leave your weapon behind."

"Badge and gun. They come as a set like socks." She pointed behind her, "And shoes."

Contrite now, Red's mouth tilted, "That is Master Shelton's rule. If you wish to see him, you will be unarmed. Weapons cause Master Shelton a great deal of anxiety. We keep your belongings locked in a vault until you're ready to leave then they are returned. I'm sure if you temporarily part with your weapon, you will find Master Shelton more than happy to answer your questions."

Josh would have my ass _and_ my badge if he knew I surrendered my weapon. Seeing no other way, she turned toward the door, "I'll lock it in my car's vault to save you the trouble."

The Amazon blocked her exit, leaving Savannah staring into two formidable breasts. From behind, the redhead calmly stated, "It's no trouble, really."

The detective slowly rotated on her stocking toes. If this interview took place, obviously it would be under Shelton's rules. He certainly hired gutsy women and Josh made it clear he wanted Duke Shelton's story on record. "Gun only?" She inquired.

"Yes, ma'am," was the ever pleasant reply.

The .38 had been her safety net for years and some clod with an ego trip insisted she hand it over. But she needed answers so the gun withdrew from her belt, holster and all. Still smiling, Red transferred the weapon to the brunette's hands. She then swept the metal detector over again. It beeped and Savannah showed her the shield. The detector remained silent after that point.

Savannah's hands clamped to her hips, "Is a strip search required as well?"

Red sounded genuinely amused, "Not yet, Detective. I realize this is quite an invasion of your privacy but we do strive to keep our employer happy just as you do yours." She waved Savannah to the living room doorway, "This way please."

A feeling of being followed caused her to glance over her shoulder. The Amazon followed close behind. Were they afraid she'd lift something – or try to escape somehow? Being boxed in brought her claustrophobia to the surface and a small thread of panic began winding through her gut. *Deep breath,* she told herself. *I can handle this bizarre situation. I can handle Duke Shelton. He's just a man.*

Red guided her to a spacious living room, filled with priceless and ornate decorations and paintings. Sculptures of women adorned antique tables along the walls. The twelve foot walls intimidated a visitor within seconds although they were covered in beautiful paintings and drawings. Chairs were scarce as there were only three in the room, a rust colored recliner and two smaller recliners, the latter sat together with an end table between them. The large rust recliner sat opposite them with its own end table, obviously situated for the head of household, Duke Shelton.

Besides the antique tables with their nude sculptures and the sparse furniture, the large room seemed surprisingly empty. Only a large oriental rug covered the middle of the floor. Red motioned to one of the smaller recliners, "Please be seated. Master Shelton will be with you momentarily."

Thanking Red, she eased into the comfortable chair. The Amazon stood guard at the door until two other women appeared in another doorway. Then, in military precision, she swiveled and strode from the room.

Only a minute passed when Savannah saw one woman bow her head, greeting, "Master Shelton."

Savannah squirmed. It was not only officially weird but unnerving to see women so subservient – and not resisting the normal urge *not* to be. She switched to the other woman who repeated the same greeting.

Duke Shelton entered the room as a king admiring his kingdom. His chin lifted as he passed the girls and when he made eye contact with Savannah, his handsome face softened and he threw a predatory smile her way.

According to her background check, Duke was thirty-three, six feet and two whole inches. What the background hadn't mentioned were chilling ice blue eyes and dark, wavy hair just long enough to curl at his collar. He looked like a normal, everyday guy probably getting ready for a round of golf. His royal blue polo shirt molded perfectly to the curves of his chest and his khakis fit snugly on his hips. Did dominants dress this way? Because if they did, in her years on the job she obviously arrested the dummies that *thought* they were into that lifestyle.

Duke approached then extended his hand, "Duke Shelton and you're Detective Savannah Prince. You've made quite a name for yourself over the past five years."

She was lost, "Excuse me?" Actually she wondered which names he'd heard. Since being on the job, a cop kind of accumulated certain reputations. Hers was mostly as a no-nonsense hard-ass.

"Well, you were promoted to detective after solving the Brewster murder five years ago. All in all, you're very successful at your job and have the commendations to prove it." Each word fell from his lips reverently, as though her abilities rated up there with Sherlock Holmes.

Hearing her accomplishments rattled off by a stranger not connected to the department flattered her but also made her uneasy. Without showing the latter, she shook his hand, noticing his grasp felt firm and nearly restrictive, "Well, Mr. Shelton, it seems as though you know me better than I know you."

The predatory glint appeared again, making her squirm *again*, especially as he brought her hand to his lips and kissed, "Oh, Detective, I know about you alright. You've been snooping around about me so turnabout's fair play I'd think."

She wondered how he found out about the background check. The obvious reason was he had a contact inside the department. The thought didn't promote warm and fuzzy feelings. It set her on edge.

"May I call you Savannah?" he inquired.

"You may call me Detective Prince."

Duke situated himself directly across from her, snuggling into the thick cushions of his easy chair, "Detective it is. You're wondering why I had my people investigate you and the reason is less sinister than you might think. I doubt you allow just any stranger in your home. You prefer to know that person before they enter your residence. Well, I like to know the person *very* well before opening my door to them. And from a scant," he glanced at his watch, "two hours I've learned your name is Savannah Charlene Prince, Charlene also being your mother's name and that you are related to the Prince family of Augusta, renowned for their apple and pecan orchards. Also in my search I found you attended Cross Creek High School in Augusta where your grades were mediocre. Where you *did* excel was in the sport of golf. You won Georgia Junior Champion twice and graduated high school with three state championships to your name." He paused just long enough for the information to sink in, "When you joined the police academy, you were the best shot in a graduating class of twenty-three men and nine women. You, my dear, would be a formidable foe. As for your personal life, you are married though," he winked, "it's a big secret since you married your partner Ennis Daniel Rutherford. I would broach the subject of your health but I consider myself a gentleman. I will only go so far as to inquire if you're feeling better now."

I could use a very stiff drink and probably several refills. But she promised Ennis she'd abstain. Plus, if she drank on duty, suspension was in her near future, with dismissal not far behind. She'd just have to endure this blatant invasion of her privacy sober. His last statement basically knocked her cold. Her breast cancer, not to mention her marriage should have been practically impossible to uncover yet Duke stated it as common knowledge. If he wanted her off guard, he succeeded. She merely nodded in response.

Duke smiled at her disbelief, "Give me two more hours and I'll know your favorite flower and what you had for breakfast." He winked, "Well, maybe not the latter but you get the idea. Point is, I wanted to determine your mindset about my lifestyle."

"Pardon me?" The question was simple, plus it was the only

thing her overwhelmed mind produced besides "You son of a bitch."

"You shouldn't play coy, dear. It's not your style. If any other officer or detective walked in my house, it would thoroughly scandalize them at my lifestyle."

"You're sure I'm not? That business in the entry wasn't pleasant."

"True. But you handled it with an aplomb no other officer would have." He stated proudly, "I rather enjoyed watching you spar with Angelique and the girls."

She looked at the two women standing guard. With their vision trained straight ahead like scantily clad military recruits, they acted as though they heard nothing. Duke continued, "I live an alternative lifestyle, Detective. In this town, with the police and public, it makes me a pariah. This is why I live in seclusion. You do not approve of my lifestyle but I trust you are professional enough to overlook it."

"I'm here to do a job, not judge, Mr. Shelton."

"I prefer Master Shelton."

"I prefer *Mister* Shelton. I have a few questions about..."

"You are also the sister of author Georgia Prince, who incidentally included my lifestyle in a recent book."

"A most unflattering portrayal of your lifestyle, I might add."

He ignored her statement, "I have all her books. The girls love them and read them but only after I have read them, of course."

Savannah had no reaction. It was common knowledge that she and Georgia were sisters and Georgia's success wasn't exactly a secret. "She'll be glad to know you enjoy her writing."

Duke chuckled, "She knows. I met Georgia years ago. Lovely, lovely woman. Very intelligent and creative in many ways."

Now this caught her attention. He met Georgia? Why didn't she ever mention it? The only reason would be if Georgia's meeting went as well as Savannah's entrance had. Talking about her sister with him increased Savannah's uneasiness. He spoke as though he knew Georgia personally. She tried to retain her stoic manner, "She is a talented writer."

Duke held her gaze, "She's talented at more than writing."

"Mr. Shelton, you obviously want to tell me something so please do so."

"Tell me how you truly feel about my lifestyle and I'll tell you."

She cursed under her breath. He wasn't talking about Georgia or answering her questions until she admitted the truth. And how did she phrase it without sounding like a sanctimonious conservative freak and alienating him? "I don't approve but I've seen worse now what about my sister?"

He leaned back with a contented sigh. He retrieved a cigar, snipped off the end with a silver guillotine, then struck a match. Lighting the cigar, he retained solid eye contact with her, the flame's reflection dancing in his blue eyes, "She presents herself as such an angel but I know the truth. She can actually be fairly wicked if it serves her."

The description stung Savannah like salt in an open wound. Imagining her sister even meeting this asshole made her shiver.

He lazily drew on the cigar, "What was she, twenty-two, twenty-four? She came to me for insight into my world. Research for a book she said. I explained I'd show her, not tell her but she'd have to show up every day for at least a month."

Savannah accessed her memory. Being sixteen at the time, she remembered there *had* been a time when Georgia was unreachable during the day and sometimes at night to the point the entire family wondered where she was. The times Savannah spoke to her, Georgia told her she was grieving their grandfather who passed away earlier that year. She added that she was also tired of their father preaching at her to get married or get a real job. A sudden memory popped into Savannah's mind of Georgia weeping on the phone, "I've found someone but neither Mama or Daddy will approve. He's a very charming, thoughtful man."

Savannah shivered at the man perhaps being Duke Shelton. Georgia was right, however. The quickest way to give their parents a stroke was to announce she was living with a dominant. They'd have no clue what it meant but once they learned, she'd have been written out of their lives, especially R.J.'s. Even learning about their relationship now, Savannah questioned her sister's mental stability back then. She now glanced at Shelton in a different way. What had attracted her sister to this man? A man that forced women into submission. "A charming, thoughtful man," Georgia said. Charming, maybe, but thoughtful? He seemed far more controlling and selfish than her sister's impression.

Duke saw the wheels in her mind cranking and ultimately seizing up, "I'm sure she never mentioned me. But I was so very fond of Beauty…"

Savannah curbed a chuckle. He'd called Georgia "Beauty" by mistake. He really *did* have too many women to contend with, "You mean Georgia?"

"No, I mean Beauty. That is my pet name for her. I wanted that woman like my next breath. But," he shrugged.

"What happened? She get tired of being bossed around?"

He frowned, a stream of smoke jetted from his lips, "I'm not at liberty to divulge that information. If Beauty chooses to disclose it, that's her decision. I did no physical harm to her so please stop looking at me as though I did." The frown eased and his tone gentled, "Tell her to drop by sometime. I'd like to have a drink with her."

She sensed his longing for Georgia and it made her edgy. After so many years, some of the pain should have subsided – but in Duke's case it seemed to focus his sights more on the lost prize. Georgia left him and Savannah prayed it was due to her senses finally returning. She knew the next stop on her schedule that day but she needed to approach Georgia alone, without Dane in the house.

Hoping to align Duke to the present day, she mentioned Dane, "Then maybe you can meet her fiancé." True, the title was premature since Dane had yet to offer a formal proposal but Shelton need not know.

But somehow he did, "Aren't you the eager one. Dane Rutherford, isn't it? According to my sources, the fellow hasn't popped the question quite yet." He sat back, amused, "Two brothers marrying two sisters. Interesting. I'd still like to see her whether she's 'nearly' engaged or not. You know, it amazes me. Such diverse personalities, you and Beauty."

Savannah chose not to further his blatant attempt to change the subject but he carried on anyway, "You're stubborn and outgoing, she's reserved and quiet."

Georgia reserved and quiet? Ha. Of all the descriptions, those two fit Georgia like square pegs in a round hole. Her older sister was obstinate, harrying and loud when she wanted to be, which mostly occurred in situations involving Savannah's health or life choices…

She re-saddled the horse she'd been given by Cole and Josh Hunter, "Back to why I'm here, do you recognize these women?" Savannah fished out the photos, offered them to him.

He did not take them but his vision never left hers, "Maybe."

"You didn't look," she pushed the photos at him.

He finally took them in hand. A smile played at his mouth as if enjoying their banter, "Rather presumptuous of you, Detective."

"No, it's not. You never looked at them."

"May I ask why you think I'd recognize or know any of them?"

As irritating as Shelton was, he had a valid point. She'd been volunteered by Cole to do the interview. She hadn't wanted to meet the crazy dominant, much less spend one second in his lair. Shelton's scrutiny bore down on her, made her not only nervous but angry. The ice blue eyes locked on her with a soft, solid gaze that demanded her full attention. They actually made her worm in her seat. What the hell, she thought. It was Cole's cornball idea anyway. "My colleague believes you do."

Shelton drew on the cigar, "Interesting choice of words, my dear. You said 'colleague', not 'we' or 'I' which indicates you aren't in total agreement with his assumption."

"The truth is I don't know what to believe and the only reason I'm here is because you won't allow men in your home."

Duke laughed, "Drew the short straw, didn't you? Personally I'm pleased you did. I find you enchanting, intriguing while delectably beautiful. In my opinion, a man can never go wrong with that combination. Allow me to set the record straight. I don't permit *most* men in my house. I actually have men working for me so they must enter the house under certain circumstances. It is on rare occasion I allow another man inside and it depends on who he is. For example, your 'colleague' Cole Jordan will not be permitted to step foot in my home. He has a personal vendetta against me. Detective, I ask for a simple favor. Inquire about his wife. I invite you to come back afterward and ask your questions if you feel they are warranted."

"He's married?" she croaked. That lying, cheating bastard, she wanted to say. Coming onto her while being "holy matrimonied", that sucked and not just for her but especially his wife. Then a brainstorm hit, "Wait. Is that why he dislikes you? Something regarding his wife? He never let on he's married."

"*Was* married and you are far more diplomatic than necessary. He doesn't dislike me, he abhors me."

She'd never been accused of diplomacy, not in her entire life. Her gut told her to be careful around Duke Shelton. His personality swung to whatever the occasion called for. He went from swagger to charm in a heartbeat. He tried to put her at ease, to show her he wasn't a monster. It failed miserably, "Abhors you why? What about his wife?"

He reached for his brandy, took a small sip, "His version first, then mine." He winked, "Forces you to come back and gives me the opportunity to lavish a pretty lady in attention."

As if he didn't have enough "pretty ladies" to choose from, she thought. It was then she realized how he loved to catch people off guard. Ennis called her beautiful but he was her husband. Most men regarded her as nice-looking, she supposed, but few ever slapped the label "pretty" or "beautiful" on her. "Mr. Shelton, what kind of cars do you own?"

"Many different types. Each serves its own purpose."

"Any as old as five to ten years old?"

"Maybe one or two."

"May I look at them?"

He tapped in ash into the ashtray, "How thoughtful of you to ask but no, not without a warrant."

"Innocent people usually don't mind," she hinted.

"Then color me innocent *and* savvy. Next question." He was playing with her, according to his smile, and enjoying every second of it.

His attitude, however, was getting on her nerves, "How many men work for you?"

"At least a dozen. Why? Don't I tickle your fancy? I'm sure given half a chance, I can change your mind." He waggled his brow, "I'd like to be granted that chance, if you will."

Overlooking the remark and suggestive smile, she forged on, "What jobs do the men have? What do they do for you?"

"Anything I ask. They should. I pay them well for their work."

The man was a trial and the worst part – he delighted in her exasperation. She tried not to ground the words out, "Specifics, please."

Leaning back, he crossed his legs and sighed, feigning boredom, "Drivers, security, gardeners, maintenance, things of that nature. My turn. Does your husband satisfy you in bed?"

Savannah audibly choked. Any and all reason flew from her mind at the speed of light. She stared at Duke is if he wandered from his mother ship.

A stream of smoke jetted from his lips. A tiny smile curved them, "I think he probably does. Tell me, do you ever spice things up during lovemaking?"

Outrage darkened her expression, "That is *so* not your business."

Duke laughed freely, "I'll bet his favorite trick is to pin you down. With such a spirited, independent woman, he probably feels more in control, at least for a brief time. That's as far as you'll go, judging by your personality. You still like to retain a semblance of control."

She unsuccessfully fought back the blush creeping into her cheeks. This was a veritable hell, she groaned to herself, and getting worse every minute. She'd never tell Duke he was right. Occasionally Ennis did tend to hold her down during their lovemaking and yes she did enjoy it – to a degree. To be honest, she'd pinned *him* a few times too but Duke's intuition failed him in that regard. "Back to my questions. Your drivers just drive you around or do they pick up and deliver too?"

"Savannah, ask what you desire of me. As delightful as this banter is, I'd rather skip the unpleasantries so we can move on to other subjects."

"Where were you yesterday morning between nine and ten? And can all of your male employees be accounted for during that time?"

"My male employees were all doing their jobs, my drivers driving, gardeners gardening, maintenance workers maintaining. As for me, I was teaching a particularly willful lady the punishment for such behavior. "

"How did you punish her for being 'willful'?"

He winked, "I have my ways, my dear. They are extraordinarily persuasive."

Ugh. She mentally rolled her eyes. She never doubted the effectiveness of his punishments. Beating and abuse had a convincing track record of success.

Her brain kicked up the abuse a notch. Horrific scenes played out in her mind, "Did it include a free breast reduction surgery and carving a number," she pointed to her right shoulder, "right about here?"

For an instant, contempt flared in his eyes, "Logic dictates I should be insulted, if not livid, by your question, not to mention the manner in which you presented it. But I realize you're doing your job and have been swayed by Cole Jordan."

"There are some undeniable connections between you and the victims, Mr. Shelton. How do you explain that?"

"I can't but I did not kill anyone."

Since she lacked evidence to counter him with, she regrouped her thoughts, referred to her notes, "So your drivers were off the property between nine and ten?"

He chuckled, "You make it sound sinister. They ran errands for me. My girls wanted Krispy Kreme. My drivers fulfilled their wishes."

"I'll need to talk to the men."

"I don't think so. They're busy, as I said, doing their jobs."

"I can find them, bring them in for questioning."

Her thinly veiled threat only amused him, "You could but you won't. You will go to the doughnut shop and ask the employees. When they confirm the driver's alibi, you will not need to question them. If you did *that*, my dear, could be considered harassment in some circles."

"Which ones? The rich circles? Because I'm not on the socially elite payroll, I'm a civil servant in the business of finding a killer."

"Then I suggest you look elsewhere." He eased back into the chair and snapped his fingers. The closest woman, a brunette dressed in a sheer green body wrap, nodded, "Yes, Master Shelton," and left the room.

Savannah felt a wave of nausea roll through. Picturing her older sister at the beck and call of this arrogant jerk turned her stomach. No wonder Georgia never mentioned it. She was too embarrassed. Less than a minute later, the woman appeared with two glasses. One was placed at his left hand, the other placed on the table to Savannah's right. Savannah looked at Duke but his face was blocked by the pictures as he flipped through them, cigar in mouth. A plume of smoke snaked back and forth above the photos, "It's your label of bourbon, Detective. And, like your sister, you have impeccable taste. Please indulge."

"Thanks but I'm still on duty."

The photos lowered and a smile curled around the cigar. Humorously, he remarked, "You break departmental rules but refuse to have one simple drink while on duty?"

Savannah did not answer.

Duke's eyes widened slightly, "Ah, I see. Your silence speaks volumes." He snapped his fingers again. The same girl came forth. He told her, "Bring Detective Prince a non-alcoholic beverage instead. No need to supply temptation, right, my dear?" He didn't break his visual hold, "Do not disappoint my girl, Detective. She strives to please everyone. Of course they all do or they are disciplined."

Savannah's expression flattened. Why did every reference to dominance and submission automatically flash a likeness of Georgia in her mind? It tormented her with pictures of whips, restraints, floggers and her sister kneeling to receive whatever "discipline" he spoke of. The toll grew heavy on her stomach. Any minute she'd hurl in his face, "Disciplined how?"

Duke cocked one brow, "Nothing they don't agree to in writing, Detective, be assured."

Shifting her vision, she witnessed the distressed look on the girl's face that was shielded from Shelton's view only by her long dark hair. She faced Savannah with head bowed, "Ma'am, what is your preference?"

Savannah looked at Duke and sensed they were sizing the other up. Daring the other to take another step further in this twisted game. She didn't, "Water is fine, thank you."

Once the woman exited the room, Savannah bent forward in her seat, her lip curling in disgust, "Written permission for discipline? What, do they sign a release stating that Master Shelton may beat them any time he pleases?" She bitterly spat the words, "Did you humiliate my sister the same way?"

"Such harsh words, Detective. I don't humiliate my girls. I discipline them when necessary and as for your sister, she should tell you the capacity of our relationship. All I'll say is Beauty did sign a written agreement." His last statement emerged as a warning, "And you forget, *she* came to *me*."

Yes, and I'd love to forget that fact too. Savannah reminded herself to calm down. Her revulsion was showing and he successfully silenced her by stating Georgia's choice to see him. Better to return to the investigation and take it up with Georgia later, "You've looked at the photos –"

"Patience, Detective." He turned his attention to her angered posture, "Patience is learned with discipline. And you'll have to learn that by addressing Cole Jordan about his wife then returning tomorrow to hear my side. And you will return because his story, he will claim, is connected to your case."

And speaking of the case, "Your record includes arrests for sexual battery and sexual assault –"

"And if you chose to investigate further – which I'm expecting you did – you also know the women withdrew the complaints."

Hardly. "They refused to testify at trial. They never withdrew the complaints."

"It was their choice just as coming to me was their choice."

"Was it also their choice to take refuge from you too? No one can locate them. What did you do, threaten them or pay them off?"

Duke feigned injury, "Detective Prince, I am sincerely distressed that you believe such nonsense. Let me explain it plainly once more. Women come to me for training in submission. They sign an agreement, I sign one also. When their training is complete, they are free to leave. Some prefer to stay and I welcome them to do so. They are held to their contracts while in my home as I am held to mine regarding them."

"I'd like to see one of those contracts."

"There's only one way you will. Train as my submissive."

Repulsed at the mere notion, Savannah replied, "Never."

He gave a nonchalant shrug, "What a pity. I could do wonders with you. With that long, dark hair of yours, I already have a pet name in mind. Won't you give it more thought? The experience will be life changing and pleasurable beyond your wildest dreams."

She tried redirecting the conversation, "Is it a legal contract? Is it written by a lawyer or jotted on a cocktail napkin? There's nothing keeping you from breaking the agreement –"

"Trust, Detective," Duke showed a hint of frustration. "Something you lack, obviously, and that's a shame. I trust my girls, they trust me."

"That last one's a little iffy, isn't it? You control their lives so they have no choice."

"Your insinuation insults me, Savannah, and I've been nothing but a courteous host. There's no reason for being rude and churlish. As I've said, after the girls leave this house, their lives are their own, as evidenced by your sister. If I killed the women who left me, why is Beauty still alive? Of all the women I've known, she was dearest to me and yet she left me. If I murdered women, who would you reason to be the first target?"

His words stirred such a riotous storm inside, she fought herself from outright attacking him. He purposefully goaded her and before compromising the case, Savannah stood up and plucked the photos from his hand, "My partner will be in touch. It's best you speak with him and you *will* speak with him because I refuse to come back here again."

"Stay where you are, Savannah," Duke commanded.

She stopped but only to turn and judge his expression. It was deadly serious as was hers so she set him straight on one pertinent fact. "You do *not* tell me what to do. I am not one of your girls."

"You are upset by my comment about your sister. I regret that. I was, however, making a point." He placed the cigar between his lips, "Now come along," he waved her to him. "I'll show you what you're wanting to see."

Wary, Savannah asked, "What do I want to see?"

"My rooms, of course. You were sent here to see if I'm a murderer so you might as well see what my instruments of death are." He laughed but she found no reserve to join him. Murder wasn't funny, at least not her side of it. Seeing the women after they'd been tortured and butchered wasn't exactly a hilarious sight.

She stopped, "I'd rather not –"

"But you will because everyone will want to know details when you return. Come," he waved to her again. "I promise not to bite. Yet."

He led her down a long hallway with subdued lighting. Black iron sconces with flame bulbs lit the way past what she recognized as a library followed by a game room. At the end of the hallway, he turned left into a room. "This is my playroom. As you can see, it's well equipped for my lifestyle. Feel free to roam."

And throw up too? Because that was a fair possibility. The expansive room with dark, heavy wood furniture had the ambience of a dungeon. She saw restraints hanging from a stone wall while others lined a rustic looking cabinet. Along that cabinet were sex toys for every possible orifice and next to them – adding to the charm – were instruments to inflict sincere pain. She recognized a bullwhip, a riding crop and variety of canes and floggers.

Savannah's breast began itching and aching. The rash was coming back and she didn't have any cream with her. Adding to her misery was the nausea from the scene before her. Tables with restraints, chairs and benches outfitted with outlandish phallic-shaped pieces pushed her stomach to the brink. "Why the hell are you showing me this?"

"To show you what I do, and what I do it with."

"Believe it or not, I've run across similar items in my career, just not so many in one room. Comes with the territory of being a cop. You meet all kinds of people."

He dismissed her statement, instead walking to the cabinet – which she wished he hadn't. He lifted the bullwhip, snaked it back and forth casually then wound up and lashed it at her feet. The resounding crack startled her. She gave him a warning glare.

"If one doesn't practice with it," he stated, "it can do serious damage to a person."

"Hence the name 'bullwhip'. Do not do that again, Shelton, or you'll be wearing handcuffs and I promise the experience won't be pleasurable."

He looped the whip in his hand, sat it aside. He lifted the riding crop in his hand, "This is exquisite. You might even like it." He neared her with it, forcing her a step back.

He tilted it toward her, "It can caress as well as sting. A lot like you, I imagine."

"Are you finished? This isn't doing anything but making me physically ill." She rolled her shoulder, hoping to relieve the constant itching from the rash. It didn't work.

He returned the crop then retrieved a bamboo cane. He whipped it back and forth, the sharp swishing sliced the air. "Now this one, *this one*," he said, impressed, "will put a person in their place."

Savannah stepped back once more, her vision trained on the cane. She rolled her shoulder again, put her hands behind her back and clasped them hard. The sound of the thin rod cutting through the air brought back memories – painful ones.

Duke neared her, the corners of his mouth lifting, "What's wrong, Detective? Did I find the right instrument to grab your attention?"

She swallowed hard, tried to stand her ground, "Put it away right now."

He ignored her, "Everyone has their weakness. Some people fear the whip, others the crop. You," he focused on her wide blue eyes, "you fear the cane or something very similar."

If suffering from the rash wasn't enough, the predatory glint in Shelton's eyes drove her to say, "I need the restroom. May I?"

"Of course." Duke called one of his women, "Escort Detective Prince to the restroom."

"Yes, Master Shelton," the brunette turned to Savannah. "This way, ma'am."

"Detective," Duke called. "Rhiannon will provide you with whatever you require."

They didn't make barf bags that big, she thought, following the tall, slender woman down the hallway and around the corner. This area of the house resembled a dungeon and it made her uneasy.

Rhiannon stopped by a doorway, "What may Rhiannon bring you, ma'am?"

Savannah peeked in the room, saw a towel on the towel bar, "Everything's present and accounted for. Thank you."

"Yes, ma'am. I'll be outside if you need anything."

She nodded then slipped in the room, locking the door behind her. She took a deep, shaky breath. Shrugging out of her jacket, she followed it with her blouse. When she slid her left arm out of her bra, she winced at the sight of her breast. The damn rash turned bright red and outlined the pattern of her bra. Running her hands under cold water, she slung the excess in the sink then pressed her cool fingers and palm to the rash. An almost instant relief replaced the hot scratchy sensation. She repeated the action until, instead of wanting to claw the daylights out of the rash, she wanted to throttle Duke Shelton for aggravating and scaring her. She didn't scare easily but the sight of the cane blindsided her. Images of razor thin willow branches raced back, along with her father's furious temper. Bending her over a chair, bed or table – whatever was handy – to flail her with.

Savannah cringed from the memories. "Damn you," she cursed Shelton under her breath. "Damn you for forcing me to remember."

She took a nearby hand towel, dried her hands and fanned her breast with it. She sighed with relief. It wouldn't last long but maybe long enough to return to the station for her cream. After dressing again, she straightened her jacket, looked in the mirror. "What am I doing here?" she whispered to her reflection. "He enjoys making me uncomfortable. I don't need this." She glanced at her breast that panged its agreement. "Maybe Ennis is right. Maybe I came back too early."

A soft knock on the door broke her train of thought. It was Rhiannon, "Ma'am, do you need anything?"

Savannah folded the towel, sat it aside then took one last calming breath. Upon opening the door, she saw the woman standing a respectable distance from it. "I'm fine, thank you," she told Rhiannon.

"Master Shelton is concerned. He fears you're not feeling well."

He'd be correct... "I'm fine, really. Where is he?"

"In the great room, ma'am. I'll escort you, if you please."

She followed the woman back to the living room. They entered the room, Rhiannon stopped, greeted Duke in the usual manner while Savannah strode to Duke. He rose from his seat, took her hand, held it in his warm grasp. "My dear, I must apologize for upsetting you. I tend to forget that my passion for this lifestyle isn't always met with the same enthusiasm." He motioned toward her chair and the table beside it, "I had ginger ale brought to settle any discomfort I may have caused."

Savannah wasn't sure how to react. One minute he delighted in taunting her, the next he apologized profusely.

Duke bent closer, "Unless your discomfort comes from another source. I understand that some women suffer a variety of problems during treatment. I have a fine physician who can look –"

"I'm okay. Thank you for the offer though. Actually, I'd like to talk to some of the women if I could."

"Be my guest. Which one first? Will Jade do?"

She nodded. That's all she currently trusted herself to do. A pang of sickness rolled through her stomach and despite the cool air conditioning circulating around her, she began breaking a sweat. God, she'd be glad when this chore was finished…

He called Jade in, asked her to sit down, "The detective will be asking you questions. Answer her and be proper and respectful."

Savannah recognized her as one of the guards at the doors. The slim, golden haired woman bowed her head as she sat in the recliner beside Savannah.

The detective's vision volleyed between Jade and Duke, the latter not moving from his easy chair. "I'd like to speak with her alone."

"Not possible. I shall remain where I am just as Jade will remain where she is. Proceed with your questions."

Savannah realized the effort was futile. With Duke sitting in the same room, the woman's candidness – if she were to have any – evaporated with his statement. But she went ahead anyway, "What is your name? Your real name?"

Not expecting the invasive inquiry, Jade nearly looked Shelton in the eyes. Duke shook his head, "Jade is all you need to know. Next."

Savannah sighed, rubbed her temple. It was going to be a very long day at this rate. "How long have you been with Mr. Shelton?"

"Two years, four months and three days."

The preciseness of the answer caught her by surprise.

Incarceration brought those type of decisive answers but then Shelton's lifestyle could be considered incarceration anyway, at least in her opinion. "What kind of..." her question trailed to silence. How the hell did she phrase this one? "How does he deal with your infractions, things of that nature?"

"Master Shelton punishes me."

"What is considered an infraction or breaking the rules?"

Duke cleared his throat, "Need to know basis, Detective. If you want answers, complete the forms for training."

The glint in his eyes dared her to accept. He continued, "The minimum is a month. I give special rates to civil servants of our fine city."

Discount beatings, she thought. Gee, Daddy gave free ones at home and I wasn't very fond of them then... She snorted her disapproval then returned to questioning Jade, "How does he punish you? That's not classified, is it?"

"There are different tools for different offenses, Detective," Shelton interjected. "For instance –"

"I'm asking Jade. Please let her answer."

Jade waited, her hands folded in her lap. Duke reached across, patted them, nodded. The woman, without looking directly at Savannah, replied, "Master Shelton has used many things to punish me, ma'am."

"Has he used a cane?"

"Yes, ma'am."

"What kind of cane? Wooden, acrylic, bamboo?"

"Different kinds for different infractions. Master Shelton has used them all because Jade broke the rules."

"Detective," Duke offered a suggestion, "perhaps a more direct approach would be in order. You're obviously seeking a particular answer."

Hey, I don't tell you how to do your job... The idiocy of the thought made Savannah blush. Dominating women wasn't a job, it was deviant behavior, at least to her.

Duke smiled back at her the way her cousin Bobby did when they played chess and he knew he was winning, only clawing the smug grin from Bobby's face never entered her mind, unlike with Shelton.

Regrouping her effort, she asked, "Has he beat you with a bamboo cane to the point he brought blood?"

Duke turned to his submissive whose eyes grew wide. Her throat worked as if to speak but nothing emerged. He touched her arm, motioned for her to leave. To Savannah he said, "I believe you've gotten your answer. I have unintentionally brought blood to a few of their backsides but the offender quickly changed her behavior accordingly."

"Who the hell wouldn't after being beaten? Especially with a cane."

"Did you change your behavior, Savannah?"

The question rolled so quick, so smoothly off his tongue, her mouth opened to
speak before it occurred to her what he'd said. She swallowed her reply, the glare returning to her features. Her cheeks flushed, the heat becoming unbearable. How did he know? How could he possibly know

her past?

"It was written not only on your face but your posture when I showed you my collection. You clasped your hands behind you as if to protect your backside. You flinched when I specifically showed you the bamboo cane. Did he use a hickory or willow limb?"

Savannah rubbed at her temple again. The ache worsened as Duke Shelton brought back painful memories of her childhood. Ones she thought she'd dealt with. Ones she clearly hadn't. "I don't know what you're talking about. I need to get back to the station." She rose to her feet only to feel a wave of nausea roll through her stomach.

Duke did not stand, "Judging by your personality, you didn't change that much. You've always been independent in your thinking and actions. 'Willful' is the word I use with my girls. Your father probably used the word 'disrespectful'. He tried to beat you into submission but it didn't work. Little Savannah took the beatings and cried herself to sleep because crying in front of Daddy angered him, made the beatings worse. I don't beat my girls, Detective. I punish them but I don't scar them physically or emotionally like your father did to you."

She swallowed back the rising sickness, started toward the entry, "I've got to go."

"He did leave scars, didn't he?" Shelton pushed as he rose from his chair. Stepping behind her, he touched her lower back, "Probably here and that's very dangerous territory. It can cause serious damage to the kidneys and the tailbone is also vulnerable. Too high on the backs of the thighs and you risk nerve or muscle damage in the legs."

She started toward the entry, just to leave the house of horrors.

She just wanted out.

"When the weather's bad, the skin tightens, makes you feel stiff, doesn't it? The pain comes back, the memories with it."

She wheeled, dropping her words like bricks, "My partner will be in touch."

6

He was impressed. With her determined nature for one. Secondly, her beauty. His choices always had both. But Detective Prince seemed different in a way. He'd need more interaction to discover that difference. He never made hasty decisions. That equated buying a house without seeing it, or marrying a person without knowing them. The last notion made him smile. Marriage. Yes, he supposed he felt a connection to his women, at least for a while, but only one stayed true in his heart and she'd left far too soon to please him. Maybe the detective was the answer, the replacement he searched for. She certainly favored his beloved.

A wealth of dark hair pulled into a ponytail showed independence from other female police officers who opted for a shorter style. She wanted acceptance in her job and yielded to the rules but only to a point. With her long bound hair, she warned the world that Savannah Prince refused to surrender her femininity to anyone.

She was tall – she stood at least five nine, maybe five ten, with long legs that gave her a fluid, graceful gait. She was nearly tall enough to look him directly in the eyes. She was a bit thin for his taste but he took into account the cancer and radiation treatments. Added to that was the stress of her job.

Eyes were the window to the soul, people said. Hers were full of promise and pain. Her eyes as well as her demeanor conveyed a driven woman and a stubborn one too.

He was good at assessing a woman's body. Beneath the tailored suit stood a shapely, strong, toned figure. Women like that put up an incomparable fight until he broke them over. He flinched as his erection fought for room in his slacks. Images of her on her knees begging actually threatened to be the undoing of his control and his zipper. It had been too long of a dry spell down south, he winced, so he allowed himself the fantasy of having her. How loud would she scream? How would she sound when she begged him to stop? With that sultry voice flavored with a gentle Georgia accent, he imagined the moment to be priceless. The instant she realized she was no longer in control...

7

No matter if Cole Jordan begged or Josh Hunter dragged her by her hair, she was never, *never* going back to Duke Shelton's lair. The man was unconscionable and manipulative. He was also mysterious, captivating and charismatic – three traits he used to lure a person, to lower their defenses so he could allow his contemptible side to hurt them. He'd made her bleed in a way no one saw it except her. He'd also inflamed her rash to the point she feared insanity might take hold before she could apply more cream. It kicked into high gear before she left the estate's front gates, leaving her to discreetly scratch and rub when traffic lightened up.

The instant she walked into the station, she headed to the locker room for her cream. Once she had a few moments with it in the restroom, she waited another few minutes to settle herself down and to let the itching and burning ease. Then she headed to Josh Hunter's office.

"I'm taking personal time." Her voice betrayed the emotion coursing through her and she cursed under her breath. Her hands still shook and knowing Shelton intruded and gleefully paraded around in her most private affairs caused the shaking to worsen. She needed peace and quiet. She needed time to sort it all out, to make sense of it. And she really prayed Duke Shelton wasn't a sadistic killer because she and her sister were squarely in his sights now.

Sensing her emotion, Hunter rose from his desk, closed the door, "Something happen?"

Tears welled and she dabbed them away, lying, "I'm just tired."

Josh's brow sank. He pointed to the chair beside her then leaned against his desk, "You were fine before going to Shelton's. What happened? If he tried anything, I'll drag his ass in here myself. *Sit down.*"

She eased into the chair and glanced behind her to ensure neither Ennis or Cole saw her. "He's very… unsettling. He had me investigated, knew more about me than anyone could and I can't figure out how."

"What did he say that rattled you? And don't lie to me again and say you're not rattled. It's obvious because you're tuning up to cry."

She swiped away more tears, tried to laugh off the answer, "Daddy's abuse. He said it was my reaction and posture that told him. I don't believe that, not when he knew other, very personal aspects of my life. He had to find out somehow."

Hunter crossed his arms, "I've heard he's scary but I had no idea or I wouldn't have sent you in. From what Jordan told me, though, you were the only way inside the house. Do you think Shelton killed those women?"

"He has the equipment the killer uses. He showed me every sordid sex toy and whip and cane he owns. He could be the one but I'm not exactly objective right now."

Josh gave her shoulder a squeeze, "Go home. We'll find another way at Shelton."

"Thanks. Would you tell Ennis I left?"

"You can do that. Here he comes, along with Jordan."

Oh great. She hurriedly straightened her face before the two men clogged the door. Both began firing questions at her but the mere sight of Cole set her off, "Tell me about your wife."

"Wife?" Ennis questioned. He turned on Cole like the man farted, "You're married?"

Cole replied, "Not anymore. She went to see Shelton to 'take lessons' and the son of a bitch raped her."

"Her name isn't in the file." Savannah wanted to know, "Why didn't she have him arrested?"

He shifted his weight from one foot to the other. He didn't want to answer but with all eyes on him, he realized he had to, "Because she was scared of him."

"Why was she taking lessons? Was she not submissive enough for you so she needed some tweaking in that area?"

He flushed beet red at her question. She wasn't sure if it was embarrassment or anger. Savannah bet on the latter. She was right.

Cole glared at her, "It was her decision to go. He's the one that raped her."

"Where is she now? I could talk to her about what happened," Savannah volunteered.

Cole shook his head, "She left me and I haven't heard from her."

"And it's beyond you to find her?" she asked, not bothering to hide her disbelief.

He put his hands to his hips, "Hey, she don't care enough to stay, I don't care enough to look."

"Your captain let you work on this case, knowing all this?" Josh asked.

"My captain only has so many detectives so yeah, I was picked to work it."

Hunter crossed his arms, "We'll discuss this later. I'll bring you guys up to speed about the interview. Savannah, go home."

The men asked in unison, "What happened?"

Ennis followed up, "You okay?"

"I will be." She turned to Cole, "Next time you want Shelton interviewed, break into his house and do it yourself."

8

With the rash temporarily under control, she left the station headed for Georgia's house. She needed answers and she'd likely have to drag them from her sister since Georgia kept her past to herself.

The trip seemed longer than necessary, despite the fact she hit all but two traffic lights right. The images tripped through her mind at a frightening pace. Georgia kneeling to Duke and taking commands from him. The word "surreal" didn't come close.

Turning onto a main thoroughfare, Savannah shook her head, "He's lying or trying to trick me." She decided it was a lie, plain and simple. She couldn't grasp her gorgeous, stubborn sister in that position.

After driving another ten minutes, she wheeled into the driveway. She was glad to see Dane wasn't there. They needed time to work this out privately. She walked past Georgia's prized pink and purple petunias and red hibiscus, the latter displaying at least one new flower. She could see her sister on her knees rounding out holes with a trowel, anxious to plant her newest flora but that was the *only* way she saw Georgia on her knees. Savannah rang the doorbell and waited.

A moment later the lock clicked and the door swung open. At

first sight of her sister in jeans and an amethyst pullover, Savannah decided she was correct. Duke exaggerated the degree of their friendship. Georgia fit a more domestic role rather than sex kitten to Duke Shelton.

Georgia smiled while holding the door open, "Well, this is a surprise."

Want a surprise? Try my day... She followed Georgia into the living room, "I've had a very interesting day."

Georgia poured each a glass of iced tea then handed one to her sister, "Tell me all about it."

Savannah eased into a nearby recliner, following her sister's motion to sit. Georgia sat in a rocker across from her. Savannah broached the subject cautiously, "I'm still on the case even with all your efforts to remove me." She winked, "Nice try, by the way. Anyway, the leads took us to a certain person and I got elected to interview him..." More like railroaded, she thought.

Listening intently, Georgia sat her tea on an end table. The hesitation intrigued her, "Are you making me guess or are you stalling for dramatic reasons?"

Tracing the rim of her glass, Savannah debated about mentioning the past. Causing Georgia pain wasn't her goal and certainly not the smartest move considering her sister had a fiery temper when provoked. "If I ask you something would you tell me the truth?"

The question threw Georgia, "I'm not in the habit of lying to you. What's the question?"

Slowly, Savannah reminded herself. *Tap into this information slowly. You don't want to piss her off.* "Remember when you moved to

Atlanta? You basically packed one night and were gone. When I asked why you left so quickly, you told me you were grieving Grandpa." Savannah saw Georgia's easygoing demeanor fade. Her sister leaned back and crossed her arms and legs. *She's not volunteering anything now, stupid. You've already overplayed your hand.*

"I was," was the clipped reply. "If you remember, Grandpa and I were always close. When I wasn't writing, I was helping him at the orchards."

"I remember," she softened her voice, hoping it might encourage Georgia to relax. "But after you moved, you were never home. Mama called day and night. I did too. You went off the radar for months." A thread of bitterness unintentionally laced her voice. At the time she'd felt abandoned by both Seth and Georgia. Seth left home at eighteen for the army, leaving both girls heartbroken. Then, a few years later, Georgia left abruptly with hardly a good-bye. It was akin to being left on a doorstep with a note tucked into the basket. All her life Georgia mothered her, fussed over her. The bedtime stories, bouts of sickness, helping with homework. Next to their mother, Georgia was her closest friend. The sudden loss of her confidant hurt Savannah and the resentment still showed.

Georgia tensed, "Exactly how does my past relate to your case?"

"I'm getting to it," Savannah wanted to remain calm for both their sakes. Obviously this was the first time anyone mentioned it to Georgia. The tension between them grew as Georgia levered from the rocker and marched to the brandy container on her mahogany writing desk. Savannah gradually lost time and her sister's cooperation, "I just want to know where you were during those months."

Pouring herself a drink, Georgia turned to face Savannah then leaned against the desk, "You make my absence sound positively criminal. I told you at the time I'd found someone. I was sick of Daddy's preaching about marriage and finding a real job. I recall both you and Seth encouraged me to continue writing, even if that meant leaving home."

Savannah smiled a little, recalling the time, "Well, I was kinda hoping you'd take me with you."

"You were still in school, Savannah. Mama and Daddy wouldn't have let you live with me."

"I was young but I still had hope..."

"Wouldn't have done any good anyway. Daddy always calling, wanting me married off." Georgia's lip curled, "I didn't like Allan Peterson and I wasn't marrying the goat no matter how much money he had or how much Daddy wanted me to."

Savannah remembered Allan. A small, thin man in his late twenties with thinning hair and bad allergies. Just looking at a flower made him break out into sneezing fits so having any in the house or yard was taboo – a reality that wouldn't fly in Georgia's life. His personality reminded Savannah of a glass of sour milk – you really couldn't swallow much without getting sick. She fully understood why Georgia refused to marry him. "So who were you with during those 'off the radar' months?"

Now her sister took a liberal swallow of brandy as if to brace herself, "Part of the time I was with a man named Duke."

Savannah's gut clenched. Her vision went straight to the brandy but realized drinking wouldn't erase the images – or harsh truth – from her mind. Shelton hadn't been lying after all. A sudden pang in her temple forced her to rub at it, trying to ease it. The headache would never go away at this rate, "Duke Shelton. The dominant in the big stone palace."

Georgia's hand shook upon hearing the name. Or was it the description? She wouldn't meet Savannah's gaze now, "You know him?"

"I do now. That's who I interviewed."

She sat the brandy down, "You think he killed all those women?"

"It's a possibility." Savannah studied her sister. Even at thirty-six, she was a spitting image of a twenty-eight year-old Rita Hayworth. No doubt her looks inspired Duke's nickname for her – Beauty. He was obsessed in Savannah's opinion and desperate to see Georgia again. "Duke remembers you well." She uttered the declaration to see a reaction. What she received surprised her.

Georgia shook her head with no indication of a smile, "He remembers every woman well. Women are his life, Savannah. Without them, he'd wither and expire."

Savannah's stomach begged for the brandy but had she reached for it, the move would have incited another riot with her sister. She opted to pick up the iced tea instead.

Perhaps she expected Georgia to react with more rancor – or hoped she would. Instead, she seemed somewhat melancholy – and that pissed Savannah off most of all. "You," she swallowed the anger, "still have feelings for him? Because your expression suggests –"

"It suggests nothing." Georgia's glare bored into her, making her squirm. The older sister continued, "Duke and I were not romantically involved."

Georgia's harsh tone sliced her next comment to ribbons. Savannah motioned for a refill on tea. Georgia poured with a very steady hand now. She'd regrouped, threw on her armor and visually challenged her younger sister. Savannah, however, felt properly dissected as she accepted the glass, "I wasn't implying –"

"Yes, you were but I was never in love with Duke. During the day he instructed me on his lifestyle for research. When that research concluded, I left and never went back. You know, not that it matters but I was dating a guy who *wasn't* Duke. He painted landscapes and portraits."

Savannah instinctively looked toward the stairway. Upstairs hung a painting of Georgia. It was a beautiful work showing her wavy chestnut hair draped over her bare shoulders. The artist captured a certain smile in her sister that brought it alive. Obviously the artist loved her.

Georgia nodded, as if hearing her sister's thoughts, "Yes, he painted that for me. And his name was William Davis, not Duke Shelton." She topped off her brandy with a sigh, "So don't bully me with your detective skills, Savannah. You have your past, I have mine."

"But mine hasn't endangered my life yet."

"I'm sorry, who was Toby Jackson again? Oh, *right...* The guy that nearly broke your jaw not once but several times. He also managed to send you to the emergency room as I recall."

That shut Savannah up but it also lit her temper. She'd managed to forget Toby for the most part until now. Her jaw ached at the recollection, "I really needed that, Georgia. Thanks. Thanks a lot."

"It helps to think before you speak on certain subjects. You don't think Duke's going to kill me, do you?"

Savannah refrained from describing the glint in Duke's eyes when talking about Georgia. She'd seen it before in passion killings. She'd heard one suspect admit to loving the woman so much killing her was the only way to alleviate his obsession.

Georgia studied her sister's serious expression until the ire drained from her cheeks, "*Did* he say something?"

Savannah sipped the tea, acknowledging, "It's good to know you're not truly as cavalier as you act. When you left, you obviously upset him."

Georgia shifted her weight, "But did he say something?" By her expression, Savannah knew it would take significant persuasion on her part. She began with a question, "It's been twelve years since you've seen him? Think, Georgia. If a man is still consumed with you, there might be a problem. Do you mind me asking if he hurt you? Is that why you left?"

Emptying her glass in one swallow, Georgia returned to her rocker. Her voice quiet and reserved, "I left because my research was over, not because he hurt me. He never laid a hand on me, or a whip or anything else."

9

She looked like a butterfly with outstretched wings. She was tall, with graceful curves and nice plump breasts. Locked in shackles dangling from ceiling beams and bolted to the floor, her limbs splayed out like a butterfly in flight. He loved the way she looked in them. He especially loved her breasts, their weight in his hands, the way the nipples stiffened in the cold room.

She had a fine sheen of sweat glistening from head to toe. Damp with perspiration, her short red hair clung to her scalp, giving the impression she'd run several miles in the Atlanta heat and humidity. Oh, she'd had a workout, alright. One only a few choice women got.

He stared into her eyes, drawing the scalpel down the warm flesh of her right breast, careful not to slice the tender skin. She expected it, he could tell by the tightening around her eyes. They'd tried every emotion with him. Flashes of anger changed to pleading, the pleading finally evolving to resignation. Her pretty green eyes lost the sparkle of terror he thrived on. He needed to wake her up again, to let her know whatever she imagined death to be, whenever she presumed it might come, she was wrong. Very wrong.

The blade skimmed along the flesh, a line of blood following in its wake. She cried out with a plea for him to stop. Then she glanced at her breast and tears trailed down her cheeks.

"There you are," he sang softly. "You know I demand your full attention. Do I have it now? Or do you need a bit more inspiration?"

The noises behind the gag heightened as panic rose. He nestled the blade beneath the nipple until she stood completely rigid in her bonds, so still she barely breathed. The tears came in earnest. Women always resorted to tears and by now she should have understood that tears pissed him off, "Now, what did I tell you about crying?"

He'd said it in a benign fashion, as matter-of-fact. Her reaction, however, indicated otherwise. She struggled to control the tears, to blink them back. She remembered well what he'd said and he was happy she did.

He withdrew the scalpel, seeing her body slacken a bit in the restraints, her breathing deepen. Stepping behind her, he touched the elongated welts crisscrossing her back and buttocks. She squirmed from the touch, the sting of his hand on the raw wounds. He worked her over pretty well with the cane. It hadn't taken long to break her, but then it never did. They all thought they could tolerate the pain, only to realize that the repeated strikes weakened their resolve. A quick glance at his watch revealed a record and a disappointing one at that. Ten lousy minutes. Most lasted at least twenty or thirty. Never past thirty-five. Yes, his little nurse was able to dole out pain but unable to take it. He needed a better challenge. One that tested his abilities. No one played a game because it was easy. No one was happy to defeat an easy opponent.

Where was the fun in that? He needed another woman quick.

He moved to her front, looked her squarely in the eyes, "Do you recall your first words to me?"

A frantic nod of her head followed. He saw hope mounting again as he continued, "You said I could do whatever I wanted, take whatever I wanted, as long as I didn't kill you."

She nodded again, still hoping. Scalpel in hand, he flipped the blade so it didn't cut – but continued to reinforce his point. In a gentle motion, the knife circled her right breast, "I want this." With great ceremony, he turned the blade over, "And since you said I could, I'll take them both."

10

When Ennis opened the front door, Savannah was not in sight and that worried him. After seeing her near tears at the station, he'd questioned their captain about the encounter with Shelton. Hunter relayed the basics of Savannah's visit but asked Cole to leave after a point. Then Josh dropped the bomb about Duke's "knowledge" about R.J.'s abuse. Ennis decided once more to campaign for his wife's dismissal from the case. It was too dangerous and Shelton, if he was guilty, seemed to zero in on Savannah.

Ennis headed to the bedroom and saw the closed bathroom door. He knocked and when he opened the door, clouds of steam billowed out. He waved his arm to clear the steam, "Where are you?"

"Right here, silly."

He glanced down to find her sitting in a tub full of bubbles, most of which had already dissolved to reveal his most desired areas of her body. He grinned, loosened his tie.

"You've got high hopes, don't you?" she noticed.

He unzipped his slacks, "Give me another thirty seconds and we'll see how high they can get."

"Hate to be a killjoy, but I'm not really feeling like it tonight." She stood and Ennis watched droplets of water trailed along the contours of her body. The view didn't promote G-rated feelings below his waist. What set him straight – the sight of her left breast. That morning it was a light pink, now it blazed cherry red.

She dried off and carefully patted her breasts dry. "Can you hand me the cream over there?"

Ennis shucked his slacks, followed by his shirt. The hot steam was killing him in the suit. He turned to the counter for the cream then untwisted the cap, "Allow me?"

She sounded relieved at the offer, "Thank you."

Squeezing a small amount on his fingers, he began gently applying it to the rash. Savannah closed her eyes, sighed. He massaged the cream in then put some on the underside of her breast where it really took to bothering her most times. "It looks worse," was all he said. No need to tell her the obvious. It actually looked like hell.

"It really acted up at Shelton's house. He got me pretty upset at the last." She released a quiet moan which inspired another uprising south of his border. The bright red rash and its heat against his hand, however, tamed his craving for sex. She was miserable and had been since the treatments began. He recapped the tube, sat it aside, "What did he do?" He knew what Josh told him but he wanted confirmation from her.

"Not what he did. What he said. He knew a lot about me, Ennis. It scared me." She slipped on her panties then scoffed, "I guess Cole kept you busy with tales of Duke all afternoon."

"No, when you left to interview Shelton, he left too. Said he had something to do. Came back about the same time you did."

She was quiet a moment then, "Do you think I'm churlish?"

The question took Ennis aback, "What the hell does that mean?"

"It's not flattering, believe me."

"Then no, you're not. Who said you were?" Probably Jordan, the man with no morals or tact, Ennis figured.

"Shelton."

Surprised that a stranger possessed that amount of gall, a sudden anger rose inside him, "Tell you what. Once I look that word up, I'm taking the dictionary and beating Duke Shelton to death with it." He reached for her robe then thought twice about it, "Why don't you run around like that for a while? Just put on a pair of shorts."

"Ennis Rutherford, my mama'd read me the riot act if I slunk around the house in my alltogethers."

"Your mama'd be just fine with it if she saw your rash." He swatted her behind, "Now do what I say, woman."

Tiny lines appeared at the corners of her eyes as she gifted him with an embarrassed smile, "And if we have company? Which sofa cushion do I dive under?"

Ennis slung the robe over his arm, "We'll have this on standby, just in case."

They made their way to the living room where he'd sat their supper on the dining table. He pointed to the sack, "Rocketburger, not so many jalapenos. You'd be up all night." When a case became too intense, she tended to forget her digestive tract as he discovered early in their relationship. Seeing her hugging a toilet at two in the morning didn't do either of them any good.

Savannah kissed his cheek, "Always looking out for me."

"Someone has to. Now sit and I'll serve supper." He went to an upper kitchen cabinet for two paper plates.

She peeked into the sack, grabbed a French fry and popped it in her mouth, "I talked to Lindsey earlier. She's looking forward to their trip. They've never been to Colorado."

"How long are they staying?"

"Two weeks. Leah will be lucky to keep Seth sane that long. He's so used to working all the time."

"It'll be good for him to spend that time with his kids too."

"Lindsey's really excited about going. She said she wants to see all the polar bears."

He paused before setting the plates down, "Polar bears? In Colorado? Did you tell her there weren't any?"

"No."

"Why not?"

"Because it's not my job to disillusion her," she stated as fact. "My job is to be the loving, supportive aunt that inspires her to greatness. Her parents have the sole responsibility of crushing her expectations of finding polar bears in Colorado."

Incredulous, Ennis nearly choked. He sat the plates down, began filling them with their respective orders, "I can see what my job will be when we have kids."

"Oh please," she complained good-naturedly. "You know I'll be right in there helping you. My point is Seth will tell her anyway. He doesn't foster hopes and dreams like fathers should. He's too much like Daddy in that respect. If he was smart, he'd wait for her to ask someone at the lodge and let *them* be the Scrooges."

Ennis eyed his wife, "Once we have kids, I'm keeping close tabs on you, woman. You're sneaky." He sat down, shook out his napkin and nearly had it placed when the doorbell rang.

Panicked, Savannah scrambled for the robe. To a degree she looked comical and he tried to slow her flurry of activity, "Settle down, sugar. You're twisting yourself in a knot. I'll get the door."

Their little house never promoted stalling when answering the door. Only a few feet from the dining and living rooms, the front door pretty much could be answered in a few seconds. Ennis waited for her to tie the robe around her before opening the door. He expected to see a face but stared back at a massive flower arrangement. He was sure someone held the basket but the flowers were so tall, he couldn't see the person's face.

"Savannah Prince?" The man asked since, Ennis assumed, he couldn't see through the arrangement either. At least he hoped that's why because as pretty as Savannah was, he'd still hate being called a woman.

"Hardly," Ennis replied, his tone reflecting his irritation. Who the hell was sending his wife flowers? That was *his* job which reminded him he'd fallen down on that job the past several weeks. His last delivery was after her surgery. Damn.

The guy sounded perturbed at Ennis's response, "Does she live here?" He also sounded overburdened by his load and Ennis understood why. The damned basket was crammed full of purple flowers of all kinds. That incensed him worse. The arrangement meant to overwhelm, not merely impress.

"Yes, she lives here. Who sent these things?" No sense in letting the little guy off the hook that quick.

"Dunno. I just deliver them."

The guy hefted them into his arms again and Ennis not-so-gingerly reached for them, "Lemme have 'em if they're that heavy." Once in his grasp, he realized they *were* that heavy. Of course a field of flowers tended to weigh on the cumbersome side.

"Thanks, dude." The delivery guy scurried like a mouse down the sidewalk to the delivery van.

Ennis took note of the florist just in case they needed to track down the sender. The bastard better have signed the card and signed it platonically or Ennis would put a good old fashioned hurting on him · whoever he was.

"What the…" Savannah gasped, a huge smile beginning to surface. "Ennis, you darling."

That nailed his guilt to the wall. Sending her flowers now basically would backfire, especially since he couldn't afford anything that massive. "Unfortunately I didn't send them. Wished I had though, judging by your smile."

That smile evaporated as fast as it emerged. "They're not yours?"

It pained him but he shook his head. Savannah backed away from them, "Then I don't want them. I don't know who'd send me flowers."

Ennis strode to the table and sat them down because his arms were getting tired and the urge to sneeze crept up on him. He could only imagine the confetti of petals if he ripped one into them. He mentioned, "Your birthday's not for another couple of months, and only a few people know purple is your favorite color. Gotta be someone you know, right?" He searched for a card in the mass of blooms and stems and finally located one. Her name and address were printed on the small envelope and Ennis wondered if Georgia sent them. Savannah's older sister thrived on spontaneity lately, dropping by with tasty meals or a gift here and there, so why not flowers for her sister?

Sliding the card out, he quickly realized the delivery had nothing to do with Georgia. Silently he read, "My most humble apologies, Savannah. Allow me to make amends by joining me for breakfast Saturday at ten o'clock. I'll send a car. Dress comfortably. Duke Shelton."

"Ennis, what's wrong?"

He cut his vision to her, offered her the card while scrubbing his finger under his nose. It was coming and it would be a doozy, "That son of a bitch inflamed your rash and now he's giving me one."

Savannah plucked the card from between his index and middle fingers, read it. Automatically she shook her head, "No way. Not after today, especially since he thinks I'm churlish. The bastard can kiss my –"

"Achoo!" Ennis sneezed so hard it bent him double and practically inverted himself. He grabbed his napkin, sacrificing it as an emergency tissue.

She blessed him, waited for him to blow his nose then, "Are you allergic to the flowers?"

"No, I'm allergic to the blight called Duke Shelton."

With every mention of the name, her temper simmered until she furiously ripped the card into tiny pieces and tossed them in the trash. The flowers went next to the bin, "Let's eat then we'll watch the baseball game."

Surprised at her non-reaction – personally, he felt like wringing a rich guy's neck right after he hit the Claritin, "Not going then?"

She blinked. Then blinked again, looked at him like he'd lost his mind. "Do I have 'idiot' stamped on my forehead? Shelton's not only creepy, he could be a killer. Why would I want to break bread with him?"

The answer settled his stomach and his anger. "Then let's eat and watch the baseball game."

Savannah plopped into the dining chair, scooped up her burger then stared at it. Ennis began to question if something crawled out of the thing and had the audacity to wave at her. A Rocketburger lasted mere minutes in her possession. Tonight she pensively regarded it like she wasn't sure what to do.

"Something wrong?" he asked.

"I wonder," she said, "if Seth has room for a stowaway. I could help Lindsey search for polar bears."

11

Leigh ran as fast, as hard as she could. She didn't know how long but the sun set long ago, leaving darkness behind. It felt like a lifetime since she'd freed herself and, hoping help was nearby, rushed into the humid night air only to see a dirt road and dense forest of trees that rose to the sky.

Her heart pounded fast and hard. Her lungs burned for air. Her legs felt wobbly, like her bones were going soft. Roots and branches clutched at her feet and ankles. She stumbled as exhaustion wore her down. She slowed to a staggering walk, determined to continue and get as far from the cabin as possible.

If the phone call hadn't come, he'd have cut her to shreds. Ironic, she thought, how a ringing phone – the one thing she despised – may have saved her life. She wasn't sure how long he held her captive – days, at least. She only knew he meant to kill her and in a vicious, brutal manner. Before the fortuitous call, he poised the scalpel beneath her left breast. She felt the pressure growing with each second. Then the phone rang and after a goodly amount of fussing, he unlocked the shackles and hauled her back to that horrible dust rag serving as a mattress.

She told herself not to think about it anymore. *Focus on finding help.* But the longer she plodded onward, the likelihood of that diminished like hope had for days. She didn't know the forest. Even if she had, in the dark of night, under the thick canopy of the trees, there was no moon, no constellations to guide her. She just focused on moving forward in a straight line, terrified of accidentally circling back to that place.

When the heat of exertion and the numbness of fear abandoned her, a chill crept up her bare skin. Shivering uncontrollably, she trudged forward as long as she could, stumbling in the dark as she tripped over uneven ground. After what seemed like hours she stopped, aching to rest and hoping that in the dark she couldn't be tracked. He'd be back soon, if he wasn't already there. She needed to put miles between them but her body refused to accept the fact. It wanted rest, food, most of all *peace...*

Her foot caught on a fallen branch and she tumbled down a sloping hill. She rolled over and over, trapping a frightened scream behind her lips. Praying no one heard the scuffle of dry leaves and snapping of twigs as she fell, Leigh quietly climbed the hill, careful to listen for any noise or movement. He might be waiting for her, to ambush her, just to drag her back and finish what he started.

At the top of the rise, she panicked. Which direction had she come from? She circled around, desperate for signs of her own tracks but the forest floor, covered in a thick carpet of pine straw, branches and pine cones, revealed no sign of her footprints. Standing there, trying to decide what to do, she grew more terrified she'd hear a twig snap in the distance, or see some movement, then see him emerge from the shadows.

So tired, she thought. But she had to push on. Soon, not too far, she would find a house. Food. A phone. Help.

A sound startled her. Heart pounding, she listened. Again. The snap of a twig, the crunch of leaves. Maybe it was an animal. That thought gave her no fear. She would be relieved to see anything, even a bear, lumber from between the trees. Just please. Not him... She stood absolutely still, begging fate that she would be hidden by the large tree if it was him.

Please, she quietly pleaded. Don't let it be...

Footfalls—unmistakable now – padding nearer and nearer on the leaves and pine straw. But was it a person?   Be   still.   Be   quiet. Breathing small, careful breaths so no person or animal could hear her.

Closer and closer the steps came.   A person.   Another step. Another. The next step would fall nearer, giving her away. Her heart hammered in her chest.   Each tiny breath released with tremendous restraint threatened to burst out in a shriek of terror. The footfalls ceased. Silence. She waited, not moving. Had she imagined it?

"You disappoint me. And I hate to be disappointed," the voice said from the darkness. *His* voice....

12

According to her voicemail, the call came during her radiation treatment. While she gingerly shrugged into her bra and fastened it, she'd turned the cell phone back on. The voicemail prompt beeped as she buttoned the purple blouse. She felt like a semi-made bed that day since she slept late, leaving her to scramble to find something clean – and different – to wear to work. She'd settled on the only ensemble left in her repertoire – the black suit with purple blouse.

Shrugging into her jacket, she gathered her purse and headed down the hallway with phone in hand. She glanced down to access her voicemail and slammed into a wall of white that forced her back a step to retain her footing.

A man's hand grasped her arm to steady her as he joked, "Whoa, where's the fire?"

Savannah followed the white doctor's coat to a face she'd seen on TV. Georgia would have a conniption, she thought, when Savannah told her who she'd mowed down. Her older sister developed a slight crush on a particular TV doctor to the point she never missed the show. Savannah never watched medical shows because she saw enough carnage with her job but now she struggled to put a name with Georgia's latest fantasy. McFeeney? No. McWeenie? No, that wasn't it either. McSteamy – *that* was it.

McSteamy's twin smiled at her, "Must be an important call."

Savannah apologized, "It's business. Sometimes I get carried away."

Before walking off, he winked, "Just remember, all work and no play…"

She headed to her car, debating over dialing Georgia and telling her about the encounter then decided against it. First, her sister didn't need the distraction from writing. Second, Savannah really needed to hear the voicemail. Once safely in her Camaro, she listened to the message. It was Ennis. Another body – number eight – turned up not far from the last one. He warned of the brutality of the scene, which was bloodier and more vicious than the last. He ended it with, "Boss says if you're not up to seeing it, you can head back to the station and wait for us."

Ha, she thought. Josh just didn't want her tossing her cookies on camera anymore. She fully expected Ennis lobbied to keep her away from the scene and Cole probably chimed in with him.

Ennis always looked out for her. She appreciated it and found it an endearing trait about her husband but she was getting paid to investigate homicides, not hide from them. Savannah took note of the location and turned the car in that direction. Normally, she'd drop by the station for a detective's sedan but since her treatment – or waiting for it – cost an extra precious thirty minutes, she opted to drive her own.

Traffic thinned out by ten-thirty and getting to the scene hadn't presented much of a hassle. That was, until she neared the actual scene. Bystanders and news crews clogged the street leading to the ravine. Uniformed officers manned the crime scene tape, keeping everyone out accept other officers and the medical examiner. She spotted Ennis and Cole standing by the ravine. Jordan stood with both hands on his hips. Ennis stood a moment then drew his arm across his forehead. Her husband's reaction and expression warned her that the scene was really bad.

Savannah exited the Camaro, realizing it was warmer outside than she expected. She unclipped her badge from her belt and walked to the nearest officer standing at a barrier. She flashed her badge but didn't wait for his nod before ducking under the tape.

Cole spied her and strode toward her, jamming his hand in his pocket. "Here," he said, extending a squashed brown paper bag. From the looks of it, it probably had held his breakfast.

Confused, Savannah took it from him, "What's this for?"

He was already on his way back to the body. He tossed his reply over his shoulder, "Your breakfast when it comes back up."

Judging by his sneer, he hadn't meant it in a kind way. A brief memory of the last crime scene where she'd hurled in front of everyone fired her anger. He ridiculed her without knowing the real reason for the sickness and Savannah would die before telling the self-righteous asshole.

Cole's harassment and innuendos, both sexual and non-sexual, got tiresome. Sighing, she trudged toward the ravine. She was several paces behind Ennis and glad for it. Had her husband overheard the comment, he'd have decked Jordan then and there in full view of colleagues, reporters, and news cameras.

She noticed when Ennis squatted down for a better view of the victim, he stopped short. Figuring it was something important, she hurried along. Ennis turned, lifted his hand in a "stop" gesture. Not him too, she lamented while trying to contain her irritation. She wadded the bag tighter between her hands, wishing it was Cole's head, "Ennis, I can handle this despite what Jordan thinks." Her resentment bared itself in all its hateful glory despite the fact she worked diligently to hide it. Emphasizing her point, she pushed the squished sack at Cole, "Shove this thing," she paused, telling herself to play nice, "back in your pocket."

Savannah attempted to maneuver around Ennis but he planted both hands on her shoulders, his voice nearly a whisper, "I know you can handle it but I'd rather you not. This woman is pretty chopped up and I don't want you seeing it."

She realized he protected her. His eyes betrayed him, indicating the magnitude of brutality behind him. His firm grasp refused to let her move a simple inch, much less a few feet toward the body. Still, she had a job to do, "You married me knowing my job description. The boss expects us to work this together."

"Will you listen to me? This guy is ramping up his violence and shortening the time between kills. The boss wants you at the station so you can search the missing person's reports and identify her. Jordan and I will take care of things here."

The sun beat down on her, and perspiration threatened to surface. The heat brought the insufferable itch back to her breast. She'd need the cream soon and being out in God's kingdom for all to see wasn't exactly the place to apply it... "I don't like this, Ennis. I'm supposed to be working with you."

"You will be. You'll be putting a name with the face while we gather evidence." He looked behind him and she followed his lead. Captain Hunter squatted beside the ravine, pointing at something. "Boss," Ennis called without releasing her, "she's headed back to work on the ID."

"Good idea," Hunter said. "Get her a photo right quick."

Savannah watched the tension melt from her husband's posture. He reached for his phone but she stopped him, "Makes more sense using mine." She unclipped the phone from her belt, flipped it open and handed it to him. He turned to snap a picture when she stopped him, her words quiet but meaningful, "Pass this word of warning to Mr. Jordan. He tries to oust me from my duties and, like Patton said, I'll go through him like crap through a goose."

Candace Levy cried non stop for thirty minutes. It hadn't taken Savannah long to locate the correct missing person's report since not many of the missing women had red hair. Once she matched Leigh Watney's face and address to her driver's license, the detective took a moment before calling the sister. Candace had filed the missing person's report days ago and once Savannah asked her to come to the station, Leigh's sister would know. It was one of the worst parts of being a cop.

While Candace cried, Savannah attempted to console her but as she found out early in her career, family members were inconsolable at that time in their lives. Savannah's vision drifted down to Leigh's driver's license. She was pretty with her impish grin and her red hair cut in a pixie style. The two sisters bore such a resemblance to each other that Savannah nearly mistook them for twins. The birthdates cleared that up with Candace being two years older. No matter the age difference, the two had obviously been close, much like Savannah and Georgia.

At first, Savannah tried to carefully obtain information from the hysterical woman and temporarily gave up until Candace calmed down. The tears finally slowed to a continuous trickle, allowing Savannah to make headway on the interview.

Not long after she began the interview, she saw Ennis and Cole walking to her office. The resentment from the crime scene returned. She couldn't help feeling left out earlier. Ennis meant well but sending her away only reinforced Jordan's opinion that she couldn't handle her job.

The two men approached the closed door and Savannah tamped down the animosity building since being shooed from the scene. She excused herself to go meet Ennis and Cole in the hall. If identifying the victim was her job, she'd done it but she wasn't sharing the love about interviewing the sister. That job was hers too and damn it, she meant to keep that *her* job, not theirs. She knew how to shoo people away too.

Ennis hitched his thumb at the woman, "Who's she?"

Okay, so the animosity reared up again, especially when Cole glanced at his watch. She crossed her arms, "Late for something?"

Cole's shoulders slumped, "Ease up, Prince. We were trying to help." He cut his vision to Ennis, "And this is what we get. Attitude. Who is she, Savannah?"

Her hands clenched into fists beneath her crossed arms. He wanted attitude? Look in the mirror, she wanted to say. "The victim's sister. The victim's name is Leigh Watney. Her sister Candace," Savannah pointed inside her office, "filed the missing person report yesterday."

Cole appeared impressed, "That's some good work. Quick too."

"Well, since the menfolk decided I needed a new assignment, I thought I'd better jump to it. Y'all deal with the blood and guts, I get to deal with the devastated family at the worst time in their lives."

Cole sighed and mumbled under his breath. She heard every word – *let it go already.*

Ennis took a gentler approach, "You don't need the sun or heat right now. Plus, I was trying to save you the carnage."

"It was gorier than the others," Cole agreed a bit too loud.

Savannah shushed him, "Do you mind? There's only a pane of glass separating your indelicacy from a distraught woman." Candace melted into tears the second she identified her sister and they hadn't stopped since. Savannah realized a victim's family deserved consideration and respect than Cole Jordan could muster. Some people required kid gloves, not boxing gloves.

"What did you learn about Leigh Watney?" Ennis asked.

"She was a nurse at Grady, worked the late shift the night she went missing –"

"Did she know Shelton?" Cole butted in.

That did it, "Y'know, Jordan, I've had to ask this woman some damn difficult things. I don't like throwing people in the deep end right off the bat. I was getting to it."

Refusing to back down, he appraised the weeping woman in the office, "Want me to play the bad guy? I'll ask her about him."

Savannah positioned herself between him and the door, "I want you to back off."

Cole's vision swung from the office to Savannah who crossed her arms again. She hoped the set of her jaw explained the seriousness of the request. Even if Cole ignored the warning, Ennis didn't, "Jordan, let's go get some coffee. Let Savannah do her job."

Cole seemed to have a penchant for ignoring people, she noticed. It was as if Ennis never uttered a word. She watched the wrinkles at Cole's eyes deepen as he tried for a tense smile, "That's okay. I gotta take a leak anyway." He waved his hand in a grand manner, "Have at her, babe." Then he tapped his watch, "Just remember there's a murderer out there and we're burning daylight being *delicate* with everyone."

Watching him walk away, she forced herself to take a deep breath. If throttling Cole Jordan hadn't been illegal, she'd have climbed aboard and commenced pounding.

"Calm down," Ennis said. "He's just an asshole. Remember that."

Rolling her eyes, she shook her head, "I need a minute. My rash is starting up again, no thanks to him."

Savannah went to the bathroom to apply more cream but found the longer she was away from Cole, the more relief she got from the rash.

She settled for stealing a few quiet moments in the bathroom before facing Candace again.

When she decided to venture back to her office, she couldn't locate Ennis but found Cole inside, his butt propped on the edge of her desk as he spoke to Leigh's sister. *That son of a bitch...* He glanced up and conveniently disregarded her presence and kept talking. Candace sat, head in hands, her long dark hair shielding her face. Her sobs spilled into the hallway despite the door being closed. Whatever Cole said threatened to finish the woman off.

Savannah yanked the door open, "Excuse me, Detective Jordan, but didn't we discuss this earlier?"

"Yeah well, I wanted to keep her company. While I was doing that, I thought a few questions couldn't hurt."

She waved him away from her desk. She opted for that gesture instead of the one-fingered kind, "As you clearly see, they do." She plucked a tissue from the Kleenex box on her desk, handed it to Candace.

Candace's beet red face rose to meet Savannah's, "I never thought I was putting Leigh at risk because of my association with Duke Shelton."

The female detective practically swallowed her tongue. Speech abandoned her. While she gathered her wits, her bold counterpart continued, "Candace was a client of Shelton's. Her sister dropped her off at his house a couple of times." He spoke proudly, as though he'd not only validated his current interrogation but cracked the case wide open.

Savannah finally found her voice, incredulity and all, "Did you really accuse her of endangering her sister?"

Cole gave a half shrug, "You never know what'll tickle Shelton's fancy. Maybe he liked Leigh –"

"Shut up, Cole," she ordered. "You have no clue what you're saying."

Candace tried her hand at speaking. The words came in hitches as she sobbed, "Detective Jordan said Duke killed my sister."

Savannah scowled at Cole, "There is no solid evidence implicating Duke Shelton at this time. Detective Jordan knows this." She pointed to the door, "May I see you outside, Detective?" She'd basically spat the last word, something not lost on Cole who frowned at her tone but relented anyway. In the meantime, a nervous tick twitched at her right eye. Great. First a rash, then Cole, now a nervous tick. Locusts, flies, lice and boils weren't far behind.

They stepped out and she shut the door behind them. Savannah verbally flayed him, "What part of *back off* went past you? I mean, you told her she was complicit in her sister's death? What were you thinking?"

"I was thinking maybe that's why we couldn't directly connect some victims to Shelton. Maybe they were related to his clients somehow. If you'd think a little more about the case rather than everyone's feelings, we might get somewhere."

Ennis appeared at precisely the right time – just before she belted Cole, "Stay the hell out of my office, Jordan," she warned. "You wanna make a woman cry? Call your mama." She glanced back at Ennis, "Keep him out of my way."

An hour later, Ennis leaned in her office, crooked his finger at her. It could mean only one thing. Cole struck again. The man was a walking natural disaster. Had he scared off another victim's family, destroyed evidence, run over a small child? Her heart sank at the various possibilities. Then she thought of Job. He managed to survive his trials so maybe there was hope... But until then, "What has he done now?"

At first puzzled by her question, Ennis shook his head, "For once, it's not Jordan. It's your suggestion that may have paid off. Now are you coming or do I have to sling you over my shoulder? 'Cause people will talk if that happens."

The threat (or promise) caused a tingle from her breasts that traveled below her navel. His take charge mood turned her on. But first reality took precedence, "You mean someone had video of the killer?"

"Looks like there's a chance." Ennis reached out, a wicked gleam in his eyes, "Which is it? The easy or the fun way?"

Savannah tried to control the scandalous thoughts racing through her mind as she stood up, "Better keep it easy. We can try the fun way later." She followed him down the narrow hallway and after a few turns until they arrived at the video room.

Ennis pushed the door open, "Security camera at a car lot half a block away caught the guy dumping a body."

She nearly turned around to go back to her office. Since banning Cole from the place, she regarded it as her sanctuary. "Nearly a block away? Ennis, the guy's gonna look like a sprite."

Ennis motioned for the tech to run the video, "Uniforms are still searching for more security cameras in the area that might have caught another angle."

Savannah crossed her arms. She'd hoped scouring the area for cameras might yield a better view of the killer. Granted, it was a long shot because the jerk always chose exposed, broad areas of land to dump the bodies. They were just lucky a car dealership or two decided to build there. She remembered a bank and gas station not too far from the ravine but doubted anything would come of it.

The screen lit up with a grainy black and white picture. Electronic snow obscured the scene momentarily then white lines slashed the picture in two. The latter ebbed into smaller needle-like flares but the snow equaled an electronic blizzard. With the muted lighting from the dealership competing with the blackness of night, it was a no-brainer which won out. "Ennis," she said, incredulous.

"Just watch, Negative Nellie."

Even with glasses she began to squint at the screen now, trying to focus on a car pulling next to the ravine. The trunk lid lifted as if on its own accord but the trunk – thanks to the shadows – appeared empty. The driver door opened next – she made note that the car was a four door – and watched the killer exit the car. He towered over the mid-size sedan and Savannah gauged his height as six feet, maybe a bit taller. "Foreign car?" she asked.

"My guess," her husband replied then pointed to the monitor.

She was wrong, she supposed, when she called the guy a sprite. Even with the street lamps and dealership lighting, a person could see the man was tall and muscular and looked to have short hair beneath a baseball cap. He rounded the back of the car and leaned into the trunk.

Savannah's stomach clenched with the realization of what was about to happen.

The man, his face obscured by the ball cap, lifted Leigh Watney's lifeless body from the dark abyss and carried it to the ravine. Again, shadows shrouded the man's movements. All Savannah saw was him bending down into the ravine holding Leigh's body then, after a few moments, he stood up, his arms empty. He took two long strides from the ravine, brushed off his hands and headed for the car. After closing the trunk, he got in and drove away.

"I'm sorry, but how does this help?" she asked Ennis. "There are probably millions of cars that match that general description and nearly as many men matching his."

"You're not watching," he stabbed a finger at the screen.

Savannah sighed, humored him by pointedly staring at the monitor. Ten seconds passed when a car – the killer's car – doubled back on the road and drove right in front of the security camera.

The tech stopped the tape, "That's one camera from the scene. Here's the other one, located across the lot, pointed the opposite direction." She clicked a button on another monitor and another grainy tape started playing.

Savannah watched the same car cruise right by the camera. Then it finally hit her what Ennis meant. Getting the driver's identity would be impossible but… "Is there any way we can –"

"Get a plate number?" he finished. "Maybe even a make and model? I've already asked our friend here," he waved his hand at the tech, "if she'd work on it."

She wanted to grab her husband in a breath-stealing embrace but thought better of it, at least in front of witnesses. She settled for, "Ennis, you're a genius."

He winked, "You're the genius for thinking of the cameras. I am a *patient* genius because I watch the whole movie and wait for the ending." He leaned down, whispering, "You can thank me tonight."

13

Thank God for Saturday. That was Savannah's first thought upon waking the next morning. No work, no duties, no *nothing*. The security video came up empty for a plate number though the techs remained vigilant with that task and trying to pry the killer's identity from the tape. She had the tech print photos from the tape, eight in all, hoping she could help. She stared at the photos, struggling to put together a workable description for the killer and his car or even a number to the plate. By end of shift, she managed only to develop a headache.

But it was Saturday, a free day she could spend any way she wanted and first on her list – the man lying next to her.

She snuggled against Ennis, listening to his long, deep breathing. He'd thrown back the sheet, revealing the dark hair sprinkled on his chest, the toned muscles beneath. She wanted to touch him but feared waking him. For the past few days, he'd worried himself into fitful sleep about Duke Shelton. Once she told him about her meeting – then the flowers arrived – Ennis wound up in a furious storm that ebbed into brooding.

Savannah ran her hand softly down his chest. He stirred beneath the covers, curled his arm around her back, "Mornin'."

"Good morning," she leaned closer, placed a kiss to his chest. She eased her hand down his belly to his shorts and slipped her fingers inside.

His eyes widened, his voice still sleepy and rough, "Whoa, girl, unless you're signing on for the whole ride. Takes more than eight seconds to win my prize."

The rodeo reference brought a smile, "It better because I'm buying a day pass for your playground."

Surprised, Ennis pulled her closer, "Sure you're up for it? You've been pretty tired lately."

Her brow sank with a good-natured frown, "Since when do you turn down sex? I mean, if you don't want it then…"

Ennis rolled atop her, pinned her with his weight, a smile of his own emerging, "I'll make you regret saying that."

She could say one thing without a doubt. Ennis was always a man of his word. Their time together was more than welcome after the past few months. The diagnosis, surgery and tiring treatments wore on her but she realized Ennis suffered along with her in his own way.

After their romp, they took a long, leisure shower then dressed in casual wear to lounge around the house. Savannah settled for an old faded Falcons t-shirt and jeans while Ennis opted for a Cowboys t-shirt and jeans that looked like they'd been mistaken for a duck in hunting season.

Their house, like their attire, looked quite lived in so Savannah decided to remedy the former. Their lovemaking energized her more than she'd expected and dusting furniture and cleaning windows didn't seem entirely overwhelming. Considering her crappy week at work, she preferred Cinderella work to fighting with idiots like Cole.

Ennis offered to help by vacuuming and straightening pillows on the sofa. It's all he felt qualified to do, he'd said. Savannah suspected he just wanted to watch the Braves game on TV. The little house never took long to vacuum or clean so by the time he finished, she expected he could catch the first pitch. Since her rash eased up overnight and had the decency to stay that way during their lovemaking, she felt rather lucky. The only flare up occurred in the shower so she applied a small amount of cream afterward to ward off further distress. Finally. A good day.

She was preparing to clean windows when a knock on the door interrupted her, dashing her hopes of an early start on housecleaning.

Opening the door, she found herself instinctively stepping back. A tall black man in a suit crowded the entire doorway. She faced Warren Sapp's twin. If the football player's bulk measured anywhere near this man's, she thought, no wonder people shrank back from him.

He looked down at her, "Missus Prince?"

She wasn't sure whether to answer that or not. He was big enough to grab her and drag her off under his arm. She felt much better when Ennis sidled up behind her, "Who are you?"

"I'm here for a Missus Savannah Prince." He stood aside to reveal a black stretch limousine. "I have an appointment to pick her up."

"I don't have a meeting anywhere," she was sure of it. "Especially with anyone owning a limo."

Ennis that stiffened at the reference. "You talkin' about Duke Shelton?"

Oh hell, not him again, she nearly said out loud. The breakfast. She'd forgotten all about it after hers and Ennis's romantic morning. "I'm not going. Please tell him thanks but no thanks."

"Missus, you might want to rethink that." He waved to another man, this one quite possibly bigger than the one standing before her, who opened the back door of the limousine.

Savannah squinted to see inside the car. Someone leaned forward in the seat, then turned toward the porch. It was Georgia.

"Damn," Savannah sighed. Her perfect day just got flushed. Drawing off that lovely thought, her temper fired as she stepped past Mr. Sapp, "I'm having a talk with her."

His hand wrapped around her elbow, "Missus, you'll be going with us so if you please, take what you need for the morning, and we'll get going."

"Let her go," Ennis barked.

The man did and Savannah made her way to the limo. A few neighbors wandered from their homes to get a better view of the long polished limo parked in front of the modest little house. Savannah was embarrassed at the scene. Now the neighborhood would be abuzz with gossip.

She leaned in the car to see another large man, this one sitting across from Georgia. Her sister dressed casually in Nikes, a black pullover and beige shorts. Not very formal but then Duke's card said to dress comfortably.

Savannah addressed her sister, "What are you doing? Get out of there."

The eldest moved two of her latest books from the seat to her lap, "Duke's card said you were going and I figured I should too. To prevent any misconceptions about our acquaintanceship."

"You explained it very plainly and very well the other day. Georgia," she whispered, "get out. I'll take you home."

"I've already committed to go."

"What did you tell Dane?"

"The truth. I'm meeting someone who previously helped me with research."

"But did you tell him who you were seeing? You know, a guy who loves to literally flog women and make them beg on their knees? A guy who," she reminded quietly, "is a *suspect* in a murder investigation."

"Either get in or stay home," she checked her watch. "We're going to be late. Duke hates it when guests are late."

Jeez, what did it take with this woman? "I get it, okay? I screwed up. Just get the hell out of the car." She glanced at the guy across from Georgia, hinting, "This doesn't exactly have a jolly vibe, does it? Feels more like Don Corleone's men taking their guests on a little trip to the acid factory."

Georgia refused to answer. Her sister fumed inwardly most times but never let a person doubt when they committed a major gaffe. After a few silent moments, Savannah tugged at her worn out t-shirt, "I'm not dressed to go visiting."

"That's okay, Missus," Warren's deep voice came from behind her. It startled her so bad she shot rod straight, banging her head on the door frame in the process. Backing out of the car, she turned, rubbing the back of her head. She nearly told him to back off. The words, poised on her tongue, evaporated upon facing the giant. His apology didn't hurt either.

He finished, "Our boss wants his guests comfortable."

Why, so we'll fit in the fifty-five gallon drums easier? She stared at Georgia, giving her time to change her mind and come to her senses.

Her sister patted the books in her lap, "He wants a couple of copies for his girls."

In other words, she's going to Shelton's come hell or high water... Most likely the former since Atlanta hadn't seen rains of that magnitude since pairs of animals boarded a big boat and took a cruise for forty days and forty nights. Savannah cursed under her breath, looked behind her, "Ennis, get my phone. We're leaving."

Ennis's jaw dropped, "But you said you weren't. *Remember* what you said?"

Yes, she'd said Duke Shelton might be a murderer. But, "Georgia's not changing her mind. I can't let her go alone."

Ennis, unlike his wife, didn't bother to veil his curse. He said it out loud where a few neighbors heard him. Those ventured back into their homes. The others still seemed mesmerized by the huge limo parked on the street.

He stalked into the house then back out clenching her cell phone in his hand. He took her aside, warning, "If you feel anything going wrong, call me." He bent to kiss her, "I don't like this."

"Neither do I." She touched his chest, reached for another kiss, "Love you, babe. See you soon." She turned to get in the car and felt a gentle swat on her bottom.

"You'd better," he said.

Warren piled in after her and as the car proceeded down the street, she looked back at Ennis. He stood on the curb, hands on hips, staring after them. No doubt he stood there giving the men, Duke *and* her a piece of his mind.

She wouldn't have gone if Georgia hadn't but she needed to protect her sister against a man who clearly hadn't let his obsession go.

"You ladies like a drink before we arrive?" Warren inquired. When Georgia shook her head, he passed his vision to Savannah, "We have non-alcoholic beverages as well."

Savannah rolled her eyes. Great. She hadn't expected her battle with alcohol to become common knowledge. It angered her that Duke spread the news like wildfire. It, like Georgia, was none of his business. Savannah too shook her head, "What we really want is to go home."

Warren sat back and chose not to further her remark. It seemed to be an epidemic. She glanced at Georgia who'd discovered a tactful, effective way to ignore her as well.

They rode in silence for the most part while the limousine glided to their destination. Savannah recognized the Shelton estate. An imposing black iron fence blurred past, revealing glimpses of the mansion behind old oak and maples tall enough to reach the sky.

Georgia shifted in the seat. Savannah noticed anxiety overshadowed her since the trip began. An anxiety only Savannah sensed. The car turned onto the road leading to the estate's entrance and the younger sister pled her case once more, "You can still back out. Georgia, he's obsessed with you."

Ignoring Savannah's comment, Georgia stared in the direction of the mansion. Savannah got the hint, shrugging, "But hey, I'm just a detective and that's just *my* impression of him."

There was an edge to Georgia's voice, "It's your impression that got me into this. If you hadn't assumed, I wouldn't feel the necessity to clear things up."

Savannah pressed back into the seat, surprised at her sister's passion on the subject. She hadn't opened a can of worms earlier that week, she'd blasted open a barrel of them… "Georgia, I said I was sorry. Don't feel obligated to see him because of my mistaken notion."

Georgia, still eyeing the mansion ominously, remained quiet. This side of her sister unsettled Savannah. During the trip, Georgia gradually changed. Colder, reserved, with arms folded over her chest. More transpired those many years ago than Georgia disclosed and Duke was the catalyst.

She saw Georgia take a deep breath. She built a steel shell around herself for this meeting – Savannah only hoped it was strong enough to withstand Duke.

The limo traveled to the house a little too fast for Savannah's taste. The driver parked the car in the half circle drive. Both he and Mr. Sapp exited. They stood outside the open car doors, hands extended for each sister. Neither partook of the gesture.

As they stepped out, Georgia tilted back to gaze at the massive house, the only sounds were birds twittering and oak leaves rustling in the gentle Atlanta breeze.

The eldest sister bristled, swallowed hard then started up the stairs to the porch. Savannah hurried behind. Feeling responsible for throwing Georgia into this fray again, she surely wouldn't allow her to endure it alone.

The moment their feet touched the top step, the door opened and the same woman stood, waving them inside, "Welcome, ladies. Please come in."

Savannah noted the woman focused on Georgia. They stepped inside and the Amazon leveled a cold glare on Savannah who returned the sentiment. However, when the blonde stood in front of Georgia, she bowed her head with a soft, "May I tend to your shoes?"

The sisters removed their shoes and the Amazon retrieved them. The brunette appeared again with her metal detector. Savannah lifted her arms, "I know, I know." She let the woman wave the detector around her. The brunette then stepped toward Georgia with bowed head, "I regret the invasion of your privacy, ma'am, but Master Shelton requires it."

"I remember the routine." Georgia sat the autographed books on a nearby table and held her arms out to her sides.

The brunette swept the wand over Georgia then graciously thanked her. She didn't thank Savannah, who was beginning to feel like a stepchild. They all treated Georgia with respect and reverence and treated Savannah like Cinderella before the ball.

Angelique appeared in the doorway, arms crossed and her slender body sheathed in an apricot colored dress. Calmly, but with an air of disdain, she approached Georgia, "Welcome back, Beauty. It's been a long time."

Georgia nearly stepped back but stopped, realizing Savannah stood close behind. To reassure her, Savannah placed her hand at her sister's waist. Standing a good three inches taller than Georgia, Savannah made sure Angelique witnessed her warning glance.

Georgia swallowed dryly, "Hello, Angelique. I'm only here for business."

Surprised at the tentativeness of Georgia's response, Savannah wondered what exactly transpired long ago. Georgia's body became rigid and no amount of her reassurance changed it.

The sway in Angelique's hips, the arrogant tilt of her chin told Savannah the woman knew. She knew Georgia feared her and was bound to capitalize on it. With her high heels Angelique stood taller than both sisters and as she neared, she basically towered over Georgia, "I realize why you're here. Master Shelton will be most pleased with your presence."

Savannah sensed the territorial battle shift into high gear. Angelique was so threatened by Georgia's presence, she pointedly intimidated her with anything imaginable – a fact that was about to take an even more personal aspect. Angelique pointed beside her, "I'm required to do body searches so," a stern tone weighed down the last four words, "take your place, *Beauty*."

In a bold move, Georgia met the redhead's eyes, her arms crossed, "No. Duke doesn't require body searches. You do, and I'm not about to submit to one."

Savannah volleyed her vision between her sister and Angelique. She thought it interesting Georgia used the word "submit" but had the good sense to remain silent. Unless the situation called for her intervention, she'd stay the hell out of it.

"I, unlike others," Angelique replied, "do not question Master Shelton's wishes. I obey them with grace." She folded her arms over her chest again. Her demeanor shouted an arrogance Savannah hadn't seen before. Snootiness yes, when she first met the redhead but nothing compared to the standoff between her and Georgia.

When intimation failed, Angelique tried condescension, "You have two choices. Let me search you or you may leave."

Savannah suddenly felt the power struggle tip in Georgia's favor. Angelique fought to retain the power but knew Georgia ultimately held it. Savannah stood behind her sister both for support and in case Georgia lunged. As angry and bitter as she seemed, Savannah wouldn't second guess her.

Georgia straightened, "You'll step back and let us pass. If Duke wants to see us, that is. Otherwise we're leaving, he'll be most unhappy and since he invited us, *you'll* answer for our absence."

Good one, Savannah applauded. *That'll shut Morticia's yap.* Of course she could thank herself for putting Georgia in the prickly mood but at least someone else suffered her venomous strike this time...

Surprisingly, Angelique hesitated.   Georgia challenged her authority and sought temporarily to reclaim whatever influence she had.

Angelique swiveled on her toes and strode to the dining room's doorway with a clipped, "This way, please."

Impressed with Georgia's effort and realizing she was a trembling heap from the attempt, Savannah reached forward and took her sister's hand. Grateful for the support, Georgia squeezed the hand in thanks while following Angelique to the dining room.

If Shelton's estate appeared massive from the outside, nothing compared to the interior – and all the rooms and hallways one navigated to find the dining room.

Savannah followed behind her sister who, despite being escorted, seemed to know her way to their destination. That fact still stung the younger sister, made her question if Georgia told her the truth about her relationship with Duke. How far did her research go since she recalled his house from memory, especially after so many years?

They padded over a polished stone floor until finally stopping at the dining room's entry. It didn't surprise Savannah to see that deep in the bowels of the dark, rustic mansion sat a large cherry wood table, at least eight feet long, surrounded by heavy, intimidating chairs. Above the table hung an ornate black metal wheel lined with flame-like bulbs. Shelton either liked playing up the medieval aspect or he generally enjoyed making people uneasy. She opted for the latter.

Savannah watched as a young woman, draped in a silky green wrap, bowed her head when Georgia approached – much the same way the girls did when Duke entered the room. She escorted Georgia to the head of the table, motioned to a chair beside it. Sliding the chair out, the woman motioned, "If you please, ma'am."

Her sister refused to sit, "I'd prefer another chair."

Angelique appeared at the door. "Master Shelton assigned that position to you."

Despite Angelique's corroboration, Georgia stepped away, "This is your place at the table. I'm not –"

"Sit, Beauty," the reply emerged ill-tempered. "It is Master Shelton's wish and you do not want to displease him."

The tone demanded she comply. She did but shot an aggravated glance at her sister. Savannah still reeled in the treatment Georgia received. In some ways, it was as though the Queen arrived.

Angelique turned her sights on Savannah, "Detective, Master Shelton assigned this seat to you."

Savannah's vision shifted from Georgia and Angelique to the seat across from Georgia. Duke had Georgia sitting directly to his right, Savannah to his left. He'd displaced Angelique for some reason and that worried Savannah.

The young woman with the soft voice pulled the chair out for Savannah, "If you please, ma'am."

Savannah wasn't sure whether to sit or run. Something odd transpired the past few minutes and none of it set well. Angelique held a grudge against Georgia. Savannah's guess was Duke lavished Georgia in the attention the redhead sought so eagerly to have.

Savannah shook out her napkin, placed it across her lap. She tried making eye contact with Georgia, but she pointedly refused. Georgia hid something important from her, she thought, and it revolved around

Duke and Angelique. Why wouldn't she tell her, Savannah wondered. Why wouldn't she *trust* her?

The women at the doorway suddenly stood rod straight, their heads bowed, "Master Shelton,"

Duke strode in differently this day. His lean, muscular body had the same nonchalant grace but now a confident swagger fine-tuned his stride when he caught sight of Georgia. His mood was buoyant and blissful, "Ah, Beauty. My delightful, precious Beauty has returned."

As he passed Savannah, a hint of spice drifted past. Charcoal slacks lined his long legs and a burgundy polo shirt form-fitted his strong chest and shoulders. Savannah's contempt intensified knowing that color combination was Georgia's favorite. He wore aftershave – a change from earlier in the week. He'd gone all out for Georgia, just another reason Savannah should've packed the Tums. This would test her stomach a variety of ways and her without an antacid to her name...

Duke bent, kissed Georgia's cheek, "You are lovelier than ever, my dear."

Georgia pulled away, "Duke."

He seemed hurt, "What is this? My Beauty denying me a kiss?"

"I'm not your Beauty," she said then suddenly blurted, "and I'm engaged."

Savannah's vision rose to meet Georgia's in a question. Georgia never lied to anyone about anything, at least nothing as important as hers and Dane's relationship. The fact she did wound the thread of anxiety tighter in her gut.

Duke smiled, cut his vision to Savannah, "Must be in the Prince blood to lie about such things. No wonder your father found you so troublesome."

"That does it," Savannah stood, tossed the napkin on the table. "Let's go, Georgia. I knew this was a mistake." The visit hadn't felt right to her from the beginning. It was best to leave now before something else happened.

Duke straightened, made his way to Savannah. She assumed his smile was meant to charm her. Instead, it instilled a distinct desire for her trusty .38.

He lifted her hand to his lips. The soft, warm kiss belied his expression, his thumb stroking her skin, "My dear, dear Savannah. I mean no harm or insult. My ability to joke is rather rusty at times. My apologies to you both. Let's sit and partake of this lovely meal my girls prepared." He patted her hand, "Shall we?"

Savannah looked to Georgia for the answer. Personally she could take it or leave it but her sister had a past here and it was her decision how long they stayed.

Georgia gave a hesitant nod. Savannah began to sit but Duke stepped behind her, giving her pause. He motioned for her to sit, "Relax. I'm merely doing my gentlemanly duties."

Something still felt wrong. He was too smug. Much different than earlier in the week.

He took his seat, shook out his napkin and waved his hand over the table, "Look at all the fine cuisine my girls have prepared. I told them we were having special company today and they have not disappointed."

Table brimmed with food. There were bagels, Danishes, muffins, apple galettes and a variety of other foods. How the hell could anyone eat that much?

Duke snapped his fingers. Seconds later yet another young woman appeared with a tray of drinks. Angelique followed behind, instructing, "These are for Beauty, these for her sister."

The girl placed a cup of coffee at Georgia's right hand, a glass of orange juice to her left. She then placed a glass of milk at Savannah's right hand and orange juice at her left. Where was her coffee? The one thing she truly needed that morning and it was missing. It figured, she thought then chalked it up to some bizarre penance on Duke's behalf.

She stared longingly at the brimming cup sitting in front of her sister, the steam rising from the rich smelling brew.

Duke saw her confusion, "Sorry, my dear. With your condition you really need to drink healthier than coffee. According to my sources, you enjoy orange juice and the occasional low fat milk. Beauty, on the other hand, may have coffee."

"Thanks for your concern," the detective deadpanned, staring at the milk. She wasn't one to stay stocked up on it except for Ennis who could drink a cow dry in minutes. "Occasional" should have read "practically never."

The dominant winked at her, lifted his coffee cup, "Shall we toast to a long, prosperous friendship?"

Georgia stirred cream into her coffee, and hesitantly joined him. Savannah opted for the orange juice, but really didn't want to toast to anything but a speedy return home.

The three toasted to friendship and Duke settled back, his excitement neared giddiness, "Now, I've the most wonderful surprise. I know Beauty prefers peach French toast and she shall have it, as will you, my dear. But just to liven the meal up, I had my chef prepare Piperade with Serrano ham. She can bring me to my knees with that meal."

If that was another attempt at a joke, Savannah wanted to say, his ability wasn't just rusty, it had fallen completely apart. She settled for a quizzical look that asked "What the hell is Piperade?"

Sensing this, he continued, "Piperade is a blend of eggs, bell peppers, tomatoes, onion, garlic and Serrano ham. As I've been told, you are a ham connoisseur so I expect a genuine critique later."

She agreed to provide one though she doubted her opinion mattered. Duke placated her, probably to keep her from mouthing off about being there in the first place.

Duke directed his attention to Georgia, "You came bearing gifts, I see. Always so generous and thoughtful. That's why I'll be partial to you until my dying breath."

Which could come sooner than you think if you touch my sister, Savannah thought with a tense smile.

Georgia replied, "They are advance copies of my new book. I thought the girls might like them."

Duke lifted one brow, "Signed, I trust?"

Georgia broke into a more relaxed smile, "Of course." She took another sip of her coffee much to Savannah's envy. The eldest sister's good mood faded as she glanced at her sister, "I'm afraid Savannah has the wrong impression of our friendship."

The dominant's other brow rose to meet the other, "Is that so? How unfortunate. I admit my explanation fell far short. After all, our written agreements are still valid and since she is your sister, I encouraged her to speak with you first. If you elect to tell her the capacity of our relationship, I shall yield to your judgment. If further explanation is required, I shall strive to eliminate any and all erroneous beliefs."

"She thinks I was your submissive and that you beat me with whips, chains and everything short of the kitchen sink. I told her none of it was true."

The blood rushed to Savannah's face. She hadn't expected her sister to swing the accusation like a baseball bat.

A hearty laugh broke the uneasy silence. Duke found it humorous for some sordid reason, "Two sisters with very active and clever imaginations. Savannah, my dear, nothing would have pleased me more than for Beauty to submit to me. Still wouldn't mind it today. But as she said, nothing happened with the distinct exception of my tutoring her on the fine art of dominance and submission. Hands-*off* tutoring to be more specific. It isn't as unsavory as people think. At some point, I do hope you'll reconsider my offer of training. You'd be a most compelling submissive. I believe you'd keep me on my toes."

"While you kept me on my knees, no doubt," Savannah struck back. She jumped as pain registered at her shin. Savannah peered across the table, seeing Georgia glare at her. Incredulous that Georgia kicked her, Savannah returned the heated expression.

Duke winked at Savannah again, "Savannah is entitled to express herself. I find her spirit stimulating."

Sneering back at her sister, Savannah retrieved her napkin and smoothed it across her lap, "Then you'll find this absolutely thrilling. I asked Cole about his wife. He said you raped her."

Georgia audibly choked at the accusation. Savannah looked at her and after a few moments, the older sister regained her composure. The scowl returned, basically spearing Savannah with another warning.

Duke, however, took no offense, "As I imagined he would. What your colleague neglected to say was *he* enjoyed rough sex. His wife came to me with the belief I'd train her how to bear it. My services do not include teaching a woman how to endure rape."

She hated discussing the case in front of Georgia who already appeared on the verge of exploding. Still, she needed to know Duke's version and he promised to give it. "Why would she want to endure it? Did she ever tell you?"

"To please her husband. But once I saw the bruises on her lovely face, I advised her to report the beast. Savannah, you don't understand. This woman was naturally submissive, dare I say perilously subservient, in all areas of her life. When faced with such compliance, I wonder if abuse isn't the cause. Most who train to be submissive require instruction, at least to some degree. This woman never made solid eye contact, always spoke softly and possessed the most reserved demeanor I'd ever encountered. She felt inadequate to meet her husband's demands. I explained that unless she agreed to and enjoyed his treatment of her during their intimacy, it was nothing short of sexual assault." He paused to sip from his juice glass.

Savannah never expected Duke to open up like a book and as it turned out, he still had plenty to say. "Cole Jordan did everything – paid bills, did the grocery shopping and bought her clothes – all so she never had to leave the house. She was only there as an outlet for his brutality. When I mentioned the authorities, she wilted before me in tears. She was an abused woman who was scared to take action and being new in town didn't help."

"Where was she from?"

"They moved here from Washington State. Renton, I believe. She asked me if she reported him, where could she go? I gave her phone numbers for local shelters and various other addresses to assist her."

"What happened after that?"

"I never saw her again. I assumed her husband ensured that she remained in the house after he discovered she came to me."

"Master Shelton, breakfast is ready to serve." The announcement came from a new face, this one as pretty as the others but her hair was pulled back in a ponytail and by her attire, Savannah knew she was the chef. She remained at the door, awaiting instructions.

Delight washed over Duke, "My guests are eager to try your creation, my dear." He looked to the redhead standing by the door, "Angelique, help Aurora with the plates."

"So you never had a sexual encounter with his wife?" Savannah asked when the chef stepped from of the room.

"Detective, please," Angelique scolded. "You are a guest –"

Duke lifted one hand, silencing her.

Angelique bowed her head, "Apologies, Master Shelton. I shall retrieve the plates with Aurora."

Duke returned his attention to Savannah, "I did not touch her."

"But your lifestyle promotes kinky sex which sometimes includes rape and physical punishment if the woman fights or refuses…"

"Savannah, don't," Georgia literally pleaded. Leaning closer to her sister, she finished, "Angelique is right. We're guests."

Duke's voice remained even and gentle, "It is alright, Beauty. Your sister has questions and I promised answers. My lifestyle is my business, Savannah. However, I did mention contracts, did I not? Each one is drawn up on a person to person basis, what they need and want, what I require from them –"

"Does it include sexual assault? You've been arrested –"

"And not convicted." He smiled what she considered an arrogant smile, "If any woman truly believes I've violated her, she can have me arrested. If I were truly guilty, my dear, I'd be in prison."

"Only if the victim makes it to trial. The women," she reminded, "have disappeared into thin air. All except two who we found raped and butchered. It seems that all the women who accuse you end up missing or dead –"

"Savannah Charlene," Georgia scolded with such vehemence it closed Savannah's mouth instantly.

Duke seemed pleased with Georgia's dressing down, "Allow me to reiterate once more. I did not have sexual relations with Cole Jordan's wife."

Savannah did a mental eye roll at his wording. A certain president used those words in regard to a woman and the entire country saw how honest he was…

Aurora and Angelique brought out two large plates. Angelique directed her as to whose plate was whose which Savannah thought odd. It was the same meal, wasn't it? Or had Duke made another change to Savannah's diet like he had with the coffee? Probably low fat something or other, she assumed, and she'd rather eat dirt than low fat food.

Once the plates were distributed, Angelique presented Duke's to him then sat at the table to eat, "Master Shelton hopes you enjoy your meal."

Thinking she'd have to choke down the food, Savannah opted for a small bite. She'd never been fond of highfalutin meals with strange or foreign names. She preferred her eggs fried or scrambled or occasionally boiled, not tossed into a hodgepodge of other food.

The first nibble tasted deceptively good. She detected a hint of bell pepper and onion and garlic, but nothing overwhelmed the general taste. She tried another bite, this one equally as delicious. Okay, so he lived a disgusting lifestyle. He thrived on control. His attitude even made her sick but he had brilliant taste in décor (which worried her to some degree) and he certainly hired a gifted chef to fill his belly each day.

Across the table, Georgia dug into the omelet with more assurance than she. But then she began chewing slowly and Savannah wondered if she tried to analyze the ingredients. Attempting to salve the rift between them, Savannah suggested, "Just ask for the recipe. Then you can go home and dabble to your heart's content."

Instead of answering, Georgia touched her throat and coughed a petite, diminutive cough like someone who swallowed wrong and tried not to let on. Georgia's cough worsened and that sent up a red flag.

"Are you okay?" Savannah asked.

With unblinking calm, Angelique suggested, "Perhaps Beauty should indulge in a sip of water."

The redhead's composure unnerved Savannah. It reminded her of a predator sizing up its prey. She turned back to Georgia whose labored breathing developed a slight wheezing when she drew breath.

Savannah rose to her feet, "Georgia, answer me. Are you okay?"

When her sister spoke, it was to Duke. "Is there seafood in this?"

Savannah cursed under her breath. The mere mention of seafood terrified her. In her younger years, Georgia's reaction to seafood had been particularly frightening. By the time the family arrived at the hospital, Georgia's throat began to close and her face had a bluish tinge. Seth tended to his seven year-old sister in the waiting room while R.J. and Charlene stayed with Georgia in the emergency room. Savannah remembered how scared she was at the time, and her fear returned now as her sister's face grew pale and sweaty.

Savannah looked at Duke, "Did you put seafood in the omelet?"

Offended now, he inquired, "You're accusing me of spiking her food?"

Her glare answered him. One small bite of seafood, one drop of the oil sent Georgia into a tailspin. Savannah prayed her sister still kept an Epipen in her purse. The epinephrine auto-injector might be the only thing that saved her until they arrived at the hospital. Savannah knew time was critical and hurried toward Georgia's purse, "Hold on, hon, and try to stay calm. I'll find your Epipen."

Gutting it for the lifesaving epinephrine took precedence over any orderliness in the handbag and she figured Georgia wouldn't bitch her out for destroying the purse's tidiness.

Once retrieved, she removed the safety cap and handed it to Georgia who clutched the Epipen in her fist. The panic on her sister's face sent Savannah's fear soaring. Memories flooded back from childhood, setting in hard like the allergy had Georgia.

Once Georgia administered the injection in her thigh, Savannah rounded on Duke, enunciating each word carefully, "Did you put seafood in her omelet?"

"Of course not. Only a monster would poison someone with such an allergy."

The man thrived on controlling women and abusing them, her brain screamed. *He* was responsible, she was sure of it but, "If you didn't, you know who did. Now, have your driver take us to the hospital or I'll call 911."

With unnerving calm, Duke Shelton appraised Georgia's condition. Savannah's blood pressure mounted at his composed demeanor. "What are you waiting for?" she demanded. If he truly understood the danger he was in, he'd race to the phone – or the door – for his driver.

When he faltered for a decision, Savannah made it for him by grabbing her cell phone and hurriedly dialed 911. "This is Detective Savannah Prince of the Atlanta Police–"

Duke ripped the phone from her hand, closed it. "You will not bring the authorities to this property."

Savannah stalked toward him, stopping just short of running him over, "Give me my phone. I have to help my sister since you won't."

He held his ground, "I never said I wouldn't help." He offered Savannah the phone which she angrily plucked from his grasp. He addressed Aurora, "Send for Michael. He'll be taking Beauty and her sister to the hospital right away."

Savannah took another look at Georgia who still struggled for air, then she turned back to Duke, "That driver better have rockets on his ass or lead in his foot because we're getting to that hospital in record time."

14

Columbia Memorial had been the closest facility to the Shelton estate. Over the last six weeks, Savannah grew to learn the areas of the hospital and its hallways by heart. The aggravation of the daily radiation treatments were nearly over and Savannah thanked God for it but that day she thanked God the place was so close by when Georgia needed it.

For thirty minutes, Savannah stood outside the emergency room doors, praying her sister would be okay and plotting and planning all manner of harm and indignities for Duke Shelton. When the doctor informed her of Georgia's improving condition, she finally relaxed for the first time in nearly an hour.

Upon their arrival, she'd called Ennis and Dane. Forty minutes later, Ennis arrived as panicked and angry as she'd been. What happened, he wanted to know. When she explained the situation, Ennis made a point of reminding her "it was stupid to go see Shelton".

"Duh, Ennis," she snapped, "but I couldn't let her go alone. She'd have died in that house as concerned as he was."

Ennis shook his head, "It's neither here nor there, I guess. I'm just glad she'll be okay."

Down the hall, Dane rounded the corner in such a rush he nearly skidded into a nurse. Dressed in his customary cowboy attire of boots, jeans, button down shirt and a Stetson, Ennis's older brother caught the interest of several staff, especially the one he nearly T-boned.

The Rutherford brothers favored enough that a complete stranger realized they were kin. Indeed, as he spoke to the nurse, she turned in Ennis's direction then back to Dane.

Savannah overheard bits of the mostly one-sided conversation and heard the alarmed nuance in Dane's usual composed voice. She waved at him, hoping to gain his attention – and finally succeeded.

Savannah realized she and Dane shared more than the same age – they both loved Georgia with all their heart but if he didn't calm down, Dane would find himself in the hospital too. The sound of cowboy boots echoed through the hallway as he approached. He removed his gray Stetson, "How is she?"

Savannah replied, "They're getting her blood pressure back up –"

His brown eyes widened, "Blood pressure? Oh my God…"

She wanted him to calm down. He'd keel over from a stroke at this rate so she kept her voice even, "Dane, the doctor said she'll be okay. Her pressure dropped because of the reaction. They're giving her something for nausea and to help her breathing. The doctor said he expected to keep her until this evening then she can go home."

Dane blew out a breath, "You're okay, right? I mean, you don't have an allergy, do you?"

"No, just Georgia."

Frustrated now, he scrubbed a hand through his hair, "What

happened? Did this guy decide to serve clams for breakfast? Why didn't she opt out of eating if that was the case?"

She pointed to a cowlick standing at attention on his head, "He served an omelet with ham."

Dane's brow sank as he combed his hair with his fingers, "I don't understand. How does seafood fit in with ham and eggs?"

From the corner of her eye, she watched Ennis frantically shake his head, mouthing "no" to her. His expression and demeanor held a warning – do not, under any circumstances, tell Dane. But why didn't he want his brother to know? Dane would just nag her until she explained. "The food had to be spiked somehow," she said.

Turning her attention back to Dane, she began to understand why Ennis begged her not to speak up.

Dane Rutherford stood a bit taller than his younger brother. His shoulders were broader and when he loomed over a person, he *loomed*, "Spiked? The guy did this on purpose? He knew about the allergy?"

Ennis clamped his hands to his hips. She read his expression perfectly. *See what you've done?* Savannah tried to bale herself out, "Dane, I don't know if he –"

"Don't lie to me, Peach," he stepped forward which forced her to step back. He took another step and another until he practically backed her against the wall. "Did he know?"

She peered around Dane's shoulder to Ennis. *Like to help me here?* No, evidently he decided against throwing her a lifeline. She jumped into the deep end by herself so he'd let her flail. Fine. "Yes, he knew about the allergy, but Dane –"

"What's his name? Where does he live?"

Savannah recognized this tone. She'd heard it enough from Ennis. It spelled big trouble. The kind people got arrested for, the kind that came with prison sentences.

He moved closer to her to intimidate her, she assumed. Dane was certainly imposing but she also realized he wouldn't hurt her. Still, she put a hand to his chest, a sign that was far enough. "Let me handle it."

Dane's chest swelled against her hand, and his heart pounded against her fingers. He was furious. "Tell me his name, Savannah."

"No. Dane, calm down. You're working yourself up and it's not helping Georgia." She figured a minor guilt trip might do the trick. If he thought his behavior affected Georgia, he'd calm down.

It seemed to work – sort of. He eased onto a nearby bench and she joined him. "I know you're angry," she said, "and so am I. But frontier justice will only get you arrested." She turned to Ennis. If he refused to help her, maybe he'd help his brother, "Like to get him some coffee, tea? Maybe Valium?"

Still clearly miffed, Ennis marched in the direction of the vending machines.

Dane shook his head, "Peach, I gotta do something," he wiped a shaky hand down his face. "I'll lose it if this guy walks."

Savannah took his hand, "He won't walk, I promise."

Dane's vision met hers. She prayed he read her unspoken vow but he was too angry. The violence in his eyes flared again, "You can't promise that. He's a rich bastard who can buy his way out of trouble."

That fact didn't make her giddy with joy either. She tightened her grip on his hand and lowered her voice to a whisper, "He can't buy me, Dane. Do you understand? He can't buy *me*."

A plethora of emotions crossed his features. When the weight of her words hit, his eyes widened, "Peach, you'll get fired if you hurt that son of a bitch. I can slit his throat just as –"

"But you won't because he won't let you in his house. He will let me in."

"What are you gonna do? I can't let you go over there and kill him. That's my job."

"I won't kill him but I'll make Duke Shelton wish he was dead. You take care of Georgia. The only thing I need from you and Ennis is my car…"

Savannah and Ennis spent the night at Georgia's. Savannah stayed to help her sister and Ennis to keep Dane under control. Ennis told her from far back about Dane's temper and how protective he was over women.

"A little like you?" she accused and that seemed to shut him up.

Morning dawned with no one getting sleep except Georgia. Dane followed through on getting Savannah's Camaro. Ennis took his brother to pick up the car and, according to Dane, asked plenty of questions about why she needed it right away. Dane never said why.

She had no gun and her identification and license were still at home. All she had was her cell phone but Savannah didn't need much for what she was planning – just pent-up rage and her bare hands.

The gates to Shelton's estate swung open within seconds of her announcing her presence. The Camaro screeched to a stop on the driveway. Running up the stairs she was surprised when the front door swung open with the same ease as the front gates.

The woman – Aurora, she remembered – tried to stop her but she barged past, "Where's Duke?"

"Detective, I implore you, please remove your shoes..."

Her shoes were the last thing they should worry about, Savannah reflected just as the tall Amazon appeared and stepped in her path. The woman's voice lacked the civility of Aurora's, "You will remove your shoes and weapon before entering this house."

Savannah leveled a withering scowl on the woman that neither backed her off or intimidated her. With one good shove, Savannah pushed past her, "Where is he?"

By the time she walked into the living room with his attendants in tow, Duke Shelton stood by the fireplace, his demeanor only slightly rattled, "I'm glad you're here, Savannah. I've been threatened and I need protection."

The rage building for nearly twenty-four hours spilled over as she stormed toward him, "Then you're asking the wrong person." She drew back her fist then swung with the intention of knocking out as many teeth as possible.

Long before her fist met its target, his large hand grasped her wrist, twisting her arm behind her back. To ward off any defensive move, he bore down on the nerve in her shoulder with his other hand.

The resulting pain sent her to her knees. "Let me go, you bastard," she whimpered. "I'm a police officer."

Duke remained calm, "At this point, you're an intruder trying to harm me. I'm not foolish enough to release you."

She struggled to gain any leverage against the hold but both hands solidified their grasp. He addressed her as he would a petulant child, "You will remain in this position until I decide otherwise. Since you refuse to converse in a civilized manner, I will assume you are also armed."

"I'm not," she replied, pain still evident in her voice.

"And I do not believe you. Aurora, summon the boys."

The quiet, unassuming woman regarded Savannah much like she would a rampaging lion whose tranquilizer dart failed to work. Taking a wide berth around the detective, Aurora's fear evolved from obedient submissive to plain old frightened female. Savannah was glad her rage affected someone because Duke certainly never flinched.

While they waited, she still squirmed without success. Duke sighed, "You disappoint me, Savannah. I thought we had a rapport."

"Not when you try to kill my sister."

"You're accusing me of attempted murder?" He found the idea funny for some reason, "You sound like Cole Jordan."

"Maybe he's right after all. Maybe you are the killer. Georgia spent most of the day in the hospital because of you."

"Your accusation is unfounded. If you'd reclaim your rational mind, you'd realize you have no proof that I tried to kill her. What happened to Beauty was an accident. Do you understand, Savannah? *An accident.*"

The two huge black men from the day before entered the living room. Duke gave the nerve in her shoulder another squeeze – for good measure, she assumed – then directed them to her, "Keep a tight hold on her. Otherwise I might not survive."

Well muscled arms slid beneath hers, strong hands held her wrists behind her back much like Duke had. Each man kept her arms high and taut against her back as they dragged her to her feet. Once gaining her footing, Savannah reared back and launched her foot at Duke's chin. She wanted some retribution for what he'd done to Georgia. Her sister was miserable for most of the day and night, just because she wanted to keep Duke Shelton happy.

His reflexes surprised her again when, as her foot reached the height of the kick, he seized the ankle, held it steady the unwieldy angle. Pain shot through her leg and back at the strain.

Duke pushed her leg an inch higher to reinforce his point, "One more contemptuous act and I shall use my hobble for the same reason police officers use them."

He waved the Amazon over, finally releasing Savannah's leg, "Search her. And if she moves, retrieve that hobble." Duke's eyes narrowed at Savannah, "I'll attend to you momentarily and if permitted I'd attend to you with cane in hand. A lesson well earned and well learned."

The woman began to pat down her waist but Duke stopped her, "Thoroughly. Do it thoroughly. She surrendered her right to privacy when she threw that punch."

The hands returned to Savannah's back, this time slipping beneath the t-shirt to feel the waist of her jeans. The fingers and palms slid up her back then traveled around her front then down each leg. Judging by the methodical inspection, Savannah wondered if the Amazon previously worked in law enforcement.

The woman reached inside each pocket, back then front, and retrieved Savannah's car and house keys then her cell phone. Without speaking, she held them for Duke to see.

He gestured to a nearby table, "Put them there." He stepped to Savannah's side and out of her attack range, "Now to our business. Before you stormed into my house, I was planning to ask for your help regarding Dane Rutherford. He called the house and made serious threats regarding my life and general health. My original idea *was* to allow you to handle this situation but in light of your deplorable behavior, I've decided to call your superior and press charges against Mr. Rutherford. I'm still deciding what I'll do about you."

His threat temporarily ebbed her boiling anger. He was going to press charges against Dane. No telling what Ennis's brother said to him, but she figured he blistered Duke's ears. It sure scared him enough to take action. She had to fix the situation and quick, "Don't. Dane's a good man –"

He lifted an open hand, hushing her, "He may have meant well but his intentions are quite clear as are yours." Duke turned to Aurora, "Get me the phone."

"Shelton, don't ruin Dane's life. Georgia loves him." The notion fostered her anger again, "But that's your problem isn't it? She loves someone other than you."

"You," was the harsh warning, "are in sore need of training. Not submissive training either. You need training in everyday, acceptable manners. If the Rutherford temper is comparable to yours, your children will be explosive."

Aurora appeared, handed him the phone. Savannah tried to stop him, "What do you want? How can I stop you from reporting Dane?"

His thumb, poised over the keypad, paused. "You think you can bargain with me or beg me not to turn that beast in? After that mortifying scene a minute ago?"

"You tried to kill Georgia. What did you expect me to do?"

Duke shrugged, "Well, then it's settled." He began dialing a number then waited, his vision strictly on her, "Yes, I need to speak to a Captain Joshua Hunter please. Yes, I'll hold."

One thing about Shelton. He didn't bluff. If she didn't hurry, not only Dane would be flushed but her too. "Shelton, hang up," she pulled against the men's hold but they reinforced their grasp. The egotistic asshole was ignoring her, "*Please* hang up."

Amused at her attempt, Duke covered the mouthpiece, "I'm not in the habit of making deals but I'll make an exception. I can either report Dane Rutherford or you. Which will it be?"

Savannah stared back at his unyielding expression. She assumed he gifted that particular grim appearance to any woman defying him. She wasn't under his control contract-wise but thanks to her temper and Dane's stupidity, Duke gained more power than she ever imagined. He made it clear – one of them had to pay for both sins.

"Quickly, please," he urged. "I'm on hold."

"Keep Dane out of it," she said.

His voice was cold and exact, "Then I will report you. I hope your brother-in-law appreciates your sacrifice. Now that we've concluded our business, I expect you to leave my estate like a lady. That means my men will drive your car outside the gates then you will be escorted to your vehicle. During that time, I trust you will not try to maim or injure my men, or the results of my phone call will be far worse than you ever imagined." Duke pointed to the door, "Get her out of here."

She didn't make a scene or a fuss this time. One man grabbed the keys and phone and shoved the latter in her pocket. As they carted her to the door, their grasp never wavered. She heard Duke on the phone, "Captain Hunter, this is Duke Shelton. I'm calling to inform you of a serious breach of professional ethics by one of your detectives. The name? Savannah Prince..."

15

Once Shelton's men unceremoniously dumped her at her car, they stood guard at the gates to ensure she departed their company. Driving away, she rubbed her aching shoulder, cursing the magnanimous giants and their rough handling. She'd lost it, she admitted that but her sister's life had been endangered. Any self-respecting human would have done the same thing, just with more planning – and a gun.

For one fleeting instant, Savannah entertained the thought of just going home and sleeping off the whole rotten week. Then her phone rang. She groaned, shook her head. That didn't take long, she thought.

"Come see me now, Savannah. You know why." Her boss left no question about his mood.

Traffic held her up for twenty minutes, giving her plenty of time to entertain various scenarios awaiting her. She picked up her phone to inform Josh of the traffic situation and decided against it. He was already mad enough. He wouldn't want excuses for any problem – even ones she wasn't responsible for.

After thirty minutes of fighting her way through Atlanta's congestion, she stepped inside the station house. As she passed the desk sergeant, he snickered, "Hey, Prince, you're a coupla days late celebrating

Casual Friday."

Her attire had been the last thing on her mind. The old shirt and jeans probably did look on the verge of hobo garb. None of her colleagues saw her in such disarray until today. She made a strict effort to dress nicely or at least keep it one step above tacky before gracing them with her presence.

The sergeant's taunting normally set her off. She'd volley back a snide comment about his paperwork – or lack thereof. Today she just kept walking.

Before she turned the corner toward Hunter's office, the sergeant offered his sympathies, "Sorry to hear about your sister. She better today?"

That caught her off guard, "How'd you find out?"

"Heard about it on the early news. You know she can't fart in this city without someone finding out. She's too popular."

Oh, for God's sake, it never ends… Her temple suddenly panged followed by visions of her career circling the drain. The harsh truth intruded, explaining it past circling the drain about an hour ago – it was already fish food and why? Because Duke was jealous of Georgia and Dane.

She slowed her pace to Josh's office, thinking through the situation. If he heard about the allergy – and subsequent hospital stay – maybe he'd realize why she'd lost her temper with Shelton. Of course, his voice hadn't betrayed the slightest degree of empathy or general regard for her feelings. It mostly sounded like she'd be missing about five pounds of ass – and a badge and gun – once he finished with her…

A low whistle broke her concentration. She sneered at the image of Cole Jordan who hustled up beside her with the brilliant realization, "Captain's real pissed at you. What'd you do?"

Savannah tried waving it off, fairly certain that, "You wouldn't understand." She drew a deep breath before rounding the corner. No need in letting Josh Hunter see her so nervous. He'd know she was, but she wanted to retain at least a shred of dignity before being reamed out. She fully expected a suspension from the job. Duke's rant probably left little room for honest employment anywhere in the tri-state area, much less keeping her law enforcement career in tact. The next option stopped her cold. Maybe Shelton threatened to sue the department or worse, file a civil lawsuit against her. She rolled her eyes. *I've screwed myself all the way to China...*

Turning the corner, she saw Josh peer up from reading. His vision locked on hers. His whole face evolved into a living storm cloud. He rose from the seat, crooked his finger at her.

Taking stock behind her, she noticed Cole Jordan lingering down the hall a ways, just far enough not to suffer shrapnel from the explosion.

Neither spoke as she stepped in her captain's office and shut the door. All Hunter said was, "Blinds too."

With a pull of a string, Savannah lowered the Venetian blinds. *Oh goody. No witnesses to my execution...* She faced her superior officer who looked ready to throttle her. She began, "Do I get a last request before –"

"Sit the hell down," he pointed to the chair beside her.

She sat down. No need to aggravate the problem since he already appeared on the verge of a heart attack.

Hunter remained standing behind his desk, hands clamped to the sides, probably to prevent himself from committing murder. "I'll just spell it out since you obviously require simplicity."

She watched his fingers repeatedly grip and release the wooden desktop as his face darkened to a fair shade of plum. Wisely she remained silent.

"The chief knows about Georgia's trip to the hospital yesterday. He saw it on the news this morning. Now if that's where it had ended, you wouldn't be here, would you?"

Savannah pursed her lips, a sign she understood he really didn't want or require an answer.

"When a limousine delivers a famous author to the hospital, the press figures they've got a story for page three. When, a day later, that author's sister – a police officer – assaults a wealthy citizen, the press figures 'Page One Material'. See where I'm going?"

"The press knows about this morning?" she blurted. God, she'd not only lose her job but be forced into complete relocation. Rogue cop, the headlines would read then be followed by calls for lynching, not just dismissal. "For the record, I never laid a hand on Shelton. I never got a chance."

Hunter's withering glare shut her up. He stood straight, crossed his arms, "The *chief* knows about it, Savannah. Shelton called him and described in detail how you charged in and had to be restrained. How you were *out of control.* See where I'm going *now?*"

Indeed. The mere notion of the chief hearing the awful details –

likely spiced up by Shelton – had her shrinking down in the chair, her vision shifting to the closed door with images of Cole and other officers listening in. Her cheeks burned with embarrassment. Moments earlier, the station buzzed with voices and the usual clamor. Although Josh hadn't yelled, she suspected the news spread through the place like a wildfire. She blamed Cole for this, but then, she blamed Cole for everything these days. "Shelton knew about that allergy. I asked Georgia and she said he knew. I went crazy, okay? But he wasn't even flustered over her reaction – one that could have easily killed her. What would you have done?"

The captain fisted his hands then decided clamping them to his desk still worked better than lunging at her, "Well, I *wouldn't* have attacked him. He has every right to file a complaint on you. At the very least, you should be suspended."

Well. That settled it. Duke basically removed her from her job for a while, the rat bastard. "I don't have my gun or shield. I'll have to go home for them."

"I tremble to think what might've happened if you'd had your gun. The point is he didn't file a complaint. He could have but chose not to for whatever reason. He does want you punished and I assured him I'd take disciplinary action. Before I decide what purgatory to send you to, answer this. Did you try to hit him?"

He already knew the answer but Savannah couldn't bring herself to meet his gaze. Josh continued, "Did you try to kick him?"

Why was he asking these questions? Shelton had half a dozen or more witnesses to her actions. Before her mouth sank her deeper into trouble, she allowed her silence to answer him.

He sighed, "Damn it, Savannah. What were you thinking?"

"I was thinking he tried to kill Georgia and someone oughta do the same to him." She made no apologies and certainly didn't intend to. She expected Josh Hunter, of all people, to understand her intent – and maybe even her meltdown. Georgia was her sister and *his* good friend.

"Here's what will happen. I'm taking you off the case. Ennis and Mathis will work with Jordan on it. You'll be back at your desk for two weeks."

"Desk duty again?" she groused.

"Well, let's see what else is on the menu besides suspension. How about doing paperwork at the sergeant's desk?"

Savannah groaned, rubbed at her temples that began throbbing now. *Boil me in oil, use thumbscrews, tie me to an anthill and smear peanut butter in my ears but don't assign me to the sergeant's desk...*

"Those are your choices. Suspension, desk duty or sergeant's desk and that one will require your uniform. And by the way, why are you bitching at me? You're the one who attempted a field goal with a citizen's head. You have no recourse. I should make you wear your uniform and give you meter maid duty for a month."

She hoped he meant it as a joke. She also hoped her expression telegraphed her feelings on the subject of punishment in general *and* donning that hot, uncomfortable uniform.

Hunter backed down, "But I won't if you explain why, after I ordered you to stay away from Shelton, you went back there and took Georgia with you."

She sat straighter in the chair, "That's not my fault. She insisted on accepting his stupid breakfast invitation. I planned on staying home. Ask Ennis. I only went to protect her and I'm glad I did."

Josh evidently realized the futility of the conversation, "Which one of the disciplinary actions are you choosing?"

Suspension was out of the question. She didn't need another one on her record and she and the desk sergeant disliked each other just enough she'd purposefully smash her hand to avoid paperwork within a mile of him. "Desk duty again," she huffed.

"Fine. Here's the cherry on your day. Shelton promised to file harassment charges against you if you so much as sneeze in his direction. That means if you contact him in any respect, I'll take your badge and gun and give them to someone with common sense. Now if you can find your way home without mugging any other residents, you're also taking a few days off to emotionally realign yourself."

If her jaw bounced on the floor, she didn't feel it. At the moment she felt nothing except anger regarding the duplicitous act, "What? I just assigned myself to desk duty. I can't get into trouble behind a desk."

"Normally, I'd agree but this is you we're talking about."

"Please don't send me home. I promise, I'm fine."

Again, Captain Hunter leaned over his desk, looked eye to eye with her, "Is that a joke? Go home, Savannah. You needed more time to recover and you refused to take it."

That riled her temper, "That's not fair. That asshole in the mansion has issues with women, I can't help that. Cole is the one who recommended I interview him and you stood behind that recommendation."

"A decision I regret but it doesn't change the fact you went back to Shelton's house after I told you to stay away. And in your murderous daze, did you consider the possibility he didn't poison Georgia? He's not the only person in the house."

No, frankly, she hadn't. Her ire focused strictly on Shelton where she assumed it belonged. "I suppose one of the women could have. Maybe Angelique since she's jealous of Georgia, or another of the women could have. Either way, I made my point."

"You sure did. A bad one. Stay away from him." He rounded his desk to square off with her, "Are you hearing me, Detective? He's off limits to you. If I hear that you've contacted him in any manner, I'll relieve you of duty and make it permanent."

16

His newest acquisition was another disappointment. The last one – Leigh – at least showed initiative by escaping. This one though… This new one lacked the fire he searched for – needed to find. His ultimate contender needed strength, not just of body but of mind. Someone to make it fun again. He'd experienced that only once in his life. All the others gave in too quick, too easily. He hated quitters. His mother had been one. She'd quit at everything she ever tried, particularly raising her children. Her only real interest revolved around men and he'd cured her of that passion permanently.

The TV across the room was too loud so he turned it down. It was all garbage anyway. Politics, talk about the heat, very little about him. Obviously city officials weren't keen on alerting the citizens of the dangers lurking in their city.

When he glanced up again, he noticed the gathering of police officials at a podium. He ran the volume up to discover the press conference was about him. What do you know, he thought. Maybe they do care, after all.

He was about to switch off the set when the camera panned

across three detectives. He recognized one as Cole Jordan, the detective first given the case. Standing beside him was a younger detective, Detective Rutherford, who, judging by the distance he put between himself and Jordan, did not like his colleague. An older, fat detective stood beside Rutherford, wearing half-glasses and frowning at the reporters.

He missed seeing the female detective. He'd begun watching the news just to see her lovely face, to hear her spirited comments. She showed plenty of potential. It was a shame she wasn't there anymore. On second thought, without her slaving over the details of his work, he could initiate her when the time came. A surge of excitement renewed the smile on his face. Perhaps her job instilled the right amount of strength to satisfy his appetite. Never let them see you cry, the saying went, and female cops couldn't afford to cry – at least on the job.

The chief continued on, making promises the citizens – and he – knew he'd fail to keep. He yammered on about the murders, the lack of suspects and finally implored the public to call some lame tip line if they "had any information" regarding the case.

Well, he thought, that was the advantage to being intelligent, to having a plan. No one ever saw anything so no one could help. Cops like the chief were lazy and arrogant but then most cops were. They signed up to be heroes, to Lord it over ordinary citizens who remained content being ordinary. They used their badges to enforce their authority. They carried guns to dispense their own justice. They used all those plus their attitudes to get their way.

He, on the other hand, needed none of those. He possessed

enough charm to lure the ladies, enough swagger to fend off encroachment by other men, and enough power and savvy to control people without a gun or badge.

Sliding a DVD into the player, he pushed the play button and smiled. Detective Prince wound her way through a throng of reporters, her hair pulled back in the usual ponytail. Personally he preferred her hair down. He liked the way her dark tresses draped past her shoulders in loose S-shaped waves. It gave her a more attractive appearance. His body reacted to her confident stride, her assertive expression and her feisty retort to a reporter.

He needed to see her again. Would see her again. In fact, he decided, tomorrow was perfect.

17

Savannah rolled out of bed at a respectable eight thirty the next morning. No need to hurry for work so she opted to clean the house – something else Shelton managed to delay, like her future promotion and pay raise. Savannah just thanked God she still retained a job after Josh Hunter finished with her.

During the night the skies opened up with a veritable flood. Morning brought gunmetal gray clouds and a serious threat of another downpour. She was glad she could stay home.

After a shower, she set her sights on a couple of eggs and slice of toast for breakfast. She'd make the best of her "sabbatical" – as Ennis called it – so why not treat herself to a fine breakfast? While Cole Jordan ate Fruit Loops and trudged off to supposedly find a killer, she'd indulge in the finest of morning meals and relax if she damn well wanted.

Dressed in her robe and slippers, she cracked two eggs in a bowl. Then she decided on three. Extravagant, yes, but her feelings still stung from Josh's tongue-lashing. She took her lumps about trying to beat Shelton senseless but not about accompanying Georgia for protection – which she'd done a sorry job of.

Guilt nested in her brain day and night about that failure. She'd stood no chance of predicting Shelton's actions – common sense and Ennis told her that – but she still faulted herself for not doing so.

She needed to realign herself mentally and there was only two ways to do it. Running or dragging out her golf clubs to polish them. The former made no sense because of her fatigue and rash. So she decided after breakfast to find her golf clubs. It always calmed her down in her younger years. Maybe the magic lingered in the motion of babying her clubs. Then she'd damn well go hit some balls – golf balls or Cole's or Shelton's, it really didn't matter to her.

The phone rang just as the skillet heated to the perfect temperature for scrambling eggs. She sighed. Why did it never fail? The instant she made a decision – one that kept her out of trouble – someone changed it for her.

She answered on the fourth ring and once she realized the caller's identity, she wished she'd let the machine pick up.

"Savannah, my dear," Duke Shelton's smooth voice greeted.

Her grip on the spatula tightened, "What do you want?"

"I'm sending a car for you. I need –"

"Stop right there. Recall your driver because I've been forbidden to see you, speak to you or think about you. Understand? I will *not* lose my job because of you." As an added aggravation, her breast itched. The rash, under control the last several hours, kicked into high gear with Duke Shelton's call. Until then, she hadn't made the connection but every time she interacted with him, the rash flared up to an insane degree.

She rubbed her breast with her wrist, allowing the terrycloth robe to do the scratching. She prayed the irritation subsided. It didn't.

Duke chuckled, "Oh, Savannah. Your dramatics amuse me. Yesterday was a bad day, yes. Let's call today," he hesitated a moment then, "a mulligan, shall we?"

The golf reference left her cold, "'Fraid you didn't hear me, Mr. Shelton. I'm not allowed to see you. My boss, you know, the one you called yesterday? He told me to stay home, to stay away from you and believe it or not, I will."

"First of all, my dear, your boss went lightly on you because I instructed him to. You wanted off that case anyway. Beauty wanted you off the case as well. I did you a favor."

Her shoulder ached in remembrance of his harsh grasp, "Gee, why doesn't it feel like one?"

"Second, he need not know of our meeting today and won't if you don't mention it."

She poured the eggs into the skillet, tucked the phone between her shoulder and ear, "The Irish call that blarney and I call it a vulgar term for manure but I'm not saying that word because I'm in enough trouble as it is. I'm not coming to see you and that's final."

Duke's voice hardened, "That's not final. If you do not comply, I will call your boss again and concoct a tale that will have you suspended until you're forty. That will give you plenty of time to consider your defiance."

He used words that grated her raw – comply, defiance – probably to fuel her temper enough to lose it and get her fired.

Staring at the spatula, Savannah wondered if he'd ever been hit with one because she really wanted to test drive it on him. She stood at the stove, simmering much like the eggs in the pan.

"Now," his tone softened, "be a good girl and be ready by ten o'clock. I actually have business to discuss with you. Oh, and don't bring a weapon. You will be searched before being allowed in my presence. A precaution I believe you can appreciate."

Oh, the nerve of him... She sat the spatula down before she threw it, "I have to be somewhere at nine-thirty. Even if my day were free, I would never step foot inside your house again, believe me."

"Never say never, my dear. Since I insist on this meeting, my driver will escort you to the hospital for your treatment as soon as we conclude our business."

If she hadn't needed the phone, she'd have slammed it against the wall. The man infuriated her with his demands and assumptions, "Not that I care but what business could we possibly have?"

"Your brother-in-law insists on harassing me. I sent Beauty flowers as an apology for the fiasco Saturday. He took great exception to the gesture, of course, but he's overstepped his bounds. You and I will mend fences while finding a remedy for Dane Rutherford. Ten o'clock. See you shortly after, my dear."

With that, Duke Shelton hung up, leaving her speechless and her eggs beginning to brown. She quickly scooped them into a waiting plate, sat the pan aside. The son of a bitch, she seethed. Not only did he coerce her into seeing him again, she'd be late with her treatment because of it. She called the hospital to reschedule then dialed Dane, "Stop harassing Duke Shelton. I know you're upset he sent flowers, Dane, but the man has enough money to sue us all out of sight. If he leaves Georgia alone, leave *him* alone, okay?"

Once she finally pried a reluctant agreement from him, she hung up and waited. Waited for, perhaps, her whole career to end without her being present for the occasion.

A light drizzle began to fall by the time the limo arrived. Warren Sapp's twin met her at the door with an umbrella. His smile disarmed her. The day before he seemed strangely eager to drown her in the nearest puddle or shoot her just to save time. Now he approached with an umbrella that she regarded with caution since it would make a decent weapon. One good swing and she'd end up in the neighbor's hibiscus.

Her escorts in the limo were precisely the same men who picked her and Georgia up Saturday – and the same ones who ungraciously dumped Savannah beside her Camaro just twenty four hours earlier.

The ride was quiet but courteous as Warren sat across from her. He resumed calling her "Missus" and offered her a "non-alcoholic" beverage. It was as if nothing transpired the day before, especially nothing as momentous as their near brush with premature unemployment. No boss, no job.

The driver hurried the trip along. If he feared another explosion from her, Warren could easily remedy the problem by throwing open the door and heaving her out at fifty-five miles per hour. Problem instantly solved.

The limousine glided down streets and highways, through and

around traffic until pulling in front of the iron gates at Shelton's estate. She looked at her watch. 10:25. She rescheduled the treatment for 12:30 so she hoped Shelton sped things along. The meeting was ridiculous anyway. It's not like she could control Dane. Only Georgia stood a chance at that. All Savannah could do was ask him to play nice.

Angelique met her in the entry, along with the two black men and the gargantuan Amazon dressed in her white pantsuit. Well, she thought, somebody certainly remembered yesterday. The four closed in, giving her little space to move, much less throw a punch – which she assumed they feared.

Angelique stood directly in front of her, arms crossed, her mood and stance resonated a temper as fiery as her hair, "You will be searched for weapons. Stand legs apart and arms out to your sides. Aurora, search the detective's purse."

Savannah held her gaze but stood as directed, her hand reluctantly offering the purse to Aurora. The Amazon stepped behind her, her hands skimming along her sides and felt along the waist of her jeans. She patted the front pockets then slid her hands into them. Savannah squirmed at the invasion but held her anger in check, "My cell phone and keys *again*."

The Amazon retrieved both, presented them to Angelique and only when the redhead nodded did the woman replace them. The hands resumed their work, moving down Savannah's back to her bottom then they squeezed. Savannah's lip curled at the shameless indelicacy of the touch. It felt more sexual than businesslike and it was enough to spring her temper forth. She wheeled on the Amazon, "There's no need to humiliate me. I was invited, no, *summoned* –"

"Silence, Detective," Angelique's voice echoed through the entry.

Savannah rounded on the redhead just as quick, ready to brace her too. Angelique stepped closer, one finely arched brow lifting, "You will resume the position and complete this procedure or be shown the door."

"Lucky for me I can find it myself," she snatched her purse from Aurora's grasp and turned to leave but the Amazon and two men to blocked her way.

Fingernails equivalent to talons dug deep into Savannah's forearm, causing her to wince. Angelique spun her around to face her, "You are the most willful, disrespectful creature I've encountered. Thirty minutes with me and you'd appreciate the value of compliance."

"Angelique," a man's voice scolded. It was Duke. He sat in the living room, Savannah assumed, sipping brandy and smoking his usual Cuban cigar.

The redhead, surprisingly, disregarded the warning, "Unfortunately I suspect beating you is the only way to enforce obedience."

"*Angelique*," this warning now came from the doorway.

Savannah observed the withering glare Shelton aimed at his wife. Once Angelique faced him, he commanded, "Upstairs this instant. I will deal with you later." He motioned to the Amazon, "And lock the door. I want no further interruptions."

Duke waved the men off, "I'm sure we'll be fine." Then turned to Savannah, "Won't we?"

She tucked her purse under her arm, "Depends. Is there a body cavity search involved?"

Duke tried to break the tension by chuckling, "I apologize for Angelique. She's protective of me and sometimes loses focus of her position in the household."

"I don't see how you need protecting." She rubbed her shoulder, "Your Vulcan Death Grip is quite memorable."

"I regret having to employ it." His hand made a sweeping motion toward the living room, "If you please, my dear."

She noticed he chose not to blame her for his "employment" of the move. They made their way into the living room where he offered her a seat then eased into his usual chair, retrieved his cigar.

After she sat, he waved Aurora over. It still irked Savannah to see women at the beck and call of a man but didn't have long to ruminate on it when Aurora appeared holding a tray. On it sat a Double Fudge Yoo-Hoo and a file folder. Savannah did not partake of either.

"Come now, my dear. I've done my homework and the Double Fudge is your favorite. As for the file, consider it a bonus."

"A bonus what? Screw job?" she accused. "I don't want that thing. I can tell it's bad news."

Duke smiled, "Not even if it concerns Cole Jordan?" He instructed Aurora to place the drink and the file on the table beside Savannah. The woman left the room but not without regarding Savannah with caution. *At least I made an impression on someone. Duke acts like I beat him in a game of chess, not tried to beat his head in...*

Shelton stared with an intensity that made her squirm, "Tempting, isn't it? You don't like him and with good reason. He's disrespectful, treats you poorly and says things to set your temper ablaze and he does it all deliberately. That file could shed a ray of light on him, Savannah. *About* him. It won't answer all your questions but it might help."

She took the Yoo-Hoo in hand, "Say I take that home and read it. What kind of somersaults am I signing up for as payment?"

He laughed the laugh she hated, the one saying that he, not just Cole, thought he was superior to her. Pouring cognac in a crystal goblet, he replied, "Absolutely nothing. Call it a peace offering of sorts."

"I thought it was a bonus *of sorts.* Can't be both. What'll it cost me, Shelton? Up front with it because I'm probably leaving that thing here anyway."

A half-shrug later he stated, "I've told you there are no strings. Take the file and learn. Don't take the file and stay frustrated. Up to you. Now, while you think on it, let's talk about Dane Rutherford."

Reaching out to her, he offered her a note. Its crumpled state indicated an unpleasant encounter with someone's clenched fist. Savannah took great pains to smooth the note flat, "Do you treat all your mail with such compassion?"

He wasn't amused, "Mr. Rutherford handed the envelope to the chef as she arrived for work so technically it's not mail." He swirled the cognac in the crystal goblet then sipped somewhat pensively, "Apparently, he didn't trust the postal service with such crucial information."

She referred to the note, "Leave Georgia alone or your concubines will bury you." Savannah's heart sank. Dane's temper rivaled his younger brother's when his "girl" was involved. The note continued, "If I hear you've contacted her, I'll kill you."

She thought she saw Duke's hand tremble slightly while gulping a large swallow of cognac. He retrieved something from his pocket and dropped it in her hand, "This was with it."

The metal object felt fairly heavy in her palm. It was warm from being in his pocket and when he withdrew his hand, she stared at a beautiful gold bracelet. She handled the jewelry with care while straightening it across her palm. The engraved nameplate circled in small diamonds read "Beauty" in an elegant script. Turning it over, she silently read the inscription, "Forever, Duke."

Developments like this made her sick. She hated being blindsided and this one bowled her over. Studying it, Savannah saw signs of wear – a clear indication Georgia had worn it or maybe even dropped it and stepped on it. If she'd had the damn bracelet all this time, why didn't Georgia tell her about it and *why*, for God's sake, did she show it to Dane?

Duke watched her fingers play over the gold links. "I insist you arrest him," he said.

Ah, the payment for the file. No strings, he'd said. Right. Not that she ever believed him but it would have been nice to do homework on Cole Jordan. That file held answers only Shelton's contacts could dig up. "I'm not arresting Dane. I should, however, haul your ass in for slipping seafood in Georgia's breakfast." *Get my drift, asshole?*

Duke briefly contemplated a response then, "Surely your exercise routine involves more than jumping to conclusions. I told you I did nothing of the sort."

"If that's the truth then you need to re-evaluate your household because the seafood didn't just leap in there itself." She reached for the Yoo-Hoo. No need to waste a perfectly good beverage.

Disregarding her accusation, Duke sipped his cognac and chose to redirect the conversation, "Somehow that bracelet left Beauty's possession and ended up in his. And it's not been treated well while out of my custody. Notice the scratches along her name. It was in pristine condition when last I saw it."

To humor him, Savannah looked again. She angled it toward the light. Yes, the top and underside of the nameplate was peppered with small but noticeable scratches. It looked stepped on, thrown and generally abused. If Dane kept poking sticks at Duke, he'd be in jail a very long time if Shelton had a say in the matter and Savannah had a feeling he did.

"The sentimental value is priceless. But for your records, it cost one thousand dollars."

Savannah nearly choked, scrambling to set the Yoo-Hoo down before spilling it on the golden extravagance. She dangled the bracelet at him, motioning for him to take it. One grand for a bracelet? He either liked tossing money away on jewelry or he... She swallowed hard at the idea. Or he thought he honestly loved Georgia. Forcing words past her lips, she inquired, "Did the bracelet just scream 'buy me'?"

Duke chuckled, "I had it made for her, my dear. With hopes

she'd stay with me, to be mine."

She refused to delve too deep into *that* comment. She was still wearing off the one thousand dollar shock. "You tried to buy her love. It didn't work. What a surprise."

Offended at the accusation, he rose and with purposeful strides, he stopped at the fireplace a few yards away, "I don't buy a woman's love no more than I debase myself with blackmail."

Savannah couldn't help herself. She laughed. "You should acquaint yourself with Webster and his dictionary. I didn't come here voluntarily. Furthermore I'm *not* arresting Dane in exchange for the file on Cole." She waited for her statement to sink in then, "Are you that upset at Dane or is it because Georgia doesn't love you?"

"I'm angry with him for destroying the bracelet. I'm disappointed in Beauty and I hate to be disappointed."

She stood, pulled her phone from her pocket, "I'm settling this argument once and for all. I've got an appointment to keep and somehow that will be more pleasant than playing verbal ping pong with you."

She dialed Georgia's number. Her sister answered on the third ring. Savannah explained where she was then asked about the bracelet. "How did the bracelet get included with Dane's message?"

Savannah, expecting a mundane reply, felt her anger rise once her sister concluded her response. Gripping the phone hard enough to break it, Savannah stated, "Say that again. You're on speakerphone with His Majesty." She mashed the speakerphone button, wishing it was Duke's head. Her sister repeated, "Angelique called me, told me to return the bracelet and to stay away from Duke. I told Dane where to find it, to box it up and send it back."

"Angelique say anything else?" Savannah stared straight at Duke who never showed the slightest bit of unease.

"Without actually confessing, she said my allergy was the last thing I should worry about if I came near Duke again."

"And when Dane found the bracelet, did he treat it like the crown jewels?"

Georgia hesitated. Savannah figured she'd try to sweeten up Dane's treatment of the bracelet. What Georgia didn't realize, Savannah didn't care and by the time she finished with Duke, neither would he. When the eldest finally spoke, it was tentatively, "He didn't exactly bubble-wrap it, no."

"Thanks, hon. We'll talk later." Savannah clicked off, took one step toward Duke, "Let's talk compromise, Shelton."

Duke stood his ground as he had the day before, even as she stood face to face, only a foot away. Her tone refused argument, "I should arrest your jealous, bitchy wife, or whatever you call her, for attempted murder. She knew about Georgia's allergy so that makes it premeditated. I'll march right up those stairs, kick the door in and drag her ass to jail. And what will you do? You'll probably call your henchmen to restrain me all over again, call my boss, get me fired and let me sell trinkets to tourists for a living. You can do that, Shelton, or you can keep that bitch," she pointed upstairs, "under control and leave Dane Rutherford alone." She hadn't realized until the conclusion of her speech but she'd practically shouted the last in his face. And he hadn't even blinked. Blood roared in her ears, her heart pounded in her chest and he hadn't the common decency to break a sweat. The fact made her double her fist, the anticipated results kept her from throwing a punch.

"I understand your anger, Savannah. I also understand why you want to haul Angelique to jail but you should take into consideration one thing: my love for Beauty. Do you honestly believe I'd let anyone harm her without suffering consequences?"

Oh, she wanted to hit him. She wanted to knock him down and put her foot on his throat just to shut him up. "What, did you send her to bed without supper?"

Duke stepped forward which sent her back a step, "I have punishments that meet the severity of any infraction."

"I can't wait to hear your punishment for attempted murder."

He stepped forward again, "My contract prohibits me from disclosing such information but be assured Angelique will be harshly punished for her actions. You will have no need to arrest her, or, as you so quaintly stated, I will call your boss and you'll be selling trinkets to tourists by week's end."

Savannah stopped, leaving Duke looming over her like a storm cloud. She refused to retreat another inch until he agreed to leave her family alone. "You leave Dane and Georgia alone and we'll have no reason to interact with each other again. You screw me on this and I will come back and drag Angelique out the front gates by her hair and toss her into a squad car."

"Agreed. Now, my driver will take you to the hospital for your treatment. Don't forget the file on Cole Jordan. Read it at your leisure."

She turned on her heel and grabbed her purse from the chair, "I don't want it."

"Savannah," his voice carried through the room like thunder. "You will take the file."

She kept walking, "I won't be indebted to you. Forget it."

18

Ennis learned to gauge his wife's day by the house's condition. If things weren't exactly up to par, she'd had a decent day. If the place was as tidy as a drill sergeant's barracks, she'd had a rough one. The neat freak award belonged to Georgia. Nothing in her home stayed out of place for long. It resembled a showplace, no dust, no clutter, no way. Savannah, on the other hand, kept the house tidy but not fanatically so. She never panicked if impromptu company arrived. She moved a few things, fluffed a pillow and vowed to feed the visitors, her theory being it was difficult to flap their jaws criticizing while they were busy chewing.

When he stepped in the house, he knew Savannah had had a really rotten day. Freshly dusted furniture and a spotless kitchen told the story. The fact the new book he began reading sat on the side table instead of in his chair detailed the abysmal state of her day. The lone sign of visible chaos sat on the dining table. Papers were scattered across it, all in an orderly jumble that only Savannah could understand.

Ennis moved closer to it, wondering if the mass of documents triggered the housecleaning frenzy. He placed his jacket across the back of a dining chair, loosened his tie then unbuttoned the top button of his shirt which had been strangling him much the way he wanted to strangle Cole for the past week.

Besides the day's mail consisting of a couple of bills and two catalogs, he spied an open file folder amid the scattered pages. For a short time, Ennis remembered back a couple of months. Before her surgery, Savannah had a similar folder on the table while her laptop computer searched for her oncologist, Dr. Wyatt. She wanted his background to make sure he hadn't killed anyone during surgery or been sued for malpractice. One thing about his wife: she leaned toward the morbid side but she was damn thorough. Perhaps a bit too thorough...

Ennis picked up a page from the table. "Cole Jordan's background?" he questioned under his breath. "Son of a bitch." He slammed the paper to the table, "Savannah! Where the hell are you?"

A crashing noise came from their infinitesimal guest room. Following a string of colorful cursing not heard since Seth's last tirade, Ennis raced to the room, praying he hadn't caused the upheaval. By the time he reached the doorway, he saw Savannah standing with one hand wrapped around a golf bag's carrying strap, her other hand rubbing her head. She stared at a broken trophy scattered on the floor. Upon closer inspection, it was a golfing trophy – one that Ennis had never seen and wondered where it came from. Peering into the closet, he saw a toppled box on the shelf that had dumped the trophy out. It also threatened to dump two others.

"What is it? Is the house on fire?" Savannah asked in a manner suggesting a fully engulfed structure was his only salvation from her temper. She leaned the golf bag against the wall and commenced struggling with the trophy box to keep the contents from littering the floor.

She was about four inches too short to right the box so Ennis rushed to help before her anger boiled over. She mumbled a thanks then turned her attention to the golf bag that began toppling to the floor like the trophy had. Once she leaned it in the corner, she turned, hands on hips, "Why did you yell?"

Ennis watched her flinch and rub the top of her head. The trophy whacked her good and he wondered what bothered her more, a headache, the broken trophy or his yelling. "You okay?" he asked.

Gathering the pieces of her award, she replied, "Besides the dent in my head, I'm fine."

He pointed to the golf bag, "What are you doing with that?"

"Bronzing it. What do you *think* I'm doing with it? Why did you yell at me?"

Since her mood excluded chit-chat, he returned to the original subject, "Why are you looking into Cole Jordan?"

"I'm not. The file was a gift of sorts."

"A gift from whom?" The glare she leveled on him normally would have backed him off but probing into another cop's life and career only caused trouble, usually for the investigating cop.

She shouldered past him holding the trophy remnants, "Duke Shelton."

He supposed it was a knee jerk reaction but Ennis grabbed her arm, a bit too hard according to her wince, "You went to see him?"

"He's a friggin' blackmailer. He threatened me with a longer suspension if I didn't."

Savannah tugged at her arm. Ennis held on, "He's still a valid suspect for these killings. You could've been –" he stopped to rephrase. She knew she ran a risk going there, she didn't need a lecture about that. "You're not on the case, remember? Josh removed you *because* of your interaction with Shelton. Do you know how much trouble you could be in?"

She yanked on her arm, finally freeing it, "I told you I didn't have a choice."

"Because he threatened you? Tell Hunter. He'll take care of it."

"Yeah. Probably by firing me. Look, it wasn't just that, okay?"

"I hope it's a better reason than a threat of suspension which Shelton can't follow through on."

"He did a fair job this last time, didn't he?"

"What was so important you risked your job and your life?"

Savannah marched to the dining table and dumped the broken pieces next to the folder, "How's this? I was keeping your brother out of jail."

Quite certain his wife would fall short on reasonable explanations, he already had a response poised on his tongue. Her reply shut that response down cold. "Dane?"

She stalked past him again, this time headed for the utility room. The small room was big enough only for a washer and dryer and had two cabinets above the appliances. She opened one door, found the glue and headed back to the table. She finally confirmed, "Yes, Dane. He's been threatening Shelton all week. He wanted Dane arrested for trespass and harassment. I talked him out of it and I hope I convinced your brother to cool off."

Ennis tamped down the innate urge to punch his brother. He understood Dane's anger, of course, but threatening one of the richest people in Atlanta showed he suffered from the usual lack of common sense. Ennis would deal with Dane later. For now though, "And what does Shelton want in return for that file? It ain't free, no matter what you think." His Texas twang burst forth in all its glory as happened every time his anger flared. He prayed his wife realized the name of the creek she was up and the fact she had no oars within a hundred miles.

Savannah sat at the table and busied herself fitting the trophy back together. "I know it 'ain't free', Ennis," she shot the words like arrows. Her steady hands contradicted her foul mood. She dabbed glue to the gold figurine and set it atop the metal and walnut wood trophy.

Ennis glanced at the award that had "Georgia State Champion" engraved on a gold plate, the year beneath that. She'd won awards, he knew that, he'd just never seen them. Now he feared she blamed him for the broken one in front of her. Judging by her disposition, the possibility was more than probable.

"I'm not going back and I'm not Duke's law enforcement toady either. He can try to pry favors but I tried to give that thing," she nodded to the file, "back to him. It was sitting in the car when I left the estate. The two men – you know, the behemoths that work for him? They essentially shoved it in my hands before driving away."

"Ever thought about tossing it back at them before they left?"

Her lips pursed, her eyes narrowed. She carefully sat the glue and trophy down to turn her full attention to him. "Actually, yes. Then I thought, why should I? That thing explains Cole Jordan to a tee. His disdain for women. His attitude on the job. Duke found things out I could never dig up."

"Have you considered the fact Duke Shelton did the same to you? That he dug so deep into your past that when he calls in that favor, you'll have no choice but pony up? The man works on leverage." He noticed she reached over and rubbed her breast. The rash flared up due to heat – external and internal – and right now she was steamed.

"Ennis, it's sweet of you to think so highly of me. To believe I have a shady past but people with the financial means can buy the shovel to dig up my past, however shady or sunny."

"Toby Jackson?" He felt sure that she'd forgotten about her abusive ex-boyfriend, the one that put her in the hospital at least once.

Savannah shrugged, "So what? Every woman has a bad relationship. He's a bastard who hits women. They're a dime a dozen." She scratched at her breast again, this time harder.

"Stop that. You'll make it worse. At the risk of you leaping from that chair and strangling me, how about excessive force complaints? You have a few of those on your record."

Ignoring his warning, she scratched once more, "And if you've been in law enforcement long enough, you do. People hate being arrested."

"Use the cream if it's bothering you." He hated carrying on two separate conversations nearly as much as seeing her claw her breast, "So what about *my* past? He's probably dug into mine too. He knew about our marriage, your health issues so I know he's burrowing into my past."

To his surprise, Savannah chuckled, "And what will he find? That you were a Boy Scout and helped old ladies cross the street in Vega, Texas? For Heaven's sake, Ennis, you don't have a past. You've been a good boy all your life. Face it, there's nothing scandalous about you."

Ennis clenched his jaw, trapping a heated reply. He begged to differ but he had a past, alright, and the last thing he needed was some rich asshole finding out about it. Savannah wasn't familiar with all his screw-ups and he worked hard at keeping them under wraps. His biggest mistake eventually sent him away from home in search of a new life. He'd found it in Atlanta, with his new partner and now wife. If she learned what drove him from home, she'd divorce him on the spot.

Her cavalier mind-set angered him but he supposed he deserved it. As long as she'd known him he'd attempted to be nothing short of a perfectly genteel male, though his temper did rear up occasionally. It wasn't surprising she scoffed at the idea of him having a dark secret. He bit back his anger, "It's not necessarily about me or you. What about your father's abuse?"

Her brow furrowed as she worked. Ennis wasn't sure if it was concentration on her task or frustration with him. He'd bet both. "It's old news," she said. "It's all over Augusta about Daddy being a mean drunk."

Okay then, "What if Shelton investigates Georgia or Seth? What if he finds a nugget to blackmail you with? He will search until he finds it."

"Ennis, I'll handle Shelton if he calls in any favor. Relax."

Easy for her to say. She wouldn't be lying awake nights worrying that Shelton prepared the mother of all favors. Or worse, he planned to abduct her, rape her and... Shaking his head, he gathered the file together, "I'm taking this back to him. If he won't take it, I'll shove it in his ear."

Savannah gave him a look that questioned his sanity – then scratched her breast again, "It's too late. I took it, I read it and you should too. If you think I have a colored past with my job, try Cole Jordan."

Now that got his attention. His wife also made a valid point. Once the file left Shelton's possession, the damage was done.

Savannah resumed fixing the trophy but couldn't quite fit one piece together. Ennis sat down, reached for it, "Go get your cream and I'll work with this."

As she headed to the bathroom, he looked the trophy over. Georgia mentioned three state championships but the box in the closet held more than three trophies.

Savannah returned, her hand beneath her shirt, rubbing the cream onto the rash. Relief washed over her expression and Ennis prayed that her mood improved too. He tried to diffuse their earlier argument, motioned to the trophy, "How come you never display these?"

"They remind me of a future I foolishly flushed down the toilet."

He tested the piece's fit then applied glue, "You could still hit the golf course once in a while. Wouldn't hurt you."

"That's why I brought out my clubs. Being tossed off the case kinda gives me more regular hours now."

Ennis fit the tiny golf club back into the little lady's hands, "There. Nearly good as new. Sorry about it breaking."

Sadness replaced the earlier relief, "Just a matter of time before one broke. I'll put it back in the box once it dries."

Ennis decided not to argue. He realized it hurt her to relive her high school golfing days. According to Georgia, she'd been a veritable prodigy with the clubs and even entertained playing college golf. Her mother's breast cancer derailed the plans, stealing not only her mother but the dream of college and perhaps professional golf. "Well," he compromised, "don't you dare put those clubs away."

Ennis turned his attention to the documents and papers across from him. He gathered a couple. Savannah stood in silence while he perused them. Cole Jordan grew up in Renton, Washington, a small town that later became a suburb of Seattle. His father divorced his mother when Cole was four. Cole's grades were less than stellar but he excelled at athletics. Years later, his grades squeaked by enough to grab a diploma – but just barely.

A bolt of fear shot down his spine. If Shelton researched Jordan this thoroughly and successfully, he was surely privy to Ennis's past and the one incident he never wanted Savannah to discover.

Ennis glanced back at the page. A few years after the divorce, Cole's mother remarried. The second marriage was to an abusive drunk. At that point, a pang of awareness hit Ennis. Had the abusive drunken stepfather aspect sparked Savannah's interest? And if so, why? R.J. was an abusive drunk and she turned out fine. Cole turned into a pile of refuse everyone avoided at all costs.

He returned to the document. The stepfather had two sons and a daughter from a previous marriage. The daughter killed herself after accusing Cole of molesting her, a charge that was never fully investigated, according to the document. The oldest son died at seventeen in a hunting accident. The younger son and Cole got along and after a point they left home to live together.

Cole joined the Renton P.D. and after four years on the job, transferred to Atlanta. He married Janine Faulkner and they'd been married nine months when she went missing.

Without speaking, Savannah slid a particular paper toward him. Taking the hint, Ennis picked it up. It was a report on Jordan's history with the Renton Police Department. He'd had plenty of grievances filed against him, mostly by women.

After reading those and two more incidents of sexual harassment complaints from female officers, Ennis laid the page down, "Okay, he's definitely got a problem and definitely with women." Ennis felt his gut tighten. It wasn't safe for Savannah to be around Cole. From what he read, he really hated women and used them for his own gratification, however crude. "Now we know about him. Try to relax and for God's sakes, don't poke sticks at him."

Savannah tensed, "And it's okay he pokes 'em at me?"

Ennis patted the air, trying to settle her down, "I didn't say that."

"I have a friend in the records department," she said almost accusingly. She was winding up for a fastball and to emphasize her point, she hurled the next statement like one, "You won't believe this one."

He wanted to remind her to calm down but that would only

exacerbate the problem. Instead, he let her continue, "You'll never guess what Mr. Sensitivity was investigating before the murders began."

Oh, he had an idea. Especially the way her hands shook at her sides and her voice deepened to a growl. He knew precisely, "Rape cases."

Her mouth, already open and primed to answer, slowly closed. Her anger subsided a trifle, "How'd you know?"

He nodded to her hands. She glanced down, seeing the two white knots that normally served as hands. Unrolling her fists, she sighed, "You're right. I need to relax."

"You're not on the case anymore so use this time off to get over your rash."

She gathered the papers into an insanely neat pile. The move reminded him of Georgia's neat freak ways. It came naturally for the older sister whereas Savannah's maddening efficiency reared up when she was upset. Cole's past still festered with her and until the case was solved and Jordan was out of their lives, it would.

Ennis watched her place the papers in the file and close it. She separated the mail – bills from junk – then took the bills and the file to the desk in the living room. The bills went in their designated slot, the file she tossed in a drawer and slid it shut a bit too hard.

Ennis tried again. This time he considered his words before speaking, "Babe, I'm not bossing you. I don't like Jordan and that file reinforces why. If you're not around him, he can't bother you."

His delicate approach appeared to work. Her shoulders slackened and she rubbed her forehead, "You're right. You know, I've been thinking about the case. Shelton's got a private physician. We need to see if he or she has access to sedatives. It would explain why no one sees the women abducted. They're not snatched off the street, they're disabled at his house."

Ennis couldn't believe his ears. No matter how he begged, she still charged ahead with the case she had no business in. "Please stop thinking about it."

"I can't. We –" she stopped to rephrase, "You and Mathis should concentrate on the medical field. Since the killer has access to sedatives only hospitals use, if it isn't Shelton, you need to cover the other bases too. I planned to check hospitals and clinics before I got tossed off the case. Some place is missing these drugs. They don't just walk out by themselves."

Ennis placed his hands on her shoulders, hoping it might shut her up. Every syllable stressed her out worse and no, she didn't shut up, "It might be worth –"

He cut her off with a kiss. Her lips softened beneath his, her eyes drifted closed. He pulled back until his lips lightly brushed hers, "I'll check it out. You've got to stop thinking about the case *and* Jordan. You've got enough to deal with. In fact, why don't you and Georgia get together tomorrow if she feels like it? Spend the day talking or shopping or whatever sisters do."

The muscles beneath his fingertips loosened and she sighed, "You're a genius, Ennis Rutherford. Anyone ever tell you that?"

He chuckled, "Only my brothers but I don't believe they meant it in a flattering way." Just as she finally relaxed, Ennis's phone rang and just as quickly, he felt her go rigid again. Ennis rolled his eyes, "Stop getting so uptight."

When he answered his phone, it was their colleague John Mathis, "I think we got another one. The woman's fiancé filed a missing person report today. She's been gone the mandatory twenty-four hours."

"What makes you think it's another victim?"

"Fits the profile. Brunette, long hair and a local businesswoman. From her picture, I'm tellin' ya, she's the ninth victim. We just ain't found her yet."

19

She took Ennis's suggestion and invited Georgia out the next day. After Savannah's radiation treatment, they went to the mall then to see a movie. Expecting the caliber of Sabrina or Moonstruck, the sisters both emerged less than impressed but they had their shopping successes to fall back on. They mostly window shopped but managed to find a pair of shoes for themselves and a couple of football related trinkets for their men.

Savannah packed the loot in the trunk and drove to Piedmont Park for a leisure walk. She parked in a quieter area that normally served as her designated running track. Before her surgery, she frequented the park three times a week to run. Parking near the hedgerow she used for a mile marker, Savannah longed for those days again. Soon, she vowed. Soon she'd bask in the sunshine without a rash, sweat out the day's problems with a good run and sleep like a baby knowing the radiation treatments were finished.

A quick visual revealed a less populated park than she expected. Even after rush hour the park wasn't as crowded as usual. Then she remembered the basketball and hockey teams had home games that night. Atlantans were nothing if not loyal to their sports teams. Though none actually won a championship in several years, residents clung to hope the way Scarlett clung to Rhett – and had just as much success to show for it.

In a way, the quiet park pleased Savannah. It allowed her and Georgia a peaceful evening together, something they'd not enjoyed in a long time. She glanced at her watch to gauge the time. They'd have a stretch of time before Savannah needed to get home and fix supper. She'd get Georgia home before seven or eight since she hated seeing her sister drive in the dark.

The day's diminishing heat weighed down the air with a somewhat drier and less penetrating humidity. It was just comfortable enough for a short walk. The two began their trek, found a comfortable pace. "I had fun today," Georgia said.

"Me too. We don't do this enough." She took a long, deep breath and with it familiar aromas wafted in on the sultry evening breeze. The smell of freshly cut grass mingled with hickory smoked barbeque, the latter drifting in from a restaurant a block away. She considered buying a mess of it for their supper then remembered Ennis preferred Texas barbeque made from beef rather than Georgia barbeque made from pork.

Oblivious to Savannah's inner debate, Georgia furthered their conversation, asking, "When do you have time? You're always working. That's why the last few months have been hard on you. The surgery and treatments and all."

It had been a whirlwind few months, yes. About the time she caught her breath, something else cropped up. Between everything

Georgia mentioned plus juggling bills and appointments, contacting the insurance company and trying to actually *work* in the meantime, it had been a nightmare. "I'll make more time for us. This experience has taught me valuable lessons like to appreciate my family more."

They stepped aside for two joggers to pass. The evening sun dipped behind the downtown buildings, giving a soft orange glow to the surroundings and a blush to the tree leaves. Before her diagnosis, Savannah would have overlooked such beauty. Now she took time to treasure nature's glory. It was a gorgeous evening, she thought. One she'd remember for a long time.

"How's Ennis coping with you back in the race again?" her sister wanted to know.

Savannah hadn't told her sister about her mandatory time off or the purgatory of desk duty. She wouldn't tell her either. She'd leave her blissfully ignorant, "He's better now. He wanted me to take more time off but with my medical bills rolling in, I really couldn't afford to." The second it fell from her mouth, she wished the words back. Georgia would volunteer funds now, forcing her to tactfully refuse.

Indeed, Georgia braced her with her best "Mama" expression, "I can help you with those. Don't sacrifice your health because of those bills. I have the money."

"I appreciate the offer but we're okay. I really do need my normal routine back. He'll mother hen me, like someone else I know."

She started forward but Georgia stopped her, saying, "Savannah, let me help. Insurance only pays so much and my book is doing really well."

Savannah smiled, tugged her along by the elbow, "Stop campaigning. I'll ask if I need it but I don't right now." Hell would freeze before she asked her sister for money. She expected the offer at some point. Any mention of money troubles and Georgia became instant benefactor. As always Georgia offered monetary help and as always, Savannah thanked her and declined.

"You know," Georgia said, "it wouldn't kill you to ask for help once in a while. Mama always said you were stubborn enough to argue with a fence post."

Savannah's grin widened, "Personally, I think you're prettier than a fence post and a lot more fun too."

The two casually meandered toward Savannah's Camaro parked down the block. "Dane coming back soon?" she asked Georgia.

"Next week. He didn't want to go but they needed to truss up the cattle or something."

They both shared a laugh since neither understood the intricacies of ranch life. When the ranch in Texas came up in conversation, both Dane and Ennis seemed to speak in a foreign language so the sisters just pretended to understand by nodding.

As the sun sank further behind the horizon of buildings, the Camaro's image dimmed in the distance. Savannah glanced at her watch, "I'll bet Ennis is on his head. He gets cranky if I don't feed him before eight."

"So does Dane," Georgia said with a hint of humor. "They're more alike than we realized."

"I know it's getting dark but do you have time to eat a bite with us?" Savannah turned to present a pouty frown, hoping to convince her to stay and eat. Then, from the corner of her eye, she saw Georgia collapse to the ground.

Panic set in when Savannah realized someone stood right behind them. She bent to help Georgia up but a storm of electricity suddenly shot along every nerve, painfully contracting the muscles in her body. She crumpled to the grass beside her sister. It felt like a bolt of lightning struck her. In the back of her mind it registered that she'd been shot with a Taser. She recognized the pain and reaction from an earlier training exercise. Fifty thousand volts of stopping power robbed her of neuromuscular control with the first current lasting seven seconds. Several, shorter bursts would follow every thirty seconds. In the safety of the police station with other officers holding a person, it still hurt like hell but their pride took the biggest hit. They felt vulnerable but they relied on their fellow officers for physical safety. But for two women in the park with no officers, no witnesses, no nothing, all the lifelines disappeared.

From the corner of her eye, she saw a man wearing a ski mask place a strip of duct tape over Georgia's mouth. He then bound her hands behind her with flex cuffs.

The jolt from the Taser stopped. Savannah's body slackened against the grass, the muscles twitching and jerking involuntarily. The shock disoriented her and she willed herself to fight back. Her arms and hands refused to obey her brain. Her whole body had disowned her.

A knee planted itself in her back. Two strong hands encircled her wrists, pulled them behind her back and bound them with flex cuffs.

The other figure lifted Georgia, carried her to a nearby car.

Savannah tried to cry out for her sister but her attacker clamped a leather encased hand over her mouth. Fingers dug into her cheeks until he replaced his hold with a strip of duct tape.

A sting in her forearm arched her against the attacker's knee. He administered an injection, struggling to hold her as she fought against him. She had to help Georgia who now resided in the back seat of a dark colored sedan. A flash of headlights illuminated the trunk and as a gray curtain descended on Savannah's consciousness, a silver emblem glinted against the light. Her vision dove toward the license plate. Remember the plate, she told herself, remember…

Her cell phone rang with the Elvis tune "Kiss Me Quick". Ennis was calling. Strong hands slipped beneath Savannah's arms and began dragging her through the damp grass.

"*Say that you will leave me never,*" Elvis sang as she strained to reach the phone on her belt. "*Kiss me quick because I love you so…*"

The drug began to fog her vision, cloud her brain. Savannah struggled to keep her eyes open but like movement and speech, the battle remained futile.

He released her, braced his foot against her hip. One good shove rolled her into a cool moist area. Dampness seeped through her clothes to her skin. He'd pushed her beneath the nearby hedge which meant no one would see her for hours, probably until daylight dawned once more. She tried to remain conscious but blackness pulled her under quickly now. A hand at her waist startled her. He took her cell phone, turned it off then tossed it beside her. The final insult came when she heard him rummaging her purse. A moment later, he dropped it at her feet then crouched beside her, his voice a mere whisper, "Goodbye, Detective."

Ennis glanced at his watch for the fourth time in ten minutes. He pulled the living room curtains back. Street lamps had been burning for an hour or more.

He'd received only one message from Savannah that day. It arrived shortly after four thirty. She and Georgia were going to a movie, she'd said. A chick flick, he remembered thinking. Savannah went on to say that Georgia would join them for supper and they'd be home around six or so.

It was seven forty-two. It wasn't like his wife to not call if she was late. If Georgia planned to eat supper with them, Savannah never wanted her sister out late for safety reasons. When he drove up to see Georgia's Tahoe in the driveway without Savannah's Camaro beside it, he knew something was off.

The worst part: his gut feeling. It said that "something" wasn't just off but completely awry. Not wasting another minute, he headed out to find them. On the way, he dialed Georgia's cell phone – might as well give his wife's a rest since he'd loaded it up with messages the past two hours or so.

His sister-in-law's phone went to voicemail as well, rooting his uneasiness deeper, "Georgia, it's Ennis. Where are you? I'm worried sick and Savannah's not picking up. Give me a call."

He tried to figure out which theater they went to. The movie wasn't a big release as he recalled but he never kept up with movies. He drove past one theater with no luck then remembered his phone could access theater listings. He pulled over to plug in the name. The movie played at two places, one on the south end of town and one close to Piedmont Park. He opted for the Piedmont Park listing since it was closer to home.

He swung by the theater to find no red Camaro so he did the only thing that came to mind. He drove to Piedmont Park. Savannah used the park to run and keep in shape. He knew exactly where she parked and why she preferred the spot. It had a hedgerow she measured distance with. She ran four to five miles and the hedge was the start and finish line.

He circled the park once and quickly located Savannah's Camaro. He inched the Dodge Ram behind the sports car, threw the truck in Park and before getting out, armed himself with the .38, his badge and flashlight.

Traffic drove past, their headlights briefly bathing the Camaro in light. Ennis saw no one in the driver's seat. He aimed the flashlight beam through the window to reveal nothing out of the ordinary. Swinging the light to the back seat, he saw nothing out of place there either. He carried a set of her keys as a precaution, just as she carried a duplicate to his Ram. Sliding the key into the trunk lock, he twisted, letting the lid lift skyward. A quick perusal revealed a few shopping bags filled with shoes and knickknacks, a spare tire and small tool box. The hair on the back of his neck rose, and his ominous feeling escalated to a full scale alarm.

He dialed Savannah's cell number again while slamming the

trunk. It rang three times before transferring to voicemail, "Fourth message, babe. Call me."

Using the flashlight, he ventured into the park. Her usual route began where he now stood. She took the pathway completely around the park so Ennis started there.

He made it thirty yards ahead, sweeping the beam back and forth across bushes, grass and people when his phone rang. Ennis answered it on the second ring, "Where have you been?"

"Detective Rutherford? This is Officer David Harris. You need to come to the south end of Piedmont Park. It's in regards to your partner."

Ennis took off running. *This* was the bad feeling plaguing him all evening. When a cop called, it was bad.

Rounding a stand of trees, he saw three patrol units and an ambulance assembled in one giant mass, their emergency lights reflecting off buildings and onlookers and illuminating the whole block. An officer stood next to a hedgerow and as he neared, Ennis saw another officer, then another, all interviewing bystanders.

"What happened? Where's Savannah?" he demanded, his mind racing to remember the cop's name who'd just called. "Where's Harris? He called me."

A young uniform cop pointed to an older officer standing by a tree. Ennis rushed toward him and as he neared, the base of the tree drew his attention. Placed precisely in front of it was a police ID and alongside it, a detective's badge.

Ennis knew by the badge's number it belonged to Savannah. Her picture ID confirmed it.

Harris proceeded, "Guy walkin' his dog found them here and called us. We did a search and found her bound and unconscious under that hedge," he pointed. "You were her emergency contact so we called you."

He looked to the ambulance, "Where is she? Is she okay?"

"She's in the ambulance. Not sure of her condition."

Ennis scrambled to make sense of it all. The day started off so well. She'd sounded ecstatic on the phone when she left the earlier message. What went wrong? "She was with her sister Georgia. Where's she?" Normally muggers snatched purses and ran like hell. And they'd covet a cop's badge, not leave it behind and they *never* took time to tie up their victims...

Harris's brow sank, "We didn't find anyone but Detective Prince. Could the sister have left then someone jumped Prince when she was alone?"

"No. Georgia's car is at Savannah's house. She was with her." He grabbed his phone, dialed the station to inform his captain of the attack and the fact Georgia was missing. Once he clicked off, he instructed the officer, "Grab some evidence bags. I want her phone, badge and ID, *everything* you found and I'll take it with me. I have to go with Savannah."

20

Someone was gonna get killed. Hog-tied and branded then killed if Ennis ever found out who attacked his wife and abducted Georgia. Columbia Memorial emergency room personnel shooed him out while they tended to Savannah, which left him fending for himself until their colleague John Mathis arrived. Ennis handed over what little evidence Officer Harris bagged – Savannah's badge and ID, her cell phone, the flex cuffs binding her hands, and the strip of duct tape used for a gag.

He updated Mathis on what he knew – which wasn't much – and Mathis informed him that he'd contacted the city, county and state police about Georgia. John glanced at this watch, "I'm surprised their brother ain't here."

"He's on vacation with his family in Colorado."

Mathis considered the answer but not long, "Don't you think you should call him? One of his sisters is laid up in the hospital, the other one's missing."

Ennis didn't want to deal with Seth. Seth was too much like their father. Extraordinarily temperamental and sometimes too judgmental of people.   There were moments Ennis still considered himself an "out-law" instead of an "in-law" and there were moments Seth reinforced that belief.   Ennis decided to let silence answer John's statement.

The rotund detective emphasized, "She's been *abducted*, Ennis. Snatched off the street.   Brothers wanna know this stuff."

"I'll call him later," Ennis promised a bit too harshly.   He realized delaying the phone call certainly wouldn't ingratiate himself with Seth. Their brother would hit the roof *then* probably Ennis once he returned home after learning of the night's events.   Ennis refused to call Dane right away either.   He wanted to focus his efforts on getting Savannah on her feet and finding Georgia safe and sound.

Mathis shrugged, "Whatever you wanna do.   Personally, he's one guy I would not want pissed at me."

The doctor stepped through the emergency room doors, mercifully ending the conversation about Seth.   Ennis's initial appraisal of the doctor was less than stellar.   He looked like that pretty boy on Dane and Georgia's favorite medical show, the guy that needed a razor and the one all the ladies mooned over – surprisingly even Georgia.   The mid-thirties McSteamy doppel-ganger and his two day beard was attractive enough to make women swoon and attractive enough to make husbands seethe.   Real doctors never looked that way, Ennis thought.   At least none he'd ever seen.

The doctor's vision bounced from Mathis to Ennis, "Detective Rutherford?"

Ennis nodded, shook his hand.   He received a solid handshake in return, surprising for a man of his profession. Most physicians refused to lock onto another man's hand and give it a decent shake for fear of bruising themselves. The doctor introduced himself, "Dr. Holland. Your partner is doing fine. Wearing off a sedative so she'll be out a while and pretty groggy when she wakes up."

Relief washed over him – but so did a fair amount of confusion, "So he didn't overdose her, just knocked her out?"

"That's correct. There were marks on her back from what looks like Taser probes being ripped from the skin. We cleaned them to prevent infection."

The longer the doctor spoke, the angrier Ennis grew. Prior to that night, the only time Savannah had been shot with a Taser was during a training exercise. Every police officer was required to participate, regardless of rank. Uniforms zapped other uniform officers, detectives zapped detectives. He dreaded it because there were only a few detectives at their precinct and when it came Savannah's turn, no one stepped forward to pull the trigger. He and Mathis flipped a coin and Ennis lost, leaving him to zap his own wife which he doubted would play well later that night in bed. He waited for Mathis and another detective to hold Savannah securely in anticipation of her collapsing because there was no "if" about it. If the Taser brought down a two hundred pound man, its effects would drop her meager one thirty on its ass. Fifty thousand volts coursing through a body disabled and disoriented anyone. He'd pulled the trigger and she yelped, her knees buckling under her. When she recovered, she called it the worst five seconds of her life.

She was right. He remembered when it was his turn he couldn't remember the time frame shortly before or after being zapped. Standing was a joke as his muscles refused to cooperate and he ended up on his hands and knees – and wasn't very stable on those either.

Ennis thanked Dr. Holland, "When can I see her?"

"Anytime but don't expect much. She's still sleeping it off. When she wakes up, I'll check her vitals. If she's doing okay, I'll release her." Holland possessed an air of authority and appearance of one who demanded instant obedience. As he sauntered to a nearby nurse's kiosk, Ennis was struck with sudden disdain. Doctors. They all thought they were God. Holland didn't realize Savannah didn't need a doctor's permission to walk out and go home. If anyone could shake a doctor's self-assurance, it was her. She'd defy God to leave a hospital, whether she was fully clothed or draped in their customary tacky little gown that covered two square inches of flesh.

"Bastard's getting bolder," Mathis mumbled. "It's the first public abduction we know of."

The same thing occurred to Ennis. If the killer felt comfortable enough to snatch a well known author from a park it meant no woman was safe any time of day. "And when he attacks a cop, it means his confidence is building fast. We gotta catch this asshole, Mathis. We gotta get Georgia back before…"

"I know, Ennis. I know." Mathis pointed to the emergency room doors, "Try to concentrate on her right now. When she wakes up, all hell is gonna break loose and you're the only one who can contain it."

"Pardon me for interrupting," Holland had approached without either cop noticing. They turned to face him. Mathis looked peeved that the guy snuck up behind them, Ennis just didn't care.

Holland continued, "I was curious if you had any suspects in this case."

"Why?" Ennis asked. What did it matter to him? The killer only targeted pretty women, not pretty men.

The doctor's brow plunged between his eyes, evidently unhappy that his question was met with another question, "Because I read the papers. Someone used a Taser to disable your partner then administered a sedative. That fits the profile for the Ravine Killer. Since Detective Prince was not abducted I assumed someone might have interrupted the killer and perhaps got a look at him."

Both detectives stared at him. Ennis debated on whether to tell him nothing and walk off or flat tell him to mind his own business. He opted for silence.

Holland crossed his arms, "I have a sister and don't want this – or worse – happening to her."

Mathis took over, "Listen, doc. You concentrate on your job, we'll concentrate on ours. Best thing you can do is tell your sister not to be out alone. Ever."

"How's Savannah?" a new voice entered the conversation. It was Josh Hunter.

"Sleeping off a sedative," Ennis answered and let Mathis update him on what happened. With Mathis and Hunter following behind, he pushed through the emergency room doors and searched out Savannah's cubicle. Sweeping the curtain back, he took a physical account of his wife. Besides her deep slumber, the first thing he noticed were the marks on her wrists left by the flex cuffs. The attacker pulled them so tight the plastic dug into the skin.

Faint discoloration on her cheeks left an outline of a man's hand. The bastard held her so tight she'd have bruises. The image inflamed him further, "That son of a bitch better pray some other cop finds him. I'll kill him on sight."

Savannah moved, her eyes barely opened. Ennis noticed they seemed unfocused as she searched the room, "Ennis."

Ennis took her hand, grateful she was awake, "Right here, sugar. You had me worried, so worried about you." He stroked the soft skin of her hand, relishing the warm velvet feel of it. Ennis closed his eyes as the harsh reality of the night set in. He could have lost her. The harsher reality was: he may not have lost Savannah, but Savannah lost Georgia and knowing his wife, she'd blame herself.

Her vision roamed the room until finding Hunter and Mathis. Both nodded and her boss suggested, "You need to rest. We'll get your statement later."

"We need her statement now," Mathis corrected then shrank back at Ennis's narrowed glare. He defended his statement, "I'm doing my job here. Faster we catch this asshole, quicker she can rest."

"He's right," her words were slow, lethargic. "Did you find Georgia?"

All three men broke eye contact with her. Ennis couldn't bear to see her expression but heard the sadness in her voice, "I had to ask. There were two men, both white," she paused for Mathis to retrieve his notepad. He scribbled as she spoke, "Both dressed in black, wearing ski masks. They were tall, over six feet and the one that spoke only whispered but didn't have an accent I could hear. They drove a new car, a four door. They put Georgia in the back seat."

"Color?" Mathis asked. Ennis let John take over the questioning. Not only was he more objective but entirely more composed.

"Blue or black. It was getting dark so it was hard to tell."

Ennis gave John Mathis credit. He waited patiently for her to continue without his usual efforts to speed things along. John treated her with a gentleness Ennis never realized he had, "They say anything weird, anything that caught your attention?"

"Not really. He knew I was a detective but he could have recognized me from the news conference."

"They shock you both, sedate you both?"

She drew a deep, slow breath that told Ennis the sedative still had a strong grip on her. Her speech sounded sluggish and drunk and her eyes made small measured movements. "Shocked us, sedated me," she said. "Bastard shocked me twice. I could barely remember my name." The first signs of emotion crept into Savannah's voice. She wiped away growing tears, "They just carried her off and I couldn't help her."

"Mathis, give her a break," Ennis said. "She's been through a lot."

Mathis whispered back, "I'll bet Georgia's going through more."

"Cut it out," Josh warned. "Savannah's doing the best she can."

Movement from the corner of his eye snapped Ennis's attention from his wife. Cole Jordan ran by the emergency cubicle then promptly applied the brakes, skidding past. Seconds later he appeared at the foot of her bed, "I just heard. Are you okay?"

The question ruffled Ennis, "She's in the hospital. What do you think?"

Cole zeroed in on Savannah, "What'd you see? What did he look like? What direction did he go?"

"Calm down, Jordan," Hunter scolded. "Mathis is getting the information."

Cole read over John's shoulder, "Two white guys with ski masks. If they were wearing ski masks, how could you tell they were white?"

Even with the sedation, the question pricked Savannah's ire, "It wasn't *that* dark, Cole. They were white."

"Could it have been Shelton's guys?"

Jordan's hope verged on insanity to Ennis. Like someone waiting to hear the last lottery number to see if they won the jackpot.

She thought a minute, rubbed her temple then sighed, "I don't know how many white men work for him. Do you?"

Dr. Holland drew the curtain back, forcing Ennis to the foot of the bed with Cole. The doctor flashed Savannah a half-smile, "I'll check your vitals and if you pass, I'll release you tonight."

He gathered a blood pressure cuff from a wall mounted wire cage and told the men, "Don't let me interrupt." He wrapped the cuff around her arm.

Ennis watched as the doctor pumped the cuff, then saw Savannah flinch. Holland patted her arm with an apology. Oh yeah, Ennis frowned. Husbands hated this guy.

"AFID," she suddenly chirped, seemingly halfway surprised with herself. "Tasers have AFID. We can trace them to the buyer, at least."

Mathis peered over his glasses, "Is she saying aphids?"

Josh rolled his eyes, "AFID, John. Not aphids. The anti-felon identification system Taser International uses." He told Mathis, "Have forensics search the area for them."

In his panic, Ennis never thought about AFID. In her semi-conscious state, Savannah remembered the little pieces of paper with serial numbers. When someone discharged a Taser, it released dozens of them, so many that the shooter couldn't possibly gather them all. Using those, they could track down the buyer who, in a perfect world, would turn out to be the killer. But as the night proved, the world was anything but perfect.

Holland retrieved a penlight from his coat pocket, "Judging from that conversation, you're doing much better. Your cognitive skills are sharper than before. Now open your eyes wide for me."

Ennis wondered how that might work. She could barely keep them open, much less open them wide. Savannah managed what she could and Holland used his thumb to lift the lid slightly higher. Sweeping the small shaft of light across each pupil, Ennis awaited the results. From his perspective, the pupils still looked too dilated to send her home. Maybe she needed an overnight stay to wear off the sedative. She wouldn't like it but he'd feel better about it. "How's she doing?"

Holland smiled back at Ennis, "Passing grades so far."

He didn't like this guy. He was too good looking for anyone to take him seriously. As if Holland heard every doubt, he pocketed the penlight, faced Ennis. The smile disappeared, "She'll be groggy, dizzy and sleep a lot but it's safe to send her home."

Directing the conversation back to the case, Mathis offered his opinion, "Could be they can't handle two women at once. One might get away or draw attention. Who knows?"

"Or," Josh chimed in, "they know it's instant death penalty if they kill a cop."

The doctor waggled a stethoscope at her, "Time to check the ticker."

Savannah pursed her lips but capitulated anyway. Holland's movie star smile returned, "Relax. I don't bite."

She tried, Ennis noticed, but hospitals drove her nuts. Savannah rubbed her eyes while Holland pressed the stethoscope between her breasts. "These guys," she said, "don't care about capital punishment because they don't believe they'll get caught."

"Detective, please," Holland lifted a finger to his lips, shushing her. She obliged while he made another attempt with the stethoscope. Evidently pleased with the result, he jotted a note on her chart, "I'll start the paperwork for your release."

Savannah thanked him, closed her eyes. Ennis assumed she drifted back to sleep. After a few seconds she mumbled, "Seven," then a moment passed then, "the letter A."

"What the hell's that?" Cole wanted to know.

"Part of the license plate," she replied.

The information pleased and impressed Mathis as he wrote, "Hey, Prince, you got a good noggin on you, even after being hit with lightning."

"You serious?" Cole continued. "You actually got a piece of the plate?"

She nodded, still deep in thought, "The lights of a nearby car flashed across it. There may have been an S or an eight." Savannah opened her eyes. They looked tired and sad, "I don't know. I could be wrong but the first two I'd stake my life on. The trunk's emblem was silver, round. I couldn't see it clearly though."

Ennis was at a loss for words. First that she remembered part of the license plate and caught a glimpse of the car's insignia. Second that she looked so helpless. She tried to help Georgia and felt responsible for not protecting her.

Savannah sat up in bed, yanked the blanket free then draped it around her. She swayed then blinked her eyes a few times, obviously dizzy from the sudden movement.

Ennis put a hand to her shoulder, "Stay put. The doctor hasn't released you yet. And I wish he wouldn't."

Savannah argued, "I have to look for her. Where I don't know, but I have to try."

Oh sure, Ennis thought. *In* your *condition...* All four men shook their heads. Josh spoke first, "Let me be clear. You're already off this case so I'd better not hear of you rattling Duke Shelton's cage or anyone else's. Let Mathis and Jordan work on it."

Cole volunteered, "I'll run a search on the plate number."

Ennis felt left out, like the last kid picked for the team, "What about me?"

Josh shook his head again, "Your partner was assaulted so I don't exactly expect you to be impartial on this case. Especially after that crack about you killing these guys on sight." He pointed at Savannah, "Ennis, your new job is keeping her at home and under control."

21

What started as a long night dragged on minute by tedious minute. Ennis tried to drift off, to gain restful sleep but every conceivable sound prevented it. The clock in the living room ticked a little louder than normal. A thunderstorm rolled in to provide its own symphony of noise. Flashes of lightning illuminated the bedroom followed by sharp, splitting thunder that rattled the windows. Wind howled against their small house, pummeling it with sheets of rain verging on hail. Storms typically never bothered Ennis but with the night's events, sleep was a desire not to be fulfilled.

Unlike Ennis, Savannah slept through the whole ruckus. He held her close just in case she awoke with a start. Ennis imagined everyone in Atlanta had done that at least once during the raging storm – everyone, that was, but his wife.

He spooned against her until he felt her heartbeat against his chest. He needed her closeness now, to feel her warmth, to touch her, to hear her breathing. She was with him, not with some lunatic killer, he had to remind himself. She was safe.

Reality told him his wife may have escaped the kidnapping and torture but her sister hadn't.   That presented a whole new set of problems.   Once awake, Savannah would want to go find her sister. Ennis understood why but he also planned to explain the cold hard facts. No one knew where to find Georgia.

Stroking Savannah's hair, Ennis considered *himself* fortunate she was spared.   Until they found Georgia – hopefully alive – he'd keep that to himself.   Savannah stirred against him then relaxed, her breathing returning to a slow, steady rhythm.   Ennis closed his eyes, happy that for now her restlessness ceased.

The phone rang around nine.   It was Cole, "How's she doing?"

Ennis kept his voice down, "Still sleeping."

"When she wakes up, ask her if she's sure about the license plate. I ran the plate numbers she remembered and came up empty."

Empty sounded like Cole's head.   The moron had to be kidding, "Not a single hit?"

"Well, yeah," Cole said in a manner questioning Ennis's sanity. "It only gave me fifteen hundred cars to weed through.   Just ask her if she remembers anything else about it but only when she feels up to it.   Did Hunter assign security detail to the house?"

Feeling her snuggle against him, Ennis eased his hand down her arm, whispering, "Patrol unit at the curb."

"If you need a breather, I could spell you.   I'll crash on the couch and let you get some sleep."

"Thanks for offering but I got it covered."

Cole capitulated, "Two cops are better than one, at least that's what my old girlfriend used to say…"

Cole wasn't long for the world if they allowed the man in their house. Either he or Savannah would strangle him. They had enough to deal with and didn't need an abrasive, horny cop in their midst.

"It was a joke, Rutherford. Lighten up. If you need any help, call me. And don't forget to ask her about that plate."

He'd be happy to when she woke up. Rousing her now would only cause the cruel reality to come screaming back. Carefully slipping out of bed, he went to the kitchen to prepare breakfast.

He cracked a few eggs into a bowl and whipped a splash of milk in. He'd seen his mama do it and when Savannah did the same, he figured why question success. If it had been a normal morning, he'd have tossed some canned biscuits on a baking sheet and shoved them in the oven. That was as far as his culinary talent extended: eggs and canned biscuits. With their lives lately, he opted for simplicity because persuading Savannah to eat would be a trial by itself.

During the radiation treatments, her pig-headedness set harder than a pit bull's jaws. In those six weeks of treatment her appetite all but disappeared, causing her to drop an alarming amount of weight. Georgia prepared delicious meals for her sister, trying to tempt her to eat. It worked most of the time. Unfortunately Ennis's coaxing ability paled in comparison to Georgia's. Being the maternal type, she lectured Savannah before pushing a plate of food at her. Savannah didn't like the scolding but ate the meal. Pushy as she was at the time, Georgia was a godsend to him – and to her sister…

He certainly lacked Georgia's influence and tact. If Savannah went on a hunger strike, nothing short of holding her down and force feeding her would work – and he'd require a battalion of soldiers to help in the effort.

Ennis's vision settled on his wife's purse sitting on the dining table. After forensics finished with hers and Georgia's belongings, Mathis dropped them by earlier. Ennis sat both purses on the table and hadn't taken time to brush the grass and debris from them. Now he took the opportunity to do that plus rummage both to ensure no pertinent cards went missing.

He put the frying pan aside, waiting to scramble the eggs. With Savannah still sawing logs, breakfast went on hold anyway.

A perusal of Georgia's purse revealed her driver's license, Social Security card, various credit cards and eighty-two dollars in cash. A veritable treasure for thieves but the men who took Georgia only wanted her, not money, not identification cards or credit cards. Just Georgia.

He sat Georgia's purse aside and unclasped Savannah's. He found everything including her credit cards, all where she normally kept them. He didn't know how much cash she carried but he found fifty-six dollars.

Rummaging further, he found mascara, a mirror, a small tube of hand cream, and a comb. In the side pocket, he found Savannah's notepad open to a name. In hurried cursive it read "Dr. Susan Swersky" and above the name, "Shelton's Dr. 12 yrs ago." Ennis flipped through the notepad for additional entries but found none.

At first he wondered why she hadn't shared the tidbit with him earlier. Then it hit him: the phrase "12 years ago" meant she obtained the name through Georgia when the older sister and Duke were acquaintances. The name they sought sat in his hand, another key to perhaps finding Georgia before it was too late. But that was also assuming Shelton was the killer or connected to the killer somehow.

Ennis dialed John Mathis, "Savannah got the name of Shelton's private physician twelve years ago. The name's Dr. Susan Swersky."

"You kidding me?" John's skeptical side emerged. "I don't even have the same doc from *five* years ago. What makes you think this psycho kept his for twelve years or more?"

"He's paranoid so he's not going to break in a new physician. Run a background, find out if she has access to the sedatives the killer is using. Did forensics find the AFID tags from the Taser?"

"Yeah, they said there were so many it looked like confetti from a party."

"Did you contact Taser International?"

"What am I? A rookie? According to their records, the Tasers were bought by the first victim Andrea Peters so they're not law enforcement X26 or M26. She bought a boatload of cartridges too."

Did he hear that right? Tasers? Not one individual Taser but more than one? "Tasers as in plural?"

"She musta been like Noah. Only shopped in pairs 'cause she bought two and then accessorized them with twelve cartridges."

Ennis nearly choked, "Was she saving up for a rainy day? Who needs two Tasers and twelve cartridges?"

"She'd been mugged four months prior to buying the units. Guess she wanted a backup or twelve. Or she suffered from that hoarding disease Kleptomania or whatever. One's good but a dozen's better."

Ennis debated about correcting Mathis on the Klepto remark. He decided to let it slide. From the corner of his eye, he saw Savannah trudge into the living room, her eyes still heavy from sleep. After a painful stretch, she yawned, rubbing her eyes with balled fists.

"Gotta go," he told Mathis. "Thanks for checking on everything." He rushed to steady Savannah since she leaned a few degrees short of tipping completely over. "How're you feeling?" he asked.

"Like a Junebug after flying into a bug zapper." She eased into a dining room chair, took one look at the chaos once serving as an organized purse but never said a word. Ennis hurried back to the eggs, switched on the burner, "Want coffee before breakfast?"

She shook her head, "No thanks. And I'm not hungry so don't fix me anything."

So it began. He sighed, resigning himself to a long struggle. He'd prepare the meal anyway with hopes of tempting her. In the meantime, he mentally rummaged around for Georgia's successful tricks. He'd try guilt if nothing else came to mind. When all else failed, try guilt, he thought. That's what his brothers did.

Her speech remained sluggish and thick, "Heard anything about Georgia?"

Ennis hated to answer that question but shook his head anyway. If he'd heard good news, she knew he'd have awakened her.

While the eggs cooked, he popped two slices of bread into the toaster. He opened an upper cabinet and took out a jar of homemade apricot preserves his mother sent them for Christmas. She'd sent half a dozen different kinds but Savannah preferred the apricot. He prayed it enticed her enough to eat because guilt remained his only other option and guilt, like nitroglycerin, required a delicate touch or it would explode in his face.

He changed the subject, "I've got Mathis doing background on Shelton's doctor. I found the note in your purse. I hope you don't mind me nosin' through it."

Savannah shook her head, her vision resting on Georgia's purse. He knew she wanted news of her sister and he had none to give. Ennis stirred the eggs with a spatula, "Jordan ran the partial plate and came up dry." The first spark of ire lit her expression. Any mention of Cole Jordan and she bristled. Ennis rephrased, "I meant it gave him a multitude of hits. He wanted to know if you remembered anything else about the car, plate or emblem."

"I was being electrocuted at the time. Tell Jordan I'm sorry for not being more mindful of things."

"Sugar, calm down," he scooped the eggs onto a plate. "You did fine. At least he's helping. That's more than either of us really expected." He fetched the salt and pepper, "Mathis said the Taser cartridges were bought by the first victim so the unit wasn't a law enforcement model."

She rubbed her face, "When someone pulls the trigger, you can't really tell a difference, believe me."

Keeping the conversation going didn't seem like a priority to her and his abilities to carry one were dreadful anyway so he concerned himself with her breakfast. After placing two pieces of apricot-topped toast on her plate, he returned to the kitchen, "I'll get your coffee."

"I'm not hungry."

"Savannah, you will eat," he demanded. "I even used Ma's apricot jam on your toast. You want to break her heart and not eat it?" Guilt – carefully crafted guilt. That was his only solution to break Savannah's stubborn streak. It worked for Georgia and Ennis prayed it worked for him too. He poured a cup of coffee, spooned a touch of sugar in it then stirred in cream. "You're worried about Georgia, we all are, but she'd tan your hide if you didn't eat." So what if he sprinkled an extra dose of guilt on her? She wasn't wasting away on his watch. He sat the cup next to the plate, "So eat."

Savannah met his vision with her trademark headstrong frown. One that without words specifically stated he couldn't, *wouldn't* boss her around.

Ennis countered it with his own look, punctuated with hands on his hips. He counted five seconds before she sighed.

She finally relented, "I'll try but don't get mad if I can't eat much."

She shook salt and pepper over the eggs then retreated to a pensive mood. The fork raked slowly through the eggs. Before taking a bite, she stopped, repeating the same account from the night before, "Round silver emblem. There are too many brands fitting that category but I couldn't get a better look. It was so brief, just an instant. The plate is still the same, I can't recall anything new." She chewed slowly, deliberately then she sat the fork down, "Maybe Mathis should try the plate search. He knows Georgia, he'll work harder to find it."

He made a mental note to tell Mathis. Their friend and colleague wouldn't mind taking over that part of the investigation. God knew Cole Jordan twiddled his thumbs so long nearly a dozen women were dead because of it. If the killer kept this pace, a dozen would pass by before the end of the following week.

"I need to call Seth."

Ennis nearly groaned. He expected the subject sooner or later but now? He dreaded calling Seth Prince like he'd dread being lit on fire. The girls' brother possessed a temper comparable to their father's and on occasion rivaled and soared past Savannah's. "Babe, settle down first. Let's not be hasty about making calls yet."

Clarity suddenly focused Savannah's eyes. Their piercing blue zeroed in on him and not in a good way. Clearly she disapproved of his proposal, "If he finds out before I tell him, do you realize what could happen to me? My brother's disposition verges on psychotic when he's angry. And not that he has a favorite sister, but I really don't want to discover which one he'd rather see dead, especially by his own hand."

"Oh, Seth wouldn't hurt you."

Her expression said otherwise. Maybe she knew something he didn't but Seth, as strange as he was, cherished his siblings.

"His sister is missing," she reminded. "His other sister is sitting on her ass doing nothing to help. How's that gonna sound to him?"

"When he finds out you were assaulted too, I think that'll buy you a reprieve. Plus, you've been ordered to stay away from the investigation."

"And Seth will be spitting nails. He's a man of action, not

inaction. He'll come home and start looking for her while I 'follow orders' and grow roots at home."

"I'll make you a deal. Hold off on calling him until tonight. Give yourself time to recover from last night."

She thought a moment then capitulated, "I'll call tonight."

22

The scent of honeysuckle drifted past when he neared her.   Her features – like the younger sister's – reminded him of Rita Hayworth. Skimming his fingers down her smooth back and belly revealed not only a slim, shapely figure but a firm, toned one.   She had slender, sleekly muscled legs and plump, beautiful breasts – considerably larger than the sister's – that begged for his attention.

Something about Georgia trumped his immediate desire for Savannah.   Perhaps it was her stunning beauty.   Men spent their lives obsessing over such visions of graceful elegance and upon first glance, he found himself enchanted.   Or maybe it was her quiet strength.   With Georgia's allergic reaction, Savannah's aggressive and demanding tone left people scattering in every direction, following her orders.   But with her sister, Savannah exhibited a gentler, composed and assuring quality.   He assumed it was for Georgia's benefit.   Savannah's effort was valiant but unnecessary since Georgia, for the most part, kept her cool and for such a severe reaction, that took guts.   The older sister's quiet strength coupled with her beauty must have convinced him to leave Savannah behind.

It surprised him that what tan lines Georgia had faded during the colder months. A woman so beautiful normally visited a tanning salon. No matter whether Georgia tanned in the sunshine or tanning bed, her skin was the perfect color to him. But her skin, while perfect in color, was anything but flawless. A small number of elongated scars on her backside were the only imperfections. Her father had been cruel to her, tried to beat her into compliance.

He could have saved her father the trouble. Beautiful Georgia merely needed the right inspiration to comply – though parents seldom resorted to threats of disfigurement or disembowelment.

Once he stripped her clothes, he placed her in "his playroom". The room with his restraints hanging from the ceiling, the ones bolted into the floor. The room containing the tools of his trade. He kept the room cold to keep their minds and bodies alert, on edge. One insignificant strike of his cane commanded Georgia's attention. Another reinforced he wanted quick answers to his questions. By the third rather lenient blow, she'd begun crying, but it emphasized his point. Now, one touch startled her to a rigid stance, her body trembling, her shaky voice pleading for mercy.

The terror so vivid in her misty green eyes enhanced her loveliness. He truly prized this part. The exquisite sight of her eyes brimming with tears and rounded with fear of what he might do next. Her heart pounded so hard he saw it pulsing at her neck. When he touched her anywhere, her body stiffened, the raging heartbeat hammering against his fingertips.

Three scarlet welts striped her buttocks. None bled or threatened to. That would soon change, especially if she refused to follow his precise *instructions.*

"You remember what you're supposed to do?" he asked, his tone calm and even.

The color drained from her face. She snuffled back more tears, the reply not quick like he desired. He stepped behind her, lifted the cane again. As if on cue she winced and her body arched, pulling against her bonds, trying to escape the blow. The blow never came.

"I can't. Please don't make me do this," she begged through her tears.

He laid the cane down, moved to face her. Her shoulders and upper chest glistened with a fine sheen of sweat. Dark waves framed her face and a few stray curls clung to her temples. That and her quick ragged breaths conjured thoughts of sex and how beautiful she probably looked when she came. As gorgeous as she was, his goal wasn't to make her come. She was merely a means to an end now. His blunder, he supposed, was that he misjudged her potential. Quiet strength was overrated. He needed the steel determination she lacked. He needed a woman who would oppose him, challenge him with an iron will that begged him to break her. Georgia failed him._ Blinded by her beauty, he wanted her to be Eva.

He eyed her plump, pretty breasts then slid his vision past her navel, "I'm not making you do anything. You have a choice. You can do this for me and save yourself pain or you can refuse." He retrieved his trusty scalpel from a nearby cabinet, touched her stomach with it, "And you know what will happen if you refuse."

"Anything, please," she gulped, trying to control her tears.

"Anything else except this."

He bore down somewhat on the blade, "Is that your answer?"

She squirmed in the restraints, trying to pull away but failing, "No."

His stare drilled her, "I'm asking a small favor. One phone call for your life. In most cases, it's considered a simple decision." He let the blade linger at her soft belly a moment. He'd never disemboweled anyone before and truthfully he dreaded the cleanup. If Georgia dilly-dallied much longer her option would be violently removed as her clothes had been. "Do it or I'll make the call and the only thing they hear is you dying while your intestines spill out on the floor. Do you really want that?"

"No."

He retrieved her cell phone sitting next to his scalpel. "Home or cell number?"

"Cell," her voice quavered. An involuntary shiver raked her body, rattling the chains restraining her.

He thumbed a few buttons on the phone to access the contact list. He scrolled down until settling on one name, one number. Before dialing, he warned, "It's on speakerphone. Don't screw up." To discourage her from doing so, he stepped behind her again. He placed the scalpel beneath her left breast, closing his eyes at the warm velvet skin brushing his thumb. Perfect breasts, he thought. Too bad Georgia's strength and spirit hadn't lived up to those wondrous gifts.

In the end they all sold out. For whatever reason – to please him momentarily, to prevent pain, to live a moment longer – they all sold out. With the distinct exception of pain prevention, he couldn't figure out why Georgia did. He supposed if someone held a scalpel to his balls and threatened to cut them off, he'd sell out too and not just his sister but his mother, grandmother and her little dog too.

The phone rang twice before a woman answered, "Prince."

"Savannah, it's me."

"Georgia, are you okay?" He heard the hope, the excitement rise in the sister's voice. She asked, "Where are you? I'll come get you."

Earlier, Georgia agreed to say she escaped and for her sister to pick her up before he found her. If Leigh left him anything, it was that idea and he'd use it to lure the sister to him. To that he added Georgia should tell her sister to come alone. Women like Georgia prized themselves on modesty. It mortified them to imagine running around naked and having the cavalry arrive. Since he lacked any real knowledge about the sister, he figured using the modesty angle might keep other cops at bay. And in case the detective ignored Georgia's warning, he had quite an infallible backup plan...

"Georgia?" Panic laced Savannah's voice. "Are you there? Where are you?"

His body reacted to the fear. She was the challenge he searched for. His next Eva. He silently berated himself for making the wrong choice. He should have taken her when he had the chance.

His erection pressed against Georgia's back. She swallowed hard, making him wonder if she felt it. He hadn't been this hard for a long time. The others stirred his desire for them, for their pain. Savannah aroused him with a plethora of possibilities. The biggest – she held the *potential for being even better and stronger than Eva…*

With her warm back against his chest, he felt Georgia's shallow rapid breathing. Come on. Say it. Stick with the script or else… *He'd chosen a secluded location within a half hour's drive of his house. With mild sedation, his newly acquired gift would remain docile during the ride.*

His current problem resided with Georgia. He admired her efforts to protect her sister but how many times did he have to warn this bitch to follow directions? Her hesitation fueled his anger and he struggled to keep his temper under control. He'd sternly and specifically explained the consequences of delaying her answers. Stalling equaled refusal, he said. He applied some pressure on the blade nestled at her breast.

She stiffened against him, "I'm here. I…" She shook her head. Attempts to subdue her weeping failed, "I love you, honey."

For her sake, he hoped she reconsidered reneging on their deal. Even as Savannah returned the sentiment, he worried Georgia changed her mind.

"Where are you? At Duke's? Just give me an idea of your location so I can help…" The younger sister persisted, her panic so palpable his erection threatened to burst free. He closed his eyes, relishing every terrified syllable she spoke, "Georgia, please give me something."

The crying increased, hot tears fell on his forearm as she replied, "He's coming for you. Don't leave the house –"

He slammed the phone closed, threw it across the room,

shattering it into pieces – the same fate his plan just met.

Wrapping his arm across her waist, he held her nakedness against him as she wept. He leaned to her ear, promising, "That will not save her. Nothing will save her and nothing will save you."

23

It was a race for the door after Georgia's call and for once Ennis thanked God Cole Jordan was there. The second the call was severed, Savannah raced for the dining table for her keys.

Cole watched in amazement as she flew past him. He turned to Ennis with palms up, shrugging, "What do I do?"

Seriously? He had to *ask*? If Ennis needed confirmation Jordan was an idiot, that did it. Ennis wasn't letting Savannah exit the house after that call, knowing Georgia probably suffered immeasurably after warning Savannah of the trap. He could only imagine the thoughts and images going through his wife's mind and none of them mixed with driving. Ennis uttered a blistering curse then enlightened his dim-witted colleague, "*Stop her.*"

Jordan's expression flattened, "You paying for my seein' eye dog when she scratches my eyes out?"

Evidently he sensed Ennis wouldn't so he opted to simply block the front door. Ennis rolled his eyes. The coward. Yes, when angered or determined, Savannah proved to be an expert at verbal battle. If it escalated to physical violence, the occasion either warranted it or was a knee-jerk reaction on her part. On any other day, Ennis doubted she'd lash out physically but today... For all his bragging, it turned out Cole was as full of crap as a Christmas goose. He was actually scared of a woman. Of course Savannah wasn't the typical female either, Ennis admitted that. She presented quite a challenge when angered – he guessed Jordan sensed that too. But still, "Jordan, man up and physically *grab* her."

Savannah's blue eyes dared Cole to touch her. Then her fingers closed around the keys. *Uh-oh...* Ennis realized he underestimated the situation. The temptation of slamming her fist into Cole's face sounded appealing but adding fury and car keys to the equation meant she'd slice him to pieces. Maybe the seeing eye dog wasn't a joke after all...

"Dude," Cole pressed against the door, hands at his sides, "how 'bout a little help?"

Ennis raced to her, his vision never straying from her hand, "Savannah, Georgia told you to stay home. Listen to her."

She tensed and Ennis stopped a respectable distance from her reach. Under the circumstances, he'd play it safe and stand back in case she decided to swing.

"Do not tell me," she warned, "I cannot look for my sister." Savannah wheeled to Ennis and he saw Cole slacken against the door, visibly grateful she directed her anger at someone else.

She finished, "Georgia's in trouble and I have to help."

When the call came in, Savannah switched it to speakerphone. All three heard the terror in Georgia's voice, the uncontrollable weeping. When the call disconnected, Ennis anticipated the upcoming quarrel. He *hadn't* anticipated the physical nature of it, and that's where he screwed up. "You can't go," he grasped her elbow to reach for her keys.

A declaration of war. That's what the move constituted. Judging by her glare, she considered his touch a provocation. She stepped toward him with a look that made him shut his mouth and swallow hard. He'd seen the look one other time but she'd been drinking then. Unfortunately, liquor changed her temperament to malicious and even violent – the one trait of her father's Ennis wished heredity had skipped. Today she ran purely on adrenaline, fear and rage and that combination was equally potent.

The hand holding the keys lifted but she thankfully used it to point, not attack, "Try stopping me. Just try it, Ennis. This is my sister we're talking about, not some stranger off the street. *My sister.*" She slung his hand away and marched to the door.

Ennis took her arm again, this time with a firmer grasp. She spun to face him, her blistering scowl telegraphing how close to the edge she felt. Ennis took the opportunity to snatch the keys from her hand. She grimaced as they ripped from her grasp but it did little to extinguish her temper. Savannah liked to slap more than punch. In the past, she'd never actually hit him but she'd tried to lay a very persuasive palm across his cheek once. It wasn't something he wanted a repeat of but her fingers opened, ready to smack him. Ennis caught her wrist, "Where are you planning to go?"

She struggled against his grasp until meeting his vision, "Let go of me."

Her blue eyes, blazing and brimming with tears, broke his heart all over again but he kept a strict hold on her – too harsh, in his opinion – but her emotional anguish and anger overrode any pain he caused. He said, "I'm not letting go so you might as well answer my question. Do you have any clue where she is?"

"You know I don't!" she shouted at him, finally surrendering to his hold.

Ennis heard a crack in her anger. The emotion boiled to the surface as rage but she was hurt, confused, and felt hopeless like he did. His voice softened, "That's my point. You don't know where to look. Let's see if John can back trace the call. Let's stay here in case she calls again."

"I have to try." Tears rolled down her cheeks, "Don't you understand? I can't leave her alone with this bastard. I have to try."

"But you can't. No one knows her location." He felt the tension in her arms gradually melt away. Ennis drew a deep breath, praying the confrontation was over.

"You couldn't have helped her anyway," Cole said, still guarding the door. "They made sure you couldn't."

On rare occasion Cole Jordan dug up a gem. One that mattered. That one really counted, at least to Ennis. It showed that somewhere inside that sexist lump of flesh, Jordan possessed a speck of a heart. "He's right," Ennis agreed.

From a significant distance, Cole assured, "Mathis and I will work day and night to find her, I promise."

Ennis felt her pull away. He debated over letting go. If she ran for the door again, maybe Cole could muster the balls to grab her this time. Sure enough, Savannah shoved him away so hard it sent him back a step but when he caught sight of her pale features, he released her immediately. She bolted to the bathroom, the sound of heaving following soon after.

Ennis cringed and saw Cole join in the effort. The Zone 3 cop sighed, "That's my cue. I gotta get back to work anyway. I'll let you know if we find anything."

24

Ennis knew she loved and revered Georgia like a child would a mother. Plenty of times he heard her refer to Georgia as a surrogate mother, someone to talk to, confess to, and fuss and laugh with. He couldn't count the times she'd called Georgia "Mama", either as a warning to silence a lecture or as a term of endearment, its meaning private and shared only between the sisters.

Shortly after Cole left, Savannah piled into bed, less her breakfast and coffee. He waited by the phone for news from Cole or Mathis, hopeful they'd get a lead on Georgia. He prayed she'd be found alive. He couldn't bear to think what might happen if she wasn't...

The phone rang at three o'clock. Picking up the receiver, Ennis heard a siren in the background as Mathis asked, "Prince isn't nearby is she?"

Dread set in. Sirens were never good news and John's ominous question set his gut into another tailspin. Ennis replied, "She's in bed. Why?"

"Good. I'm calling you before it hits the news. They found another body. I'm on my way there."

Now *his* breakfast crept up his throat. If the victim turned out to be Georgia, John's call was the precursor to Savannah's meltdown. Ennis never saw his wife so inconsolable and despondent. He held her as she cried, trying to assure her and give her hope. In his heart he feared the same. When Georgia warned Savannah about the trap, the killer more than likely leveled his rage at her. If the body was her sister's, how would he tell Savannah? If Georgia was dead, how *could* he tell her? Ennis scrubbed a hand through his hair, "I won't tell her till she wakes up."

"Try not telling her at all. The boss is firm – she better not show up at the scene. That's an edict from God, Rutherford. Keep her home."

Hunter's callous approach grated on Ennis. Forcing Savannah to endure the news was bad enough. Forcing her to stay home and not allowing her to be there for her sister was outrageous. He understood both sides – Josh's and Savannah's – and felt torn between them. No, seeing her sister's mutilated body wouldn't be wise but no army in the world stood a chance of holding her back either. "You tell Hunter if Georgia turns up dead, I'll be lucky to keep my wife sane. She worships her sister."

In the background the siren wailed and Mathis pounded the horn, yelling out the window, "Same to you, asshole." He returned to his conversation, his voice softening, "Ennis, I know it's rough on her, on both of you. I ain't stupid. To be honest, I think the boss is afraid it *is* Georgia. Can you imagine how Prince would react if she saw her sister like that?"

"Yes," he replied, as grim images of the previous victims clawed their way back. And if anything could destroy Savannah, losing Georgia would – especially in such a brutal manner.

"I'll keep you updated," Mathis said. "Oh yeah. Checked on that Dr. Swersky for you. She does have access to the sedatives used on the victims. Once we identify the victim, I'll do more digging. Gotta go." Before he clicked off, he pounded the horn again, yelling at another motorist, "There's a reason I'm driving like this – what's your excuse?"

Ennis stared at the phone in his hand. Besides Savannah, there were two other people he dreaded talking to. One was their father R.J., the other was Seth. When their brother left town, he actually had a smile on his face. Like gold and diamonds, smiles were rare for Seth Prince. Once returning from the army, he opened a self-defense studio, mostly to help educate and train women against such attacks. Being a workaholic, Seth cultivated the business into a success so prying him away took iron perseverance and his wife Leah possessed an abundance of it. He agreed to turn his business over to a colleague for a couple of weeks to spend some family time in Colorado. They'd gone on vacation to sightsee. Now they'd probably come back to a funeral…

Then Ennis thought about Dane. His brother and Georgia had grown particularly close the past year. So close he'd heard Dane mention marriage for the first time in his life. For Dane Rutherford to hanker for a wedding, it had to be a special woman. Ennis couldn't think of a more exceptional woman for his brother. His heart squeezed in his chest and he rubbed at it to ease the sensation.

"Who was that?"

Ennis flinched. When he looked up, his wife was propped

against the living room door for stability. Heavy lidded and thick speech aside, she seemed halfway awake. Her tone verged on hopeful and Ennis rubbed harder at his chest, wishing away the pain – not only for him but mostly for his wife. He couldn't bring himself to tell her. Instead he shored up his best poker face, "No one you should worry about."

"Ennis, who was it?" She took a step and staggered toward the kitchen like a drunk on a binge.

Ennis rushed to steady her. He slipped his arm around her, redirected her to the bedroom, "Babe, you need to rest."

When her red swollen eyes met his vision, there was a vacancy in them that warned him she toed a thin line. She cried herself dry earlier, and now her eyes just plain tired. Her brow crinkled, "What happened to your hair?"

Ennis smoothed it into place, forgetting that he'd basically yanked himself bald during John's call. "I accidentally scruffed it up."

"Who was on the phone?" She repeated. As usual, she treated the question the way a bulldog nagged on a bone. She wasn't letting it go.

"Mathis. He was checking in, seeing how you were." He prayed the lame answer worked. Maybe, he thought, she's exhausted enough to accept it. Their colleague and friend cared, however a random inquiry about a person's health was unusual.

"John called about me?"

Ennis deciphered the mumbled attempt at a question. He nodded. Savannah never broke eye contact which unnerved him. His wife possessed an uncanny knack for ferreting out lies and half-truths that any child would detest and any parent would envy. She analyzed people very well by studying their expressions, most especially their eyes. But at the current time it was difficult to discern between scrutiny or whether she just stared blankly. When her brow dipped, he realized it was the former. He sucked at poker for a reason, he decided, and it had nothing to do with the cards.

"You're lying." With tearful wounded eyes, she slid the accusation like a knife to his heart, "Mathis doesn't do that. What did he say and tell me the truth."

He tried to divert the conversation once more, "You need rest. You're still recovering from the radiation treatments. Dr. Wyatt told you to take it easy."

"Wyatt's sister wasn't abducted by a serial killer." Anger surfaced through her weariness. She rubbed her eyes with balled fists, "What did Mathis say?"

Ennis touched her arm but she shrugged away, "Don't. Not until you tell me what's happened."

He hadn't had time to prepare a softer approach to the subject. Of course how did one tell a person their sister – a person they loved dearly – was probably dead in a ditch? "Sit down first," he pointed to a dining chair. Her already short temper unleashed a smidgen of its ferocity – he didn't need the full blown storm. Frustration coupled with guilt and anger weighed her down, he told himself. And this news... It would crush her.

He wrapped his hand around her arm with a firmness that refused argument. Savannah unexpectedly stopped, "You want me to sit down." The inflection hit hard. She knew what was coming. "No," she tried to pull away. "No, no, no, Georgia's okay. She's not gone…" Her voice wavered, "She's *not*."

Ennis brought her into his embrace even as she fought against it. "Sugar, settle down," he pleaded. "There's no guarantee it's her. Mathis was on his way to the scene."

Savannah shoved against his chest, violently breaking the embrace, "She's not dead!"

Ennis stood, dumbfounded. "I never said she was. *Mathis hasn't seen the victim.* I just wanted to prepare you for the news that they found another body." He prayed the emphasis hit the common sense part of her brain.

Savannah turned then stumbled sideways until bracing herself against a chair. Steadying herself, she tramped into the bedroom, mumbling to herself.

The battle began in earnest now, forcing Ennis to fashion an emergency brake out of words. If that failed, he'd have to physically stop her and pray his jaw survived her wrath. "What are you doing?" Ennis already knew the answer but asking might buy him a few extra seconds. God knew he sure needed them. That and a fourteen ton weight to anchor his wife to the house.

"I'm going to the scene," she said. "I have to see if it's her."

Ennis stepped in the bedroom, surprised to see her already dressed. She wore jeans and a very well worn Braves t-shirt that she swore to God would never be seen in public until the team won another World Series. For a person two degrees short of unconscious, the woman sobered up quick – with one exception. "Your shirt's on backwards," he told her.

Savannah glanced down, appraised the situation then pulled the shirt over her head, turned it and slipped it on again. The Braves trademark tomahawk graced her chest instead of her back now. Whether the shirt was on correctly or not didn't really matter because, "You can't go."

She wheeled with a molten glare capable of blinding most people, "The hell I can't. That could be my sister." She fought rising tears, dabbing them before they fell, "And if she's the victim, I don't want her to be alone for several reasons. One, those reporters will exploit her a second time. Two, I can't leave her…"

Ennis watched her lip tremble as tears slipped down her cheeks. He reached for her, to hold and console her but she shrugged past him, heading for the front door. Next, the search for the Camaro keys began. He'd hidden them for exactly that reason. The moment she regained consciousness, he expected her to look for Georgia. He stopped her the only way he knew how. Prevent her from driving.

"Where are my keys?" Savannah rounded on him as if *he'd* abducted Georgia. "Hand them over now."

Her fire had him debating over stepping back. Once she reached a particular level of anger, most people scrapped the debating part and retreated. Ennis didn't. He also didn't offer her the keys.

Savannah uttered a searing curse she rarely used because God highly disapproved. Then, "Ennis, do *not* do this. Give me the damn keys." She suddenly wobbled on unsteady legs. He reached to support her. This time she accepted the help.

He tried to reason with her again, "You're unable to drive. Hell, you're about to fall over."

Instead of whopping him, she wrapped her fists in his shirt and in the process ripped a good deal of hair from his chest. He flinched, wondering what hurt worse, a punch in the jaw or that.

She reminded, "She's my sister, Ennis. I have to go."

Impossible. That was his wife. Completely impossible. She'd go even if she had to walk to the scene. So he quickly formulated an solution. He'd drive her to the scene, but call Mathis on the way to forewarn him. Maybe a slew of uniforms could subdue her if she bolted for the victim – which he knew she would. "I'll drive you on one condition. You stay in my truck at all times and I'll look at the victim, see if it's Georgia. If the boss sees you near that ravine, he'll have your badge." He braced her shoulders, "Do you understand? You'll lose your job."

With her nod, Ennis assumed they agreed on it before they left. He tried calling Mathis but the detective's phone went to voicemail. So much for the forewarning, he thought grimly. He needed directions and had depended on John for them. When Mathis didn't pick up, Ennis called the station to learn the victim's location.

Traffic picked up as they approached and they passed by camera crews from every TV station in Atlanta and at least three national channels.

John Mathis, Cole Jordan and Josh Hunter gathered near a ravine, along with a couple of uniform officers. Yellow crime scene tape cordoned off the area from the media and mass of bystanders straining for a glimpse of the body.

Ennis drove up to the crime scene tape, turned to his wife, "Stay in the truck."

She rolled down the window to get a better look at the scene. Fortunately the victim remained well hidden in the ravine. "Savannah," he cautioned, "don't let me catch you outside this truck. I'm only thinking of you, and I'm trying to save your job."

"I'll stay," was the halfhearted promise.

Ennis climbed out and into the muggy heat. Josh Hunter stood a good five feet from the ravine while instructing the forensics team on what to collect as potential evidence. The instant he locked vision with Ennis, frustration clouded his expression, "I'm two seconds away from suspending you both. Where is she? She can't see the body."

The statement hit Ennis like a fist. Was it Georgia? Ennis hitched his thumb toward his truck, "Told her to stay put." He stepped nearer to the ravine until the ashen flesh of a leg came into view. Ennis forced his vision toward the head.

Josh blocked his view, "Ennis, don't. Go back to your truck and manhandle her. She's about to bolt."

But Ennis had to know. He promised Savannah he'd find out. If that meant identifying her sister's body to save her the horror, he'd do it.

"Grab her," Captain Hunter shouted at someone behind Ennis.

From the corner of his eye, Ennis saw officers descend on his wife who'd broken *her* promise and scrambled for the ravine. Bystanders lifted cell phones to snap pictures and media shouldered cameras and began recording the scene as it unfolded.

Ennis looked back to see two uniformed officers and Cole Jordan subdue her wild fighting. She clawed for an inch of freedom, giving the cops a struggle they hadn't anticipated.

"Is it Georgia?" She cried, "Is it her?"

Her cries broke his heart. He forced his vision back to the ravine, wiped a hand across his forehead and tried to brace himself. In respect of her sister – if it was her – Ennis moved closer to the victim's head. The woman's long chestnut hair splayed across the dirt valley. The color matched Georgia's perfectly. If he had to identify her by only the hair, he'd swear it was Georgia. He took a deep breath and muttered a quiet prayer before glancing at the woman's face.

What he saw nearly buckled his knees. Tears welled in his eyes. They blinded him until he swiped them away with the back of his hand. He turned to Savannah who continued battling the officers and Jordan for freedom. She finally broke free, raced toward the ravine, tears streaming down her face. Ennis caught her in his embrace, "It's not Georgia." He tightened his hold as she basically collapsed in his arms, "Thank God it's not her."

25

It was time. Ennis wasted enough of it – well not wasted but *waited* until he had no other choice but call Seth. Lindsey painted a psychedelic fish magnet that held the number to the Breckenridge resort. He'd avoided that number like the plague and realized the continual stalling would send Seth's temper and animosity soaring. Since their brother already teetered on the south side of sane anyway, Ennis reconsidered his original plan to wait. Since childhood, his brothers maintained he wasn't the sharpest tool in the shed. Today he had to agree.

Savannah resigned herself to a shower – this after Josh Hunter threatened her within an inch of her life. Taking her aside, he dispensed with being her boss and lectured her as an older brother might. A livid older brother but judging from the conversation, he struck plenty of nerves with his female detective. She'd come home silent and nearly whipped. Ennis overheard just enough to realize Josh spoke calmly but effectively and finished the dressing-down with yet another threat to take her gun and badge. One more slip-up, he'd said. One and she'd be unemployed – no excuses, no mercy, no job.

While Savannah showered, Ennis planned to take the

opportunity to inform Seth and his family of the recent developments. While he was at it, he'd tell Dane that his sweetheart was missing… Rethinking on it, maybe the truth sounded better. Brutal as it was, Ennis didn't want anyone accusing him of hiding anything if the worst happened. He'd leave Dane for last though. Growing up with him, he knew his personality better than Seth's. Savannah's brother, no matter how long they'd been acquainted, always put him on edge. It was as if he considered Ennis on probation with the marriage to his little sister. As Josh warned Savannah, one slip-up and she was through. Ennis felt the same threat from Seth and considering their brother was an ex-army Ranger, those type threats didn't instill the greatest of confidence in a person. Seth was trained to kill people hundreds of different ways and if he held Ennis even a shred responsible for Georgia's kidnapping, he *was* really toast.

With the phone number in hand, he dialed the area code slowly because he was, quite frankly, scared of Seth Prince. He'd never tell Savannah but she probably knew it. She could handle her brother better than Ennis but allowing her to notify him of the situation was the sign of a true chicken. Ennis might have been afraid but he wasn't heartless.

His finger stood, poised over the next number. The same queasiness awakened in his gut. This was it. Once he finished dialing, he was locked in. In that time, Georgia could be found alive and he'd be on the phone telling her brother she was kidnapped and possibly dead. He dialed anyway. Again, his finger froze above the next number. Cripes, was he *this* big a coward? Seth needed to know about his sister, his conscience prodded. Just do it.

He dialed the next two numbers quickly hoping like medicine, if he did it fast, the misery would soon pass. On the last number, divine intervention saved him. The doorbell rang. Since it occurred at exactly the same instant, Ennis took it as a sign that Georgia was still alive. Gladly he sat the phone down and as luck would have it, the shower shut off, validating the fact the phone call really wasn't necessary right then. *Yes, Ennis, you're a big fat coward, but an optimistic one...*

He opened the door to see Cole Jordan leaning against the door frame, hands jammed in his jeans pockets and chewing on a toothpick. "She calm yet?" he asked.

Without offering him entry, Ennis shrugged, "Best as anyone can expect." And one look at Cole would obliterate whatever calm she mustered in the last hour or two. Jordan hadn't been kind to Savannah at the scene. Instead of helping the uniforms restrain her, he'd manhandled her into an embarrassing and painful position. She came home with a bruised ego and body. Cole's grasp left red marks that surely would darken to bruises before morning.

"I want to run something by her." He straightened, removed the toothpick and used it to point inside, "Mind if I come in?"

Yes, actually I do... "Make it brief," he mumbled, stepped aside.

Cole sauntered in, gave the place a once over, "Nice place. Meant to tell her that earlier but it didn't seem the time."

"What's your business with her?"

He saw Cole's vision flit around the room then land squarely on the phone number on the dining table. The goldfish leered up at him and Ennis hoped the ceramic doodad told the brash cop to mind his own business.

"Asking a question is all. Hey, how'd she take that roughing up by the captain?"

"How would you?" Ennis bit back.

Cole cocked an eyebrow and Ennis sensed he enjoyed ruffling feathers more than breathing. If that was the case, he'd cure Mr. Jordan of the latter real quick. Cole pulled a chair out from the table, plopped in it, "No offense, Ennis. It's idle chit-chat till she gets here."

"Savannah!" Ennis blurted then regretted it. He'd let the bastard under his skin. Mr. Jordan better speak his peace quick, he thought, before Savannah hauled out of the bedroom, picked his peas and handed them to him.

Ennis marched to the bedroom door, knocked twice, "We've got company."

"Who?"

"Cole Jordan."

"Tell him to go away." Her tone described her disgruntlement over Cole's rough handling. "Better yet, tell him to go to hell."

Ennis also detected a desire for payback in her reply and in her mood lately, it was probably safer to keep the two separated. He'd stand guard outside the door in case she bolted out to strangle Cole. "He wants to ask you something."

"And I want to tell him something. It involves cramming his attitude *and* his Half Nelson where the sun don't shine. Get him out of here, Ennis."

Jordan's move wasn't exactly a Half Nelson but it brought her under control rather effectively. When Ennis turned to see Cole's treatment of his wife, he'd raced toward them to level a special threat on the Zone 3 detective. One that had Savannah released within a second of its delivery.

"Hey," Cole's voice came from right behind Ennis's left shoulder, startling him. Jordan ignored Ennis's scowl to offer, "Do you want to look for your sister?"

That really pissed Ennis off. First that he endangered Savannah by inviting her on a wild goose chase and second, that the lummox had no manners regarding privacy. "Get back in the living room. No one invited you in here."

Cole shrugged, "Coulda shouted it, like you did her name. Didn't think it was proper though."

"Neither is sneaking up on people." Ennis stabbed a finger into the living room, "Back."

The bedroom door swung open. Savannah, her hair still damp from the shower, had dressed in jeans and another t-shirt, this one pink and donned correctly. "Did he mention Georgia?" The anger magically disappeared. Replacing it – hope.

"Not in so many words." He could see where this was headed. He didn't approve either. Her eyes, once dull and heavy with despair, now sparkled with eagerness. One simple reference to Georgia removed any insult Jordan subjected her to but Ennis still stung over it. He gently took her arm, "Don't fall for any lines or charm. He's a jerk and you know it."

"The man has no charm but if he's willing to help find Georgia –

"

He tightened his grasp, "Use your gut. Hunter warned you about getting involved. He finds out you are and your career is over. He made that crystal clear."

Her anger swapped from Cole to Ennis, "My sister's life is more important than my career."

Ennis held both arms now, trying to shake some sense into her, "You don't know where she is and neither does he. And if he does, that means he's withholding information."

According to her expression, Savannah debated his argument. Suddenly his gut tightened, telling him that despite common sense and his best efforts, she'd still haul out the door with Jordan. He used what he thought was more logic, "Think, babe. You didn't trust him from day one."

"Jordan," she called, her vision strictly on Ennis, "why are you offering to help me?"

Shoes padded across the carpet until Cole peeked around the corner, "Uh, well, after that scene today, I figured I'd keep you busy doing other things. Only trying to help."

"Where are you planning to go?" she demanded, probably more for Ennis than herself.

Cole felt comfortable standing in the hallway now, Ennis assumed, because Savannah hadn't launched at him. Jordan replied, "Shelton's got property outside of town I want to check out."

Uh-huh. Ennis crossed his arms, "And you're just now telling us this?"

"Hey, I was doing my homework when we got the call about the body. One of my buddies just found the paperwork on the property. Gimme a break, guys. I'm trying to catch a killer," he glanced at Savannah, "and I'm one detective short."

"Where is this property?" Ennis inquired, arms crossed.

"North of town. It'll take a while to get there so I brought my luxury car."

What was it, Ennis wondered, a burned out Fiat? Any time Cole Jordan attempted to joke, the punch line held an entirely different meaning. That didn't rattle him as much as seeing Savannah squeeze past him and head toward her off duty gun. He felt pretty sure she wouldn't shoot Jordan – yet – but the alternative bothered him more. She was leaving with the bum.

Ennis followed her with Cole close behind. Savannah already armed herself and dropped her cell phone in her pocket. Ennis stepped in front of her, "Think about this. You'll get fired and that's the best case scenario. You could get hurt or killed if you manage to run across this nutcase."

She met his vision. Her sadness faded, leaving sheer determination in its place. She'd find Georgia or die doing it, the look said and also added that he should step aside or regret not doing so.

Hands on hips, Ennis frowned down at her, "For the record, I don't approve of this. You're signing up for trouble one way or another."

"Duly noted," she replied, waving Jordan out the door with her, "Let's go."

26

"You two fight like you're married," Cole said, merging into highway traffic.

"We've been partners long enough we probably are married," was all she said. Wearing off the anger and hurt of Ennis's attitude would take a while. If Dane was in trouble, Ennis would go anywhere and go with *anyone* to find him. Why should she be different? Okay, so she and Jordan clashed most times but he'd offered to help find Georgia. Ennis hadn't and she refused to sit at home and wait, no matter what Josh Hunter said.

Now she sat in a black late seventies Cougar XR7, complete with 8-track player. The thing was a veritable battleship and Savannah wondered where in the confines of Atlanta, Georgia he'd found it and more to the point where did he find a place big enough to anchor it?

From the outside it looked decently cared for. The car's paint dulled over the years but the cougar hood ornament still had chrome on it.

The interior was a different story. It resembled a repository for empty fast food containers, old newspapers and mud. Even with her busy schedule her Camaro never reached that level of disgrace. It was neither mint nor spotless but she attempted to keep it neat, not one step above Dumpster.

She was surprised the 8-track player wasn't employed as a sandwich holder then realized Cole wasn't into sandwiches. He preferred hamburgers, judging by the Burger King wrappers in the seat and floorboard. She scooched away from them.

Cole saw her, slid his sunglasses down his nose to peer at her, "You don't like my car? It's old but it's got cup holders."

Yeah, and a cracked wood veneer dash, enough trash for three garbage bins and a smell akin to the city dump. His prized aftermarket cup holder currently stored a milkshake and what appeared to be McDonald's coffee. She didn't venture a guess on their ages. Maybe late teens, early twenties… "No, it's fine," she replied and discreetly scooted a stray wrapper aside.

"It's my roustabout. When I go places it might get dirty."

Might get dirty? The interior needed a professional overhaul from a detailing crew and he was worried about crud on the outside? Unbelievable.

The car glided into the exit lane. Curious, she asked, "You told Ennis the property was north of town. This exit takes us west."

"It is north of town. I'm taking this road then swinging back north. Trying to avoid traffic this way."

That comment convinced her Cole Jordan couldn't find his way out of a paper bag. Avoiding traffic in Atlanta? Fat chance. Every road, avenue and boulevard remained crammed or congested for hours, then if one had the luck of the Irish or prayed just right, they could squeak through traffic in a half hour at best. The only answer was traveling rural roads which really made no sense at all unless you intentionally headed to the country. "How far is this place?" she asked. "In the boondocks?"

"Shelton's property is *way* out there and it's probably buried in fifteen tons of mud."

Well, she conceded, at least it will match the mud on the car mats and the carpet and the smudge on the passenger door and...

They drove for another twenty minutes after leaving the city's bottlenecks. Savannah admitted the old Cougar drifted over bumps and dips in the road much easier than her Camaro. It almost seemed like they floated. She saw the exit headed north and pointed, "Slow down. This is the exit you want."

For the last several minutes, Cole leaned back with his hand propped on the steering wheel. He shook his head, "Nah. There's one up ahead."

"Cole, I've lived here forever. There is no other exit onto a major highway. Slow down and take this one." She hated it when people assumed she had dirt for brains. She was born in Georgia, raised in Augusta but made trips in and around Atlanta all her life. Without literally bashing it into his concrete skull, she'd tried to be gentle, diplomatic. Clearly it hadn't worked.

"You need to chill out, love. How 'bout some music?" He reached down to the console between them, felt around and dredged up an 8-track tape, "You like Black Sabbath, Lynyrd Skynyrd or are you more of an ABBA or Wild Cherry kinda girl?" He shoved a Black

Sabbath tape in the player's gaping slot. On the faded spine it read "Live Evil". A moment passed when a familiar guitar riff blasted from the speakers. After a few more seconds, she recognized it as "Iron Man" but that didn't mean she liked it. When the singing – or supposed singing – began, she cringed. Cole turned down the volume somewhat, "Not a metalhead, huh?"

The lyrics came through loud and clear despite the volume being a tad lower than jackhammer level. She decided Cole Jordan would never grow up. He was and always would be fifteen years old, still believing blondes had more fun and that armpit farting was funny.

"Nobody wants him," Cole sang aloud, "they just turn their heads, nobody helps him, now he has his revenge…"

She did a mental eye roll. Great. Stuck with an idiot on the trip from hell. She propped her elbow on the window, leaned her head into her hand and suffered his dying cat rendition of the song. "In case you're wondering," she raised her voice above the music, "there's a turn off ahead. It'll take us north but since it turns into a dirt road later, it'll be messy."

He belted out another verse of the song, making her cringe. Guess he wasn't interested in the advice. "Jordan, take this exit now," she insisted. "We'll be wandering all over the countryside and we'll never find that property."

"Savannah, I've got it. Trust me. I know where the hell I'm going."

But she didn't trust him. They'd just passed their only major exit north. She pulled her phone from her jeans pocket.

Cole's easygoing demeanor faded slightly, "What are you doing?"

"Calling Ennis. Maybe he can find a back road for us."

"Put the phone away, will ya? Cripes, women are all alike. You think men can't find their asses with two hands and a road map."

Something told her Cole wouldn't recognize a map to save his life. Lord, she pitied his wife. No wonder the woman left him. They probably went out for a burger and ended up in Alabama – all because he wouldn't stop and ask directions. "I want to find Georgia. We're wasting time."

He motioned for her to put the phone back in her pocket and added a "please." Cole sighed, "I'm trying to avoid getting stuck, okay? This battlewagon may glide but it sinks too. The north side had a deluge last night and I didn't remember it until a few minutes ago."

Still, "Wouldn't finding another cutback be smart? Ennis can look one up."

Cole stretched a little, "Give me ten minutes. If I haven't found another road, call him. Just stop going all female on me."

The comment grated on her. Cole and women. Oil and water. Gasoline and matches. All the same. Ugh. She wanted to find her sister and the clod was probably getting them lost. "If Shelton's as paranoid about this property as he is about his mansion, he'll have people patrolling it and I'm assuming they'll be armed. All I have is my .38. How about you?"

"A .45," a lazy grin crossed his lips. "Listen, stop worrying. They're not gonna screw with cops. Trust me already."

That was easier said than done. The only reason she agreed to come along was the possibility of finding Georgia. The thought of her sister made her reach for her phone to call Ennis.

Looking at his watch, Cole reminded, "Only been three minutes. Put it up."

"Maybe he's heard something about Georgia. It's not always about you, you know."

His hand covered her wrist, "You're just determined to make this trip ugly, aren't you? If he'd heard something, he'd have called. Calling him will only make him more anxious than he is. He didn't want you coming along anyway."

Savannah traded hands with the phone, flipped it open, "Not knowing my whereabouts will make him worse."

Cole's hand returned to the steering wheel, "Give me the allotted time then you can call him. By then I might need a back road, who knows?"

All she saw was a forest of trees around them. Exactly where would a back road be? "You have a good feeling about Shelton's property?"

Cole turned to her, grinning behind the sunglasses, "I've got a hunch this'll pay off like a slot machine." He slowed the car for an impending turn. The road had no sign, just a narrow hidden entrance overshadowed by tall pine trees. The place gave her the creeps, but not as much as the fact Cole seemed to know exactly where the hidden road was, "This won't take us north."

"It's worth a shot though, right?"

An uneasiness rose the longer they drove. Number one, she

hadn't seen another car for several miles, indicating they were further from the city than she thought. Number two, if her sister was being held in a dense forest like this, no one could even find her unless they knew the surrounding area well. Savannah didn't, of course, because she never had occasion to travel this far outside Atlanta – not by the back roads at least.

Wild trees grew onto the sides of the dirt road, their limbs arching over and intertwining to block most of the sun. Smaller trees and underbrush stretched like bony fingers scraping the sides of Cole's car.

"You okay?" he asked.

Not exactly. Her claustrophobia crept to the surface the further they traveled the narrow road. She tried not to fidget. She tried to stay composed and practice the breath control method Seth taught her. Her brother, being an Army Ranger, learned tricks to manipulate his breathing and heart rate and tried to instruct her how to apply them during her panic attacks. She took a deep breath, counted to four then exhaled slowly. She continued the process even as the trees seemed to close in around them, confining them in a tunnel of limbs and branches.

Her lungs constricted like a giant invisible fist squeezed them, preventing air from entering. The exercises weren't working. If anything, her condition worsened so she closed her eyes. Maybe removing the visual image of the encroaching trees might help.

Cole took his foot off the accelerator, "Savannah?"

She hadn't answered his question. Before he caught wind of her crisis, she nodded, forcing the lie past her lips, "I'm fine."

"Music making you nervous?" He ejected the tape and with the exception of leaves and small limbs rasping the sides of the Cougar, the ride was silent.

The sounds amplified with her eyes closed, painting a vivid picture of her ongoing predicament. The breathing exercises failed miserably this time, probably due to the stress of Georgia's situation and the fact Savannah felt trapped by a full grown teenager in his car.

She needed to hear Ennis's voice. He always found a way to calm her down during her attacks. Usually with physical contact – holding her hand or a simple kiss. Now she relied on the rich timbre of his baritone voice, the words he used, the love he felt for her.

Savannah reached for her phone again. Cole clenched his teeth, "Damn it, woman. Stop harping about back roads. Put the phone up or I'll toss it out the window."

His little hissy fit riled her but finding a solution to her panic was foremost in her mind, "I need to talk to Ennis."

Cole brought the car to a stop. He shoved the gearshift into park, removed his sunglasses then faced her. She assumed the glare was supposed to intimidate but the surroundings presented a more ominous threat. That and the fact her lungs shrunk to the size of marbles...

"No, you don't. He's not your keeper," he stated flatly. "You're not with him right now, you're with me so deal with it." A flare of anger hardened his voice, "Georgia's probably dead by now anyway. You know it and I know it. Hand me the phone and while you're at it, give me your gun."

She sat, still attempting to gain the upper hand on her runaway heart and not go crazy in the meantime. What was he saying anyway? He wasn't making sense. He'd been the one to give her hope and a place to search for Georgia. As for his demand for the phone and gun, he could shove it. Savannah threw open the door, hoping fresh air would ease the tightness in her chest. "What is your problem?" When she brought her hand back from opening the door, she inconspicuously reached for her .38. Cole Jordan was an asshole but he hadn't stooped to such outrageous demands until now. She may have been half deranged with panic but she wasn't completely stupid.

Turning to him, she drew back, seeing the barrel of a .45 aimed at her. Cole held his other hand palm up, "Your gun first then the phone."

Savannah kept her .38 next to her thigh. "Why the hell are you pointing a gun at me? Are you nuts?" She realized he was a few bricks short anyway but for him to draw down on her was insane.

"Just do what I say. Hand over your gun."

She eased one leg out of the car, "Whatever's going through your mind, you'd best reel it back in. I pushed your buttons, you pushed mine. Let's call a truce and take a breath." Slowly, she swung out of the car, praying he wasn't trigger happy.

"Savannah," he called.

Purposefully not turning around, she listened for the car door. The claustrophobia gradually took a back seat to the growing danger of Cole Jordan. Something went horribly awry the last several minutes and she had to keep her wits or risk being shot.

He opened his door and she heard approaching footsteps around the front of the car. She turned, seeing Cole still stood a few yards away, the gun still aimed at her, "Hand 'em over."

"I'm not surrendering my weapon." Her intuition failed her but her gun wouldn't. Her .38 was in plain sight but still lowered unlike his .45. She wasn't about to tempt him into shooting her, at least not by aiming a weapon at him.

She sure hated to get shot because of a stupid move. But then, Ennis had tried to warn her, hadn't he? I don't trust Jordan as far as I could throw him, he'd said. He's a snake, she remembered saying. A snake with a vicious grin and a gun pointed right at her chest.

Savannah needed to call Ennis but couldn't keep watch on Cole and dial home. So she raised the .38.

Cole chuckled, "Put the gun down, Savannah. You're not gonna shoot me."

"You're sure?" She reinforced her grip with both hands. "Shelton doesn't even have property north of town, does he? You lied about the whole thing."

The corners of Cole's mouth lifted, "Are you getting paranoid on me?" He slowly stepped closer, "Nah, you're not paranoid. You're *scared.*"

"Don't come any closer," she warned, giving a quick glance behind her. She stood near the ravine and couldn't step backward without falling.

"Imagine that," he seemed amused by the idea. He moved closer, "What part of this is scaring you? The fact we're all alone in the middle of nowhere, the fact I'm pointing a gun at you or the fact you're not going home alive?"

She wanted to call Ennis for help. She should have heeded her husband's foresight – hell, even her own gut feeling but her concern for Georgia overrode her better judgment. "Do not come any closer, Cole. I *will* shoot you."

"Women cops always freeze up. You're not shooting anyone, least of all me."

The blast echoed through the dense foliage. The acrid smell of gunpowder hung in the stale humidity as Cole Jordan clapped a hand over his right shoulder, a blistering curse falling from his lips.

Savannah hoped the shot derailed his misconceptions about her. Women cops didn't freeze up when their lives were threatened. They fought like any other terrified human being.

Though she succeeded in not "freezing up", her blood ran cold when his vision met hers. "You think your sister suffered," he said, "wait till I get my hands on you." He transferred the gun to his left hand.

Savannah dove into the ravine, stumbled then regained her footing to run toward the woods. A gunshot split the silence. Cole's effort barely missed her, the round embedding itself in a nearby tree. He fired again, the bullet struck the ground in front of her, spraying dirt at her feet.

She dodged behind a tree to hide, catch her breath and figure out how to alert Ennis without getting dead in the process. She tuned her hearing to any noise, especially sounds of footsteps nearing her. *Call Ennis... Put space between you and Cole and dial home...*

"You're not going anywhere," Cole shouted from the road. "You might as well give up."

Savannah's heart pounded in her chest and ears. Move or be killed, her brain screamed at her. Cole wouldn't wait forever. And he didn't. Footsteps tramping over pine straw and snapping twigs forced her into action. She lunged from behind the tree. Less than a second passed when another shot rang out.

Pain registered at her calf. She forced herself to swallow the cry and started running again, this time with a noticeable limp.

"I got plenty of ammo left. You just keep running." His voice sounded closer, the footsteps faster. Cole was coming after her.

She raised her .38. Cole lifted the .45 and pulled the trigger without aiming. A bullet zipped past her.

Savannah concentrated on keeping her footing in the thick growth of pine straw and branches. She ducked limbs, hid behind trees while trying to track Cole by sight or sound. She'd try calling Ennis. Her hand shook while thumbing through the contact list. Pressing her back against another tree, she focused on finding the number – one she should know by heart. Finally the familiar phone number flashed on the screen. Home. Ennis. Safety. Savannah dialed then realized the deafening silence around her. No footsteps, no threats, no hard breaths. Nothing.

She turned to search for Cole when a pain tore through her back. For a split-second, she assumed she'd been shot. Then a storm of lightning struck her, painfully contracting her muscles. A Taser.

She collapsed on the ground, the gun and phone slipping from her grasp. The fiery pain stopped as abruptly as it started. From somewhere nearby she heard Ennis calling her name. She cried his name, fully intending to follow it with a plea to save her from Cole Jordan. The debilitating pain jolted her again, effectively foiling the attempt as her muscles shuddered and tensed so tight she could barely breathe.

Two feet came into view. Cole reached down and retrieved the cell phone, closed then pocketed it. "I warned you," he scolded, "but like a typical woman, you didn't listen." He released the trigger on the Taser and Savannah fell limp against the moist ground. Gathering her bearings became impossible. The world spun as her body tried in vain to relax.

He rolled her onto her stomach. She implored her body to move and gradually she pulled her legs beneath her in a feeble effort to stand.

Cole shook his head, "You're kidding, right?"

He squatted beside her, Taser in hand, "I've read about people like you. You never give up. Normally, I'd consider that admirable, but in this case, I think you're stupid. Here's why."

He pressed the trigger again, and before she could plead for him to stop, the crippling pain engulfed her body. Savannah heard herself cry out, her jaw locked like the rest of her body, and she felt alive with fire.

"They say it can't kill you." Cole casually continued, "I've heard of people getting zapped a dozen times without dying." He leaned closer, "So you keep squirming and we might break a record."

She doubted it. The instant he released the trigger, she lay motionless except for the involuntary twitching along her legs and arms. Boneless and sapped of energy, she struggled to generate a coherent thought. Escape? Yeah, right. Cole would fry her again and again until she gave up or died. Being shot multiple times with a Taser produced scarring or death. Dead didn't help her and it sure wouldn't help find Georgia.

"Done yet?" Cole waggled the Taser in front of her, "Or do you need a booster?"

Savannah didn't move or speak. She allowed her stillness to answer his question. In the process of his sadistic binge, she'd bitten her tongue and judging by the taste in her mouth, she'd gnashed it pretty hard. She tried to spit, to rid herself of the taste and felt a small trail dribble out.

Cole grasped her left arm and flopped it behind her back. Cold metal cinched down on her wrist. He brought her right hand into the other cuff, locked it in. "I gotta say you're a tough one to bring down. I believe you are my best trophy to date."

He stood and rolled her to her back with his foot. The trees above continued spinning. She couldn't move or stand if she had to. She saw Cole reach to his back pocket.

Her vision blurred as he bent down blaming, "It's your fault, you know."

The sensation of a soft cloth on her face startled her. He wiped the blood from her mouth and chin, "If only you hadn't remembered the license plate."

27

"Are you tracking her cell phone yet?" Ennis asked Mathis.

"Started a few minutes ago."

"What?" Ennis nearly shouted into the phone. It wasn't so much incredulous as cross. "I called you right after she left. What took so long?"

Mathis sighed, "Lemme explain it to you. I told the boss what happened, that she took off with Jordan. The boss hit the roof. He described in detail everything Prince was including fired. Then I had to sweet talk him into letting me track her. I had better success talking my ex-wife into letting me have the car during our divorce."

Ennis shoved a hand through his hair, closed the fingers in it. He was so close to pulling out a clump, he could scream. He did the next best thing. He uttered a searing curse that included God's name and not in a particularly good way. "Did you get a fix on Savannah at all?"

"'Fraid not. It's like the battery's been removed. It's not just turned off, it's dead. I'm telling you, Rutherford, I'd hate bein' her when the boss sees her. He's so pissed he'll hardly speak. You know how hard it is to understand sign language?"

"Hunter should realize the danger she's in –"

"Ennis, that's his point. She put herself in this jackpot. Everyone told her to plant herself at home and she defied them. He's tired of her going rogue on him."

Ennis cradled the phone on his shoulder, slid his .38 onto his belt, "I should've gone with her. I let her walk out the door with that son of a bitch. Now look what's happened."

"Did Jordan say exactly where this place was?" Mathis stopped a moment, "Hey, Rutherford, it's back. Her phone just came on and it's in the city again. Call her and let me know what's going on."

Ennis disconnected with Mathis and dialed Savannah's number. A ray of hope finally beamed bright in his heart until a man answered on the second ring. "Yeah?" the gruff voice asked. It also sounded breathless.

"Who is this?" The new voice threw him momentarily. Then recognition followed shortly after. If Mathis thought Hunter was pissed, he should have seen Ennis, "Jordan, where's my –" he stopped himself. He nearly said "wife" and re-geared his brain. "Where's Savannah?" Savannah screaming for help, her phone dying, now a breathless Cole Jordan answered her phone – it all added up to Ennis killing a particular detective from Zone 3 – but not before he literally wrung every detail from him first.

"It all happened so fast. I tried to help her."

Cole's remorse fell on deaf ears. What didn't – the words: I tried to help her. "What happened? Is she okay?"

"It has to be Shelton. First Georgia, now Savannah, it all makes sense."

Ennis uttered the same curse as before, realizing he had a lot of apologizing to do to God, "Jordan, tell me what happened."

He drew a shaky breath, "They went straight for her. I tried to help her but they basically knocked me out. All I remember is them running after her and they fried her with a Taser and carried her off. I couldn't do anything. I'm so sorry."

A deep and primal rage rose in Ennis. He watched her walk out with this monkey. She'd gone against Ennis's advice as he essentially pleaded with his wife to stay home. He'd never trusted Cole Jordan. She hadn't either and it surprised him when she crawled into his car to look for Georgia. The love for her sister overrode her better judgment and now she was as defenseless as Georgia. "How do you know Shelton is responsible?" His voice telegraphed the boiling anger beneath the surface. "Give me proof."

"One of them mentioned his name. Listen, don't worry. I'm on my way to his house right now. I'll bust down the door to get her back. Sit tight and I'll have her and Georgia back soon."

"Stay the hell away from Shelton, hear me? Drop her phone at the station and tell the boss what's happened."

"But I'm nearly there. The sooner I get in the house, the less he can do to her."

"Jordan, let *me* handle Shelton." He slid his badge onto his belt, "Savannah is my partner and I think my visit might have more of an impact."

"We could bust down the door together if you want."

"You've done enough," Ennis resisted the urge to expound on the subject. Instead he opted to hang up. Ever since the detective appeared, he and Savannah had their share of trouble privately *and* on the job.

He wondered *how* hard Cole fought to help Savannah. Since her repeated rebuffs, Cole's personality darkened, turned colder. Only when he appeared at the door offering to search for Georgia did he thaw out. Ennis feared Cole might try to jump her in the car. If he tried, her self-defense moves would have kicked in.

What he never took into consideration: someone kidnapping her, especially while in the company of another cop. Who's that stupid, he wondered. Who was stupid enough to kidnap a cop in broad daylight? And who jumped two cops at once? Evidently a rich, arrogant son of a bitch who believed he was above the law. Ennis set out to remedy that belief...

28

Savannah drifted back to consciousness. Her muscles felt bunched and strained, her head foggy and muddled. Vague memories floated back of bullets flying, a Taser being used and a less than joyful ride in the back of an old smelly Cougar. More memories followed: A dark blue Maxima parked in front of a cabin shrouded in a dense forest. Someone carrying her into the cabin. Taser probes yanked from her flesh. A pain in her forearm, this one an injection.

In the midst of it, she'd sworn she saw Georgia in the same room. Her sister was tied to a bed. If she remembered correctly, a kitchen/dining area sat off to the right upon entering the place. To the left was a small living room used as a makeshift bedroom. There was a small bed – where Georgia was – a table beside it and a heavy rustic chair close by. There was a doorway into another room but the door was closed.

There were two men, not just Cole. The other made it a point to call her "Detective". He hadn't exactly sounded like Duke Shelton but then her ears weren't quite tuned after being hit repeatedly with lightning.

Her leg ached and she remembered a bullet grazing her calf. Strangely though, her calf felt bandaged. What the hell was going on?

The room felt cold. An air conditioner in the window blasted an icy breeze across her bare flesh and she tried to voice her protest. It was then she noticed her mouth refused to open. She pushed her tongue past her teeth but hit a blockade. Once she realized she was gagged and bound to a chair, a groan emerged. She'd really screwed up this time. She should have listened to Ennis – or been more accurate with her aim.

A musty smell drifted into her nose. Another odor mixed with it, this one more subdued but identifiable – blood.

Her eyes gradually opened and locked on Georgia across the way. Savannah saw her sister lying on an old bed, her naked body splayed out, her wrists tied to the headboard, her ankles to the footboard. Thankfully Georgia was still alive but the time with the men took its toll. She looked scared and exhausted. Georgia tried for a small tentative smile, prompting a nod from Savannah. What had they done to her and was she okay, she wanted to ask Georgia. From Savannah's position, it appeared that, for now, her sister escaped the horrendous beatings the other victims suffered. She only prayed the men hadn't sexually violated her. Those wounds haunted the body and mind of the victim where they remained hidden from plain view of others.

"Your sister is fine, Detective," a man assured from across the room. "Just a few marks, nothing serious. I'm saving the best for you."

She turned in the direction of the strangely familiar voice but another man stepped in front of her. Her line of sight was his crotch and according to the bulge in it, he had very high hopes. Calloused fingers traced her jaw, tipped her chin up. A bare-chested Cole. His shoulder was bandaged where she'd grazed him with her shot. He grimaced as he reached forward, his fingertips trailing around her breast, stroking it.

She squirmed away from the touch, cursing the nervy bastard. His hand squeezed her breast then moved downward until nestling between her thighs, "I've been waiting a long time for you."

Savannah fought against the bold caress, her angry threat muffled by the gag. A sharp pain across her cheek ceased all thought except retreating from another assault. Cole sure knew how to backhand a person. It felt like a brick connecting with her cheek.

"I'll take that fire outta you, bitch." He promised then cracked his knuckles, "Try that again and see what you get."

"She's not intimidated by you," the mystery man laughed. "She never has been."

"I'll fix that," Cole promised.

Mystery Man rose from his seat, started toward her, "We both know who impresses the ladies and it's not you."

Savannah tried to focus on him. All she saw was a white t-shirt stretched over broad muscular shoulders and jeans that hugged firm hips and legs. This man worked out, kept himself lean and fit.

Blinking a few times, the cloudy film over her eyes stubbornly refused to completely clear. He had short dark hair and a neatly trimmed week long beard. His dark eyes centered on her, "Your sister is lucky you joined us when you did. I was getting impatient and bored. The other women know how I cure my boredom and she," he pointed to Georgia, "was about to find out." The hair on the back of her neck stood up at his unsettling, yet gentle tone, "Well, let's have another look at your leg. With you and Cole trying to kill each other, I'm surprised either of you survived the ride here. I'm just grateful he didn't accidentally kill you. He's not the best shot in the world."

"Hey," Cole argued, "I'm a great shot. I didn't see you out there ducking bullets from *her*."

Peeling the bandage off her calf, Mystery Man rolled his eyes, "Yes, yes, I've heard all about it – a hundred times." He gave her a conspiratorial wink, "Cole, shut up before *I* put a bullet in you." His fingers tenderly probed around the wound, and Savannah flinched from the soreness. The man's grasp slightly tightened, "Hold still, Detective."

The gentle quality of his voice, the way he said "Detective"… She forced herself to focus, to clear the cobwebs from her brain. She knew this man, met him recently, saw him a few other times. He medicated the wound then applied a new bandage. His mannerisms and proficiency finally sparked his identity. The doctor at the hospital.

A memory emerged from the fog. After the seafood fiasco at Duke's, Georgia gushed over the fact "McSteamy" regularly checked on her although he wasn't her attending physician. He also noted how protective Savannah was and how she had the staff running in all directions. At that time Georgia found him and his remarks charming to the point she wished Atlanta's McSteamy was her attending physician. Savannah figured her sister's fascination with the man had long vanished by now.

McSteamy. Savannah would hate the name forever regardless of never seeing the show. But what was *this* guy's name? Dr. Harper. No,

Dr. Hollis. No, that wasn't right either. Holland! Yes! Dr. Jeffrey Holland. Mr. I Don't Bite. Maybe not but he'd sure perfected torture and murder.

He patted her knee, smiled up at her, "It looks good."

"You done playing doctor with her? She shot *me*, y'know." Cole stepped toward her, his hand drawn back to hit her.

Jeffrey caught him by the wrist, "Stop whining. I tended to your shoulder. You won't die."

"The bitch tried to kill me. I owe her."

"Not now. Get any bright ideas about breaking routine and being shot by a woman will be the least of your concerns."

Cole stared down at her, his hand easing up the inside of her thigh, "I've got special plans for you."

She twisted away from his touch. Through her clouded vision she saw him swing back again and when his hand struck her, her cry died behind the gag. He leaned closer, "Listen to me."

Savannah shied from him, fearing another attack. His large fingers grasped her jaw, forced her vision to his, "Your attitude dictates how long you suffer before you die. Keep that in mind before refusing any kindness I might offer. And don't think your partner will save you. He's really busy right now. He's out for Shelton's blood because he's convinced the pervert has you locked up in that big old house. Of course he's had plenty of help coming to that conclusion." Cole's temper suddenly flared, "Shelton wants to rape my wife then deny it?"

"And you were so gentle with her yourself," Holland gibed.

"She was *my* wife, not his," Cole shot back then turned back to

Savannah. "Shelton'll pay for what he did and your partner's gonna serve up justice. He's gonna kill Shelton and it'll be too late because you'll already be dead."

29

As it turned out, Ennis had driven past the gates to Shelton's sprawling estate many times without realizing who lived there. He passed a grove of old oaks and mentally counted the trees leading to the entrance. An expanse of large, mature trees along with a tall iron and brick fence framed the Shelton estate on each side, nestling the enormous twelve thousand square foot mansion in secrecy of oaks, maples and pines.

It was a perfect place for a freak that hurt and killed women – remote and hidden. The idea of Savannah suffering those cruelties sent his temper soaring. If she was in that house, he'd kick in every door until he found her.

After Cole's phone call, he piled into his Dodge Ram but not before checking his gun for a full compliment of ammunition. And if he ran out of bullets, he'd use his fists.

Savannah told him all about the illustrious Master Shelton and the inner workings of his household. She purged the filth from her mind by detailing every oddity and perversity she encountered in the house. The information literally nauseated him but he took careful note of it all and now he'd shoot his way to her if he had to.

He wheeled the Ram around the corner onto a paved side road leading to the entrance. The sprawling property only instilled the fact she was in that enormous house begging for her life. Shelton's ornate privacy fence had surveillance cameras mounted at particular intervals to monitor traffic – and individuals – around the property. To most residents or tourists, the place looked like something out of a historic novel. To Ennis it looked like a maze. God only knew how many rooms the two story mansion had – and he intended to bull through every one of them.

The Ram came to a screeching halt a few inches from the closed gates. He thumbed the intercom button and thrust his badge at the camera above.

"Yes?" a female voice inquired.

He dropped the words like stones, "Open the gates."

"I'm sorry. You don't have an appointment."

Ennis shoved the shield back on his belt, glared at the camera, "I want to see Duke Shelton right now. Open the gates."

"Sir, I do not have authorization to do so. If you'll –"

"Lady, you tell Shelton if those gates don't open in the next ten seconds, I'm bustin' 'em down." He made a show of pointing to his watch and revving the Ram's engine.

Four then five seconds passed when a heavy metallic click sounded followed by a mechanical motor. The two iron gates began their laborious task of swinging open.

It took only a minute to drive to the main house. He bounded up the stairs and pounded on the front door with the force he wanted to punch Shelton's face.

The door opened to reveal a woman dressed in a sheer orange gown. Flanking her were two other women much taller than she. They also displayed a certain degree of anger toward their visitor.

Ennis yanked open the door and bulled inside, "Where is he?"

"Detective, please calm down and remain in the reception area," a tall blonde in a white pantsuit instructed. "You will not be allowed to see Master Shelton in your current frame of mind."

Every word scalded him. Allowed? He was the friggin' police. "So you'd rather me plow through the lot of you to get to him? Fine." He shouldered his way between the three but felt a hand on his wrist as he passed by. Ennis wheeled to face the golden-haired female his height. Maybe she hadn't heard him clearly, "I've never hit a woman in my life but I'll make an exception if you don't let go." He slung her hand away and marched into the living room, "Shelton!"

His shouting caused the women at both doorways to jump. Ennis stalked to each one, looking down hallways, searching for Duke. "Shelton!"

"Detective," another woman approached. This one had red hair. He remembered Savannah mentioning her. Angelique. The bitch that poisoned Georgia.

Angelique remained a few feet away, her voice calm, "If you'll have a seat, I'll tell Master Shelton you are here. But I implore you to lower your voice and check your anger."

He finally realized Duke Shelton wasn't about to show his face until he displayed a modicum of composure. He planted his hands on his hips, "Fine. Just get him."

Angelique walked through a nearby doorway, whispered something to the scantily clad "guard" then disappeared down a hallway. Ennis paced the living room. Instead of one woman per door as Savannah described, his tirade managed to circle the wagons. Three muscular Amazons sent the sheer dressed women away and replaced them to stand guard. All in white pantsuits, they looked like Charlie's Angels on steroids. He now had nine women staring at him as he paced and waited.

"Welcome, Detective Rutherford," a jovial voice greeted. As Ennis wheeled, Duke Shelton swept his hand in a grand gesture to a nearby chair, "It's a joy to finally meet Savannah's husband."

He looked like an asshole, Ennis thought as he approached Shelton, his rage mounting once more. He looked like someone who'd hurt women and seeing the man provoked a monumental tidal wave of rage unfamiliar to Ennis. He literally felt like beating a person to death. For now he settled for grabbing a fistful of Duke's shirt, "Where's my partner? I want her and Georgia back now."

Without attempting to put an ounce of space between them, Duke inquired with ease, "Would you mind releasing me so we can speak man to man?"

"That would be a stretch for you," he let Duke go with a shove. "You bring her to me right now and I won't shoot you. That's the deal."

The dominant acquired a humorous expression, "Then I'm afraid there's no deal."

Ennis drew the .38 and leveled it between Duke's eyes. The

master's smile faded, "Easy, Detective. I only meant I do not have Savannah. I like the girl but not enough to kidnap her. And before you impulsively pull that trigger, please know I do not have Beauty either."

The gun never wavered, "Your cavalier attitude'll get you killed, Shelton. She and Georgia are either here or at your property north of town." It took every ounce of self control not to pull the trigger, "You *do* have property out there, don't you?" Ennis dared Duke to deny it. He wanted Shelton to trip up so he *could* pull the trigger. Then and only then would Ennis feel slightly vindicated.

"Yes, I own property there but if you'll take a moment to gather your wits, you'll realize that one phone call would reveal there's no dwelling on the site. I bought it for conservation. As a retreat of sorts."

"I'll bet." Ennis's anger boiled to an explosive level, "A retreat to rape and kill. If the girls aren't there then they're in this house. Take me to them or I'll turn this place inside out looking for 'em."

"You'll do no such thing. First of all it's invasion of privacy. Second, if I chose to, I could call your superior and claim you're trespassing. I'm getting rather weary of you and your wife threatening my wellbeing. I should call and have you charged with harassment. Before you assume I'm bluffing, Savannah would tell you I do not participate in such behavior."

His berating and its delivery drove Ennis to brace Duke harder, his finger bore down on the trigger as his teeth gnashed so hard his head ached. Shelton's arrogance would tempt any red blooded male to knock him into the next universe. "Call my boss then you'll find out a bullet travels faster than a patrol car. You'll be dead before dispatch is called."

Duke's vision volleyed between Ennis and the shaking hand holding the gun. Ennis watched him swallow, blink then return to meet his vision. Duke's tone remained calm, "You're not leaving my house until you search it, are you?"

"You can bet your ass I'm not."

Duke sighed, "Very well then. But I go with you. I will not allow further upset to my girls by letting you stampede into their rooms."

Ennis didn't care. He only wanted results and if he had to rifle the whole henhouse, he would – no matter the cost. "Whatever. I'm calling the station to have officers search your property north of town. Tell me where it is."

"Pushy, aren't you? How does Savannah tolerate you since she herself is a dominant personality?"

"Worry about yourself right now. Keep pecking at me and pissing me off and 'your girls' will need a new master. Let's go."

30

Holland stood right behind her. Savannah felt his warmth against her shoulders and back, smelled a hint of his cologne as he leaned to her ear, "It didn't work, did it, Detective?"

Savannah used Georgia to gauge her situation. Her sister watched him and, without consciously realizing it, her eyes told Savannah whether to brace herself or not.

For the time she'd been there and awake, Savannah carefully tried to loosen the ropes binding her wrists. She quickly learned the effort was futile. The ropes held tight and what the old rustic chair lacked in comfort and style, it made up for in strength and substance. No storm dared to sweep the bastard away or swallow it whole. The chair would choke it to death. Whoever crafted it obviously ran out of patience or muscle since coarse flat-sided logs served as the seat and a backrest. Slivers of unevenly sanded wood abraded her upper back, leaving her lower back unscathed but freezing in the air conditioned room.

In her efforts to free herself, she'd been spotted by the evil doctor while Cole watched a basketball game on TV. Trying to free herself hadn't amounted to much except having the tape removed from her mouth. That and now Dr. Death hovered behind her, asking questions he already knew the answers to.

Holland possessed a composed manner that comforted her in the hospital. During the chaos with Ennis, Mathis, Hunter and Cole, he'd been the only source of calm. Now she realized the composure wasn't a natural one. It was unbalanced and once alone with him, it didn't soothe, it scared the bejeezus out of a person.

"Answer me, Detective. It didn't work, did it?" he whispered the question against her ear. He might as well have shouted since she practically jumped out of her skin.

Savannah had a feeling Jeffrey Holland rarely shouted. His methods of getting a woman's attention far outshined any use of his voice.

Georgia's eyes flared wide and Savannah braced herself for whatever Holland prepared to do.

Holland leaned closer, his stubble rasping her ear, "You don't want to speak? Fine. Let me help you with that." Cold fingers closed around her throat, the iron grasp choking off her air.

Georgia cried out but the thick gag muffled her efforts. She was surely telling Savannah to answer Holland, to do anything to make him release her.

"In case you need a reminder, Detective, your life is literally in my hands," his tone maintained the same unflappable quality, as if nothing in the world bothered him because he was in control. His tightening grip proved it, "Surely you're not naïve enough to think I'll kill you this early in our relationship – but make no mistake. I can and will make you utterly miserable before I do finally kill you."

Georgia continued to scream and thrash and Savannah struggled for a wisp of air. She wanted to convey that she *was* trying to stop him but his grasp, if she hadn't noticed, cut off her ability to communicate. A gray curtain descended over her consciousness when she heard him ask, "Would you like another chance? I'm a reasonable man, Detective. If you'd like a second chance, you'll get one."

She tried to nod. Fighting for one meager breath failed and she saw the gray curtain dimming to black just as he released her. A long, deep gasp filled the room's silence. The ringing in her ears magnified for a time, and little pinpoints of light danced across her vision as she fought to fill her lungs.

"Let's try this again," Holland said. "Did your efforts to escape work?"

She pushed her answer past her raw, aching throat, "No."

"Take my advice. To avoid further grief, answer my questions in a timely manner. That means without hesitation. Understand?"

"Yes." The pained, whispered reply seemed to satisfy him. Maybe the worst was over for now. Maybe she'd pacified his need for control temporarily so she could prepare for whatever came next. It didn't work.

She gasped as his cold hand swept across her lower back, the icy fingers trailing along the scars striping her back from hip to hip.

"Where did you get the scars?" he asked. "Your sister has a few but not... like... this."

The light sweeping motion of his hand made her impulsively

shiver. She was about to answer when he continued, "This is the work of an angry father, isn't it? An angry father punishing a very bad little girl. You must've been a terror for him to mark you up this way. Were you a bad girl, Detective? Did you deserve these beatings?"

The air conditioning soon became unbearable and making things worse, Holland's latex covered hands were inconceivably frigid.

"You're hesitating again." He reached around, cupped her right breast in his hand. It felt like he plunged her tender flesh in ice. "Did you deserve them?"

"No," she replied and with the inflection, gave him a piece of her mind. Struggling against his touch caused the fingers to tighten on her breast. She heard the smile in his voice, "That's what all bad girls say and you know what? They do deserve it. Because they'll grow up to be demanding, manipulative control freaks if Daddy doesn't beat it out of them. Guess what, Detective?"

She should answer him but instead she channeled her energy into bracing for whatever came next. A quick flash of pain wrenched a cry from her as he brutally twisted the nipple. *That* no woman could ever prepare for. She cringed, trying to wear off the swell of pain rolling through her.

He reminded, "That's your cue to say what."

Pulling against the ropes, she fisted her shaking hands, wishing she could break free. Clenching her teeth against the pain, she snapped, "What?"

"Your daddy failed. It's up to me now." He stood up, put a hand to her shoulder, "Take her in there," he told Cole.

Georgia immediately reacted to those four simple words. She writhed against her bonds, her panicked screams muted by the gag. Her head shook side to side, warning Savannah "in there" wasn't a nice place to be.

If she could muster enough energy, Savannah would use the opportunity to attack Cole. One good shot to the groin was all she needed to temporarily disable him. Past that, she wasn't sure what to do. Going after Jeffrey meant leaving Cole recovering from her assault which also left Georgia vulnerable.

Cole approached Savannah then thought twice, "I'm not touching her without some insurance."

She shifted her vision across the way. Holland busied himself behind the kitchen counter. He never looked up, "Cole, are you saying a woman can overpower you?"

Cole's eyes narrowed at Jeffrey though the latter didn't see it. "I'm saying you want her in there, take her yourself. She's a fighter and a decent shot too if you remember."

"I *remember* Tasers work on her. I also *remember* a scar on her left breast and the rash that hasn't completely healed. That spells breast cancer and radiation treatments. That translates to a weakened physical capacity. So if that woman can kick your ass in her condition, you deserve it."

Cole shifted the glare to Savannah, "Give me any trouble and I'll beat you beyond recognition."

On a normal day – like one where she wasn't tied to a chair – that comment warranted at least a decent slap. But she chose to remain still and quiet while his fingers worked fast and efficiently with the knots. Cole wasn't a genius but he was stronger than her and she needed to wait for her opportunity.

From the corner of her eye, she saw his vision flick toward hers, silently warning her to behave. She sat motionless, her body as relaxed as possible to show she'd play nice.

Cole untied the last knot and the instant the rope fell free, she launched her foot into his groin so hard sharp bolts of pain traveled up her toes and calf. He stumbled back with a yelp, his hands instinctively cradling his crotch.

She rose from the chair and grimaced as her weight settled on her wounded leg. Her vision darted around the room for a viable weapon because unless Jeffrey was a complete fool, he realized something bad transpired between her and Cole and with the schoolgirl shriek Jordan unleashed, it was clear who'd won the battle.

Time quickly ran out and desperation forced her to use the only option available. A folding chair propped against the wall. It struck her as odd that Jeffrey still hunkered behind the counter and rummaged a cabinet, evidently unconcerned with his partner's spirited cursing.

Savannah approached Jeffrey from behind and swung the chair over her head.

"Detective, you can't kill us both," he bluntly stated.

His placid approach to nearly getting his head bashed in caused her to pause. He continued, "You're outnumbered for one. For another, Cole may be a bumbling idiot but I suspect he's standing behind you about now and he's not happy." Jeffrey stood, turned to her. He was smiling.

Just to wipe that grin from his face, she swung the chair with all her strength.

Holland leaned back, ducking the attack. The chair slammed into the counter, leaving a sizeable dent in its wake.

An immense pain exploded in her back, staggering her and literally stealing her breath. Cole's huge fist – or perhaps his foot – buried itself into her right kidney.

She fell against Jeffrey, clung to his broad shoulders for stability and the warmth from his body. He wrapped his arm around her, holding her to him. The blow robbed her breath but more importantly it crushed her will to fight for a brief time.

Jeffrey stepped back with her in his embrace, his voice holding a warning for Cole, "Enough." Tipping her head back, he saw the tears gathering in her eyes, "You made your point."

His other hand slid beneath her knees and Jeffrey effortlessly lifted her into his arms. Savannah tried to fight, willed herself to but her body refused. He carried her past Cole and then Georgia who still struggled for freedom. The door to "in there" was closed. Georgia's screams intensified, giving Savannah a clearer idea of how terrified her sister was of the mystery room. She tried to wrestle herself from Jeffrey's hold but found his embrace growing restrictive.

Cole reached past, opened the door for them. Jeffrey smiled down at her, "Welcome to my playroom, Detective."

The overpowering smell of copper mixed with bleach overwhelmed her senses. Large amounts of blood had been spilled in the room, and the men used bleach to clean up. To her right, a large plasma TV hung on the wall. Next to it: a video camera on a tripod. To her left was a silver surgical tray loaded with instruments found in every operating room. Behind that was a smaller table with one lone instrument – a rattan cane.

The room was painted stark white, the floor bare concrete with numerous bloodstains discoloring it. Above the stains hung two chains ending with steel cuffs and padlocks. Situated beneath those were two more steel cuffs, one for each ankle.

Savannah implored her body to react, to try to fight, but the pain radiated through her body. Cole's blow had been ruthless and very effective.

Jeffrey carried her to the restraints bolted to the floor. Cole secured her left ankle first. The click of the padlock registered a finality that spilled the growing tears down her cheeks. There was nothing she could do now. Nothing but wait – and suffer.

Cole spread her ankles, locked the right one in the other restraint. A steel cuff snapped closed around her right wrist followed by the small padlock. Once her left wrist was secured both men stood back, visibly proud. She stood spread-eagled before them, the embarrassment overshadowed by the feeling of total vulnerability. Fear compounded by dread set in along with the truth. They could do anything they wanted and no one could stop them.

Holland moved behind her and she tried to catch a glimpse of his location. She heard a click then a cold breeze swept across her. Another air conditioner. During her brief trek in Jeffrey's arms, she'd soaked in his body heat, savored every degree of it. Now she was back to freezing and her body almost immediately began shivering.

Cole drew his fingers down her throat, trailed them between her breasts in a slow, deliberate manner. They traveled along her hip then swung down and brushed between her open thighs, "I owe you big time, bitch."

"Leave her alone," Holland ordered. He waited for Cole to leave the room then stood to face her, "So you don't think we're impolite hosts, we'll provide you entertainment before we begin." Jeffrey approached the video camera and pushed the play button. He turned and winked, "Enjoy."

Savannah wasn't sure what he meant. She only knew they would record her beatings, mutilation and rape. Then it finally occurred to her. They recorded *every* woman.

Without looking up, she heard moans. A woman in pain. A sudden, shrill scream startled Savannah, forcing her vision to the TV in front of her. Leigh Watney stood in the same spot she now occupied, her arms and legs outstretched and shackled. Bloody welts crisscrossed Leigh's belly, breasts and thighs. Jeffrey stood behind her with his usual smile. He drew back with the cane and Savannah heard it slash the air before connecting with Leigh's back. Sickness crept up her throat at the woman's scream. She tried to swallow it down but blow after blow, scream after scream etched into Savannah's brain until she felt certain she'd go mad. Finally they stopped, leaving the room silent save for Leigh's weeping and shuddering moans.

Cole stepped into the picture, "My turn yet?"

Jeffrey didn't look happy but moved aside, "Once, just to shut you up. Then I take over." He sat the cane down and walked away. Savannah heard the door close.

Cole neared Leigh who'd been beaten so viciously her face was swelled on one side. He touched her wounded breast which brought another cry from the woman. Savannah cringed, turned away. She knew what was coming.

Chains jingled and she heard Leigh pleading with Cole. One brief glance revealed Cole unlocking the woman's wrists. He forcibly bent her over to reveal bloody wounds crisscrossing her back from shoulders to her bottom. Leigh used what strength remained to fight Cole but Jeffrey's beating left her weak, her will nearly broken. Cole stepped behind Leigh and Savannah closed her eyes, swallowed hard.

As Cole raped Leigh, the sounds overwhelmed Savannah, the woman's misery and pleas providing their own agony. In an attempt to block the horrific images and sounds, she began searching her mind for biblical verses. One in particular raced to the forefront. Her mother often recited it, saying it gave her comfort.

Savannah concentrated her efforts to speak each word carefully and loud enough to drown out Leigh's rape, "The Lord is my light and my salvation, whom shall I fear? The Lord is the stronghold of my life, of whom shall I be afraid?"

She repeated it until other verses came to mind and she recited them over and over to combat Leigh's cries and Cole's brutality.

She wasn't sure how long the tape played but as she recited the verses, the cold air tightened her muscles, the chains rattling from the uncontrollable tremors. She prayed for the video to stop, prayed for some peace from the terror of it but she knew the truth. She'd never get Leigh Watney's screams out of her brain.

The door opened and Jeffrey walked in, Cole behind him. Latex gloves encased Jeffrey's hands and he'd changed to an older pair of jeans and a white t-shirt with the Columbia Memorial insignia.

Cole mercifully shut the video off, removed a memory card and replaced it with another, "You like our matinée?"

Her stomach still boiled with nausea and she supposed it translated in her expression. Jeffrey chuckled, "I guess it's an acquired taste."

Cole stood behind the camera, repositioned it at her. Savannah saw a tiny red light blink on. Cole stepped around for a front row seat, "Give us your best smile right now cause it'll be the last time you smile about anything."

A cold touch on her shoulder slid down the slope of her back to and bottom. Jeffrey. "So you're a religious woman, are you?"

Chills rose along her body and she shivered, "Yes."

He leaned closer until she felt his warmth against her back, "That's good. Because you'll be calling for God's help soon enough." He stepped back, gave her shoulder a squeeze, then eased his hand down one side of her back then the other, "You've got good muscle tone, Detective. Not slight like the others. I think I'll put you through my paces, see how you do. First though, we have some business to attend to. Cole says you've been snooping into his life."

"I don't understand," she stammered. "Snooping how?" A

moment passed when she heard him moving items on the surgical tray.

Savannah braced herself but Jeffrey merely lifted an object to her vision: the rattan cane. "Don't disappoint me, Detective. I want my answers quick but I also want honesty. Answer me honestly. Why did you do a background on Cole?"

"I – I don't know what you mean. I didn't do any background on him."

He stepped in front of her, dragging the cane's tip around one nipple then the other, then eased it down her belly, "You are only delaying the inevitable – and compounding it as well – when you lie. Someone made inquiries into his life and you're the only one that fits the bill."

The tiny muscles in her stomach quivered and tensed from the light stroke of the cane. As it passed her navel to travel further down, she swallowed hard, "It wasn't me, I swear. If you check it out, you'll realize that."

The cane's journey halted at the crown of her pubic hair, "Then allow me to 'check it out'. *Tell me* who poked about in Cole's life."

Savannah may have been a lot of things, some of them not too flattering. But the one thing she could honestly say – she wasn't a rat. Giving them Shelton's name wouldn't change anything. The two men wanted to exercise their control over her but that part stayed to herself.

Jeffrey reinforced that fact as the cane struck sharply against her left thigh. Savannah gasped with pain and surprise. The blow shot a fiery bolt of pain through her leg that spread into her stomach.

Glancing down, she saw a raised welt striping her thigh, the dark pink flesh deepening to scarlet red. The residual ache throbbed to her toes.

Cole leaned against the wall, "Was it Duke Shelton?"

"Be quiet, loudmouth, and let her tell us," Jeffrey warned. When he faced Savannah again, she regretted the fact Cole stoked his temper. "I want the name now, Detective."

"Why does it matter?" she asked.

Jeffrey moved closer until his chest brushed her breasts, their faces only inches apart. He studied her a moment then softly proceeded, "You like pushing your luck, don't you? There's a time and place for nobility, Detective. Now is not that time. Tell me the name or you'll discover how little patience I possess."

Cole needled Jeffrey with his own words, "Looks like you can't intimidate her either. Listen, it had to be Shelton 'cause she's not smart enough to get an in-depth background on anyone."

Cole's condescension infuriated her. After all, it was *his* fault she and Shelton met. Savannah struggled against the chains, "You're the one who sent me to interview him. I'd never have gotten that information if –" She suddenly yelped, arching from an intense knifing pain across her shoulder blades. Her knees buckled from the penetrating, all encompassing ache, leaving her fighting to regroup her bearings and control. Not even R.J. resorted to beating her across the shoulders. It reverberated throughout her body, settling in her stomach and making her sick. Jeffrey's assault surprised her but it certainly shut her up.

"Careful, Detective," Jeffrey warned, watching her blink away tears and struggle back to her feet. He finished, "Your insolence will be repaid in kind, remember that." He slid a finger along the welt across her shoulder blades. She strained from his touch, grimacing at the raw stinging. Jeffrey continued, "Let's assume Shelton gave you the file. From his generosity I assume you discovered Cole's connection to me."

Truthfully, she didn't care about any connection. She only wanted the pain in her shoulders and back to ease. Jeffrey's hand moved down her back again as if deciding where to strike next. "I didn't bring blood with that one," he gave notice, "but the next one, well, I can't promise anything if you don't answer me."

"I never made a connection because there was no Jeffrey Holland mentioned. There was a Jeffrey something-or-other but not a Jeffrey Holland." Savannah spoke quickly, almost too fast. She'd do nearly anything to avoid being struck again but for all her effort, she still saw him step back into position. *No, no, please no...* "It's the truth. How could I make a connection with that?"

Her postscript seemed to satisfy him. Rounding her front, he lowered the cane to his side, "The file say anything about Cole's siblings?"

Wonderful. A test. And even an idiot could guess the consequences of giving a wrong answer. She strained to recall the file's contents. "Two siblings," she quickly answered. Her mind raced for the key to stop the beatings. *Keep him busy with conversation and maybe it will work for a while.* "No, three," she corrected. "Two stepbrothers and a stepsister."

"Very good. Did it say what happened to them?"

"The sister killed herself and one of the boys died. An accident, I think."

"Hunting accident. What did it say about the other boy?"

In that time, a sheen of perspiration formed on her face and neck. She shouldered off what she could. Instant regret set in as the motion only drove the pain deeper, "Something about him and Cole getting along, I don't remember exactly."

"Good enough. Now, Detective, I'll let you in on a secret. I changed my name several years ago so if the file failed to list my current name, that's why. Nothing like a fresh start, don't you agree?" He continued without allowing her a chance to speak, "Would you like to know another secret only Cole and I are privy to?"

"Yes." *Just keep talking and I'll keep listening. It's easier and better than bleeding…*

"My sister didn't kill herself and my brother didn't die in a hunting accident. Guess what happened."

Savannah saw it in his eyes. They conveyed a dark unfathomable evil. One so potent and pure her blood ran cold. Before he struck her again – this time probably as hard as he could – she replied, "You killed them."

Jeffrey turned to Cole, "And you said women make lousy cops." He swiveled back to Savannah with a sense of pride, "You'll be happy to know *I* never underestimated you. I told Cole you'd eventually figure it out. Then I told him because of that, you were a threat to us." He stepped closer, his eyes searching her face, sensing her fear, "I don't like threats." Jeffrey moved behind her again, "That license plate sealed your fate, I'm afraid."

He tapped the cane against his palm. The sound caused her to tense, preparing for another blow. She heard the smile in his voice, "We're going to take this nice and slow, the way I like it."

Savannah shuddered at the memory of the previous victims. The pain etched into their faces, the horrors they suffered. Jeffrey's victims almost certainly prayed for a swift death but he happily prolonged their suffering and kept them alive to endure excruciating, unspeakable acts. Now it was her turn unless fate or God intervened.

He stood to her side, gave the cane a few practice swings then raised it high above his shoulder and brought it down hard against her flesh.

A subdued cry spilled from her lips. It hurt but she'd suffered worse from her father's tantrums. R.J. had a wicked flick to his wrist that cut into a person. There were times when she couldn't sit comfortably for days, others required medication to prevent infection because they bled.

The cane struck her again, this time harder. She struggled not to scream. Jeffrey was only warming up, she cautioned herself. Things would soon get worse, much worse judging from the other victims. The feeling in her hands long since disappeared even as she balled her fists tighter. She tried to focus on Bible verses she'd memorized, "Trust the Lord. He is your helper and your shield…"

"Where is He now, Detective? He's not helping you. No one is and no one will," the voice taunted as the cane met her flesh again.

She trapped a scream behind her clenched teeth. Perspiration rose all along her body. The pain grew in enormity, every nerve vibrated from the repeated blows.

She heard Georgia crying and screaming in the other room. Visions of her childhood flashed by. Georgia begging R.J. to stop beating Savannah and her crying when he refused. Savannah concentrated on finding that one place, that one nook in her brain, to retreat to during this nightmare. As a child and teen, she carved one out strictly from necessity. Now that inner refuge disappeared, leaving her to bear the brunt of Holland's cruelty.

Jeffrey's voice came from behind, "I'm not your father. I *want* to hear you scream."

A drop of sweat trickled down her forehead, stung her eye. It was coming at some point, he'd make sure of it. The one that broke her silence.

The pain compared to a red hot poker pressed against her backside. It flowed through her veins and muscles like her blood was on fire. *Don't give in to it. Don't give in...* "For whosoever shall call upon the name of the Lord shall be saved."

The words barely left her trembling lips when she heard it. The swishing noise sliced the air just before the crack of rattan connected with flesh. Razor sharp agony so fierce and intense tore a scream from her depths. Tears fell in its wake as her knees gave way.

Her whole body shook, her heart pounded, her mind emptied of everything except the unbearable agony flooding her system.

"Call upon the Lord, Detective," he taunted near her shoulder. "See if He saves you."

His cold hand swept across her hot, stinging buttocks, making her arch away from his touch. He held his gloved palm to her face. Blood streaked his fingers. "Does it look like God is in this room?"

Savannah gritted her teeth so hard her jaw ached. She wouldn't give in to the bastard. She'd survived her father's beatings, she'd survive this. She survived her mother's death, cancer and more in her life. She *would* survive this.

She concentrated on her breathing. During the beating, it evolved into short shallow breaths. The last strike worsened it, forcing her to remember to breathe long, deep breaths for two reasons. One, she needed it. Two, her focus began returning albeit vaguely, and she needed to wear off whatever pain she could before he struck again.

Stepping in front of her, his vision swept her from head to toe, "No one is immune, Detective. Everyone eventually succumbs to the pain and judging by your reaction, you're about there." He swept away her tears, "The others couldn't handle two without begging for me to stop. You haven't uttered one plea, not even to your God."

Yes, she had. She'd prayed until her prayers ran on rims. God *was* in that room, she told herself, and He'd help her through this. He'd give her the strength to survive.

The cane gently tapped against her lower back but Savannah jumped as though he'd struck her. He positioned the cane just above her hips, "Did you scream like that when your father hit you here?"

A slow moving swell rolled from her back through her legs. She gnashed her teeth, tried to will it away but the throbbing clawed to the bone. Her inability to tolerate it provoked a harsh reply, "What do you think?" Her father's attacks were drunken fits so he flailed anywhere the limb might reach. This man, the one who vowed to kill her, would strike her there deliberately.

He didn't speak for several seconds. Savannah knew right away she'd chosen possibly the worst response on record. In a tense, clipped voice, Jeffrey replied, "Let's find out what I think."

It sounded like a pistol shot when it hit but the sound failed to compare to the shattering pain. The cane landed hard above her left hip and whipped around to strike her lower back and right hip. Her scream filled the room's silence, a flash of white engulfed her brain that gave way to a gray curtain veiling her consciousness. She fought the overwhelming darkness, forced herself to remain awake.

"Want me to expound on what I think?" he wanted to know.

She'd collapsed, leaving her wrists to support her weight. Struggling to stand, she gulped for air, trying to fill her lungs, "No." It was unbearable. Standing, breathing, talking, thinking, even simply existing was impossible at this rate, she thought. Her shoulders shook as she surrendered to the overwhelming urge to weep. It was worse, so much worse than her father's rage.

"Still feeling sassy?" Cole asked. "'Cause you don't look it."

Screw you, she nearly muttered between sobs.

"He asked you a question, Detective. Answer him." Jeffrey slowly drew the cane's tip along the throbbing welt across her shoulders. He skimmed along every wound, leaving another wave of anguish in its wake.

He wanted an answer? Fine. Her tear-filled vision rose to see Jordan's smug features. Then the bastard smiled at her. That was the last straw. She refused to lose her dignity. She'd endured R.J.'s abuse and all the other shit she'd been dealt in life and she'd be damned if these two stole her self-respect. Though it wasn't the smartest move she'd ever made, she uttered the granddaddy to "screw you", not only to exercise her blue streak but to show the assholes Savannah Prince – no, Savannah *Rutherford* didn't give up.

Cole's features flushed as red as the blood on her backside. He pushed to his feet, marched toward Jeffrey, "Gimme that thing. I'll teach the bitch a lesson she'll never forget."

Jeffrey yanked the cane from his stepbrother's grasp, "Back off. She's mine and she's about to discover my patience is at its end." He moved back again.

Savannah closed her eyes and felt more tears slip down her cheeks. She tensed up and she clenched her teeth, bracing herself for the worst...

31

Futile. Desperate. Clueless. The words haunted Ennis. The girls were nowhere in the Shelton house. He'd searched every room, nook and cranny, and any place a person might be stashed and came up empty.

Though not pleased with the invasion of his privacy, Shelton methodically walked him through every step of the place to prove his point – Savannah and Georgia were not there.

Darkness descended on Atlanta in that time. When it came to locating the missing or abducted, nighttime equaled impossible. The department would probably send the extra officers home until morning to begin searching again. That gave the killer plenty of time with the girls.

In the middle of his frantic quest around the house, Duke Shelton surprisingly offered his help. He realized the police worked overtime to find the girls, he'd said, but they also must abide by the law. Not that he was suggesting anyone *break* the law, he stressed, but his men were equipped, trained and willing to aid in the hunt. All he required from Ennis, he said, was a nod.

Ennis prided himself on thinking things through. Granted, there were times his heart ruled his brain but mostly he managed to maintain a levelheaded approach to things. This time, however, he nodded without any consideration to the decision. He needed help and more to the point, Savannah and Georgia needed it and if it came from the most unlikely source this side of Satan, so be it.

Standing in the middle of the opulent living room, Ennis felt torn between searching for them himself or staying put like Duke asked him to. Shelton warned him – as Ennis had Savannah – that leaving only amounted to trouble.

Ennis's phone rang and he checked the Caller ID. It was Mathis, "There's nothing on his property but land. No buildings, nothing. Unless he's got an underground tunnel system like a mole, we're outta luck." He continued, "They're calling off the extra officers until early morning but the boss brought in the nightshift detectives to help with phone calls. They're contacting hospitals and clinics about any missing meds and we're hoping to get a lead off that."

"How's that going?"

"All but three places got back with us so far. Nothing promising yet."

"What three are left?" Ennis asked then heard John shuffling papers.

After a moment, Mathis replied, "Grady Memorial, Columbia Memorial and a health clinic on Peachtree N.E."

The second name rang a bell with Ennis, "Columbia is where Savannah got her radiation treatments." Another revelation hit him, "It's also where they took Georgia for her allergy that day. Look closer at that hospital."

For the first time, John sounded hopeful, "I'll have the guys check all the employees. But," he reminded, "it'll take a while, Ennis."

"I know. Just work as fast as you can." He hung up from Mathis and his thoughts returned to Cole. Where were Savannah and Jordan when they were ambushed? Ennis tried Jordan's cell number to ask him but with every attempt, it went to voicemail. Ennis closed the phone, jammed it back on his belt with a mumbled curse. He'd just have to wait for Mathis to call him.

While Duke relaxed in his recliner, Ennis paced the floor, searching his memory for clues he missed or inadvertently ignored. He dissected every conversation for any trace of help.

"Detective, I implore you to sit down," Duke sighed. "If pacing was the answer, you'd have found Savannah and Beauty by now. Why don't you indulge in a cup of coffee? It might distract you from pacing." Shelton pointed behind Ennis.

Ennis turned to see a woman, her long golden hair flowing past her shoulders. She was dressed in a sheer green wrap that revealed more than it concealed. His mama would have thrown a robe around her. His brothers would have stood in mute lust. Ennis respectfully kept his vision above the woman's shoulders despite the fact she carried a silver tray at waist level.

The rich aroma of coffee wafted past, enticing him to partake. He needed a jolt of caffeine but it wasn't worth glancing down for it. He aimed his vision strictly at the woman's face, "No coffee, thanks."

Duke leaned forward, assessed the tray's contents, "Detective

Rutherford prefers his coffee black, I believe."

The woman bowed her head, "My apologies, Master Shelton."

"No need to apologize, Chantal. Just leave the cup for the detective and take the sugar and cream back."

Ennis watched the precise movements she made, setting the cup on a small table neighboring another recliner. He thanked her but didn't intend to drink it. Everything about the Shelton household screamed luxury and that made Ennis skittish. If he accidentally dropped the delicate cup, he'd probably owe Shelton a thousand bucks to replace it.

The dominant sighed again, "Please sit. You're tiring me."

Duke's request brought him from his thoughts, "When he called, Jordan said your men ambushed them."

"And as you learned in your rather crude exploration of my residence, it was a lie. I do not ask my men to abduct women. The women voluntarily come to me and they set the rules as to what they desire from my training. If we agree, we sign a contract. If we do not, they are free to find a dominant that does."

Ennis took that at face value, went back to picking apart conversations he'd had with Savannah. She'd mentioned a private physician and Ennis recalled the name Susan Swersky. It was a hell of a long shot but, "Does your physician have ties to any area hospitals?"

The question sparked Shelton's ire, "Now you're being absurd. I assume you've dug into her life as you've dug into mine so it's rather obvious she does not."

Ennis watched him snip the end of a cigar then painstakingly light it. The motion took a small eternity that not only lit the cigar but

Ennis's temper. He was about to speak when Duke lifted one finger to shush him. That incensed him more.

Shelton leveled a soft but strict caution, "So do not think you can bull through my whole household with your badge labeling everyone a murderer."

Ennis stalked toward him, hands on hips, "I don't have to. You've already got one of those and her name is Angelique. She oughta be in jail for what she did to Georgia."

"And I assume your wife informed you why Angelique is not incarcerated. It was Savannah's idea to strike a deal."

And there it was. Dane's crazy ways. The Rutherford brothers suffered from an unpolished and, at times, abrupt demeanor that usually befell them when a woman was involved. They'd fought amongst themselves a few times, accusing each other of muscling in on their girl or trying to sabotage a relationship. With age it diminished among *them* but it redirected itself onto society. If a Rutherford got into trouble, a woman was involved and the brother felt threatened by another male. Ennis hadn't quite managed to corral his streak but at least he tried. Dane didn't even have a fence to corral his and it seemed he didn't want one… But still, "My brother was protecting the woman he loves. That's different than poisoning someone."

"Threatening to kill me is different how? If he had access to my house, I'd be dead. I regret what happened to Beauty and I deplore Angelique's behavior but I remedied it, be assured."

Ennis doubted that. He doubted a lot of things lately. Starting at Christmas with Savannah's diagnosis, nothing made sense anymore.

Their lives stayed in constant turmoil. He only prayed this nightmare ended soon and ended well.

Duke continued, "It's admirable to defend someone you love, don't misunderstand me. Just defend them in a less homicidal fashion. Your brother is quick to anger. You," he tilted his hand in a so-so motion, "not so much, except today of course but I'm overlooking that. Actually, it's not surprising Savannah chose you. You're good-looking, strong and protective. Most of all, you seemed to represent what she never thought existed: a man who isn't violent toward women."

"I was raised to respect women, not hit them."

Duke picked up on his unspoken accusation, "Your distaste in my lifestyle isn't surprising since you're from the Bible Belt. Born on a ranch outside Vega, Texas. I hear you were quite the football star at your high school. A veritable hero on the field as I understand."

Oh crap. Here it came. He warned Savannah it would happen. The dreaded background on anyone associated with the Ravine case. Shelton's nosiness undoubtedly uncovered the one thing Ennis prayed stayed buried and it was only a matter of time until he mentioned it.

"You chose law enforcement to be a different kind of hero, didn't you?"

Ennis nodded. It was on the tip of Shelton's tongue, he could feel it. The man ached to mention it, to needle him with it and possibly blackmail him.

The dominant tapped an ash into the ashtray, "Too bad it didn't work out that way."

Ennis remained quiet. This wasn't how he imagined his life.

Discussing his past with a rich bastard who prided himself on raising hell with people. That information should have been private – and past history. Shelton exhumed his painful past for some reason and Ennis figured he'd find a clever way to use it as payment for his "help".

How exactly *would* Shelton use the information? Though it probably wouldn't affect Ennis's employment, it would definitely, in his opinion, destroy his marriage. Why would Shelton wreck a perfectly good marriage, unless it was payback for poking a gun in his face. Shelton said he'd ignore his stupidity but Ennis wouldn't underestimate him.

Duke continued, "It's quite a testimonial to a woman's ability to forgive. I'd never have guessed Savannah would overlook such behavior, especially in the man she married and trusted was gentle and kind."

"Don't go there, Shelton."

"Go where?" he asked, feigning innocence.

Ennis rounded on him, "You know where. You did a background on me like you did Savannah. I know you read the report but it's not what you think. Just drop it."

"I'm curious. For a woman so determined to ruin someone, Ms. Roberts dropped the charges unexpectedly. No reason given. Interesting."

Ennis felt like grabbing his gun and finishing the job. Shelton kept pushing and prodding him but everyone had a limit. Ennis reached his, "Stop nosing into my business."

Duke studied his frown. After a long moment, the truth dawned, "You never told Savannah about this, did you?"

The bastard got personal and quick. No wonder Savannah's rash flared up every time she was around him.

Duke shrugged, "Fair enough then. You haven't told your wife of it, neither will I but keep this in mind. If she should discover this on her own, how will it affect your marriage? Its very foundation is love and trust and if you remove the latter, will the former be enough to sustain you through that turbulent time? Most people value honesty but Savannah demands it. You run an enormous risk by keeping your secret from her."

Ennis couldn't believe it. "I'm getting morality lessons from a guy who ties women up and beats them. Incredible."

"Relax, Detective. Your secret is safe with me. It is your choice not to tell your wife but I would reconsider that strategy if Savannah survives this ordeal."

He wanted to strangle Duke Shelton for one, mentioning the whole mess and two, for not having faith in Savannah. Ennis clung to his faith and confidence in his wife, despite the odds being against her and Georgia. She possessed an incredible resourcefulness and intelligence. If an opportunity arose, Savannah would take advantage of it. But she also needed some help, "Are your guys ever gonna call with news?"

Duke nodded, "Give them time. If she and Beauty are to be found, they will find them."

32

"Hang on, honey," a voice called from what seemed miles away. "We'll be home soon."

Savannah swore the voice belonged to her mother. The soothing tone assured her home wasn't far away but what home exactly? The relentless pain racking her body refused to ease so was her mother promising something more spiritual rather than a street address? *Mama, help me,* she pleaded. *God's not listening. You said He'd listen...*

Jeffrey had been right. God wasn't in that room. As much as she prayed and begged for His mercy, Holland slammed the cane harder against her already torn, bleeding flesh. The screams stripped her throat raw. God hadn't heard them, her despondent weeping or her cries for mercy.

Maybe God tested her the way He had Job and unlike Job, maybe she failed. Maybe all her sins caught up with her and when God tested her, He'd decided she wasn't worth His time. He hadn't eased her anguish one bit, convincing her the monster had been right. Jeffrey mocked her faith, ridiculing her for begging "her God" to save her. She should have been begging him instead, he said. He was real, God wasn't.

He was in charge of her pain, of her *life*, not God.

"God can hear you," the voice continued. "Don't give up."

She wanted to be strong like her mother. Charlene lived her life never giving in to anything, not even cancer. Even in her last days, she fought to stay alive, to tell everyone around her she loved them – and what she expected of them. In a quiet moment alone with her youngest daughter, she told Savannah she admired her strength but in troubled times, even the strongest person needed God. "Rely on His strength," she'd said. "He will see you through."

Savannah tried to be strong. She'd try one more time. She'd ask God to shed the pain rooted deep in her body and to help her and Georgia survive. The waves of fire continued burning along every nerve, and for an instant, she realized the degree of pain required to welcome death. It wasn't only the unbearable pain but the relentless suffering. The cancer must have hurt worse, she told herself. And her mother withstood it all without tears, without whining, without surrendering.

Her muscles contracted from the constant agony. She felt her resolve slipping. So close to giving in. The cancer was worse, she repeated again. *Be strong like Mama...*

Ennis's handsome image floated in. He accused her of being headstrong but he surpassed her when striving toward a goal. He'd search every square mile of Atlanta, probably the state of Georgia, until finding them. He would exhaust every lead and still not give up. Savannah clung to that hope, making it her lifeline. He would search until finding them – hopefully alive. She was grateful their paths crossed in life. She'd given up on meeting a gentle, decent man and truly falling in love. After her dealings with Toby Jackson, she resigned herself to growing old alone. But now she'd experienced true love, the kind that made people silly with joy, the kind that tore at a heart when tragedy struck. They'd seen each other through tough times, staying true to their vows about sickness and health. The writers neglected to insert a passage about abduction by serial killers but she figured it fell into an all inclusive "for better or worse" category. She just prayed the "until death do us part" was many years away, not a few days.

Savannah whimpered as a burning pain bolted across her back. Sweat migrated into the open wound, reminding her of the cruel turn her life suddenly took.

A different thought emerged through the haze of her mind. If, through all his efforts, Ennis didn't find them alive, what would he bury her in? After her diagnosis, she'd rummaged her closet in search of appropriate burial apparel – just in case. He'd stopped her in mid-search, demanding she be more optimistic. Optimism had its place, she supposed. Now didn't seem to fit the bill.

As another wave of pain swept through her body, she prayed for her mother's strength. She felt herself impulsively strain against the bonds confining her to the hard wooden chair then realized she was shivering uncontrollably.

"Savannah, stay strong. Ennis is waiting."

Once the muted ringing subsided in her ears, she recognized the voice as Georgia's, not her mother's. Was she hallucinating? Georgia spent the entire time silenced with tape over her mouth. How could she speak? Must be a delusion, she groaned. *Great. Now I'm losing my mind too.*

Savannah recalled a phone ringing and Jeffrey drawing up a sizeable injection. He'd assured Cole it would keep her quiet until his return a few hours later. Well, it made her sleep a while but the pain was back and felt like her body would explode from it.

Her trembling only intensified it. Perspiration chilled her while afflicting her with a new agony: salt in the bleeding welts on her back and bottom. She was going crazy and her mind and body chose the slowest, most agonizing route possible.

Savannah groaned again. This time a different voice spoke, "Pipe down over there. I'm watching the news."

Cole. The son of a bitch laughed when Jeffrey thrashed her with the cane. His threats of "what came next" accentuated with a crotch hike failed to frighten her the way Jeffrey's mere presence did. If Cole believed his threat of sexual assault mattered, he was a bigger fool than anyone imagined. By the time he managed to grow an erection, she'd be long dead. Jeffrey's ability with a cane put any other sadist to shame. One more session with that bastard and she'd throw herself on the friggin' cane and impale herself.

As a kid, she avoided sitting when possible, and only slept on her belly until R.J.'s rant healed. Jeffrey, however, plopped her down in the chair, cringing from the scream she belted out. That, and Cole's insistence, convinced Jeffrey to sedate her. Now the seeping wounds bonded her to the seat tighter than superglue. Another nightmare awaited her when they peeled her off of it.

Cole complained, "Stop your bitching."

"She's in pain," the voice snapped.

No, she wasn't hallucinating. That was definitely Georgia and when she used that particular tone with Savannah, she shrank back from her older sister. Somehow, though, it failed to deter Cole, "I'll bet she is."

The bastard. There was a smile in his voice. He really believed his time with her was coming but Jeffrey kept denying him and putting him off. She wondered what the difference was. According to the video they forced on her, the two took turns with their own special hell for women. Jeffrey beat them, Cole raped them. But Jeffrey refused Cole his turn with her.

"Can't you give her something to ease it?" Georgia pushed. "He's got to have something over there."

Yes, Savannah wanted to say, but it wasn't anything to relieve pain. Holland only cared about causing it, not easing it.

"Want me to seal you up again? I don't care if she's hurting, get it? So shut up," Cole warned. Savannah heard footsteps approach. Cole sounded closer, "Besides, *I* got a different way to shut her up."

Fear laced Georgia's voice, "He said he'd kill you if you touched her."

"Then it looks like Little Miss Sunshine keeps giving us her nice warm glow. Shut up already. It's like being married again only with two wives. I'll bet those Mormon guys live on Valium."

The unmistakable sound of an open hand meeting flesh focused Savannah's attention on her sister. Georgia whimpered from the backhand. Cole grumbled, "Besides, he didn't say I couldn't touch you, did he?"

One thought soared to the forefront of Savannah's consciousness. *Protect Georgia.* She moaned, hoping to divert his attention away from her sister. A new flash of pain joined the dissension throughout her body. Cole decided to exercise his backhand on her, "Shut your whining up, bitch." He walked away complaining, "Damn liar. He said it would keep her quiet for at least four hours. She woke up in three."

The blow stunned her temporarily but at least she'd helped Georgia momentarily. It also served to awaken more nerves, making them throb in concert with the others. It was getting so hard to bear... Too hard.

Across the room, Savannah heard a local newscaster report the time and date. It was early morning and she'd been with the men sixteen hours. Jeffrey and Cole kept their victims for days. The mere idea of spending that amount of time being beaten and tortured brought a surge of tears to the surface.

"Savannah," her sister called again. "Think of Ennis. He's looking for us. He won't stop until he finds us..."

She knew that but where the hell would he start? In the meantime, the two bastards could do whatever they desired.

She sniffed back more tears and smelled a hint of rain. The sound grew from a gentle shower to a pelting deluge. She prayed the rain washed out the road, preventing Jeffrey from arriving until she'd recouped some strength. All she needed was to ease the pain and get a decent opportunity at Cole. She'd rip that smile from his face and shove it up his...

The commercial break ended and the newscaster proceeded with the day's headlines. Savannah listened closer, tried to hear over the downpour outside. She swore she heard him say Georgia's name, followed by her own. A roll of thunder drowned out part of the report but she heard the word "abducted" then a phone number for the police.

The public now knew the next intended victims of the Ravine Killer but they, like her husband, didn't know where to begin searching. No one ever saw anything when the Ravine Killer struck. He, no, *they* were too careful. And, like she, the public never suspected a handsome, genial doctor name Jeffrey Holland of being a killer...

33

A noise outside woke Savannah. She wasn't sure how long she slept but the rain had stopped, leaving the air thick and heavy with humidity. Turning to the source of the sound, Savannah winced the second she moved. Her wounds cranked up the orchestra again, playing the symphony of pain she'd managed to ease to a dull roar. Instead of scouting out the noise herself, she glanced at Georgia, using her as a visual barometer on the situation. Her sister stared wide-eyed at the front door. Savannah searched the room. Cole sat at the dining table, pecking away on a laptop. That meant only one thing. Jeffrey was back.

The cabin's door slammed open like a gunshot. Jeffrey stormed in, his wrath aimed at Cole, "You dumb son of a bitch!"

Cole immediately stood, retreated from him, "What?"

Jeff slapped a copy of the Journal-Constitution and USA Today against Cole's chest, "This. You didn't tell me *she*," he pointed to Georgia, "was a celebrity. The whole world is looking for her!"

"She's not that famous, is she?" he tried to calm his stepbrother down. "I've never heard of her."

"Like that matters now." Jeffrey's hands clenched and released in a way that told Savannah Cole's jaw might be in jeopardy. *Hit him*, she silently urged. *And hit him hard.* If the two tangled with each other, they'd leave her and Georgia alone.

Jeffrey's tirade intensified, "That's all I heard at the hospital." He leveled a withering glare at Georgia, "Where is Georgia Prince?" Then he turned it on Cole, "We know, don't we? Look at the damn paper!"

In a slow measured move, Cole apprehensively unfolded the newspaper. From Savannah's position she saw a large photo of Georgia with a large headline "Atlanta Author and Sister Abducted." In slightly smaller print read, "Police searching for Georgia Prince and sister Atlanta Police Detective Savannah Prince". Below Georgia's picture was one of Savannah in uniform. She always hated that picture. It looked too much like a funeral announcement. She nearly groaned at the irony of it.

To appease his stepbrother, Cole gave the USA Today a cursory glance. Savannah again saw Georgia's picture near the bottom beneath the headline "Renowned Atlanta Author Abducted." Cole folded the papers to hide the headlines, "How did I know it would explode into this? I didn't think –"

"You're right. You didn't think, Cole. We have to get rid of them today. If you're capable of reading that rag, it says they're widening the search north *and* west of the city. Guess where that takes them? And guess what else that means? You're not touching her," he jabbed his finger at Savannah. "You screwed up, you pay."

Cole was furious, "Killin' 'em will be quick. Just cut their throats. *But I want my time.*"

"No, we do this my way now." Jeffrey riffled the papers, settling on the Atlanta one, "Read that article, genius. In fact, read the third paragraph out loud." Jeffrey removed his blue dress shirt, revealing his strong muscled physique. It took regular workouts and lifting weights to maintain a body like that, Savannah thought. Or perhaps beating women and carrying their mutilated bodies to a ravine kept him fit. Whatever the reason, he was a man to carefully consider before attacking him. Strategy, not strength, would bring him down.

Jeffrey grabbed a white t-shirt from the table, stretched it over his chest. He removed his khaki slacks, replacing them with a pair of worn jeans that he tucked the t-shirt into.

Cole had been reading silently during the time then began reciting the article, "Witnesses saw two men dressed in black at Piedmont Park Monday evening. One witness described seeing two men in dark clothes carrying something to a car then quickly driving away…"

Jeffrey put his hands on his hips, "You know what that something was, don't you, Einstein? It was Georgia Prince. And the witness? That old man walking his dog. And if she," he now pointed to Savannah, "saw the license plate, he might have too."

"Then why didn't he come forward with it?"

"Maybe it slipped his mind and that rag jogged it for him today. How should I know?" Unable to curtail his temper any longer, Jeffrey fisted Cole's shirt and shoved him against the wall. Cole's head struck the wall with such force the sound echoed through the cabin. "What I do know," Jeffrey continued, "is I never should have listened to you. We deviated from our plan. We went to a public place and then you wanted to flaunt your ego at the detective. Leave her badge in plain view. I was foolish for listening to you, Cole but be assured, it won't happen again."

Savannah slanted her vision to Georgia who stared wide-eyed at the pair. Let them fight, Savannah tried to tell her. It was good that the two were at odds. At least they weren't leveling their rage at her or Georgia. Savannah shook her head and mouthed "calm down".

The muscles in Jeffrey's arms bulged as he pushed Cole flush against the wall, his shirt still bunched in his fists. Savannah heard the hard breaths, the words squeezed between clenched teeth as Jeffrey continued, "We have to get rid of them both now. Because of your greed and insatiable sex drive, I'm deprived of *my* pleasure, Cole. The news stations and newspapers are splashing their pictures everywhere. You can't turn on a TV without seeing one of them. That screws up my plans. Do you remember how much I hate that?"

"I remember." Cole glared down at Savannah, "But I'm taking what I want before we finish 'em off."

Jeffrey slammed him so hard against the wall Savannah flinched. Yes, Holland clearly had a fierce temper she'd not anticipated – and the muscle to back it up. His fists blanched as he held on to his stepbrother, "You got us into this jam so you sacrifice. I don't want them found so we have to be careful. If we can get rid of 'em and not get caught, I might let *you* live."

Jeffrey stalked to the dining table. He withdrew a vial from the leather bag, tilted it to the light, "I don't have much left." He shoved his hand inside again, a frown darkening his fair skin. His vision settled on Savannah as he tossed a prescription bottle at Cole, "Give her two."

Cole studied the name on the bottle, shrugged then opened it.

Savannah caught sight of the name. They were sleeping pills.

He shook two pills into his palm but Savannah pursed her lips tight. Cole's open hand swung back, "Wanna play rough? Fine."

A hand on Cole's shoulder startled him, sent him back a step. "You're pathetic," Jeffrey told him. "You have no clue how to handle her." His narrowed vision settled on Savannah and a vicious grin surfaced, "But I do." His voice settled into the familiar calm that sent a shiver down her back. The same tone that reminded her of the pain he inflicted earlier without breaking a sweat, "You *will* take the pills, Detective." He lifted a shining scalpel to her vision. He dragged the blade gently down her throat to her left breast.

She gasped when the cold blade traced the surgery scar. The nipple tightened painfully as he trailed the stainless steel around it, careful not to nick the skin.

"Unless," he added, "you want to watch me cut your sister apart."

Savannah tried to contain every spiteful word dangling on her tongue. He left no doubt that he'd follow through on his monstrous threat. Despite being short on time, he'd make their deaths as agonizing as possible and torturing them in front of each other probably presented too much temptation.

Then it hit her. When he focused on one person, his attention stayed there until something or someone interrupted him. She'd try to divert the conversation away from them and onto, "Don't you think you let Cole off easy?"

Her question caught him off-guard. Jeffrey's eyes searched her face as if trying to reach into her thoughts, "What?"

Her voice remained matter-of-fact despite her pounding heart, "He's ruined everything for you and all you do is shove him around?" From the corner of her eye, she watched Cole bull toward her.

Cole's hand clenched into a fist, "Why you –"

Jeffrey extended his arm, blocking Cole's approach, "She's got a point."

"You're kidding, right? After what I've done for you and you're listening to that bitch?"

"Shut up and step away, Cole. The detective and I have some things to discuss."

Georgia's expression questioned her sister's sanity. She questioned herself too but seeing her sister suffer didn't rate too highly with her either. She had to draw his attention onto Cole and away from them.

Jeffrey lifted the scalpel, "What do you think is a fitting punishment for my stepbrother?" He turned the blunt side to her throat beneath her right ear. The cold steel trailed across her throat to her other ear, making her shudder. He asked, "Should I make it quick and cut his throat?"

He lightly drew the scalpel down her belly. The blade played back and forth through her pubic hair, haphazardly cutting the coarse hair until the frigid steel slipped deeper between the tender flesh. Sheer fright swept through her and she struggled to retain fragile control and not tip the situation any further awry. Another stellar decision, she berated. She was an idiot beyond compare. She'd seen the victims after Jeffrey finished with them. He sliced and mutilated them *exactly* where the scalpel rested.

The corners of Jeffrey's mouth lifted, "Or should I take my time removing the offending appendage since it rules his brain?"

Her breathing dried to a shaky whisper. She wasn't sure if she could answer if he forced her to. One tiny movement and pain took on a whole different meaning.

"Your decision, Detective. Quick or slow?"

She sat frozen, breathing small, shallow breaths and unable to speak. She glanced down at his hand, silently pleading with him to carefully remove the blade.

His expression stilled, "Now that you mention it, I believe I was easy on *you*. I don't recall you begging *me* for mercy. You begged your God and I think you owe me."

He withdrew the scalpel, allowing Savannah to slowly release her pent up breath. Pain suddenly exploded in her head and with it, her cry splintered the silence. He'd backhanded her with a strength that put Cole to shame.

"You think you can screw with me?" His fingers fisted in her hair and directed her vision to Georgia, "Here's the deal, Detective. You screw with me, I screw with her." He brought the scalpel eye level, "And I owe *you* one as of right now."

He stripped off a section of tape and covered her mouth, smothering her pleas to stop. The plan backfired, her brain screamed. He was going after Georgia again and judging by his expression, nothing was stopping him. How did she help her sister now?

The scalpel glinted between his fingers. Georgia's eyes widened as she writhed against her bonds, crying and screaming against the gag.

"Don't blame me," he said then pointed the blade at Savannah. "Blame her. She signed you up for this."

Sitting next to her on the narrow bed, his free hand touched Georgia's throat then eased down to her right breast, traced it with his index finger. He cocked his vision to Savannah as he caressed Georgia, "Nice. Warm, plump, beautiful." Giving the flesh an appreciative squeeze, he said, "Flawless, even. These I can work with. These are my canvas, Detective." He wagged the scalpel between his thumb and forefinger, "And this is my brush."

Georgia pulled against the ropes. Tears glistened in her eyes as the blade nestled against her right nipple.

Savannah screamed against the gag. *Come on, you bastard, listen to me! Let me talk!*

His vision locked on hers, "You sound like you want to make a deal."

She frantically nodded. Her heartbeat thundered in her chest and ears. The sheer panic coursing through her veins ebbed a degree. Maybe she'd managed to slow down the situation enough to think and re-gear her plan. Strategy not strength, she reminded herself. She had to be careful because if Jeffrey suspected anything amiss, he'd go straight for Georgia again. *Be calm. Think before you speak.* Georgia's earlier and less-than-tactful suggestion popped into her mind. Savannah decided to try it. Talking with Jeffrey equated to playing chess. Every move had a countermove, every remark did too.

Jeffrey removed the knife, stepped closer to Savannah. He ripped the tape from her mouth, seemingly satisfied with her cringe, "What's your offer?"

"You want me to take the pills, I'll take them. Just don't hurt my sister."

"That's all you've got? Sorry, Detective. No deal," he reached up to replace the tape.

She struggled away, speaking before he silenced her again, "What do you want? What will it take for you to leave her alone?"

"More than taking the pills." His hand glided down her arm to her wrist. His ravenous stare settled on her left breast, causing an uneasy feeling to rise in the pit of her stomach. Memories of the victims clawed their way to her consciousness. Their breasts sliced off, leaving bloody gaping circles in their place.

Jeffrey's vision shifted to her right breast, held it in his palm, "You want your sister spared. What are you willing to give in return?"

Savannah refused to look at Georgia. From the corner of her vision, she saw her sister vehemently shaking her head. She couldn't bring herself to speak. He wanted an answer but offering an actual part of herself? Who could honestly answer that question? Instead, she dropped each word like a stone, "What do you want?"

An insidious smile crawled across his lips, "To make you beg. I want to make you beg *me*, not your God. And believe me, I *will* hear those words from you before you die."

It was, at that point, she felt the sharp edge of the scalpel nudge against her right nipple. She squeezed her eyes shut, swallowed hard, trying to prepare for the unbearable pain.

"No," he demanded, "open your eyes. Look at me."

Savannah couldn't.   The sickness grew in her belly with the realization of what was about to happen. The scalpel hadn't moved and nausea already crept up her throat.

"I said look at me!" he shouted.

When she opened her eyes, she saw her sister crying. Georgia was on the verge of hysterics and Savannah wanted to calm her down but all thought ceased when she felt a sudden pressure below her collarbone followed by a slicing sensation. A cry tore from her depths as the blade sank into her flesh and drew in a downward motion. Excruciating pain bolted through her right shoulder and it spread down her arm and into her chest like fire. Tears sprung to her eyes as she instinctively strained against her bonds. Georgia was still crying but Savannah barely heard her from the ringing in her ears.

She clenched her teeth against the pain. Her sister's horrified stare forced Savannah to assess the damage. Blood dripped from a wound below her shoulder that trickled down her breast. Jeffrey looked satisfied with the three inch slice below her collarbone. An unmistakable number "1". It was the beginning of a long agonizing journey to death. She was going to be victim number ten.

Jeffrey walked to the dining table. When he returned, he held Cole's .45 at his side. She met a fiery gaze that melted straight to her bones. She still hadn't begged him for mercy. She still defied him but she had a feeling that was about to change.

Jeffrey lifted the gun, "Here's what we're going to do. You're going to swallow those pills and I won't blow your brains out. You wouldn't want your sister to witness that, would you? Hasn't she seen enough?" He lowered the barrel until she stared down the dark chamber. It pressed against her forehead, right between her eyebrows.

She barely nodded, careful not to nudge his finger resting on the trigger.

"Open," he reached back to Cole for the medication.

Savannah did. He dropped the pills at the back of her throat, and before she closed her mouth, long fingers pushed them past her tongue. Fingernails scraped along her cheek into her throat. She heaved against the invasion but his fingers pushed them deep. She gagged and coughed, trying to regain control of her reflexes.

He told Cole, "Get some water. I don't want them coming back up."

Savannah turned her attention to Georgia. Tears streaked the older sister's face. She hated that Savannah took the brunt of the abuse but the younger sister remembered plenty of times when Georgia saved her from R.J.'s rage. Savannah lost count of how often her sister took the blame and the subsequent beatings associated with it.

Through the waves of pain spiraling down her arm and into her chest, Savannah tried to exhibit more calm than she actually felt. Perspiration rose along her body from the shock. Blood continued to drip from the wound. She grimaced as burning tendrils snaked to her hand, encircling every nerve along the way.

Cole held a cup of water to her lips, "Drink or I'll drown you with it."

She drank it down then glanced at Jeffrey who stood a few paces back. He watched her swallow, a smile curved his lips. Switching his vision between sisters, he began reciting a perverse rendition of a child's nursery rhyme, "Eeny, meeny, miny, moe, Catch a sister by the toe. If she hollers make her pay, 'Cause there's no hope of getting away." His dark eyes stopped on Savannah. He closed in, "You really want to be first?"

Besides "has your stay been satisfactory thus far", it rated as the dumbest question she'd ever heard but a little ray of hope continued burning. She'd still try to give Georgia a fighting chance. Maybe somehow her sister could find a way to free herself, even if Savannah couldn't.

Ignoring her sister's protests, Savannah nodded. Jeffrey's smile widened. She hated that smile.

He leaned closer to her ear, "That's too bad because I'm withdrawing my deal." He turned to Cole, "Take the sister."

34

Ennis paced the floor as he'd done for the last few hours. Surely by now Mathis and the nightshift would have found the connection. In the pit of his stomach, Ennis knew Columbia Memorial held the key to the case. They had a killer working for them – but who?

"Have you seen Jordan anywhere?" he asked Mathis when he called. "Every time I call it goes to voicemail."

John groaned. Ennis imagined him removing his glasses and rubbing his eyes. A brief pause later, Mathis answered, "That's another thing the boss hit the roof about. With Prince and her sister missing, no one can find Jordan. We've called, sent officers to his house – which ain't exactly nearby. No one's heard from or seen him."

"He never dropped off Savannah's phone?"

Mathis sighed this time, "That would fall into the category of 'seen him', Ennis. The boss is about to blow an aneurism. He needs all the help he can get and Jordan's AWOL."

They exchanged a few more words and Ennis clicked off, clipped his phone back to his belt. AWOL? His original anxiety reared up again. The way Jordan hassled Savannah. His attempts to lure her on a date, even knowing she was spoken for. The sting of her continued rejection. Even with her rejections, he never left her alone, transforming his desire into frustration and outright hostility.

Jordan was there when Georgia's call came in, warning Savannah of the trap. After the ninth victim's discovery, Cole offered to take her to search for Georgia on the premise of Shelton's "newly discovered" property. It turned out to be a lie. Shelton's property was purely land, nothing more. Jordan's phone call to Ennis nagged at him. Too convenient. It was way too convenient...

He grabbed the phone and called Mathis, "Check Jordan out. There's something hinky about him and no one can find him."

"What are you thinkin'?"

"I'm thinking I've never trusted him and isn't it odd he's in the wind after Savannah's abducted."

Mathis was quiet, as if considering the unspoken accusation. Then, "Ennis, that's a long shot. I mean the guy's a cop."

And a not a very good one – probably for a reason. "Mathis, please. You know how he treated Savannah."

He finally wrenched a begrudging "okay" from Mathis before they hung up. Ennis realized how unlikely it was but he was desperate. Georgia was missing. Savannah was missing and now Cole. Nothing added up and nothing felt right about Cole Jordan from day one.

"It's endearing, you know," Duke said.

The declaration brought Ennis out of his thoughts. He stared at Shelton, wondering where the hell he found such words and how he had the balls to actually use them. Endearing was an airy fairy term women used, not men. If Ennis uttered it within earshot of his brothers, they'd all pile on and beat him until he cussed like a rancher's son again. *Endearing.* Good God... "What are you talking about?" he asked Duke.

Without offering a prompt reply, the dominant snipped the end of a cigar, placed it in his mouth and proceeded with the long ritual of lighting it. Ennis put hands to hips, waiting. Whenever asked a question, Shelton always found a way to suspend the conversation. Ennis assumed the dominant felt uneasy with inquiries – after all, he got paid to direct people, not answer them.

Duke rotated the cigar above the flame as he puffed, "Your attachment to your wife. It's charming to see people pine over each other."

"Glad I entertain you." He pointed to the cigar, "Y'know, those things'll kill you."

Duke leaned back, gave the cigar a brief appraisal then smiled, "I like living dangerously."

Oh, and speaking of that... "Are your men doing anything to find Savannah and Georgia?" Because if they weren't, Ennis would give them all a beating surpassing the one his brothers would for saying the word *endearing.*

"Detective, I hire ex-military. Not just any ex-military. These men were special forces."

"Is that a yes?"

"Indeed." Duke lifted a bottle of brandy, "Won't you partake of one drink? Might keep you from unfraying at such an alarming rate."

Ennis watched Duke's steady hand pour brandy into a small glass.

The detective refused, "I don't want anything clouding my mind. But thanks."

Duke sighed, "Suit yourself. I shall partake because your nervous habit is grating me raw." He tilted the glass into his mouth until it emptied.

Grating him raw? *His* wife wasn't being tortured so he could afford the luxury of calm, cool and collected. Ennis couldn't, "Sorry my concern is bothering you but I love Savannah and want her and Georgia back safe."

The dominant busied himself watching the cigar smoke snake back and forth from the ashtray, "You and I are not so different."

First he criticized Ennis's worries. Evidently not content with that attack, now the man decided to insult him. *Believe me...* "We're nothing alike, Shelton."

"Come now, Detective. Stop judging my lifestyle and think. You love Savannah. I love Jade, Angelique and all my girls. It would break my heart if something happened to any one of them."

"Let me make myself clear. I married the woman of my dreams. You collect women like kids collect baseball cards."

For some reason, Duke found amusement in the strangest things, especially ones that could result in serious bodily harm. After a hearty chuckle the dominant replied, "You and Savannah are truly meant for each other. Listen, you are just as possessive of her as I am of my girls. You don't consider Savannah property but you do consider her yours, am I correct?"

Ennis thought on that a minute. Yes, he did consider Savannah his own. Their bond compared to his mother and father's. Strong through thick and thin. Fights were few, laughter was frequent. Come to think of it, Savannah had called Ennis hers, so why should he tiptoe around it? He nodded but so help him if Shelton gloated, that arrogant grin would lose a few pearly whites.

Sensing this, Duke tapped an ash from his smoke and settled for, "Then we are not so different. She chooses to stay with you because she loves you, not necessarily because of those vows she took at your wedding. My girls and I share the same arrangement except I have no ceremony to bind them to me."

"That's because there's a law against polygamy, at least where I come from."

"Your black humor reminds me of your wife's. As I said, you do belong together."

Ennis glanced at his watch. Another two hours ticked by since he'd put Mathis onto Columbia Memorial. His heart battled his brain. It's probably too late, the latter reasoned. Over twenty hours with a sadistic killer, neither sister stood a chance. They were probably both dead and if they weren't, they were wishing they were.

"Patience, Detective," Duke said, evidently reading his thoughts. "That combined with a generous amount of hope. The two together are powerful. And since you are a spiritual man, a few more prayers might be in order."

The semi-lecture offended Ennis, "I have been praying."

"Your expression suggests otherwise. It has been several hours since they were abducted, yes. But perhaps Beauty and Savannah have found their way to freedom and all we have to do is wait."

Yeah, Ennis thought. Wait and lose his mind...

35

At first, Savannah wanted to call it luck. In her heart, she called it God's intervention. When Jeffrey chose Georgia as his next victim, he probably hadn't anticipated an argument. She assumed Cole grew rather weary of his stepbrother's bullying but when he refused to untie Georgia, he also underestimated Jeffrey's temper.

Unlike most doctors, Holland possessed no reservations about slamming his precious fists into someone. The ferocity of his temper forced Savannah back in her seat with hopes the men avoided connecting with her. When the fighting subsided, Cole sat doubled on the floor, cringing like a man who'd been gifted with bruised ribs.

Jeffrey loomed over Cole then stabbed a finger at Georgia, "Bring her to the car now." In one last show of his authority, Jeffrey buried his foot in Cole's side, "And stop whining. You're worse than a woman."

Cole slowly rose to his feet, arm cradling his side. Without further protest, he did as instructed.

God's assistance revealed itself after Cole carried her sister outside. Savannah, frantic to help Georgia, began searching for a way to free herself. She still heard her sister's screams as they fought her into the car. A door slammed, muting Georgia's terrified cries. A second door closed then a third, followed by a car's engine roaring to life. The Cougar.

Before the car drove away, Savannah spied the scalpel sitting on the table to her left. She assumed in his fit of anger, Jeffrey forgot to take it with him. She knew her time was limited before he discovered his error and returned for it.

She stretched her left hand to the tabletop. Her ring finger carefully scooted the scalpel to the edge. Concentrating on small deliberate movements, she maneuvered it between her index finger and thumb with the blade resting against the rope. She sawed at the binding, flinching when the knife nicked her flesh. With careful, deliberate movements, the scalpel gradually sliced through the rope, severing it one cord at a time.

After what seemed an eternity, the rope fell away from her left wrist. Savannah quickly sliced the ropes securing her right wrist and ankles. Now for the hardest part. Getting up.

She took a deep breath, closed her eyes and rocked forward. The flesh peeled from the seat, sending swells of nausea and a tidal wave of fire through her. For Georgia's sake, she couldn't give up. Bracing herself with another breath, Savannah rose slightly from the seat. Muscles rioted against the movement, nerves screamed to life again. Her body implored her to sit down, to stop the pain and save her sanity.

Georgia needed her, she argued back. Only one person could help her and Savannah fought against the worst pain of her life to do it.

As she rose, the motion ripped the wounds open one excruciating inch at a time. Savannah clenched her teeth, trapping a scream behind them, only allowing a whimper to emerge. Perspiration crept to the surface, her chest glistened and her face felt cold and damp. *One more try. Just one more. You're Georgia's only hope.*

The last push peeled the wounds free and an expletive-laced cry spilled from her trembling lips. She steadied herself from the rising dizziness, wiped a shaky hand down her face. Nausea crept up her throat until she bent double, trying to heave the anguish from her body. Then her vision strayed to the chair. Blood covered the seat, inspiring another round of unsuccessful heaving. It was worse than she imagined. She expected a little blood but mostly swelling – dark memories of her childhood. But this... This was a massacre and the lingering sickness reminded her how relentless the beating was.

Concentrating became a challenge. The pain from her shoulder combined with the welts on her back robbed her of focus. Help. The word emerged from the shroud of pain. She needed to alert Ennis, the police, *anyone* that Georgia was in trouble.

Cradling her arm, she made her way to the kitchen area. A portable television sat on the cabinet along with dirty dishes and an empty pizza box. Cole, no doubt. He was a living pig pen. *Wait a minute... Cole.* She'd seen him at a computer earlier. Turning to the dining table, she saw the laptop still open, still on and apparently connected to the internet.

The screen displayed nude women engaging in various sexual acts. Above them, a banner flashed, inviting visitors to take advantage of the website's subscription discount. Savannah ran her finger over the mousepad to the tool bar listing several sites including the one hosting her webmail account. The page went blank for an instant then the homepage appeared, prompting her for a username and password. Using her left hand, she typed in the username "SCPrince". Skipping down to the password, her mind went as blank as the screen had seconds prior. What was her password? Any other day she'd remember it but pain began rooting deeper throughout her body, obscuring her brain, making it nearly impossible to think. *C'mon, it's a personal phrase, an address, a name. Wait, a* name...

Savannah typed her mother's maiden name and hit the enter key. Bingo. Now she called up Ennis's email address. She typed a rough guess of her location, following it with a quick set of directions then, "Killers are Cole and Dr. Jeff Holland. Come quick. Georgia's in trouble." After sending the mail and logging off, Savannah grabbed the scalpel from the dining table. It may have been a small weapon but as Holland proved, it could hurt like a bitch.

She turned to the door, hoping to find her sister before it was too late...

Ennis heard his phone ring a second time before he could answer it. The generic ringtone indicated it was probably Josh or Mathis. He'd waited and prayed to hear "All Shook Up" instead. Thanks to Savannah, he'd developed her quirk of personalizing his phone. She enjoyed assigning certain ringtones with people as a form of Caller ID.   Her father possessed an uncanny knack of calling at the wrong times and they were *all* wrong times, she said. Ennis thanked God R.J. hadn't called. He suspected her father resided at a bar in Augusta, drowning himself in scotch and remaining completely oblivious to the news.   Right now, that's exactly where Ennis wanted him, at least until this nightmare ended.

Ennis glanced at Caller ID: It was Mathis. Ennis clicked on, "Yeah."

"Nice chatting with you too," Mathis replied. "I ran the license plate."

A spark of hope glimmered in Ennis's mind, "And?"

"Over a thousand hits."

Spark officially snuffed. "Great."

"And Columbia Memorial's got their thumbs up their keisters. I get one moron after another and none of them known diddly. I sent Nelson over there to show 'em we mean business."

That made Ennis feel a little better. Kevin Nelson was a hard-ass detective no one messed with – not even other detectives. When he spoke, people listened or got a nice whop upside the head until they did. "Any news on Jordan?"

"Nothing yet but I'm going at it like I'm killing snakes over here. I'll keep working, Ennis. You know I will." Mathis was quiet a moment then, "Guess you haven't heard from her."

"Nothing. And if this guy runs on the same schedule as before, she and Georgia don't have much time left."

"Keep the faith, Ennis. They're both fighters so they ain't going easy," Mathis encouraged. "I'll call you if anything changes."

Ennis bid farewell to his colleague then stared at the phone. If they relied on a license plate to find the girls, he and Seth should probably start making other plans. Plans Ennis prepared months earlier when Savannah forced him to. When they should have been shopping for little Dylan's birthday, they were scouting burial plots. Seth's son received the fire truck he asked for but Savannah ended up the proud owner of a cemetery plot – just in case. Just in case…

Closing his eyes, he berated himself for being negative. As kooky as John Mathis was, he rarely mentioned faith of any kind and never labeled himself an optimist – but for some reason he still had hope for the girls. With over twenty years experience on the job, John Mathis had seen a lot in his career. His ability to read people verged on creepy. He'd known Savannah and Georgia longer than Ennis and knew how deep their stubborn streak ran. Despite his usual grouchy mood or cheeky remarks, Mathis genuinely cared for both sisters. He could find that friggin' plate, Ennis told himself. If anyone in the APD could ferret it out, it was Mathis. The man never lauded himself as a "footwork" detective. He specialized in "sit down" investigating. At his desk, at his computer, Mathis produced copious amounts of information – some of it actually useful. With two of his friends in danger, Ennis felt confident Mathis would do his "sit down" work until *his* keister grew roots to the chair.

The facts, though, kept getting in Ennis's way. If Mathis and Nelson failed to get the information from Columbia, that basically left the license plate. If Savannah and Georgia's survival depended solely on that, they needed more than hope and John Mathis. They needed a miracle. "Twenty-one, nearly twenty-two hours," Ennis shoved a hand through his hair. "Why can't we find them?" After a baleful glare at his phone, he clipped it back on his belt, allowing himself a mumbled curse. There were women present and his mama would have tanned his hide if he launched into the blue streak building inside him.

Ennis turned to see that Duke Shelton returned to his easy chair with his trusty stogie. Then he wondered how long the man had been there.

Duke drew off the cigar, blew a stream of smoke skyward, "I understand Savannah won three state championships in high school and several junior golf championships."

How the hell did golf figure into this chaos? Who *cared* about golf right now anyway?   If Shelton's intent was to strip the gears in Ennis's brain, it worked.

Duke smiled, "You need a temporary diversion while your detectives do their jobs. Since she's constantly on your mind, let's talk about Savannah's talent for golf. You know, it's not as placid a sport as people think, especially if someone has the aggressive style of play she does."

Normally Ennis would have questioned why Duke presumed to know her playing style. Not even Ennis was privy to that knowledge because she rarely spoke of her golfing days. The fact Shelton ran a person's life through a sieve answered the unspoken question, "She played high school golf. That's all I know," Ennis replied.

"She was quite the competitor too. It would be interesting to know the psychology behind her choice of sport. The violence of whacking something with a club."

Duke left the statement hanging as though expecting Ennis to expound on it. He didn't because Shelton, like anyone who knew about her childhood, already recognized why she probably chose it. It provided an outlet against her father's physical abuse. She couldn't hit back so she swung a club at a ball.

Duke proceeded, "A person can't just strike the ball haphazardly and expect successful results. Golf takes concentration, discipline, good judgment. From my brief encounters with her, I'd say she has all three. Well, apart from the attempt on my life. A brief lapse in judgment but everyone has an occasional one."

"And your point?"

"Whoever has Savannah will slip up. When they do, she will take advantage of it. Don't underestimate her, Detective. She's a smart girl."

Ennis's hands curled into fists. Shelton actually accused him of selling Savannah short. *Why, you arrogant son of a...*

"Master Shelton," a delicate whisper of a voice spoke behind Ennis and he turned. The same woman from earlier – Chantal, he remembered - held a tray with a variety of drinks and snacks. Ennis tried making eye contact but she averted her gaze, settling for bowing her head. Waves of golden tresses cascaded around her shoulders, crowding her gentle face.

Touched at the sentiment, Duke nodded to her, "It seems as though Chantal has a fondness for you, Detective. Why, without being asked, she's brought you an array of food and drink to help maintain your strength."

Chantal quickly explained, "Chantal meant no disrespect, Master Shelton. She merely intended to offer our guest –"

"On the contrary," Duke assured. "You make me proud by attending so dutifully to the detective." He waved Ennis toward the platter, "Please, Detective Rutherford, do her the courtesy of partaking." He leisurely tapped an ash from the cigar, "Savannah would want you to."

Upon closer inspection, the tray brimmed with a lot of his favorite food and drink. Between a glass of milk and a steaming cup of coffee were slices of three different pies – pecan, chocolate and coconut cream.

A thread of unease curled into his stomach. It found its way to his brain, saying Duke Shelton performed such a thorough background check on him, he probably knew what kind of underwear he wore. "These are all my favorites. How did you know?"

"The essence of a good woman, Detective," Duke answered. "My girls have an uncanny ability to read people."

"With a little meddling thrown in for good measure?"

The dominant shrugged, "That too. Please do eat. It's a shame to let it ruin. After all, Chantal did prepare the plate for you."

The girl's face lifted slightly. Hope sparkled in her big blue eyes. Eyes that weren't quite as blue as Savannah's but seeing them reminded them of his wife's. He supposed Savannah was right when she called him a pushover, "Can't hardly turn down pecan pie." He removed the saucer from the tray, followed by the coffee. He thanked her and received a contented nod in response. He sat down, placed the coffee on the side table. "I'm not all that hungry," he told Duke.

"Do what you can. Chantal wanted to help. She's more a motherly type. When someone is distressed, she believes food always helps."

The description reminded Ennis of Georgia. The woman cooked for an army when she got stressed out or when she knew someone else was. Give her a problem and she'd cook her way through it and whether she found a solution or not, everyone had plenty of good eats to fortify them.

Ennis spooned a small bite into his mouth. Memories of Savannah's pecan pie raced back. His wife began cooking more after her surgery and did a damn fine job of it. So fine a job, he'd gained four pounds.

The first bite of Savannah's pecan pie made his mouth water and his belly begged for more. Savannah was under the impression her culinary skills were subpar to Georgia's. How wrong she was, he told her. Even with radiation treatments sapping her energy, she continued to cook, refusing to surrender to the fatigue. She'd cooked until they had to share with Georgia and Dane, an unusual switch in roles between the sisters. Despite the side effects from the treatments, it was a glorious moment for her when Georgia praised her efforts and skill. After another bite of Chantal's pie, he sat it aside, yearning for those days again.

"Something wrong with the pie?" Duke inquired.

"It's fine," he said without going into detail. Intense guilt also set in. He sat in comfort, eating pecan pie while his wife and sister-in-law suffered indignities and cruelties they may not survive.

His phone chimed with a message. He didn't have time for messages. Most of them were junk and he wasn't wasting time with junk.

The phone chimed once more and when Ennis continued ignoring it, Duke asked, "What if it's important?"

"Who's gonna message me with anything important, Shelton? They've all got my phone number. That's what will get results, not some email."

"That racket will drive a person insane. For the love of God, check it."

Ennis scowled at him. If nothing else, the asshole really had balls. Ennis made a show of unclipping the phone from his belt and opening it, "Happy? Now it won't make a sound."

"Check it," the dominant ordered.

One more word and I'll throw it at you instead... But to appease him Ennis gave the message a nonchalant glance anyway. The second his eyes locked on the sender's name, his knees went weak. The message was from "SCPrince". And to think he'd initially discounted it as junk mail. "It's Savannah." Without looking up, he warned, "And don't gloat. I admit you were right."

Duke rose from his chair, abandoning the cigar to the ashtray, "What does it say?"

Ennis barely heard him. He carefully read the message that she'd typed in short brief sentences. He ran across the two names: Cole Jordan and Jeffrey Holland. A fury so intense built inside followed by a surge of crushing guilt. He should have known. He detested Cole Jordan from the start. Jeffrey Holland gave him the willies the instant he saw him. Ennis should have known...

"West of town," Duke said. In that short time, he approached Ennis from behind to read over his shoulder, "Unfortunately that could be anywhere."

Ennis pointed to one part of the message, "She gave us which highways and what exit to take." His brow furrowed as he reread the last part of it. Her directions were vague, her sentences unclear. Something was horribly wrong because her words ran together, some of them misspelled. He chose to believe nothing more dire than time constraint forced the drastic change. He couldn't bear to believe otherwise. "The rest of her message is confusing. What was she trying to say? All I understand is west of town."

"She gave us ambiguous directions in that regard but I'll get my men on it. If anyone can interpret them, they can." Duke leaned over a nearby table, retrieved a piece of paper and pen, "When you forward the message to your colleagues, forward it to these people too. They can begin the search ahead of us." He handed the slip of paper to Ennis who'd already begun the task of forwarding it to Mathis and Josh.

Duke clapped him on the shoulder, "See, Detective? As I said. She's a clever girl."

36

Savannah prayed Ennis read her message. He tended to ignore messages on his phone. He'd answer a call but pass over email and text messages. If he bothered to check it and followed her directions, he'd hopefully find his way to her and Georgia – or at least catch Cole and Jeffrey.

She started through the woods at a reasonable pace and had gone far enough the cabin was out of sight. She stayed close enough to the road to see oncoming traffic – if there was any – and stayed far enough in the trees she could hide if Cole and Jeffrey happened by.

The warm humid air clung to her bare skin as she wove her way through the mass of trees. Soft rolling thunder in the distance warned her another storm approached, shrinking the window of time to find Georgia.

The recent rain turned the dirt road into reddish brown sludge that helped her track Cole's Cougar. The men dispensed with using the Maxima, which confused her at first – unless the car's main purpose was for dumping bodies. That left Cole's XR-7 as the workhorse. If that was the case, Georgia might still be alive.

The air smelled of moist dirt after the rain. It softened the leaves and pine straw, silencing her steps as she traveled. The only problem: it also disguised anyone pursuing her. She navigated the thick carpet of pine needles and twigs with an occasional wince when they pricked the soles of her feet.

She pressed a hand to her right shoulder and winced again. Warm wet blood met her touch. She pitied the previous victims. They suffered more than she had and they probably welcomed death. For the first time in her life, Savannah understood why. Another roll of thunder made her glance skyward. Through the treetops she noticed the darkening sky. If it started raining, the storm would obliterate the car's tracks. If she lost those, she lost Georgia.

Noise drew her attention to the road. Off in the distance, she heard a car sloshing through mud. She hunkered behind a large tree, trapping a whimper as the wounds on her backside split open further. Sharp twigs dug into her knees, the tree's bark scraped her shoulder when she crouched against it. *Please don't let anyone see me. Please God, help me save my sister.*

Something small and cold splattered on her back. When another raindrop splashed her shoulder, it occurred to her. The storm, not Cole or Jeffrey might prevent her from finding Georgia.

The approaching car neared. Savannah recognized the XR-7's deep throbbing engine. It neared the curve in the road. Savannah peeked around the tree to see the Cougar churning its way toward her. Panic triggered an intrinsic desire to flee. *I can't stay here. They'll see me. They'll find me and kill me...*

Savannah forced herself to close her eyes a moment and she

inhaled a deep breath to calm herself. *Calm down. Georgia needs you.*

She ducked down to make herself as small as possible. The car rounded the corner and Savannah held her breath, waited and prayed. Keeping her ear tuned to the speed, she quietly released a tremulous breath when the Cougar's acceleration remained steady as it passed by. She waited another few beats then tentatively rose to her feet. Keeping her vision trained toward the Cougar's back bumper, she began her journey once more, careful not to venture near the road until the car was out of sight.

She pushed herself to progress faster down the road. Every second became precious since they'd discover her gone. Staying in the woods, she angled around the bend to see more deserted road and more trees. Another swell of panic struck her. How far away from the main road was she?

Cole ambushed her on a straighter stretch with an upcoming turn. If it was the same area, the main road was at least two miles off. It might as well have been a hundred. They had plenty of time to discover her absence and would be searching for her and that forced her to stay in the woods, making her trek a longer, slower one.

She'd made her way further down the road when the Cougar came into view. It flew through the sloppy ruts, spraying the nearby ravine with a tidal wave of mud. The car traveled too fast for her to hide from sight.

It slid to a stop and Cole threw open the door. He withdrew his .45 from his belt, aimed it at her, "Don't move."

If he thought she'd go willingly or quietly, he was a fool. She wasn't going back and nothing except killing her would stop her from saving her sister.

He carefully traversed the downward slope from the road, "On your knees."

Lacking a good hiding place for the scalpel, she folded her arms across her stomach to hide it. If she could just lure him… "I'm not going back there. I'll never go back."

Every step closer prompted his smile to widen, "I'm not saying you're going back. I'm saying get on your knees. It's *my* turn with you."

He charged ahead and shoved her, knocking her off balance. Savannah watched the scalpel tumble from her grasp and into the pine straw. She scrambled to catch herself before sprawling on her belly. Light glinted off the scalpel and she reached for it to hide it.

She hadn't anticipated Cole's blitz. She was now on her knees in the wet soggy leaves and pine straw. By his grin, he wanted more than that. By the erection in his jeans, he intended to get more than that.

Cole motioned with the gun, "Turn around."

Make me, asshole, she dared with her eyes.

Cole's jaw tightened. He swung back with the gun to backhand her. Savannah leaned back, missing the blow by a few inches. She swung the scalpel, slashing it across his arm.

Rapid-fire expletives filled the woods as he cradled his wounded arm. She swung the scalpel again. Warm blood spread beneath her fingers as she stabbed the knife deeper into his shoulder and twisted. Cole yelped and shoved her away, evidently not realizing he'd dropped his gun.

Savannah saw it at his feet. She needed that gun and while he appraised his wound, she scooped up the .45 just he glanced up. Pain and numbness prevented her from holding the gun in her right hand so she opted for her left with hopes she could shoot straight if necessary. Her first inclination was to ventilate the bastard six ways from Sunday but common sense prevailed, telling her he knew Georgia's location and getting that was a matter of how many bullets he wanted in him – and where.

Cold rain fell through the forest canopy, peppering her shoulders and back. The storm moved in faster than she anticipated, shortening her timeframe to rescue Georgia. The key to her whereabouts lay before her, whining and threatening her with all manner of defilement.

Savannah stepped back, aimed the .45 as best she could, "Where's Georgia?"

His hand pressed harder to his shoulder as he answered, "I'm not telling you."

She pointed the gun at his thigh and shot. He fell to the ground with a blistering curse. Savannah gave him another chance, "Tell me where she is."

He pressed his other hand to his leg, grimacing, "When I get my hands on you –"

She aimed between his legs and pulled the trigger. The report echoed between the trees, dirt sprayed up between his thighs. She stepped closer, "Where's my sister?"

Cole flinched and covered his groin, "You're too late. It doesn't matter where she is."

Savannah aimed, shot again. Cole grabbed his knee, screaming, "You bitch!"

How long was he willing to hold out, she wondered, because ammunition was running short and her aim was obviously askew.

"My aim gets better with practice," she lied then leveled the barrel at his privates again. "*Where is she?*"

He uttered a scathing curse, "In a barn on the main road. But you're too late."

She headed toward the Cougar, "You'd better pray I'm not or I'll come back and finish you off." And she would if he lied. If he was that stupid, she'd exhaust the ammo supply then beat him to death with the gun – but only *after* he told her exactly where Georgia was.

Savannah held the gun between her teeth while clawing her way up the mud-slick hill leading to the road. Once at the top, she gingerly eased herself into the Cougar's seat, grimacing from the pain. She pulled the heavy door closed, clicked the transmission into drive. A barn on the main road. She repeated it over and over because her mind started to cloud because of the sleeping pills.

She blinked, trying to keep her focus. Georgia needed her. Letting the pills take over meant failure. Jeffrey and Cole would kill them both, dispose of their bodies and resume abducting and killing women. Savannah had to save her sister and stop the men. No matter what Cole said, Georgia was alive. The sisters shared such a close bond, Savannah felt sure she'd know if her sister was gone.

Navigating the treacherous road proved challenging, not only because of the muddy conditions but the huge vehicle traveling it.

Adding to it was the rain that started in earnest when she approached the main road. She flipped on the wipers, letting them clear the windshield enough for her to search for a barn. The terrain around her looked like farmland. Farmland meant a barn somewhere, right? Farmers always needed barns.

She edged the Cougar onto the paved road, grateful to be rid of the mud. Then it occurred to her. Mud. A quick glance over the hood revealed the tracks from their earlier trip. Rain poured down in sheets and Savannah hurried before the rain obliterated them.

The drive began to look hopeless. She'd followed the Cougar's tracks until she wondered if they belonged to a different car. The pills impaired her thinking, making simple reasoning arduous and complex. These were their tracks, right? They came from the same road – a road that no one used on such an inclement day except two determined killers.

Far in the distance, an image came into view. She pressed the accelerator, driving faster until an old rickety barn seemed to rise from the horizon, growing closer with each second.

The barn's faded paint and poor condition gave it an abandoned appearance from the outside. Passers-by probably never noticed it, making it perfect for Jeffrey and Cole.

The fuzziness in her brain ebbed in and out, forcing her to concentrate harder. She steered the Cougar onto the side road leading toward the barn. The wheels dug deep into the mud but kept churning until she parked near the barn door.

Savannah abandoned the car, taking the gun with her. The closed door clung to rusty hinges and when she pulled it open, it creaked, objecting to the effort. Steady streams of rain slipped through cracks in the roof, creating pools of water inside. The smell of rain, rotting wood, moist dirt and hay mixed with something else Savannah couldn't immediately identify.

There were several bales of hay stacked in a back corner and rusted tools hanging on flimsy walls. Otherwise the place appeared empty. Cole lied, she fumed through the growing haze. He lied and Georgia was going to die.

Savannah leaned on her knees, taking a moment to gather her thoughts. Unless they drove Georgia back to the cabin, she had to be there, the muddy tracks outside proved it. She groaned at the pain rising in her body. Her shoulder ached and oozed more blood, every nerve inside her felt raw and alive.

She sidestepped tiny waterfalls pouring from the ceiling to investigate the rest of the barn. Muddy footprints led to the back near the hay bales. Heading toward them, the odd smell grew stronger. Sudden panic temporarily pushed the pain aside. The odor was blood and the area reeked of it.

Savannah clawed the bales aside and climbed the remainder like giant stair steps. When she glanced behind them, she stood in mute horror. The bales had been stacked to create a wall, secreting the ultimate depth of the men's perversity.

Behind the wall of hay bales stood a sturdy wooden table fashioned from two by fours and four by eights. Secured to the table by her hands and feet: Georgia. In her career, Savannah saw depravity beyond comprehension. What she saw before her not only fell into that category, it jumped to number one on the list. Inserted into Georgia's jugular vein was an IV catheter. Connected to that was a blood-filled plastic tube snaking from the IV to the floor, slowly draining Georgia of her life, each drop adding to an already spreading pool beneath the table.

For a moment Savannah stared, trying to accept the bizarre scene as reality. How did their lives evolve to this? Abducted by two psychopaths and having to fight for every breath and every *drop of blood* inside them?

Thunder cracked the air, breaking her daze. She called Georgia's name while finally pushing herself into action. Georgia was dying right in front of her – she only hoped it wasn't too late. Her sister remained still and quiet, generating a new panic in Savannah. With every drop, every second, time ran out.

Reaching down, she gently pressed her fingers against the other side of Georgia's neck. She breathed a sigh of relief when a slow but steady pulse drummed against her touch. "Georgia, wake up. Open your eyes," she pleaded.

Tears blurred her vision as her brain struggled about what to do. Georgia was alive but not conscious and she needed to do something quick before she jeopardized the former. *One step at a time*, Ennis always said. First, remove the IV.

She reached forward at the same time Georgia's lips parted to whisper, "They're..." Georgia continued to form words but they were so weak and quiet, Savannah couldn't understand them.

"It's okay, hon," she assured. "I'm getting rid of this and you'll be fine."

Georgia's eyes barely opened. She formed the words carefully, "They're... coming... back..."

"And we'll be gone. Georgia, stay still for me. Stay awake but stay still." Savannah reached down and peeled the tape from around the IV.

"Go... while you... can..."

"No," she ground the answer between her teeth. She hadn't come this far to give up and she absolutely refused to leave her sister to die. "And you can't make me leave either. For once in your life you have to listen to me. We're getting out of here before those bastards get back." She took a deep breath, tried to focus, "I'm taking this out now. Stay very still." Savannah secured the IV between her fingers and said a prayer. Carefully she slid it from the vein and once free, pressed her hand against the open wound. Warm blood trickled between her fingers and wouldn't stop. She bore down a little harder on the wound. Something was wrong. The blood wasn't clotting as quick as it should.

The pressure made Georgia wince and Savannah apologized while trying to keep the panic from her voice, "I'm sorry, honey. Give it a couple of minutes then I can let up." She hoped. She'd never seen blood refuse to clot. Maybe she wasn't applying enough pressure but her sister's expression said otherwise.

Georgia met her vision. The usual vibrant meadow green had faded from her eyes, "Can't walk... Too weak..."

"I'll carry you," Savannah vowed. That was a bold statement, her body challenged. Her brain joined in agreement. She had to try, she argued back. Georgia would not die because *she* was too weak from the treatments and Jeffrey's cruelty.

Georgia's brow dipped slightly. Savannah assumed she too disputed her promise to carry her. The faint whisper confirmed it, "You can't." Her eyes drifted shut, "Just go."

"Stop it, Georgia. I'm not leaving you so stop saying that." After another minute or two, Savannah eased her hand away from the wound in Georgia's neck. She breathed a sigh of relief, seeing the bleeding stopped. Now she began working on the knotted ropes binding Georgia's wrists and ankles. The rope fell free and she slid her arms beneath her sister's shoulders and knees.

Pain coursed through her shoulder and a wave of dizziness nearly staggered her, making her stumble for balance. Her feet sank deep into the pool of rainwater and warm, sticky blood. "Georgia, stay with me. Argue with me, for God's sake. Lecture me, bitch at me, *anything*."

But there was nothing. Georgia lay silent and motionless as her weight settled into Savannah's arms. The pressure and strain pushed her shoulder to its limit. Georgia kept herself trim and fit but the extra stress proved nearly too much. The radiation treatments sapped her energy for weeks. She hadn't had time to recoup her stamina in a few short days. Between the pain and sedatives, her strength depleted quick. Savannah clenched her teeth, channeling every ounce of power into her arms, "Come on, Georgia."

The haze clouding her brain rolled in like thick fog. Sleep threatened to overshadow consciousness, and with it Georgia's life would be lost. If her sister was right, the men would return and kill them both. Overcoming the medication was her only option – if she could.

She tried to shake the clarity back. It didn't work. Georgia still remained quiet and still in her arms, even as she struggled toward the stairs of hay. Climbing those would be the biggest challenge. "Stay with me, Georgia," she begged. "You told me to fight the cancer and I did. Now *you've* got to fight to live. I love you and I need you."

Blinking her vision clear, she headed to the first bale of hay. "I know Ennis will find us," she continued, hearing her speech slur. Her tongue refused to form words right. Her body suddenly lost its strength. She fell to her knees, trying to place her sister gently on the ground. She wasn't going to make it. The medication gradually won the battle, forcing her eyelids to slip down and encouraging sleep to steal in.

A dark curtain of gray shrouded her brain that soon blackened to midnight. Savannah felt herself falling, unable to fight the drugs any longer…

37

Ennis sat in the back seat of a brand new Mercedes-Benz SUV with Duke next to him and two of Shelton's men sitting in front. They'd traveled fifteen minutes but it felt like an hour to him. Every minute that ticked away, so did the lives of two people he loved.

They drove until they ran out of city. They drove until traffic thinned to a few straggling cars. They drove until the highway narrowed to a strip of road with trees towering on both sides. They did this in a deluge of rain Ennis feared would soon turn into a flood of biblical proportions.

He'd never traveled this far west out of Atlanta because he never needed to. Duke and his men could be driving him to Ohio and he'd never know the difference. Where the hell were they anyway, he wondered. So he asked.

Always the epitome of calm, Duke replied, "We are following Savannah's instructions the way my men have interpreted them. West of the city and this is west of the city."

Ennis begged to differ. "It's the friggin' Sherwood Forest. How the hell are we supposed to find them in this?" he asked, jerking his thumb toward the trees speeding past.

"The more I'm around you, the more I realize you and Savannah are two peas in the proverbial pod. Neither of you possess a shred of patience."

Normally, he possessed an abundance of patience but when every tick of the clock meant the difference between life and death, his patience ran dry. Ennis spoke over the downpour outside, "She's my wife, Shelton. Surely you can understand and overlook my anxiety."

"I can but we should navigate this road with great care. There are many dirt roads in this area and being from farm country, you understand how tricky muddy roads get."

The Mercedes was technically a sport utility vehicle but judging by the swanky interior, Mercedes really never intended for their vehicles to see mud, much less drive in it. Ennis drove an old Ford pickup at home – rear wheel drive – and still managed to travel places that newer cars didn't.

Duke turned to his driver, "Where are the others?"

"One took the road two miles west, the other the north road."

Shelton lifted a brow, "See, Detective? All covered. If they are anywhere near, we will find them."

Ennis stared out the windshield. The rain fell too hard and fast for the wipers to keep up. The torrent obliterated anything within a quarter mile ahead of them. It would be a miracle if they found the road, much less the girls.

Warren Sapp's twin drove the car. If they did run across Holland or Jordan, Ennis figured both men might hesitate to tangle with such a mountain of muscle. Riding shotgun was another of Duke's men, this one Caucasian and just as daunting – but not nearly as daunting as his choice of weaponry. The man toted a .50 caliber gun in one hand and a .45 on his hip. Ennis felt a bit intimidated by the former considering he carried a .38.

"Your colleagues are searching as well, am I correct?" Duke asked.

The question broke Ennis's stare on the .50 caliber gun. He nodded, "I forwarded the message to them. I only hope we find the girls first and I really hope we find those two bastards first." He pointed to the cannon on White Dude's hip, "I could make good use of that rascal."

"Now, now, Detective. Let's not be hasty," Duke scolded.

Ennis swiveled back to him, his silence demanding a decent explanation for such an outrageous remark.

Shelton smiled, "Wouldn't you rather take your time with them? Killing them on sight seems inefficient. Once you consider the torture their victims suffered, you can become quite creative about indignities to inflict upon Jordan and his doctor friend, don't you agree?"

Finally, Ennis thought. The man *finally* made sense. He'd had plenty of malicious ideas nesting in his brain since Georgia was abducted and they only escalated from then on. "Good point," he replied.

The rain let up a little and Warren switched the wipers from frenetic to a slower, more moderate setting, "There's a turnoff to the left up here. It's a dirt road so it's gonna be soup."

Ennis tried to remember Savannah's message. She'd mentioned a turnoff on the left side of the road – a dirt road. He only prayed this was the one out of dozens snaking through the dense wooded area. The driver seemed to know his way around the area which helped considering it looked like a hopeless maze to Ennis. He'd never seen so many trees in his life.

They approached a clearing ahead, with forest on the left and a flat open area on the right. Ennis peered out the right side window. It looked vaguely like farmland. A structure came into view ahead of them. As they neared the turn off, the shape down the road began resembling a barn. There was a car parked in front of it. "Keep going," Ennis said.

Duke stressed, "But Savannah's message clearly stated –"

"Stay on this road," he told Warren and pointed straight ahead, "and go to that building down the road." Ennis couldn't explain it. The building drew him, summoning him for some reason and if he'd learned anything, it was to follow his gut.

The structure became more defined as they approached. It was a barn. An old dilapidated structure held together with rust and cobwebs. Parked out front – another relic. One with four wheels. Ennis knew who it belonged to, "That's Jordan's car."

The dominant appraised the old XR-7 then shuddered, "The man certainly lacks taste in his choice of transportation."

He also had shit for brains, Ennis wanted to say. Because when he got hold of him and Holland, they'd never see another sunrise. No one got away with hurting his family, but what those two did to his wife and sister-in-law deserved a long, drawn-out beating then he'd put Jordan and Holland down like the rabid dogs they were.

The SUV pulled off the road alongside Cole's car. A cursory

glance revealed no one in the car but Ennis's vision locked on the front seat. Stripes of scarlet blood crisscrossed the driver's side seat. He warded off the encroaching dark thoughts. They'd come too far to give up now. With prayers – and luck – the girls were still alive.

He removed his .38 from its holster as Warren pulled the barn door wider. The door creaked then succumbed, leaving a gray shaft of light bathing the interior. Ennis lifted his weapon, his finger tightening on the trigger. If Jordan or Holland holed up inside, he wanted the first bullet in them to be his.

He eased inside then froze when a familiar odor drifted into his nose. It mingled with the smell of musty barn, rain, wet hay and dirt. His concern suddenly shifted from securing the place to finding the girls.

Duke's lip curled, "What is that smell?"

"Blood," Ennis replied. His eyes darted around the place, searching for signs of Savannah or Georgia but found no one. Rain pounded the roof, water leaked through the roof in small cascading waterfalls. It was too quiet. The hairs on the back of his neck stood painfully at attention. Something was wrong. Something was horribly wrong. "Savannah!" he called, praying for an answer.

He waited, tuned his hearing to even the slightest noise. He heard nothing except the raging storm outside so he raised his .38 again. No response from Savannah meant someone else probably drove the car to the barn – and they were still inside and possibly armed.

Ennis turned to see muddy footprints in the shadows. They led to the back of the barn. Duke and his men already headed that way so he followed. Halfway there he heard Duke call him from a dark, remote corner. Ennis glanced down. The muddy footprints led to where Shelton stood. The worst part of it – Duke's tone sounded grim. So grim that Ennis's worst fear came screaming to the forefront. The sisters had been with two serial killers for several hours... The overpowering smell of blood when he walked inside... No answer when he called Savannah's name...

Holstering his gun, he ran toward Shelton who stood behind a short wall of hay bales. The metallic smell of blood grew heavier as he neared. No, the scene wouldn't be good and Ennis prayed that whatever Duke found, it wasn't devastating. Wounds could heal, death was pretty much permanent.

Warren heaved the bales aside as if they were empty boxes. Once the way was clear, he stepped aside for Ennis to join Duke on the other side.

One step past the barrier and Ennis froze. In an area saturated with blood, Duke kneeled between two female figures, one was Georgia, the other faced away from Ennis. From his vantage point, he didn't immediately recognize the second figure. Only when he stepped forward to see the tiger tattoo at the small of her back did he realize the bloody, battered figure as his wife.

The dominant pressed his fingers against Georgia's neck for a pulse while Ennis stood horrified and speechless. This couldn't be the end, he told himself then asked God, *please* don't let it be. After all the work, all the help, after Savannah's valiant effort to save her sister and herself, this couldn't possibly end wrong. Duke's man had driven like his ass was on fire – or as fast as the rain allowed. Ennis prayed a million prayers for the girls to survive. If they arrived too late to save them, it would be the cruelest blow he'd ever been dealt.

As he neared them, his heart stopped its relentless pounding and settled into a slow, almost nonexistent rhythm. He watched Duke's fingers press against Savannah's neck. Ennis's brain pleaded with him to move, to join Shelton and see if the girls were alive but he turned instead, heaving from the shock and the smell.

Duke spoke again, this time with buoyant relief, "Ennis, they're alive. They're both alive."

The words spun Ennis back to the awful vision that would surely haunt him forever. How, he wanted to say? His wife looked anything but alive. He needed to see for himself but feared touching either sister.

Moving closer, Ennis held the back of his wrist under his nose to curb the smell. Crisscrossing Savannah's backside were several deep, elongated wounds, swollen to the point they split open. The trauma darkened the skin of her lower back and bottom to a dark plum, nearly purple color. A few other wounds slashed her upper back and a couple tracked across the backs of her thighs. Ennis recognized the cane marks from the previous victims.

Tears welled in his eyes as he uttered another prayer hoping Shelton was right. He bent down, pressed his fingers to Savannah's neck. Warmth met his touch and a slow pulse drummed against his fingertips. He swiped his tears away, "Thank God."

Ennis gently turned her to her back and his stomach threatened to revolt again. A three inch slice beneath her right collarbone still oozed blood, not enough to account for the soggy puddle he currently crouched in. That caused him to panic over Georgia. He swiveled to the older sister. Dried blood on her throat sent his stomach south again and Duke, evidently sensing it, reiterated, "She *is* alive but it's a miracle." He pointed toward a wooden table a few feet away. Loose ropes hung from the edges and on the floor lay a blood-filled tube with an IV catheter attached to the end.

A sympathy pain in his neck caused Ennis to rub the back of it. The thought of what the girls went through overwhelmed him. The sight of the wounds ached to his bones and the smell of blood became personal because it belonged to people he loved and cherished.

Duke draped his jacket over Savannah while Warren covered Georgia with his. The dominant stood and allowed a reserved smile to surface, "In fact, I believe this would be considered *two* miracles."

38

Kaiser-Lee Hospital sat nestled in a quieter section of Atlanta, away from traffic jams and the general din of the city. Ennis had heard about Kaiser-Lee but figured he'd never see it except from the outside. The place only served the swanky rich who paid for five star medical treatment, gourmet meals and room service. It employed the cream of the medical field crop – a crop that elevated the hospital's status to one of the top five in the southeast.

When Duke demanded his driver take the girls to Kaiser-Lee, Ennis's first thought was that his family would get that renowned five star care. His second thought: There wasn't a bank in town willing to loan him the money to pay their way out of the place…

For some reason, the name Duke Shelton set off a storm of activity akin to a frenzied but perfectly orchestrated drill. Doctors and nurses ran to retrieve gurneys that promptly rushed the sisters behind the trauma room doors. Ennis always assumed that stuff only happened on TV, never in real life. The blizzard of white coats engulfing his wife and sister-in-law changed his mind. "You own this place or something?" Ennis asked Duke.

"No but I've been known to contribute money now and again."

According to all the commotion, Shelton's contributions meant mountains of cash, not just a meager donation. And the room they assigned the sisters rivaled any suite in a luxury hotel. The place barely resembled a hospital with plasma TVs, entertainment center, internet service and gourmet meals delivered to patients *and* their families. The room even had two bathrooms decked out with designer soaps and shampoos and thick, velvety bath towels. Sure, Ennis had seen places like this for rich tourists who demanded posh surroundings during their stay. But this bill was *his* – well, technically his and Savannah's – but adding up every bell and whistle inspired a pang at his temple that nagged on him. Once she was released, he could imagine her tirade. One that might begin with, "Why take us to that hospital? There are dozens in the city." Or maybe he misjudged her. Perhaps her attitude would be more sedate now. Living through hell tended to change a person. Ennis only hoped it didn't destroy her.

Ennis paced back and forth while Duke sat quietly in the nearest recliner, watching him trek from the door to the window then back again. Since they arrived, Ennis tried to walk off the shock, to clear his mind of the images in the barn. To see his wife's injuries and sheer number of them swirled his stomach into a tumultuous storm. The dark plum color crept to the small of her back, making her tiger tattoo resemble a black light poster from the seventies. Then there was the slash at her collarbone. The number "1" carved so deep it required stitches. The number represented the beginning of the number ten or eleven, depending on which sister Jeffrey decided was next.

Savannah was strong but not even her iron will could withstand such injuries and those were only the physical wounds. He couldn't imagine the emotional trauma she'd endured. Once the wounds healed, she'd need a shrink. Hell, *anyone* would need a shrink after that.

Memories flooded back of the horrific scene. The instant he laid eyes on both women, he assumed they were dead. The blood and injuries spelled out the obvious. No one should have survived. Much as he detested Shelton's lifestyle, Ennis was – and always would be – grateful for his assistance and quick response getting them help.

He rubbed his forehead then wiped his palm down his face and jaw. The son of a bitching headache needed more than aspirin. It needed revenge. Thirty seconds – that's all he needed with both Jordan and Holland. Twenty-eight to break their jaws and a few other bones then two to shoot them dead.

"You're doing it again," Duke sighed.

Ennis stopped, "What?"

"That infernal pacing. If you're concerned about the bill, I can assure you it will be paid. You needn't worry." He lifted a brow at Ennis's frown. "Conserve your energy for Savannah. She will need you more than you can possibly imagine. Physical wounds heal rather quickly compared to emotional ones. The savagery was appalling but at least they weren't sexually assaulted. They won't have those unspeakable memories haunting them."

"They'll have enough haunting them." Ennis corrected. When she began showing signs of post traumatic stress, he'd suggest a shrink and then he'd get the granddaddy of tongue-lashings. She hated shrinks.

Georgia accepted them as an outlet if a person needed one. Savannah considered it a weakness for *herself.* He needed a way to present it so she might listen when the time came.

"Savannah is strong," Duke said. He waited for Ennis to meet his gaze before continuing, "She'll come through this."

Ennis hoped he was right. He flinched at the remembrance of the huge ugly welts as thick as his middle finger. The skin split open from the caning, her flesh swollen and discolored. "I don't know how this will affect her." Once the emergency seemed to be over, other thoughts took root in his brain. "We don't know what she went through."

Duke leaned back, his tone thoughtful, "You're right and she may never share her experience with anyone. Being a police officer, she's trained to keep others safe. I suspect from her point of view, she failed to keep her sister and herself safe. Beauty suffered at the hands of people Savannah was sworn to protect her against and I expect she suffered most because she tried to draw their attention away from Beauty."

Ennis's eyes welled with tears. That was *exactly* why. Savannah protected Georgia the only way she could – by luring Jordan and Holland away from her.

"I have a top-notch therapist," Duke offered. "She's very patient, understanding and discreet with questions when need be. I know police officers are guarded about such things since they don't want the department to find out. My therapist will maintain Savannah's utmost privacy. No one except you, Savannah and my therapist will know she went. If you'd rather I stay out of it, I'll only go so far as to alert her

Savannah might visit."

Ennis appreciated the thought but, "She won't go. I tried to get her into therapy when she was diagnosed and she refused."

"People can only endure so much, can only carry so much emotional weight without breaking. Her health issues tested her far beyond what she expected. This situation might change her mind about talking to a professional. Encourage her to. I intend to encourage them both to see a therapist because if nothing else, they need to cleanse their minds of those two brutes." He reached in his jacket for his phone, scrolled through names until settling on one. Duke retrieved a pen from his other pocket then began searching for something to write on. He tore off the corner of a Southern Lady magazine, scribbled a name and number then extended it to Ennis, "Try to convince her to go."

Ennis took the slip of paper, read the name. Dr. Lisa Coates. "Is she one of your," he cleared his throat to make his point. Saying the word "submissive" provoked the urge to puke and he had enough afflictions to contend with.

"Would it matter if she is one of my," Duke responded in kind by parroting the throat-clearing. "She's intelligent, receptive and reasonable on fees. Please don't impulsively judge her because of her association with me."

Ennis studied the slip of paper. Shelton had a point. If he convinced her to see a shrink, she'd insist on complete privacy, especially regarding the department. "And she's discreet you said."

"Exceptionally. Give her a call, talk to her yourself. See what you think."

He might do that. If Coates sounded open and easy to converse with, that was half the battle for Savannah who closed down like a maximum security prison.

He thanked Shelton who nodded, "Anything you need, anything the girls need, let me know. Savannah helped exonerate me and unfortunately she suffered greatly for it. I owe her an immense debt."

39

Ennis fought drifting off. Now that the crisis ended, his muscles relaxed and his eyelids drooped. His body ached from the pent up tension and implored him to sleep.

He could, he supposed, but Holland and Jordan still presented a legitimate threat. Ballsy as they were, Ennis wouldn't underestimate them again. With Holland's profession, all it took was smoothing talking a nurse and he might slip into the room and finish the job while Ennis snoozed.

Duke went home soon after leaving Dr. Lisa's name and number so Ennis paced the room for a while until the majority of his anxiety waned. The toxicology report revealed sleeping pills in Savannah's system and once she slept those off, the chore of recovery began, pain, soreness and all.

She winced in her sleep followed by a muted groan. He wondered if she relived the last day in her nightmares or if pain prompted the reaction. The doctors medicated her with morphine to help with the latter so more than likely she suffered flashbacks. No, Ennis would not be napping anytime soon, no matter how desperately he wanted or needed to. Hers and Georgia's safety came first.

Ennis brushed a knuckle against her hand. It finally felt warm to the touch. He needed the reassurance of her warmth and her slow, steady breathing.

They'd left Savannah on her left side – a position she'd sleep in for the next few weeks, they said. The swelling and bruising on her backside prevented her from resting on her back, and the wounds would cause her pain until they healed. Weeks. It was another facet in their new lives together. Having the physical wounds heal and hoping the emotional ones followed suit.

Savannah cringed then whimpered. Ennis scooped her hand in his, stroked it with his thumb. He tried to reassure her, to calm her and after several seconds, her face and muscles relaxed. A deep sigh later, she settled into the slow rhythmic breathing once more. Ennis released his own long breath, grateful the pain subsided.

He touched her forehead, smoothed her hair back. It was one of the few places spared wounds or bruises. Even her jaw and cheek showed discoloration fitting a blow across the face. Knowing Cole Jordan, she suffered several of them.

Exhaustion overwhelmed him. He'd think about it later. For the moment, he'd bask in the joy of having his wife and sister-in-law back. He held Savannah's hand in his and contemplated letting his eyes close…

He'd just made the decision to rest his eyes – not nap because napping meant he was off guard duty – when his phone rang. The jangling bugger startled him and he practically yanked himself in two trying to answer it without disturbing the girls.

Palming the phone, he rubbed his eyes then groaned upon sight of the caller. He'd planned on actually saying hello but the voice prohibited anything except paying attention.

"Where the hell is Georgia?" Dane ranted, "Is she okay?"

Cringing, Ennis pulled the phone from his ear as his brother continued at a volume probably heard in Canada, "I leave for a few days and she's *abducted*? What the hell happened, Ennis? *Is she okay?*"

Once he felt certain his older brother's yelling played out, Ennis tried to explain what happened. She'd be okay, he said, at least physically. He went on only to be interrupted by Dane whose rage fully recharged, "Why didn't you call me when it happened?"

His headache returned full force and if his brother kept yelling, Ennis's brain would explode, "I don't know. I should have and I'm sorry."

"I'll teach you about 'sorry', little brother, but first I need to check on Georgia. *Where is she?*"

"Kaiser-Lee Hospital. She's right here but she's asleep."

"And Peach?"

The words caught in his throat as a swell of emotion rose in his chest. He couldn't cry on the phone. He wouldn't but the tears welled of their own accord, "She'll be okay but she took some mighty hard licks."

"I'm flying out tonight." Dane's fiery temper flared again, "Try not to lose either one of 'em before I get there."

Yikes. Ennis stared at the phone in his hand, surprised it hadn't melted from Dane's wrath. Truthfully, he was surprised Dane heard about the whole thing. Being a farming and ranching family, the Rutherfords grew up keeping a close eye on the weather, not the national news. National news didn't kill their cattle, blizzards and tornadoes did. National news didn't tell them when the rains would come and ruin their wheat crop – the weather did. "Where did you hear about this anyway?" Ennis wanted to know.

"I ain't dead, little brother. I watch the news. Georgia got me in the habit of it."

That figured, Ennis thought.

"Ennis, keep 'em both safe. Tie a damn string to 'em if you have to but don't let 'em out of your sight." He hung up but not before Ennis heard his tirade continue to someone nearby – probably their mother.

Ennis paced the floor to wear off Dane's scathing call. His brother had every right to bitch him out but it didn't make it easier to accept. Since Dane called, Ennis braced himself for his mother's call. He dreaded that one most. She considered Georgia and Savannah the daughters she never had. She doted on them and spoiled them every chance she got. When his mother called, the cell phone towers would melt all the way to China.

The thought barely vanished when his phone rang again. Sucking in a deep breath, he braced himself for his mother's tirade. "Ma, I would've called you but –"

"But you didn't. Why didn't you call me, Ennis?" This time the voice held a ring of menace that caused Ennis's sphincter to pucker.

Everything from his toes to his brain shriveled, including his gonads which he assumed were history once Seth finished with him. If Ennis didn't die of a heart attack first, he'd try to worm his way out of this one but to do that, he needed his voice and that, strangely, had abandoned him.

As expected, Seth Prince was infuriated and Ennis was damn glad the man was in Colorado. That gave him a few states worth of breathing room to settle Seth down because frankly, the eldest Prince sounded mad enough to kill. "They are my sisters!" Seth's voice carried from the phone just as a nurse entered the room. Her eyes rounded at the shouting blasting from the tiny phone then went about her business – quickly.

Ennis worked his tongue, hoping pry it loose since his mouth dried to the consistency of cotton, "Everything happened too fast. I'm sorry I didn't call but we were busy trying to find them –"

Their brother uttered the Savior's name in a manner that shook Ennis to the core. People could cuss but not like Seth. The style and inflection was all his own. "You do *not* leave me out!" Seth pounded him with each word. "I could have been helping somehow. Looking for them, anything."

Ennis assumed Seth sent his wife and children out of the room before exploring the depths of his blue streak. At least he hoped so since Seth developed a fondness for one word in particular – the same one God highly frowned upon. "What you will do," their brother informed, "is explain what happened and where you locked up the sick bastard that did this. That's *after* you tell me how Georgia and Savannah are doing and what hospital they're in. Tell me every detail, Ennis. Leave anything out and I'll show you how Army Rangers deal with the likes of you. Read me?"

He supposed he deserved it. He unintentionally kept the family in the dark. In retrospect, not his smartest decision but he wanted the girls safe before fielding questions and irate brothers. To do that, all his energy needed to be focused on the search. Now he had to explain the "sick bastard" was actually two "sick bastards" and they were both still loose on society.

Describing Georgia's ordeal – what he knew of it – churned a nausea in his gut that only intensified as he began relating Savannah's wounds. Seth listened as patiently as Seth could, and when Ennis wrapped up the dissertation, their brother's anger mounted again, "My kids saw this shit on the news. Lindsey's old enough to understand what happened. She's beside herself, Ennis. I can't make her stop crying. She nearly lost two people she worships – while she was on vacation!"

The room's door swung open again. Ennis frowned at it. At this rate, the whole world would know how deep in dung he stood. Concrete dung, to be exact. The kind the mob used where the offender just disappeared and became a two minute headline on the news.

Seth only reinforced that fear, "What do I tell her now?" He basically yelled, "What can I tell my daughter to stop her tears, Ennis?"

Mathis and Hunter peeked around the door, probably questioning whether it was safe to enter. Ennis waved them in. He'd need someone to revive him after the verbal beating Seth gave him. He really wanted to end the phone fiasco, especially before Seth ripped into him again, "Tell Lindsey they're alive and safe. That's all I could tell our kids if we had any. Seth, I gotta go. My boss just stepped in." He quickly signed off, and took a second to settle his pounding heartbeat. Whew. Besides his mother, Ennis hoped no one else chose to call him that day. Then he thought of Savannah's father R.J. and his head began to pound in earnest.

"That their brother you was talkin' to?" Mathis asked.

More like talking *at* him, Ennis wanted to say. Leaning his head in his hand, he only managed a sick nod.

The rotund detective whistled long and low. "There's a man I'd hate to piss off. He ain't like these two," he pointed to Georgia and Savannah. "Well, he ain't like Georgia, kinda sorta like Savannah."

"Don't let Savannah hear you say that," Ennis warned. She flew mad if she heard anyone compare her to Seth. Savannah loved her brother but sometimes he scared her too. Her temper sent people back a step or two. Seth's sent people running for cover.

Josh stepped between the beds, looked at each sister, "How are they doing?"

Ennis described their wounds, finishing that Savannah was sleeping off sedatives and Georgia had the anticoagulant warfarin in her system. He continued with the projected recovery times and release dates for each sister. The tedium and redundancy of repeating it all kept his stomach in turmoil and his head feeling like the nail after a whack from a hammer. The horrible images from the barn branded into his brain with no hope of ever obliterating them. The bloody, discolored flesh swollen from all the brutal beatings. Savannah's whimper as he scooped her into his arms. Georgia's ashen complexion. He held a hand to his stomach.

He'd be glad when this hell was over.

"And they weren't..." Mathis jerked his head toward the two women as if Ennis understood the action. He didn't.

Mathis sighed, "How'd the rape kits turn out? Jeez, make me spell for you, why don't you?"

"They came back negative and when did this," he aped John's head-jerk, "become code for rape?"

"I was trying to be nice, Rutherford." Mathis pointed to the sisters, whispering, "You never know what they can hear."

Not wanting to fuel another argument, Ennis inquired about the cabin.

Mathis retrieved his notepad, flipped through a few pages, "Mud was so deep and thick Brazil woulda got lost in it. Once we finally got to the cabin, it was empty. Whatever computer she emailed you with was gone. A few sticks of furniture, a chair with blood on it and a bed that looked pretty ripe." He held a hand to his stomach, "But when I saw that back bedroom I nearly lost my lunch."

"Mathis," Hunter stopped him, nodded toward Ennis with a frown. "Ennis doesn't need to hear this." Josh changed the subject, "According to Columbia Memorial's records, Holland's address matches Jordan's. They were living together."

"Now they're both needles in a haystack over three million people big," Mathis added. "Gonna be hard finding them. Nearly impossible, if you ask me."

The last statement angered Ennis. Just because the girls were safe didn't mean the danger was gone. Holland and Jordan were determined, psychotic and now angry that their last two victims survived. Ennis figured if Dane and Seth knew about the rescue, so did the killers. He needed hope and flat-out told Mathis, "Give me some hope. He nearly killed my wife and her sister."

"We're still looking. That's all the hope I got for you. We're tracking down Jordan's rabbit holes and praying they're in one of 'em." He referred to his notes again, "After the cabin, we checked out Jordan's house. Your witness early in the investigation mentioned a late model dark sedan. According to DMV records, Holland owns a Majestic Blue 2008 Maxima. Prince was right about the partial plate but it would have taken me days to sort through them and find his. On a *positive* note," Mathis enunciated probably for Ennis's sake, "forensics is still working at Jordan's house. Maybe they'll come up with something."

Josh cleared his throat. With raised brow, Mathis sounded surprised, "Oh, I can tell him about this?"

"Don't be a smartass, John," their captain warned. "All I meant was Ennis doesn't need every detail."

God, it was like having kids, Ennis groused. Mathis wanted to lay things out in full color and their boss tried to spare Ennis the gruesome particulars.

"Okay then." Mathis referred to his notes again, "We *did* find a few things of importance. He claimed his wife left him?"

Ennis stopped rubbing his temple long enough to nod.

"She left him alright. We found her in the freezer along with a pork roast and –"

"John," Hunter warned again, this time in a harsher manner.

"Too much information now."

Mathis glanced over his glasses at his boss and apologized, "Anyway, we're guessing she was the first victim here."

Ennis was lost, "The first victim *here?* Does that mean there were others earlier on?"

Mathis blew out a breath, "Oh yeah and they are one sick set of Bobbsey Twins. They had spiral notebooks detailing other murders in the Seattle area. We also found dozens of DVDs documenting their torture. Each one was labeled with a victim's name."

Ennis's throat constricted. His heart squeezed painfully in his chest, "Any of them have Savannah's name?"

Hunter shook his head, "No. We're guessing they still have the recording with them."

Ennis breathed a tentative sigh of relief. He wasn't sure if the missing recording was a good or bad thing. Right now he couldn't worry about recordings or DVDs or what ifs – all he wanted was Savannah and Georgia safe and okay. "What did the notebooks say?" Ennis asked.

Hunter instantly raised a hand to stop Mathis and his incessant campaign for the unvarnished truth. Their boss answered instead, "From what little I read, their torture and mutilation was more of a ritual than anything. They'd do one thing, then another and so on, then return to square one and begin again until..." Hunter's voice trailed off then, "Something must have spooked them because none of this," he pointed at the girls, "matches the notebooks. You said they weren't sexually assaulted and that itself differs from their routine. What happened to Georgia should have happened after he –" Hunter caught himself again.

He quickly rephrased, "Anyway, just be glad they weren't with those bastards any longer than they were. Holland kept one woman, Eva Snyder, for five days before killing her. He had three DVDs with her name on them."

Ennis flinched. He couldn't imagine what Holland did to the woman for five days. One hundred and twenty hours of constant beatings, rape and being sliced apart. Ennis glanced at Savannah. Her wounds demonstrated one day with Holland. One day. An involuntary shiver raked Ennis. "How many women did they kill in Washington?"

"When Hunter and I left the house," Mathis replied, "they were up to seventeen."

40

Men's voices swirled around her, drawing her back to consciousness. Savannah tried to orient herself while sorting out vague memories. Ones of cutting herself loose with a scalpel, traipsing through the woods in the rain, a fight with Cole and finding Georgia in a barn. Were they memories or dreams? They felt so real but the harsh truth raced in. The men's voices meant they were figments of her imagination, wishful thinking that transferred to her subconscious.

But what had eased the unbearable pain? Certainly nothing Jeffrey gave her. Whatever relieved it, she was thankful – and not too excited about moving for fear of awakening the monster again.

The soft drone of rain reinforced the fact she was still at the cabin. She compelled her eyes to open, to face whatever hell awaited her. Her eyes refused to focus immediately but it didn't take long to realize she was lying on her left side. The bed was soft and she felt a sheet and blanket covering her. The air smelled crisp, clean. Nothing like wet leaves and pine woods mixed with sweat, urine and blood. If this was a dream, she'd savor it as long as possible.

Without alerting the men to her conscious state, she squinted, trying to bring the room into focus. The room was different too. Instead of plain dark wood paneling, white walls with flower paintings gave the room warmth and comfort.

Across from her was another occupied bed. Beyond that, a large wall of windows with open drapes revealed gray skies and the pelting downpour outside. The rain left glittering tracks along the window panes, blurring what looked like buildings in the distance.

One of the men spoke again, "When's she gonna wake up?"

Savannah swallowed hard. They were expecting her to be awake soon. Knowing Cole and Jeffrey, they'd find some cruel way to wake her. For now she'd fake it, try to be still and quiet – and free of pain…

"They said tonight or maybe morning. Just waitin' for the sedative to wear off."

Savannah's heart shifted from the rapid drumming fueled by fear to one filled with joy. She knew that voice and it didn't belong to either Cole or Jeffrey. It was Ennis! His delightful Texas accent never sounded so delightful, so perfect. Excitement brought her wide awake now, and tears trailed down her cheeks onto the pillow. She thanked God it wasn't a dream. It was as real as the growing ache in her back and shoulder. She was safe. Finally.

But who was in the bed next to hers? Not quite able to make out the person's profile, she squinted again, willing herself to concentrate. For one instant, Georgia's face came into focus. She was alive! Through her tears, she called to her sister but sound never emerged. Her tongue and throat were like cotton and somehow simply moving her jaw made her body ache.

She moved her hand and noticed an IV taped to the back. Her first instinct was to tear it out but she remembered Ennis's voice moments earlier. She and Georgia were safe. Safe from the evil of Jeffrey Holland and Cole Jordan.

Savannah stretched her arm further until pain shot through her shoulder like a flaming spear. She whimpered and reflexively drew back.

A second later, a face filled her vision. It belonged to an angel – and was the answer to her prayers during those long, agonizing hours.

Ennis smiled, his brown eyes warm enough to stave off a chilly winter night, "Hey, sugar. Welcome back."

He never looked so wonderful. Even with the five o'clock shadow darkening his cheeks and chin, even with his unruly hair curling over his forehead.

He placed a soft kiss above her brow, his voice smooth and honey sweet, "I'm so glad you're okay."

Being "okay" was a matter of opinion. She was alive, yes, but her body creaked with every movement. Muscles set up, her skin swelled and tightened. Her tongue felt like a giant woolen sock in her mouth and her brain felt two steps away from shriveled and dead. Pain still ran rampant through her, just at a lower volume.

Still, she needed to know her sister's condition. She remembered removing an IV from Georgia's jugular vein and applying pressure to the wound. Shortly afterward, everything went black. "Georgia," she whispered. The name, barely imperceptible to her, must have sounded the same to him.

His brow wrinkled then recognition registered, "Oh, *Georgia*. She's fine, babe." He brushed her hair back, "Don't worry, she'll be okay."

The gentle touch lulled her eyes closed. Just feeling his tender touch, knowing he was there...

"Hey, Prince," another voice startled her awake. Her eyes opened to see Ennis frown at John Mathis who, oblivious to it, gave her a cheery thumbs-up. "Good to see you back. You take all the time you need to recuperate. Hey, that's right. You'll have *plenty* of time to recuperate. What luck." He ended his merry greeting with a wink.

Recuperate? She'd just be glad to walk again without feeling like a bear attacked her. It would take weeks. She remembered that from childhood. R.J. never beat her as bad as Holland but the results were basically the same. Weeks of side-sleeping were in her immediate future along with showering instead of bathing and wearing nothing but loose clothing around the house.

Josh Hunter entered her view. He stepped beside John Mathis with his own frown directed at the rotund detective. "Take your time getting well. Work will be there when you're ready. We're just happy to see you and Georgia alive."

Savannah saw Mathis cut his vision to Ennis then added a sly grin of a man who just got his way. What subtle hint had she missed between the men? So much happened over the past few days, remembering any one detail seemed monumental. Then it finally hit her. Captain Hunter's threat. *Get involved in the case again and get in the unemployment line.* Apparently his stance on the subject changed.

Probably after seeing his detective beaten into a pile of hamburger meat helped salvage her job.   In the technical sense, she supposed she and Georgia solved the case – and both paid a huge price for it. Retaining her job was a nice consolation because at the current time she needed that health insurance and the steady income. But what she truly needed was to be able to sit and be normal again.

She tried asking a question then realized her mouth hadn't caught up to her brain yet. Ennis leaned nearer for a rerun.

She closed her eyes to concentrate, carefully enunciating each word, "Did you catch them?" Meaning Holland and Jordan.

Ennis broke eye contact. That told her all she needed to know. When he kissed her again, he offered an apology then, "They're still looking. We'll get 'em, sugar. The important thing is you and Georgia are safe."

She had to tell them what she knew, even if it took all day – which it might at the rate her mouth moved. "Jordan's wounded. I shot him. Check the hospitals."

Ennis relayed the information to Mathis who wrote it down. While he was in the note-taking mood, she'd broach another difficult subject, "There's…" She tried to clear her throat and waved Ennis closer. She wanted her words as precise as possible, "There's a recording of what Holland did to me."

He winced at the statement and his warm dark eyes shifted away. His sudden inability to meet her gaze told her he already knew it existed.

Hunter glanced around Ennis's shoulder, "We haven't found yours or Georgia's yet. When we do, we'll use discretion. There are plenty of other DVDs that will buy those bastards the death penalty." Josh tried for a comforting smile, "Your main goal is to get rest and get well. Don't muddy things up by worrying."

Mathis peered over his glasses at her, "You're better than Timex. You take one hell of a licking and keep on ticking."

The statement rendered Ennis and Hunter speechless. Impervious to their incredulity, Mathis shrugged, "What? It's a compliment. It's better than saying she's a tough broad, ain't it?"

41

Five-thirty. Ennis stared at the clock, curious how long a human could sleep. She spent the better part of two days in bed with brief breaks for bathroom visits and eating meals – if one could call half a sandwich a meal. If her injuries weren't enough to worry about, he consumed himself with her lack of appetite and now the resulting weight loss.

Adding to his worries were Savannah's sleep habits. She slept sounder than the residents at the local cemeteries. He rethought that. No, the dead didn't groan and jerk themselves awake with pain. Their pain was over, hers wasn't.

I'm going nuts here. He searched the room for something to do. He'd straightened the kitchen and living room. Taken time to sweep and remembered to pay bills. Anything to stay busy. His vision settled on the daily paper. Despite his lack of in-depth knowledge of them, he kicked back to try a crossword puzzle. It took less than five minutes to realize he was in over his head. Every answer ended up being wrong, despite every answer fitting just right in the stupid little squares. He tried again. *Four letter word for lasso. That's easy.* In each respective box he wrote an R then O, P then E. Rope. The word intersecting the O worked fine. It turned out the word intersecting the R didn't fit because he didn't know a seven letter word for "knife". And why in hell were they putting words like rope and knife in a damn crossword puzzle anyway? What was it, the serial killer edition? That thought snapped the final twig of patience he had. He tossed the paper aside with a frustrated sigh, concluding either he needed a better education or more rest. He certainly needed to rid himself of the memories of Savannah and Georgia in the old barn.

A noise from the bedroom caught his attention. Every noise did now. This sound, however, became too familiar over the last two days. Savannah whimpering herself awake. He held his breath, waiting. Would the aching keep her awake or ease enough to let her drift off again? Counting the seconds, he released the breath when she settled back to sleep.

If I ever get my hands on those bastards, Ennis vowed then realized his hand ached. Looking down, he'd squeezed it into a rock hard fist. As far as he was concerned, Jeffrey Holland and Cole Jordan were dead men walking.

His vision strayed to the golf bag leaning against the TV. She'd dragged her clubs out a week ago to polish them and use them. Ennis gnashed his teeth. Now her dream of resuming her greatest talent had to wait until the nightmare ended with the killers arrested and her physical and emotional wounds healed.

Well, he could expedite the process by helping her in one respect. Rising from the couch, he meandered toward the golf bag. Removing an iron, he appraised it, gave it a test swing then leaned it against the wall.

Unzipping a side pocket, he found a polishing cloth neatly folded, ready to use. When he removed it, an envelope followed, its corner caught on the cloth. Ennis debated about tucking it back but curiosity won out. She rarely spoke of her golfing days, leaving him intrigued even more about her past.

The return address in the upper left corner had an emblem he recognized all too well after moving to Atlanta. The logo belonged to the University of Georgia. The recipient: Savannah Prince at her home address in Augusta. He peeked into the bedroom, saw her still asleep. He opened the envelope and read. By the end of the first paragraph, he stood in stunned amazement, whispering, "A full athletic scholarship."

Once the shock subsided, he noted the date and counted back. Her senior year. The realization made Ennis wince. It was the year her mother was diagnosed with breast cancer. It didn't take him long to put the puzzle together. Savannah began drinking after her mother's diagnosis and her golf game, he assumed, took a header.

His heart broke for her. She was on the way to play for a major university when the tragic news came of her mother's condition. He stared at the five iron then looked back at the letter. His hope was after Savannah recovered, she'd proceed with golfing, at least as a diversion.

Reaching into the same pocket, he found two more letters, these from the Universities of Tennessee and Alabama, both full scholarships. The reason she tucked her trophies in the guest room and out of sight, finally registered with him. The memories were too painful to see every day.

Ennis reached in for her putter, quietly lifting it from the bag.

From the corner of his eye, he spied yet another envelope peeking from one of the other pockets. He reached in for the large package and behind it, he felt another piece of paper, this one small and lacking an envelope. He might as well throw himself into the frying pan. If she awoke while he nosed through everything, he'd claim ignorance and hope it worked.

He took everything back to the couch and leaned the putter against the cushion. He wanted to know the contents of the envelope before she woke up but first he carefully unfolded the worn piece of paper. It had seen many years, according to the faded writing and worn creases. The penmanship showed signs of a young girl trying to refine her cursive to appear as adult as the contract she wrote, "I promise to pay Grandpa Prince one dollar every year to pay for my golf clubs." At the bottom was Savannah's signature, the tentative script much different than today's confident flair. She'd signed with her first, middle and last name. Below hers was a bold, blue signature reading only, "Grandpa." Ennis smiled, folded the paper carefully, set it aside. The insight to his wife both intrigued and saddened him. Her grandfather seemed like a nice enough guy unlike his son. Ennis could only imagine how R.J. reacted. He probably fought her from dawn to dark, forbidding her to play. Knowing R.J., he called it useless and a waste of time.

Ennis turned his attention to the large envelope. The front of it had Georgia's return address on it. The recipient again was Savannah at the family home in Augusta. He opened it, turned it upside down and watched a plethora of letters and newspaper clippings litter the couch. Some letters were from Georgia, others from Seth during his time in the army. The clippings were all from the Augusta Chronicle or Atlanta

Journal Constitution. As he perused them, they highlighted her talents with headlines "Prince's Power Play" and "Augusta's Stealth Bomber". He read through them all, each describing her violent yet accurate swing. Another mentioned how "she picked opponents apart with her short game and demolished them with her driving skills." Reading the clippings gave him a new perspective into his wife. And when he saw the pictures of her, he saw a beautiful girl whose smile could break a thousand hearts.

"Ennis," she called, her voice throaty and rough from sleep.

He carefully pushed the clippings aside and rushed to the bedroom, "What is it, babe?"

"I have to get up. I'm stiff as a board."

A little alarm went off in his brain. *She'll see all your trolling and she'll be mad.* "Sure you want to? How about a quick shower to loosen up?"

She shook her head, reached for his hand. "I miss being with you."

Well, he couldn't argue with that. He'd missed every moment they were apart and worried himself dog sick since seeing the damage the men had done. Ennis took her hand, helped her up.

Savannah groaned herself to her feet. Ennis winced with her as wounds awakened with the movement.

Ennis grabbed her fluffy pink robe from the nearby chair, helped her on with it, tied it at her waist. He eased one arm around her, careful not to disturb the wounds on her back.

She took baby steps, drunken ones, as she leaned against him for support. The painkillers knocked her so far on her ass, standing became a challenge. As they slowly plodded to the living room, she pressed her hand to his stomach for stability. Her other arm wrapped across his hips, pulled him closer.

The second they stepped in the living room, her eyes trained on the chaos on the couch. He explained, "I was going to polish your clubs. I found those with the polishing cloth…"

Savannah reached for a scholarship letter, glanced at it then tossed it to the coffee table, "I oughta throw those away. Nothing came of golf anyhow."

Uh-oh… Her tone reverted back to the monotone indifference of the last few days. He wouldn't let her give up on her one and only passion. No way in hell, "I'll pack 'em away. As for the clubs, you're taking 'em out as soon as you're healed. Hear me?" He bunched some pillows together, making a soft nest for her to sit on.

She gingerly eased herself onto the couch. After another subdued groan, she settled inch by inch onto the pillows until finally releasing a long breath. "I probably stink at it now. I know how to play, the mechanics, strategies and all, but I've probably lost my touch."

"You'll do fine," he gently argued. His vision passed across the agreement she'd written so long ago. "I ran across a contract between you and your grandfather."

The mention of it didn't ruffle her as he expected. Instead she followed his vision to the paper, "Daddy threw a fit when he found out I wanted to play. I was eight years old. Grandpa Prince bought my first set of clubs with only one condition. I had to join the Georgia Junior

Golf Foundation. Daddy didn't like it but coped. When I grew out of the first set of clubs, Grandpa offered to buy another set and Daddy blew up and said if I wanted the clubs, I'd damn well pay Grandpa back and put it in writing. Grandpa got mad but agreed I could pay him one dollar a year. I wanted to pay more so I worked in the orchards to pay him off sooner."

Ennis slid his arm across her shoulders, "I like your grandpa."

"He thought the contract was ridiculous but signed it anyway. I kept it in my bag all those years for good luck." She leaned against him, staring at the golf clubs and the absolute mess he'd made. He felt her relax, something she rarely did lately, and he held her close.

She glanced beside him to see the crossword puzzle. After a quizzical look, she inquired, "Since when do you do crosswords?"

"Since you've been sleeping. Don't worry, there's no threat of me trying again."

Savannah focused on the puzzle. Glad she finally showed interest in something, Ennis handed it over then reached for her glasses on the coffee table.

She rubbed her eyes, slid on her glasses then studied the puzzle. "The word you're looking for is 'cutlass'."

Ennis handed her the pencil. Hell, if she wanted to do puzzles, he'd give her all the tools she needed. Watching her fill in the word, he nearly smiled. It disappeared when she erased "rope". "That shoulda been rope. I mean, lasso? No-brainer, right?"

"Growing up in Texas, sure. But in this case it's 'cord'." She wrote the answer in and handed it back, "Here you go."

He waved it off, "I think your brain is more geared for it than mine." He watched the genuine beginnings of a smile curve her lips. He returned the gesture, feeling the tension melt from his body. He'd just been given a rare and priceless gift. A smile. Maybe, he thought, just maybe things would return to normal.

The phone rang which told him in some cases, yes, things were returning to normal faster than he wanted. The damn thing rang off the wall since they'd been home. Ennis reached to answer it then wished he hadn't. "Is she up?" her brother asked with the chilliest reception Ennis ever received.

"Just now," was all he said.

"Let me talk to her," Seth demanded.

Ennis had had about enough of Seth Prince. For the last few days, their brother refused to acknowledge his existence unless forced to. Ennis realized he screwed up but the continual snubbing prickled him now. Before saying another word, Ennis heard Seth's wife Leah in the background, "Seth, be nice."

Ennis waited to see if Seth was capable of it. Their brother sighed, "Let me talk to Savannah *please.*" It fell far below the category of "nice" but at least he hadn't ground the words between his teeth. Ennis handed the phone to Savannah, "Seth."

He hadn't complained about Seth's aloofness however Savannah noticed it in the hospital and tried a diplomatic approach with her brother. Ennis figured it was because little Lindsey and Dylan were present, otherwise she'd have used far more colorful language with him.

As for Ennis, he chose to ignore Seth's behavior because he had more important things to worry about. Number one on his list was getting his wife help. He racked his brain for palatable ways to mention a shrink to her without losing some teeth in the process.

Ennis listened as she greeted her brother and heard him immediately launch into another campaign insisting she have someone at the house to "protect" her. Seth evidently forgot his sister's tenacity. She didn't want anyone, she said, because she had Ennis. "I trust him to protect me," she told Seth, "so stop overreacting."

Ennis noticed when a subject upset Seth, the man's voice carried like thunder. Without considering decibels or manners, he let his feelings fly and they flew loudly. This time was no different, "Savannah, Ennis would lose his shadow if it wasn't attached to him. Let me send my friend over."

Savannah's jaw set and her body tensed – not from pain either. "Don't talk about Ennis like that. You've treated him like an alley cat since you got back. He's my husband and I love and trust him."

Ennis stretched his hand out for hers and she grasped it with surprising strength. Oh yeah, she was mad. The fingers around his hand suddenly squeezed much like the words between her teeth, "Don't make me hang up on you." There was a pause then, "Then stop insulting and ignoring him. I know you're worried."

Ennis felt her body tense, this time from a sudden twinge then after a grimace, she relaxed again. "I'm fine and I only want Ennis for protection," she stated as fact. Many times Seth used his daughter as leverage to get his way. He figured it was about time Seth would bring out the kids. Seth didn't just introduce them, he hammered Savannah with them. "Let's ask your niece what she thinks," he barked at her. "You know, the niece who cried all the way from Colorado because her two aunts – who she loves more than life – nearly died."

Ennis felt his temper rising at her brother's brutal approach. At the same time, his heart sank. Just when he pried a smile from Savannah, Seth had to wreck it. Ennis remained silent since he'd experienced the quirky way the Prince siblings worked out their problems. Still, considering the last week, Seth should've shut up. What her brother probably hadn't anticipated was the emotion in her voice.

Savannah removed her glasses, swiped away growing tears, "That's below the belt, Seth. I never wanted to hurt Lindsey and you know it."

Her brother's voice softened where Ennis couldn't hear it. Whatever her brother said, it inspired more tears. Sometimes, he hated Seth's attitude. Without question, he was a younger R.J. with his "my way or the highway" approach.

Ennis leaned over, stripped a tissue from the box on the coffee table and handed it to her. She dabbed at the tears and after a few more exchanges, Savannah hung up, defeated and disgusted. She dropped the phone in her lap and sighed.

Ennis retrieved the phone, placed it back on the table, "I didn't appreciate his brutal tactics."

"Makes two of us," she said. "I don't need this. *We* don't need it. I heard the same shit from Daddy and now him. I'm sick of it."

"I'm not their favorite person right now," he confessed. And he probably never would be.

"Well, you're my favorite person and that's what counts. They can shove their opinions." She twisted the tissue between her fingers, her stare fixed somewhere beyond the coffee table.

He fought the urge to slide his arm across her shoulders because of the wound there. Instead, he slid his hand in hers again, clasping it. The simple gesture brought more tears, "He treats me like I'm nine because that's how old I was when he left home. I'm not nine, I'm an adult and I'm really tired of people telling me what to do. Holland did it, Jordan did it and now Seth." She cringed, "Most of all, I'm *really* tired of hurting."

His gut clenched at the sight of her tears, his heart ached to soothe her, comfort her, to make everything right again. Ennis tilted her chin, bringing her vision to his, "Babe, stop thinking about it. They're never coming near you again."

"You can't say that," she argued. "They're out there stalking other women, maybe even Georgia or me. No one knows."

"They'd be crazy to stay here. You have to believe it."

Judging by her reaction, he'd unintentionally triggered a sore subject with her. She shored up her composure, "Ennis, they are psychopaths. They finish what they start. If they want us, they'll come for us."

He hated bringing up the therapist angle but now seemed the best time of any. Savannah's paranoia rooted deeper every day. She reacted to every noise, however small. The phone ringing, silverware clanking in the sink, screams or gunshots on a TV show – they all tested her nerves but mostly her reflexes. No matter the sound, she reached for her gun. That's when Ennis pulled the shrink's name and number from his wallet. Savannah needed help. "Georgia went to see the doc Shelton recommended. She said the girl is pretty good."

"If Georgia needs therapy, I'm glad she went. I don't need a shrink."

Ennis refused to blast her with facts or guilt her like her brother. His method was to ease into the subject, "Consider her someone to talk to, not a shrink."

"I talk to you."

"You can always talk to me but that's not my point. You need to share your feelings with another person, someone who isn't emotionally involved."

A distinct change occurred in his wife. The tears disappeared, her body tensed and her jaw set somewhere between concrete and steel. Her body language promised she wasn't budging but if he kept pressing the issue *he* certainly would be – right off the couch.

"Why would I do that?" she wanted to know. "Why would I tell a stranger I was tied up and beat so hard my ass looks like hamburger meat? Why would I tell a stranger how it felt for that blade to sink into my flesh and slice me open just so some nutcase could carve a number into me? Tell me, Ennis. Why would I do that?"

She played hardball, fine. He would too because whether she realized it or not, her life depended on it. "Because it will haunt you until you do. You will suffer nightmares and those horrible images forever but maybe they'll become less frequent if you see this girl. If you won't do it for yourself, do it for me. I want you to go see her."

Savannah clenched her teeth, trapping whatever reply lingered on her tongue. Judging by her expression, he really didn't want to hear it anyway. He'd give her more time then try again. The incessant violent nightmares would drive her to it, he'd bet on it.

He watched her swallow the heated reply and settle for a straightforward, expletive free, "No."

42

The doorbell rang again. The caller clearly couldn't take a hint. Savannah refused to jeopardize her safety because some clod had lead in his thumb and air between his ears. Only seven short days passed since her release from the hospital and still the concept of opening the front door – *her own* front door – terrified her. What if Cole stood on the other side? What if Holland did? She proved herself against Cole. All she needed was a gun and she carried that in her bathrobe. Mortified that she'd basically become Grandma Culberson, Savannah understood the woman's paranoia. Sure, as a teenager Savannah thought Grandma had a few screws loose. Who lugged a pearl handled .38 in her apron all the time, even when she gardened? Savannah now knew the answer to that question.

As much as Cole scared Savannah, Holland frightened the bejeezus out of her. The man's cool composure never shattered except with Cole. With women, his poise remained unwavering with knowledge he could easily end their lives with one swipe of a scalpel. He remained calm and in control, no matter the woman's screams or her pleas.

The gun soon became an issue in the household. Ennis worried she'd accidentally shoot him, the mailman or paperboy. What she needed instead of that gun, he said, was to see a shrink. Even with his careful wording of "doctor" she'd bowed up for a verbal fight. She didn't need a shrink, she told him, she needed them to arrest or kill Jeffrey Holland and Cole Jordan. Then she could sleep. Then she could rest. Then her life would be normal again.

Heading toward the bedroom, the sound of the doorbell riled her, especially when the interloper took to knocking on the door too. Once the knocking ceased, she heard someone calling for her. The voice sounded deep, too deep for Holland or Jordan.

With great caution and absolute silence, she tiptoed to the door. Savannah squinted out the peephole to see a huge black man, his hands propped on a tall box.

He leaned toward the peephole which backed her away from it.

"Missus?" he called. "Are you there?"

She recognized Duke's man – the one she called Warren Sapp. Why was he banging on her door and what was in the huge box? "Just a minute," she replied to the door while retying her robe and tucking the gun deep in the pocket. No need to let the world know she was a head case right now.

Twisting the deadbolt open, she opened the door and the man smiled, "I'm glad you're home, Missus. The boss wanted me to drop this off for you."

In his black suit and shined shoes, Warren looked overdressed for such a task. Delivery men usually didn't deck out to the nines. "It's enormous," she said. "What is it?"

He heaved the box into his arms like it was light as a feather and stepped past her, "That's your job, Missus. You dig into this and you'll find out."

Mr. Warren Sapp displayed a proud grin. She would love the contents of the mystery box, it said. Really love it.

"You're looking fine," he mentioned. "Much better than the last time I saw you."

She expected so. The last time he saw her she was naked, filleted, beaten black and blue and lying in a pool of blood. Anything would have been an improvement but she thanked him anyway.

When Warren sat it down, she heard something clunk inside. That couldn't be good, she figured. Presents that clunked usually meant damaged in transit but she'd be a brave little soldier and tear into it, whatever it was.

She went to the kitchen for a knife to open the box. He called her back, saying, "You can use mine." He unfolded a pocket knife and handed it to her. Careful to slice down the tape's seam, she heard another clunk, a metallic one. *Okay, it's officially weird now. How exactly does metal break?*

Savannah glanced at Warren who still looked as excited as a kid on Christmas morning. The clanking hadn't flustered him a bit. "Need help with that?" he offered.

Handing the knife back, she replied, "Go for it, Warren."

His smile never faded but he stopped a moment then grinned

bigger, "The name's Abel, Missus. I been told I look like Warren Sapp. Is that who you meant?"

Abel. Why not? She just hoped he didn't have a brother named Cain. Abel was a sweet man – when unprovoked. "That would be the one."

He tore into the box with great enthusiasm. So much so, it backed her off a step. Yep, a nice, laid-back gentleman unless provoked *or* ripping into gifts.

Flattered at the comparison, he nodded his thanks while slicing through the cardboard with such ease, her shoulder ached with a reminder of Jeffrey's scalpel. Instinctively, she reached to touch it but managed to stop herself.

He cut the box all the way to the floor then stood up, "The boss says if these don't fit right, let him know and he'll have you fitted by a professional."

As much as she began to like Duke Shelton, Hell would freeze before she allowed someone associated with a dominant to "fit" her for anything. Considering his line of work, the mystery in the box took on a slightly darker undertone. He wouldn't be insensitive enough to send bondage equipment, she assured herself, especially knowing her stance on the subject. But what else clanked and clattered in a box from a professional dominant?

Abel folded the knife, slipped it in his pocket, "There you are, Missus. Take a look."

She prayed it was G-rated, whatever it was. Abel opened the side facing him so she stepped around the giant box and mentally braced herself.

Guardedly, she peeked in like it contained a snake about to strike. There were no snakes, no bondage equipment. Nothing she feared it might be. Taking another look, her heart skipped a beat. Her stomach fluttered in a way she hadn't felt since high school. Abel's smile had been on the money. She *loved* the contents.

Before her stood a full set of golf clubs nested inside a brand new pink golf bag. Abel motioned to her, "Go ahead, take one out."

She couldn't take them, she reminded herself. The department would kick her ass and frankly she was tired of that happening. But touching them, feeling a club in her hands again, they couldn't penalize her for that.

She chose the eight iron. Sliding the club out of the bag, she basked in how lightweight it felt. Different from her high school clubs. These were state-of-the-art gems, the newest design and material and oh, did she *crave* to use them.

Her vision wandered to the club head and the fantasy came to a grinding halt. There was leading-edge then there was the *titanium* leading-edge. She nearly choked upon sight of the insignia, "These are some of the priciest clubs available." She readjusted her grasp as if she held a piece of rare china. If she'd realized the cost, she wouldn't have allowed herself the dream of swinging such a sleek, beautiful club.

Abel's grin engulfed a good part of his face as he hoisted the golf bag into his hand, "Where do you want 'em? How about over there so you can see 'em? Boss says you need to get out more. Can't go wrong with these sweethearts."

She was still feeling up the eight iron – carefully – and still entertaining images of being on a golf course again. Then reality intruded, "Abel, you have to take these back. It's against department policy to accept gifts. Tell Duke I appreciate the thought – no, tell him I *really* appreciate the thought, but I can't."

He shook his head, "Not when you got the same look as my mama when she sees a rib roast. Boss told me to leave 'em and I think I'll leave 'em right here." He sat the bag in a corner behind a chair. Her chair. Great. So she'd see them every time she walked through the living room. Perfect.

Abel intended to follow his boss's instructions – something she'd decided to try more often herself with her own job. No need trying to convince him otherwise, she decided. "I'll take it up with Duke later."

A chuckle bubbled from his cheery smile, "You can try. Boss has a knack for getting his way."

Savannah intended to try very hard to send the beautiful clubs back. The brand new, expensive, graphite shaft, titanium head, perfectly-fitting clubs. She gave the pink golf bag a baleful glare. Why did they have to be perfect? The length could have been too short for her and they *should have been.* Most clubs were too short for her height. Duke knew she was five nine but how did he know the distance between her hands and the ground when she addressed the ball? He'd never seen her swing a club and both club length and space between the hands and ground were crucial when determining the right clubs for a person.

He knew her skill level – at least in high school – but how did he know how fast she swung a club or which club she used at the one hundred fifty yard marker? The man was like Santa Claus or God. He knew everything about her and without delving too far into that thought, it impressed and kinda scared her.

She'd give the putter a test drive before calling. Might as well enjoy them while she had them. Her shoulder prevented much movement until the stitches were removed but she'd still get the pleasure of holding a hugely expensive, magnificent club – until having them voluntarily repossessed.

A little thrill wound its way through her as she lined up an imaginary putt, gave the club a gentle swing. Then she groaned. They were *perfect…* Now they were like the hungry puppy sitting on the porch, whining for a warm place to stay. You couldn't just bring it in for one night without getting attached.

Get rid of them, her conscience demanded. *Now, before you jeopardize the job you nearly lost.*

She slid the putter back in the bag then headed straight for the phone. She'd written Duke's number on a slip of paper during the investigation and Ennis hadn't moved it. It sat there, waiting for her to contact Duke Shelton and order him to remove the generous, exquisite gift from her custody. The gift that, if she kept it, would eventually keep on giving once she healed and Jordan and Holland were caught. The absolute ideal gift and she could not keep it. Shit.

She dialed and waited. After two rings, the uppity British accent answered. She asked to speak to Duke.

"Who may I ask is calling?" the gruff tone inquired.

Some things never change, she sneered at the phone. *He's just as congenial as I remember.* "Savannah Prince."

To her amazement, the voice thawed instantly, "Yes, ma'am. Right away."

Pigs must be flying somewhere, Savannah thought and pulled the dining room curtain back to check. No airborne swine yet.

"Savannah, how wonderful to hear from you." Duke's voice had the soft lilt she remembered from their first meeting.

"Hello, Mr. Shelton."

He chuckled, "We've been through too much to continue with formalities, my dear. If you don't call me Duke, you will break my heart."

She capitulated, "Okay, you win. Thank you for the clubs. I love them but –"

"And are they acceptable?"

Acceptable? That was the understatement of the year. "They're beautiful. I'd never be able to afford them." Titanium, her brain taunted. Graphite shaft. *Are you sure you want to toss them back?* "Like I said, I love them and I appreciate the gesture but I can't accept them."

"Nonsense!" he exclaimed like it was the most outrageous thing he'd ever heard. "It's the least I could do."

"No, Duke, I *really* can't accept them. Department rules –"

"My dear, first of all they are a gift from a friend. Your birthday is coming up. Your superiors cannot argue with a birthday gift from a friend. Geminis are known to have lots of energy and like to stay busy. Those clubs will come in handy."

That's probably why Mama was always afraid to leave me alone. She was afraid I'd dismantle the blender. She applauded Duke for his diplomatic phrasing. Geminis were known for their energy but what he neglected to specify was their usual lack of dedication to activities. It was as if that sign was deemed the Attention Deficit Disorder child of the zodiac. She hoped she proved the "experts" wrong by sticking with golf in her younger years and police work later.

"Secondly, and this is just between us," Duke continued, "those clubs are also a mere pittance of my gratitude for your exonerating my name. I'm sorry you suffered to do it but remember, if it weren't for you, I'd be in jail for murder. If your superiors say one word to you, I shall intervene. Besides, I intend to make a healthy contribution to their widows and orphans fund. Now tell me. Do the clubs fit properly?"

"Somehow you know they do. I'm not sure I want to find out *how* you determined the right measurements though."

"Trade secret, I'm afraid. Couldn't tell you even if you twisted my arm." He gave a satisfied sigh, "Now, how are you healing?"

The mention of it gave her a twinge in her shoulder. "Slowly but getting there."

"And emotionally?"

She took time to think that one over. Sleeping only produced nightmares. In the daytime she investigated every sound or movement outside – but only when Ennis was home. Otherwise she stayed in with the gun. "The same," she elected to say. "Slow but getting there, I guess."

Duke's tone softened, "Did Ennis give you the name of the doctor I recommended?"

"He did but I can deal with this without a shrink."

He paused then, "Asking for help is not a sign of weakness, my dear. Asking for help is merely asking for help. She's an excellent doctor."

"I'm sure she is. I'll keep her number but I probably won't see her."

"It is your choice but I ask that you do not set your mind against going. There may come a day you find no other release from the pain."

Savannah fought from clenching her jaw. What was it with everyone? She dealt with her father's beatings without a shrink. Yes, his beatings paled in comparison but disclosing what Holland and Jordan did, exposing herself again – to another stranger – didn't set well. The last thing she wanted to do was relive the horror. Explaining the details of her ordeal forced her to relive it. She did that enough in her sleep.

To appease Duke, she agreed but in her heart, she realized he sensed the lie. With time she'd heal, she told herself. She only needed time.

43

"You get any skinnier and you'll have to run around in the shower to get wet." Dane's statement was met with a solid jab from Georgia's elbow. Dane flinched, "I was just tellin' her to gain weight. Sheesh."

Savannah didn't take offense. She'd heard it numerous times in various ways from her husband. It only stood to reason his brother would join the chorus. Dane merely chose a more colorful avenue of voicing his opinion.

Still cradling the foil covered casserole, Georgia tastefully rephrased, "What Dane means is you should eat a healthy serving of this." The older sister shrugged between her sweetie and her sister to set the thirteen by nine inch dish on the table. Georgia brought the casserole over piping hot from home. Her older sister enjoyed cooking and when the moment struck, Georgia spent hours preparing and creating meals that would feed army battalions – with plenty of leftovers. With Ennis's concern over Savannah's weight, it probably inspired Georgia to begin preparing meals to tempt her appetite. She just never expected so many meals and she sure never expected people to monitor *how much* she ate.

The air filled with the rich aroma of ham from the casserole.

Georgia certainly knew her weakness and capitalized on it. Generally anything involving ham brought Savannah front and center, fork in hand, ready to begin an embarrassing sight of obscene mindless consumption. Georgia's latest culinary delight smelled heavenly but Savannah also caught a whiff of a conspiracy – one engineered by Ennis.

Savannah followed her sister to the kitchen. Georgia already pulled two plates from the cabinet and headed to the table. "Georgia," she said, "I appreciate your efforts but you have to stop. You're wearing yourself out cooking and I'm really not hungry."

"You're eating." The older sister delivered the declaration in the same delicate manner as the German Blitz. No questions, no options, it was happening so cope.

Georgia sat the plates on the table then returned to the kitchen. Savannah's kitchen took little effort to maneuver in. It took a total of five steps to reach either end and two steps from front to back. The stove and oven were one unit which was a blessing considering the cabinets felt cramped as it was. Arranging the place was simple when she lived alone. Now that she was married, it required more plates, silverware, cookware and serving dishes. They all needed places to live and they weren't welcome in the living room or bedroom so she found ways to nip and tuck them into their respective spots. The layout would intimidate most people since the configuration took nothing short of a Rubik's Cube solution to untangle them. Georgia, on the other hand, pushed, pulled, shoved and repositioned everything in just the correct manner to release whatever she needed.

Georgia went straight to a drawer which she opened, scooped

silverware into her hand and turned to face her younger sibling, "How much do you weigh?"

Savannah cinched the robe tighter. Of all the questions… She'd hoped the big, fluffy robe might hide some of the weight loss. She hadn't expected her sister to blatantly interrogate her about it – especially in front of Dane, "Normally, that question is grounds for a fight, especially when asked in front of menfolk."

"Savannah, how much?" the older sister pressed.

For some reason Georgia's accent deepened the more frustrated she became. If she got really angry and equally perturbed, no one would be able to understand her. So Savannah decided to spare them. "One eighteen," she whispered.

"She weighs one hundred and eighteen pounds. She's a willow tree," a voice boomed from the living room. Ennis.

She'd always felt awkward about her height and the fact she considered herself gangly. With his comment, Ennis reinforced that self-consciousness whether he knew it or not.

Savannah rolled her eyes then tossed a sarcastic "thank you" at him – with the same heartfelt sentiment as her sister's German Blitz moments earlier.

Georgia marched toward the table, "That's why I keep cooking for you. And you *will* eat."

Savannah straightened, bringing herself to her full five nine height. Usually the three inch difference between her and Georgia – and Savannah's expression – backed the older sister off. This time it didn't. Georgia stared up at her, hands on her hips, "Might as well save your energy. You're not bullying me into leaving you alone. Ennis, supper's ready."

Ennis rose from his seat, conveniently ignoring his wife's scowl. Dane volleyed his vision between the two and opted to grab a cup of coffee. He poured himself a cup and sipped – most likely to look busy – then sputtered into a coughing fit. He stared at the cup in disbelief then looked to his brother for an answer.

"I meant to warn you," Ennis said then pointed to Savannah. "She brews it strong enough to raise the dead."

Carefully setting the cup down, Dane added, "Or kill weeds. You know, Peach, this coffee might be partially responsible for your loss of appetite. It's eating a hole in your gut."

Georgia, ignoring the conversation, pulled a dining chair out for her sister then placed a pillow on the seat, "Sit."

Savannah bowed up at the order but her sister countered, "Having you in the hospital with malnutrition will wear me out more than cooking for you. I said sit."

Dane watched in amazement the battle taking place. He'd seen them argue but probably not with such vehemence. Savannah still stared down at Georgia and the older sister still challenged the younger one.

Savannah sighed, slowly eased into the seat, "And you call me the bully."

Dane chuckled, "How 'bout that? Little Georgia wins the fight."

Placing a napkin in her lap, Savannah argued, "She's not so little in spirit if you haven't noticed." Her eyes bugged at the serving size of ham casserole Georgia cut for her. It could shade the entire state of

Rhode Island. "For heaven's sake, Georgia, I can't eat all that."

"You'll eat most of it because I'm going to watch you and don't quarrel with me."

"If you turn sideways, no one will see you," Ennis uttered under his breath.

He'd taken the seat beside her and basically whispered it – just not quietly enough. The statement still stirred her temper, "I get it, okay? You want me to eat. I'll do what I can."

Georgia settled into the seat across from her, "We're worried about you, that's all. You can't sleep, you won't eat and you're scared to leave the house."

"And you're feeling perfectly fine after what happened?" Savannah snapped then shoved a bite of casserole into her mouth. It was mouth-wateringly delicious but she wasn't about to let that moderate her anger.

"No, but I'm seeing a therapist. She's helping me cope. I'd like to see you go too."

That did it. Savannah dabbed the corners of her mouth with the napkin and tossed it on the table, "Is this why you came over? To drug me with good food and drag me to a shrink?"

Georgia tried her best "mama" look on her. The one that refused debate, "We can go together but yes, I want you to go. Savannah, you saw me in trouble and saved me. Now you're in trouble and I'm going to help."

"You were dying, Georgia," she explicitly clarified. "That was different."

"No, it's not."

It was, at that moment, Savannah recalled something her father said. "Georgia could nag a monk to suicide." It was rare for her to agree with R.J. on any subject but this time she did. And as much as she loved the casserole, it wasn't worth being lectured so she began the laborious task of standing up.

Georgia pointed to the chair, "Sit down and listen to me."

Just the inflection planted her back in the seat. Georgia rarely raised her voice to anyone. Savannah had a temper but Georgia's was comparable to hers in some ways. The last thing Savannah wanted was to wake that sleeping giant...

"Think I'll go watch the game," Dane wandered into the living room and sat in the chair farthest from the discussion.

Ennis stood, plate in hand, "Think I'll join him."

Fork in hand, Savannah portioned off more casserole, "Are you happy? You ran 'em off." She lifted the fork to her mouth, "This casserole is scrumptious. Thank you for making it." Okay, so she tried praising her way out of trouble. She hated for Georgia to be angry but her sister suffered tunnel vision sometimes. Once she realized no amount of pestering, bribing, feeding or yelling would force Savannah to a shrink, she'd back off. At least Savannah *hoped* she backed off.

"I'm glad you're enjoying it," the words fell softer and quieter now. Georgia switched seats to the one Ennis vacated. "Listen, I know how you feel about therapists but she's helping me and I believe she can help you. Let's make an appointment together."

"With all due respect, Georgia, I'm physically unable to go

anywhere, much less to a shrink." She saw her sister bristle albeit slightly. To tame another impending lecture, Savannah finished, "Give me some time. I need to sort things out then I might consider going." It was a lie and Georgia likely knew it. It wouldn't prevent her from nagging her about going but it shut her up in the meantime, allowing Savannah to enjoy the ham casserole without wanting to fling it at her sister.

Georgia got up, headed toward her purse. Initially, Savannah feared she'd upset her to the point she was leaving. It would have been rare that her sister huffed up to that degree but nothing had been truly normal since Jeffrey and Cole entered their lives.

Deciding to wait out Georgia's next move, Savannah returned to eating. She snapped straight at a sudden touch on her shoulder. Her heart pounded like a caged animal trying to beat its way out. She'd been jumpy ever since Jeffrey Holland. Her nerves stayed on edge with the slightest physical contact. She really needed to calm down, she told herself. Everyone present was a trusted relative, not a crazed killer. Now she only hoped Georgia hadn't taken offense to her reaction.

Clearly, she didn't since she bent down to Savannah's ear, whispering, "Tonight take this to help you sleep. Once you get rest, you'll think clearer about a therapist."

Savannah glanced down to see a small prescription bottle. Inside: a sleeping pill. Flashes of Cole holding a similar bottle raced back. Her throat convulsed at the memory of Jeffrey's fingernails scraping past her tongue into her throat, shoving the pills so deep she nearly choked on them. The relentless memories crippled her and joining them, her shoulder panged, making her rub it – a habit she'd developed whenever Jeffrey's face appeared. The physical damage was bad enough but what she lost in that cabin with Jeffrey Holland was her sense of safety, her confidence. He taught her how vulnerable she really was.

When she didn't readily accept the bottle, Georgia eased down in the chair again, sat the bottle next to Savannah's plate. She continued in a hushed voice, "You need sleep. Ennis will be beside you all night so you know it's safe."

But closing her eyes caused Jeffrey to return in the quiet dark of night. Without fail, his evil smile crept in, haunting her until she got up, surrendering her sleep night after night. The pill might ward off Jeffrey Holland at least for a few hours. A few hours of peace. She couldn't remember the last good rest she'd had. "Ennis isn't getting much sleep either. When I do drift off, he always has to wake me from nightmares."

Georgia took her hand, held it in hers, "Promise me you'll take this tonight. Get some sleep and we'll talk about the doctor later."

An inner battle raged inside her. It wasn't fair to Ennis to keep him awake or be constantly on alert for her nightmares. But could she actually swallow the pill without the panic or fear returning – without seeing Jeffrey's smile or Cole standing nearby? *It's a sleeping pill, for God's sake. Your sister is offering it to you, not forcing it down your throat.*

Georgia gave her hand a gentle squeeze, bringing her out of the dark, painful memory. Savannah blinked and a tear rolled down her cheek. If, for a few hours, the little pill provided a respite from the nightmares and terrible memories, she'd try it. Swiping away another tear, she nodded to Georgia, "I promise."

44

Savannah awoke the next morning around nine. She gave her sister credit. The sleeping pill gifted her with a dreamless slumber free of constant nightmares. She felt more refreshed than she had in a week and a half. Georgia was a true blessing. She'd fed her a delicious filling supper then provided her with a decent night's sleep. Things were looking up. Finally.

With Ennis at the store to restock their fridge and pantry with groceries, she decided to clean up. She felt better than she had in several days and wanted to show her husband she wasn't a lost cause. She understood his pleading puppy dog eyes when they asked the unspoken question: Are you alright? She held her temper at the incessant asking of, "Are you feeling okay?" Eventually the questions would lessen in number and frequency until it wasn't spoken again. All it took was time.

After taking a long shower, Savannah carefully toweled off. Since coming home, she'd learned the intricacies of performing such tasks with minimal pain. The wounds still hurt and sitting still presented a problem unless she approached it slowly and delicately.

Her vision wandered to the scar below her collarbone. It still ached and pulled when she stretched too far or reached the wrong way. It would always be there, a punishing reminder of Jeffrey's cruelty. The day she thought would be her last on earth.

She touched the scar. She'd memorized its rough texture left by the stitches. A hint of sadness shadowed her face, knowing Holland would always have that part of her – that moment in time when he brought her to the brink of giving up on life.

Shaking her head free of the memory, she assured herself work awaited her. Before long she'd be back at her desk, going through the rituals and routines every detective performed. Only *she* would treasure the busy schedule and the work. It would help fade the nightmare of Jeffrey Holland and Cole Jordan.

Now Savannah stood in the quiet of the living room, searching for a task that might aid in the quest of a normal life. Her vision settled on the old golf bag across the way. She'd left Duke's gift in the corner where Abel left it but they hardly needed attention like her old clubs. While Ennis shopped, she'd polish the diamonds of her past and perhaps indulge in a memory of her high school days. Days that held promise with the first ray of sunshine. Perfect warm afternoons that invited a person to walk the golf course and enjoy the sound of birds, the warmth of the sun on the shoulders and the satisfaction of a good round of golf. Days that she longed for.

She'd finish the job Ennis began earlier in the week. His progress took him through the putter, wedges and half the irons. Savannah slid her trusty driver from the bag. In high school, that one singular club concreted her name around the state of Georgia. One swing of the driver drew gasps from the crowd and groans from her competitors. Of all the junior golfers, her distance and accuracy with the club earned her the nickname "Augusta's Stealth Bomber".

Draping the polishing cloth across the club head, she leisurely rubbed until it gleamed. Georgia claimed she "caressed" the clubs when she cleaned them and Savannah never disputed the fact. The clubs were good to her so she felt it only right to return the favor.

She eased the cloth down the shaft to the grip. Over and over she buffed and babied until returning the driver to its former glory.

A knock on the door wilted the beginning smile on her face. She rose from the couch, retied her robe, and checked the pocket for her gun. The sleeping pill afforded her some rest but it didn't lessen her fear of strangers.

A covert peek between the living room curtains revealed a city maintenance truck parked at the curb. She moved to the door, peered out the peephole. A man in a cap and gray work uniform held a clipboard in his hands. He gave his watch an impatient glance.

When she didn't open the door, he thumbed the doorbell and accompanied it with another knock. Savannah couldn't believe she debated opening the door to a city worker, a guy just trying to make a living. Before Jeffrey and Cole, she'd have already addressed the man and found out what he wanted. Now, she feared the stranger on the opposite side of the door. She literally felt petrified to answer her own front door. *You can't be afraid forever.*

She took out her .38, unlatched the safety and kept a firm grasp on the weapon as she slid it back in the pocket.

She opened the wooden door but left the glass door as a barrier between them. The guy kept his attention on the clipboard.

The name embroidered on his shirt read "Richard". Richard needed a few lessons on dealing with the public, evidently, and she wasn't in the mood to school him, "What do you want?"

Her vision dropped to the clipboard. For a city worker, his hands appeared supple and soft – and the nails immaculately clean. She watched Richard wag the pencil between his thumb and forefinger. A flashback appeared of a scalpel playing between the fingers of a flawlessly manicured hand. Jeffrey's.

Richard's vision rose to meet hers and before the door closed, she caught sight of the city worker's face. Jeffrey Holland smiled back as he yanked the glass door open, "I want *you*, Detective."

Savannah shouldered the wooden door with all her weight, trying to force it shut before he pushed inside. The motion reverberated through her body, jarring the already tender wound at her collarbone.

For an instant, she felt Jeffrey stumble backwards. Praying it bought her just enough time, she scrambled to close and lock the door.

Almost immediately the wooden door rammed against her, driving her back into the entry. With one solid kick, Jeffrey nearly cracked the door and sent her against the entry's back wall.

Jeffrey stepped inside, sending her frantically fumbling for her gun. Pulling it from the robe, the .38 barely saw the light of day when Jeffrey swatted it away, knocking it from her hand.

He leveled a chilling glare that brought back every horrible memory from that day. The scalpel slicing into her, the cane whipping against open wounds, fighting for her own life and for Georgia's...

Jeffrey's tone remained calm, "I'm disappointed in you. Do you remember what happens when I'm disappointed?"

He reached for her arm and panic flooded her. She raced to the bathroom for her phone. She realized the meager lock stood no chance against his strength but it might slow him down long enough for her to call Ennis.

She'd left her new cell phone by the tub in case he called or she thought of something else for him to pick up at the store. Quickly dialing his number, she heard Jeffrey calling her. He remained composed with no signs of anger or impatience. That alone unnerved her. Nothing unsettled Jeffrey Holland, not the thought of being shot, not the possibility of being caught and arrested. Nothing would stop him except death.

Ennis answered on the first ring. "Ennis, he's here," she stammered then consciously tried to slow her speech down. He'd never understand her otherwise. He'd only know she was terrified but not why. "Jeffrey's here," she carefully enunciated, "and he's inside."

"Savannah," Jeffrey called again. He now stood outside the bathroom door. He sounded like a lover summoning his sweetheart, enticing her out. "This isn't the way to treat a guest."

Tears swelled in her eyes, "Ennis, hurry." Her heart hammered in her chest as she searched for a weapon to defend herself with. She saw nothing. "Please hurry –" her plea was cut short by an explosion of glass. Instinctively she ducked, feeling tiny shards pelt her robe and hair.

Jeffrey had kicked open the bathroom door, shattering the full length mirror mounted on the back.

"Savannah!" Ennis's voice blasted from the phone. "Are you okay?"

Without turning, she knew Jeffrey stood behind her. She sensed his presence and his cold, satisfied smile. One last time she begged her husband, "Hurry, Ennis," she cried. "Please –"

A touch on her shoulder silenced her except for a whimper. The memory of those hands inflicting horrific pain – unspeakable pain…

Jeffrey grabbed the cell phone from her hand and closed it, cutting off Ennis's panicked voice.

She heard him place the phone on the vanity. She tried to turn but pressure on her shoulder prevented her from it. It produced a silent demand to kneel instead. Savannah eased to the floor, "Jeffrey, please don't…"

Her plea faded as he shushed her, "No talking unless I ask a question." The harsh grasp on her shoulder gentled, "Now lose the robe."

She didn't immediately comply which brought a frighteningly composed demand, "Do as I say."

When she didn't, he tipped back her chin until their vision met, "Allow me to explain your options. One, you can do as I say without hesitation and we can make this quick. Two, you can jerk me around and I'll wait until your husband returns and," he leaned closer, "he'll be a one man audience while I cut you to pieces."

It took every ounce of courage to meet his gaze, "He'll kill you first."

An arrogant smile crossed his features. He stepped to her side, removed a bloody scalpel from his jacket, and placed it beneath her ear. Her breath caught in her throat as it nestled against her pulse. The blood-smeared blade explained Richard's brutal death in graphic detail. His was certainly quicker than hers would be, she assumed. Richard was a means to an end. She was the one that got away.

Jeffrey said, "He walks in and I position this so he can see it clearly. I'll tell him that if he doesn't follow my directions, I'll cut your throat. Now, unless he has no regard for your life, he'll follow instructions. Nice wedding picture, by the way. Such a happy couple, especially for partners on the job."

She felt Jeffrey flip the scalpel's blade so the blunt edge rested against her flesh. He drew it lightly across her neck from ear to ear. She shuddered from the cold, precise movement.

He continued, "And if you should try to speak out of turn, I'll make it so you can't. As you learned earlier, noncompliance has serious consequences."

She tensed as Jeffrey tugged at the robe, "Lose it. Now."

Stall. If she stalled long enough, Ennis would be home. Savannah slowly shrugged out of the robe, glanced at the clock on the wall. The way Ennis drove, he'd be home in a flash, she told herself. Just keep stalling…

"Hands behind you."

The command caught her short. How did she hedge her way out of this? Ennis wasn't *that* fast on the accelerator and being limited on movement wasn't a good way to escape a killer.

The brutal blow came fast, disorienting her. All she saw was the floor racing to meet her. She threw her hands out in front of her to prevent her head crashing against the tile.

His voice, once composed, suddenly turned vicious, "That's right. You like it rough." The hard sole of a boot braced against the middle of her back, holding her flat on the floor. She heard a rattle of metal then he bent down, his knee replacing his foot in her back. Cold hands gripped her left wrist, violently pulled it behind her and locked a handcuff around it. She tried to fight back but he rewarded her with his weight sinking against her spine. Once both hands were restrained, he fisted her hair, "Sit up."

She struggled to her knees, wincing as the hard tile dug into her bare flesh. Jeffrey released her, stepped back, his breathing hard, his face flushed. It was the angriest she'd seen him since bracing Cole at the cabin. His hands clamped to his hips, "Noncompliance has what, Detective?"

"Consequences," she whispered.

"Right. That means we're waiting for your husband so he gets a front row seat." He took the scalpel and placed it next to the healing wound below her right shoulder. His dark eyes never blinked, his vision never wavered as he lightly drew the sharp blade in the shape of a zero.

Savannah flinched as the blade grazed the flesh, a thin line of blood surfacing in its wake. Number ten. With the fluid movement of his hand, the scalpel drew a smooth circle next to the already half-healed "1" he carved into her at the cabin.

His attention riveted to the motion in an almost hypnotic

manner. "You think you're smarter than me, don't you, Detective?" The knife kept tracing the same pattern. "Goading me at the cabin, fighting me, arguing with me. Even now you refuse to follow my directions. I knew a woman like you a while back. Her name was Eva. She thought she was smarter too. It took me five days to break her." Jeffrey finally made eye contact, "Five long, glorious days. I wanted that for you. I wanted to see if you were stronger than Eva but you ruined it. You and your sister ruined it." The anger rose in his voice, "You think you're more intelligent than I am, that you'll find a way to escape. Not this time, Savannah. I'm making sure of it." He reached in his back pocket, brought out a silver flask, "Look what good ol' Richard left me. We'll relax with this while we wait for your husband."

Savannah watched him unscrew the lid, tilt the flask to his mouth. Halfway through, he coughed, cringing as he swallowed. He wasn't used to drinking, she thought. Which meant one thing – he was losing his composure at a frightening rate. She never saw him drink at the cabin. While Cole threw back the Wild Turkey, Jeffrey sneered at the action, finishing with a lecture about defiling himself with alcohol.

Today, Jeffrey felt different about imbibing. He took another swallow, wiped his mouth with his sleeve. Then he stepped closer, held the flask to her lips, "Drink."

"No," she whispered, praying it worked and knowing it probably wouldn't. Whatever it was, she promised Ennis she wouldn't taste alcohol again. She intended to keep that promise if possible.

Jeffrey reacted with surprising calm. The scalpel's sharp blade nestled against her left breast. His grip trembled now where earlier it held steady. "It wasn't a suggestion."

To buy herself time she had to, she told herself. She'd deal with the repercussions later. She'd beg forgiveness from Ennis later – if she survived. Her lips parted, allowing him to tip the contents into her mouth. One taste told her she was doomed.

The smooth taste of bourbon – her biggest weakness – slipped past her tongue, warming her throat all the way to her stomach. She savored the taste, the one she longed for the last few weeks. But harsh reality smothered the welcome rush with a more potent feeling. Guilt. With every swallow, she broke a solemn promise. She cried inside with the knowledge she'd sold out and betrayed Ennis.

Jeffrey finally withdrew the flask. A trail of bourbon trailed down her throat and between her breasts. Tears welled at the thought of what she'd just done.

She struggled with the craving since her diagnosis. It intensified after her initial encounter with Jeffrey and Cole. Savannah fought the thirst for bourbon as hard as she fought the two bastards. One swallow would ramp up her anger to near violence, a lot like alcohol inflamed her father's temper. The last drink she took, she *had* tried to slap Ennis and shame still weighed heavy on her.

The alcohol spread through her body and limbs with the old familiar warmth. She wanted more. Staring at the flask, knowing it was half full, she wanted another drink and she hated herself for it.

"Do you know how I remove a breast?" He took another swallow then moved the scalpel to her nipple.

She drew a shallow breath, shook her head. Uncontrollable

tremors raked her body, forcing her to concentrate on staying completely motionless. Savannah prayed Ennis arrived soon. Jeffrey was losing control and frankly, she didn't want to lose any body parts in the process.

He drew the blade softly along the flesh, careful not to cut her, "I start with the nipple. Once that's gone, I make a cut from there," he drew the blade toward her shoulder, "to here. Then I move to the bottom of the breast." He did so then drew the blade toward her nipple again, "And make another cut. I peel it like a nice firm fruit." His hand suddenly slashed the air, "Then I slice it off." Jeffrey tossed back another swallow, "I love to hear a woman scream, the anguish on her face while she begs me to stop. You," he motioned with the flask, "scream a lot like Eva. There's strength in it, not just pain. Strength that, the longer I work with you, will diminish until your scream is as pathetic as all the other women I've had. That's why I enjoy women like you. The ones that think they're stronger than me. I love proving them wrong, to show them I'm in control."

Her vision drifted to his crotch. An unmistakable erection grew beneath his jeans. Jeffrey never raped the women, Cole did, but the sight before her stirred a new fear – one that she ignorantly overlooked. With his sudden change in behavior, Jeffrey now might find pleasure in raping women before he killed them. "The police are coming. Ennis is coming. Even if you kill me, they'll find you and kill you."

Jeffrey's arrogance rooted deeper. A smug grin split his face as he stepped closer, "But most importantly I'll have killed you. *I want number ten.*"

Savannah leaned back, away from his self-satisfied smile. She tried to stall, to wait for Ennis, but the effort wore on her nerves. It seemed like an hour passed. Where was Ennis?

"I especially love the fear in a woman's eyes when I come near." He smiled at her, "It's the same fear you have right now. You're trying to hide it but you can't. I broke you just enough at the cabin that it shows in your face." He glanced at his watch, "I imagine your husband is getting close." He pressed the flask to her mouth again.

Savannah swallowed back two gulps and tried to back away. Jeffrey held the back of her head, keeping the flask against her lips, "I didn't say stop. All of it, Savannah. Every last drop."

She closed her eyes, praying she'd get her revenge before he either killed her or made her so drunk she couldn't fight. Jeffrey's smile widened, "There's a good girl. See, it's not so hard to get along."

The first drink already began working, making her woozy and slightly unsteady. On an empty stomach, the liquor went straight to her knees and head. The worst part of it: a small part of her wanted the rest of the bourbon, to drink the flask dry – and she had.

Get it together, Savannah. You're running out of time. As soon as the alcohol reached her brain, she'd be further impaired which presented its own problem.

Jeffrey seemed amused at her actions, put a hand to her shoulder, "Steady there, Detective. If you fall over and crack your head, you'll ruin my plans. Now Jeffrey says don't move or what will happen?"

"Consequences." Like dying wasn't enough.

He winked, "Right. Let me see if our guest has arrived."

Through the fog of alcohol, Savannah watched him step from the bathroom, his feet crunching over shards of the broken mirror. Trying to focus on the vanity for stability, she took that instant to pull her knees from under her and roll onto her back. Since she'd lost weight, she could easily pull her cuffed hands beneath her. She folded her legs and slid her bound hands out until they were in front of her. Now she could try to fight – if she could stand without staggering.

She pushed to her knees again and paused as her equilibrium tilted off balance. Damn the bourbon, she thought. It *was* a miracle she didn't flop backwards, bang her head and kill herself, saving Jeffrey the trouble.

She struggled to one foot while balancing on her other knee. She swayed then tried to steady herself while listening for any movement from the living room.

Savannah pushed to her feet just as Jeffrey stepped into the doorway. The same rage from the cabin emerged, "What I wouldn't give for three more days with you."

He suddenly lunged at her, the movement disoriented her, causing his image to blur for a split-second. This was it, she thought. She had to win this battle to survive.

Jeffrey sped toward her, the scalpel glinting as he charged. His arm swung back with the blade – obviously killing her slowly went on the back burner. He wanted her dead any way possible now.

Putting all her concentration into one single move, she swung her foot back, aimed for one particular spot and prayed her aim was true. For an instant, she closed her eyes, mustering every ounce of power possible.

Her foot connected with something solid, the resulting cry told her she'd hit him and hit him hard. A quick look revealed she'd hit her mark – his knee. He fell to the floor holding his leg, promising, "You're gonna pay for this."

"I already have. It's *your* turn now," she replied with more certainty than she felt. She turned to run when a grasp on her ankle yanked and slammed her face down onto the floor. The impact nearly knocked the breath from her. She pulled against the grasp, clawing at the tile for a solid grip but finding none. The hallway door stood a few feet away – freedom – and she couldn't reach it.

His hand locked around her ankle like a vise, the fingers digging into her flesh as he crawled atop her, stabbing a knee in her back to hold her.

Pain bolted down every nerve in her body from the pressure. She fought to focus on the only important objective – survival. With her cuffed hands stretched in front of her, she groped for the only weapon available – a long shard from the busted mirror. Fingers snaked through her hair and fisted, pulling her head back. Savannah saw him reach for the scalpel. She rallied her strength to twist beneath him while swinging the jagged piece of mirror. It sank deep into soft flesh, and a warm sensation spread across her palm. Blood. A yelp confirmed she buried the glass in his thigh.

Jeffrey collapsed to the floor again, grasping his leg, cursing her. As she pushed to her feet, she traversed the minefield of broken mirror and winced as tiny shards pricked the soles.

Savannah made her way into the living room, again searching for a weapon. Her panicked vision quickly scanned the room and finally stopped as sunlight beamed off the answer to her prayers. As if God sent a ray of light showing her the way, she raced to the couch, grabbing her old driver.

Her fingers closed around the grip and beyond the panic came confidence. The club saved her many times from hazards on the course. Now it would – with any luck – save her from a real hazard and with it, her life. She knew this club like she knew her family. Holding it, she remembered the weight of it in her hands and the power it possessed.

Boots scraped the bathroom floor. The sound of crunching glass warned her he was on his feet again, his anger mounting until verging on fury. He was cursing louder now, his voice nearer and stronger. The pain of her attack waned enough to spur vengeance, something she meant to dole out for what he'd done to her, to Georgia, and to all the women he'd tortured and killed.

Positioning herself near the bathroom door, she drew the club back into the familiar position – a backswing to fire a line drive down the fairway. Only this time she stopped at the apex of the swing, waiting for just the right moment to strike. She waited what seemed like forever.

The wound at her shoulder ached and pulled from the strain, making her bite back a groan. Despite the assurance of the club's power, the same intense fear flooded her. If she missed, if he ducked... Her biggest fear: if he gained control again, she wasn't just dead, he'd slice her apart slowly before allowing her to die, with or without Ennis as a witness.

She tried to slow her ragged, shallow breathing. *Don't let him hear you.* Her heart pounded against her ribs, her hands and arms trembled under the weight of the driver. Waiting.

"Savannah, when I'm done with you –" he stepped out and for an instant, their vision met.

She'd started her downswing too quick for him to react. She channeled every ounce of strength into the swing, not caring what she destroyed in the process of saving herself. The driver's head connected, the sudden stop reverberated through the shaft to her hands and up her arms. A sickening crack broke the silence and with it Jeffrey cried out. His scream echoed through the house as he fell to the floor holding his leg, "You broke my leg!"

Staring at the crippled monster, Savannah realized one thing. She had to finish the job. If she didn't, he'd come back for her until he killed her. He'd come back for Georgia and kill her too. She needed to rid the world of Jeffrey Holland for her sake and for Georgia's. It was the only way to restore not only sleep, but her peace of mind. It was the only way to restore her life.

She swung back one last time and felt her muscles react without instruction. They knew, as on the golf course, what their goal was: launch the ball as far as possible.

With a pained grimace, Jeffrey looked up and through the pain, she saw another emotion. Defiance. Staring into the monster's eyes, she sensed the arrogance in them – the taunting message. *Go ahead and kill me,* they said, *but I'll be with you forever. Until you draw your last breath you'll see me, fear me. I will still live in you day and night. I will never die.*

Savannah started her downswing again, this time with more power than the last. She meant to end the confrontation forever.

She thought she heard Jeffrey call her name, begging her to stop. Nothing short of death would stop her.

Bringing the club down with every ounce of strength in her, the reality of an abrupt stop shattered her focus. The club stopped partway down like hitting a brick wall. Something prevented her from killing Jeffrey Holland.

A hand gripped the club's shaft – a hand that tried to wrestle the driver from her grasp. In her rage, she assumed it was Cole. One couldn't exist without the other and now she had both men to battle. Again.

She struggled against him like her life depended on it because she was quite sure it did.

The intruder's grasp ripped the club from her hands and she turned to run. If she couldn't kill them, she'd run to safety. Through the cloud of fear, rage and alcohol, she kept hearing someone call her name. An arm wrapped across her waist, brought her against a hard chest. It was too late. Cole caught her and if she didn't free herself now, she was destined for a horrible death but only after Cole violated her every way imaginable.

"No!" she screamed, still wrestling and flailing against the restrictive hold.

"Savannah, stop!" the voice yelled back. The man's voice gentled unlike his hold, "It's me. Stop fighting." It took a moment to register but when she recognized the man holding her, she instantly stopped struggling and practically collapsed in his arms. Tears came in a flood as she cried in Ennis's embrace. She clung to him, holding him so tight she felt him wince.

He held her, assuring, "It's okay. I'm here and you're safe. He's never hurting you again."

45

Waterford crystal chandelier. Chippendale chairs. Handcrafted rugs that likely cost thousands of dollars. Standing in the midst of all that opulence, Savannah felt not only her gut clench but her bank account too. The rug alone probably cost more than her monthly pay. The chandelier with delicate teardrops cost more than her *house.* Her first reaction was to flee but Ennis clasped her hand tighter, probably sensing her intent. It was a mistake coming here, she'd tell him. This was so out of their league, they'd never climb out of debt.

A leather couch sat near the door. She leaned down, skimming her hand over the texture. She calculated the value to be around the cost of her Camaro's new transmission.

Ennis approached a mahogany desk that reminded Savannah of Georgia's writing desk. She *knew* how much her sister paid for the thing and the amount caused a particularly obnoxious knot to form in her throat. *Leave now while you still have some money.*

Ennis picked up a note from the desk. Savannah prayed he didn't accidentally scratch the wooden treasure in the process. Judging by his smile as he read the note aloud, he hadn't, "Please knock on door."

She had a better idea – please walk out and go home. But Ennis wouldn't. He'd follow the note's instructions because he wasn't scheduled to see Dr. Lisa Coates. *She* was – and considering the lengthy battle to get her here, only God or a fire alarm stood a decent chance of extricating him.

So far Savannah could say one thing about Dr. Coates: when she promised discretion, she meant it. The doctor arranged her schedule so they'd be alone in the office and besides the half dozen plants placed around the room, they were. The receptionist, gone for the day, left the desk perfectly organized for the next day's appointments.

Ennis was about to rap on the door when Savannah whispered, "Wait."

He turned to her, not bothering to join her cloak-and-dagger behavior, "What?"

With a wave of her hand, she hoped to signify how deep in bankruptcy they'd be if she stepped inside, "We can't afford this. It'll break us."

He knocked anyway, "You need help. Besides, she's already quoted you an hourly rate and we both agreed it's affordable."

There was that, she supposed, but any conscious, middle class human being would be intimidated by the office. It screamed "second mortgage" for new patients.

A voice came from inside the office, "Just a moment."

She pursed her lips. *Well, it's too late now.* Maybe Ennis was right. Since Jeffrey's attack, she'd not slept more than two hours at a time, and when she nodded off, nightmares crept in. Paranoia ruled her

world. She demanded to keep her gun with her at all times. She wasn't
herself, she didn't feel good, and didn't see an end in sight.

After getting up and showering that morning, Ennis prepared a
modest breakfast complete with his Mr. Cheerful mood. She managed to
choke down a scrambled egg and half a piece of toast. Mr. Cheerful's
smile lost a little wattage but all in all he seemed pleased. When she
showered, he guarded the bathroom door as she asked – and had since
the attack – until she toweled off and dressed. With Ennis standing
guard, she felt safe. No one could break in with him around. No mirrors
would splinter into a million pieces, no one would hold a knife to her
throat, or threaten to dismember her – not with Ennis on the job.

The last two weeks took their toll on her despite Jeffrey being
safely behind bars. She eased onto the couch with a weary sigh. She
looked and felt like the walking dead. Dark circles under her eyes,
constantly drifting off only to startle herself awake with images of Jeffrey
Holland. She was a wreck and before she lost her mind completely, she
lost her pride and decided to see a shrink. Duke's shrink. Not even the
knowledge of their dominant/submissive relationship mattered to her
now. She wanted her life back and if Dr. Coates held the key, she'd see
her.

Ennis joined her on the couch and leaned back. His gentle touch
kept her mind from wandering to the dark corners of her mind. Ennis
clasped her hand in his, gave it a squeeze, "I'm glad you finally agreed to
see her."

She hoped she felt the same way after the appointment. She
always hated shrinks. They pried into everything, read too much into a

simple statement and twisted things a million different ways. By the end of the session, she figured Coates would blame R.J. and Charlene for Jeffrey's attack and Cole's running loose. In a shrink's world, parents were at fault for everything.

The phone on the receptionist's desk rang, the noise jangled her nerves and she recoiled against Ennis's soothing touch. Lately she'd done a lot of that – recoiled. She refused to let Ennis out of her sight and always had to have her cell phone and gun with her even in bed. The latter ended three nights earlier at midnight when she drew her gun and nearly shot him for being "a shadow" in the dark bedroom. The next morning she made the appointment with Dr. Coates.

The door across the way opened and a woman stepped out. The tall, slender woman wore a blue pantsuit and high heels. Lisa Coates was a pretty lady with her dark, shoulder length hair and dark eyes, Savannah thought. It didn't surprise her, really. The women associated with Duke Shelton fit a particular image. Young, slender, pretty. Dr. Coates looked close to thirty-five or so, still within range of Duke's preference.

The doctor offered her new patient a gentle, pleasing smile, "Savannah?"

She nodded and tiredly rose from the couch. She gave Ennis's hand a squeeze and gifted him with as big a smile as she could muster which wasn't much.

Dr. Coates shook their hands, apologizing for the wait. She motioned Savannah into her office then told Ennis, "We'll be about an hour, maybe more."

As Savannah passed her, a small relief washed over her. She was getting help. It would get better. With time, it would. Normally she wouldn't have taken Duke's recommendation on anything but she needed someone to talk to. She didn't want to make Georgia relive the trauma and didn't like seeing Ennis get so furious when she spoke to him about it. His focal point was killing the two men and the mere mention of them incited a riot between them lately.

Georgia's appointment with Dr. Coates went surprisingly well, according to the older sister. She described Lisa as open and easy to talk to but judging by the office décor and Lisa's attire, she charged mucho bucks for the privilege of her company. Unlike the monochromatic colors and metal furniture of the department shrink's office, this place reeked of expensive, heavy wooden furniture, exotic plants and plush cream colored carpet. "It's affordable," she whispered to herself. "Do it for Ennis, for yourself."

"Have a seat," Lisa waved to a leather covered chaise lounge flanked by another expensive looking leather chair.

Four new tires and full tune-up, Savannah thought. That's what the chaise lounge cost. And the chair? *Stop it. Stop putting numbers to everything and relax.*

She eased down onto the chaise lounge. She wasn't sure whether to lie down or not. She chose not to. Then her hands felt lost so she tried folding them in her lap. They still trembled – they never stopped – but strangely her nervousness didn't stem from being in a shrink's office. It was about leaving the house, being out in public, out where Cole Jordan could see her, find her and...

Savannah sensed Dr. Coates staring at her. Clasping her hands together, she willed them to stop shaking.

"Have you ever been to a psychiatrist before?" Dr. Coates asked softly.

She swallowed then realized her feet took over the nervous habit from her hands. Instead of shaking, they tapped the floor. *Stop, stop, stop. You're safe. Ennis is just outside the door.*

"Would you feel more comfortable lying down?" the doctor suggested. "Some people prefer it."

"I'm fine, thank you," Savannah replied calmer than she felt. "To answer your other question, I've only seen the department shrink and that was under orders."

"Well, first let me assure you that whatever you say is confidential. It's different than visiting the department psychiatrist. I'm only here to help you, not evaluate you. I'd like you to be as honest as you can and as expressive as you feel comfortable being."

That would be a trick considering Savannah hated shrinks and trusted them like she trusted her father. Still, she made the appointment so she wouldn't shirk on the honesty too much. Some things remained off limits but the subject regarding Jeffrey and Cole were fair game. "I'll try but I'm not good at expressing myself. I didn't want to come here but I..." her statement trailed to silence. *I nearly shot my husband. I'm so paranoid, I nearly killed the man I love.* "I had to see someone."

The declaration inspired a smile from Coates, "I'm glad our friend convinced you to see me."

Interesting how she called Duke "friend" instead of "Master". Savannah assumed Lisa preferred the title "friend" to avoid introducing any awkwardness to the meeting.

She was surprised by Duke. The man she thought at first was a total pervert and creep ended up helping her. He wasn't her cup of tea, but he was a good man. "Do you know what happened at the cabin?" Savannah asked. Images of Jeffrey rushed in much like he charged in her front door. She swallowed hard, willed them away, "And at my house?"

Lisa settled into the seat across from her and nodded somewhat, "Some of it but only what I've read in the paper, heard on the news. Your husband told me about the incident in your home but when you're ready, you can tell me."

The doctor gave her time to get comfortable, to set her own pace for the session. What she overlooked – Savannah had no clue where to begin and said so.

"Start wherever you're comfortable. This is your time so take things at your own pace."

She was sure Georgia enlightened her on plenty of details. She also figured Duke clued her in on others. "Duke didn't tell you anything?"

Lisa shook her head, "Only that you might see me at some point. That's all." She waited a moment then, "Are you surprised he didn't?"

Savannah shrugged, "Figured he'd give you a heads up since you know each other."

"We do but we don't mix business with pleasure, so to speak. Would you like something to drink? I've got coffee, tea –"

"No thanks. Besides, lately I wouldn't accept anything but bourbon." Savannah wanted to slap herself. *Way... to... friggin'...*

go... The verbal slip was just the beginning of her downfall, she feared. Now Coates would think she was a lush – a label Savannah herself battled with every day. Was she or wasn't she an alcoholic? Was she or wasn't she turning into her father?

Lisa picked up on the silent berating, "You've been abstaining so far?"

She nodded, "It's hard." The cravings came mostly at night, when she was awake and Ennis slept. When she told Coates it was hard, she meant virtually impossible. If fear hadn't caged her inside the house, she'd have already swilled down a bottle or two.

Savannah rubbed her eyes. They still felt swollen and scratchy, "It's all I think about at night. Just one drink and I might sleep. But I promised Ennis I wouldn't and right now it's the most difficult promise I've ever made."

"It's a positive sign you're trying."

"But I broke the promise." A thin thread of anger laced her voice. "I broke it and I disappointed him."

"Did you have a choice about drinking?"

She had to say it, she had to say the name. Another hurdle blocking her path. Closing her eyes she pushed the name past her lips, "Jeffrey Holland made me. I told him no but he forced me."

"And your husband said you disappointed him by following Jeffrey's orders?"

Savannah knew by the way Coates phrased it, by her tone, she was convinced Ennis wasn't disappointed. "No, Ennis would never say that. He's too sweet."

"Then perhaps it's too harsh to blame yourself."

"I guess I feel like I disappointed him." Problem was after that drink, she wanted more. And lots of it. She'd beat herself up for wanting the stuff. Ennis kept beer in the fridge but to her, beer equaled turpentine. Even the smell was nasty. Plus, the few times she drank it, it hardly had an effect on her. Not like her precious bourbon. That stuff chased away any demon – at least for a while.

If she had anyone to talk to, to share with without upsetting them or forcing them to relive the trauma… Savannah sighed, reminding herself that was why she was there. Coates provided objective ears. These visits were a stopgap until she healed enough physically to run again or maybe even play golf. But, her mind taunted, she'd have to feel safe again for that. Everyone outside her home, outside her family, was a threat. Getting past that paranoia required help and that's where Dr. Lisa came in. Savannah shrugged again, "I can't talk to anyone about it. It'll traumatize my sister again and Ennis has anger issues when I mention it. I can't deal with these images and nightmares by myself anymore. And I *do* want to drink. I want it like my next breath." Tears welled in her eyes. She'd given up fighting them days ago. Fatigue and the nagging fear drove her to them. Now they became a part of her life. "I'm afraid I'm my father now. I don't want to be an alcoholic but I'm scared I am."

Coates handed her a tissue. Savannah dabbed the tears, struggled to retain her composure as the doctor said, "You're aware of your problem and trying to avoid alcohol. That's a major step in not becoming one. You said you promised your husband and you're keeping the promise."

She nodded, "I'm trying."

Coates referred to the papers Savannah filled out a day earlier. "You were diagnosed with breast cancer at Christmas. How's that going?"

"Better. Finished radiation just before..." her voice trailed. Memories of Jeffrey's cold hand closing over her breast brought a shiver. The feeling of the scalpel nudging against the nipple – all it took was one twitch of his hand to slice it off...

"You've been under a lot of stress for months," Dr. Lisa stated, bringing Savannah from the dreadful memories. She glanced at the papers again, continuing, "According to your forms, you haven't slept much and have nightmares."

Savannah added, "I don't feel safe anywhere and won't let Ennis out of my sight. Not a good thing when you're a cop."

"Your husband seems very supportive. That was one thing our friend mentioned. He called your relationship 'charming'."

That sounded like Duke. A tiny smile curved Savannah's lips. "Ennis is a blessing. He tolerates much more from me than he should."

Ennis sat in the quiet waiting room, the silence lulling him to lean back and relax for the first time in weeks. He thanked God Savannah decided to see Dr. Coates. It took a unified effort between him and Georgia to pry a commitment from her. That, and the fact she nearly shot his nuts off the other night.

He was grateful for Duke Shelton's recommendation but was surprised he refused to name Coates as a psychiatrist, at least in Savannah's presence. It told Ennis the man knew way too much about psychology. The term "doctor" fell softer on Savannah's ears than "psychiatrist".

Ennis heard the voices in the next room. Savannah's velvety tone wavered between tearful and monotone. Following Jeffrey's latest attack, her voice alternated between the two without variation to the buoyant lilt he loved. If he and Georgia hadn't pushed her to go, Ennis feared his wife's sanity would nosedive. Twenty-four hours a day she stayed on edge, ready to kill anyone foolish enough to merely ring the doorbell – or tiptoe to the bathroom to relieve themselves. He nearly peed his shorts when she aimed the gun at him that night. It took a few seconds – but felt like a lifetime – for her to recognize his voice, to recognize *him* and when she did, she apologized. His bladder didn't forgive so easily and for that matter neither did his bowels.

Judging by the doctor's tone, she tried to finesse more conversation from his wife. World Peace came easier than that. He certainly failed in the conversational respect. The times she mentioned the subject, he flew mad – not at her but at the two men. He wanted them both dead but *he* wanted to do the killing. He didn't apologize for grabbing the golf club from her that day. Her intention was quite clear and Holland's defiant stare hadn't helped. His unspoken promise deepened her rage and fear until it took over, wanting to obliterate any trace of the man – just to get peace.

A flash of memory brought back an unsettling thought. If he ever wondered why the Augusta Chronicle named her "The Stealth Bomber" during her high school golf days, her swing certainly illustrated why. Hearing the driver slice the air on her downswing, he realize Savannah possessed the strength of two men when armed with the club. The sickening crack of Jeffrey's leg breaking took a back seat to seeing her wind up for another whack at him, this time his head. Had the driver's massive head connected with the bastard's skull, his brains would've plastered the walls.

When Ennis seized the club's shaft, stopping its momentum became iffy. Her body twisted as she swung back and he'd seen the murder in her eyes, the terror in them. On her downswing, he'd called her name but her movement showed no indication she heard him. The only way to stop her was physically restrain her.

Ennis flinched at the recollection of her elbow slamming into his diaphragm, then finding his chin during her flailing. She fought like a wild animal to escape his grasp. Once she recognized him, she basically collapsed in his arms, her panic stretched long beyond tears.

He worked for several minutes to settle her trembling, to comfort her. Before the police arrived, he'd wrapped a robe around her but she refused to let him go. She wanted Jeffrey dead, she'd told him, to end the nightmare and erase the uncertainty from hers and Georgia's lives. *Why did you stop me*, she cried in his embrace. *Why? I could have been free...*

He tried to reach the common sense part of her brain with the explanation, "Because you couldn't have lived with yourself if you *had* killed him."

Now, a couple of weeks later, he began to wonder about that. She wasn't exactly living with Jeffrey behind bars either. In fact, her paranoia mounted to levels he never expected to see in a woman so strong and grounded. She refused to leave the house without him and stayed by his side at all times. He barely had a moment alone.

She smelled Jeffrey's aftershave at odd times, particularly at night, forcing Ennis to search the house for a monster he knew sat in jail. Jeffrey Holland and Cole Jordan plunged their lives into hell and for that Ennis could have killed them both with his bare hands – and slept well forevermore.

He'd hired a crew specializing in crime scene clean-up to mop up the blood and clean the bathroom. The thought of strangers in their house pushed Savannah to new, unseen limits and Ennis drove her to Georgia's to stay while they worked.

One of the worst ramifications of the ordeal: Savannah expressed enormous guilt for drinking when she'd promised not to. It broke Ennis's heart with each apology she offered. It wasn't her fault, he said, it was Jeffrey's. But Ennis saw her struggle with the craving. He caught the glances at his beer – a substance she avoided like the plague. He watched her turn from the TV when alcohol ads appeared. She battled the desire with a shaky resolve.

Ennis shook his head, grateful she finally made the appointment. Her stubborn streak held out longer than he expected. She contacted Dr. Coates, she said, because she feared in a moment of panic she'd mistake him for Jeffrey and kill him.

A vibration on his hip alerted him to a call. He removed the phone, looked at Caller ID and answered. It was Dane. "She go?" his brother asked.

"She's in with the doc now."

"Georgia wanted me to call. She get any sleep last night?"

"Not a wink and neither did I. I try to keep an eye on her when she's up."

"Why?" Dane wanted to know. "Afraid she'll wander off?"

Actually, he didn't know *what* she'd do. Dane seemed to pick up on his thoughts, "Listen, if it's any consolation, Georgia said this doctor's good. She said she helped her."

The news gave him hope. His muscles released another ounce of tension and he rubbed the back of his neck. Maybe Duke was right after all. After a pause, he mentioned the other thing weighing heavy on his mind, "Savannah wants to sell the house."

"I can kinda understand that after what happened. Selling the place might be a good idea."

"I'm not sure we can afford it right now. We've still got the radiation bills to pay. Soon as she calms down, then we can talk about finances."

Georgia spoke in the background, making Ennis strain to hear her. Dane relayed her statement, "Georgia knows a good realtor. If Peach doesn't settle down about it soon, give this girl a call. Got a pen?"

Sighing, Ennis realized his brother wasn't letting go of the idea. He wouldn't either if money wasn't so tight. He wrote down the name and number, stuffed the note in his pocket. "I'm all for moving, don't get me wrong. I hired some guys to clean the floor and bathroom. At least that won't detract from the selling value. And I finally got the bathroom mirror replaced last week. That seemed to help her a little."

Dane offered, "Georgia and I could lend you some cash, Ennis. If you move then Peach might improve. Get rid of the bad memories, y'know? At least not live in the same room with them."

Ennis cringed. Taking money from anyone rated at the bottom of his list, "Thanks but let us talk about it first, see what we can do." It would take more than moving to get rid of the memories. Ennis doubted anything would. He only hoped Dr. Coates managed to quiet them down.

On the way home, Ennis debated over grabbing a burger. It had been weeks since she'd indulged in her favorite, a Rocketburger. Maybe eating one would inspire happier thoughts and restore some good memories. When he asked, she only shrugged. Anticipation needled him. For the last ten minutes, they drove in silence. Had seeing the doc helped or not? Her expression gave nothing away, least of all an interest in food or basic conversation.

Then, "If you want a burger, we'll stop and get one. But I'm not hungry."

He stopped for a red light and glanced at her, seeing the same detachment he'd observed for weeks. Only when she leaned back did he notice a subtle change in her expression. It wasn't a smile. It wasn't joy. It was a brooding darkness. One he'd seen repeatedly the last few days.

Following her line of vision across the intersection, he sighed. A liquor store. He'd hoped seeing a shrink might have helped more in that area. He tried directing her attention away from the temptation across the street, "You sure? I won't police your jalepeños this time. And I'll even let you have my fries."

But her focus remained riveted at the Kroger-sized liquor store. All that alcohol. All the different labels a person could want. All the hell they'd go through if she drank one drop...

Waiting for the light to change, Savannah's demeanor changed from apathy to restless. The light was about to turn green, she sensed it and didn't want to miss her opportunity.

His fingers tightened on the wheel, expecting a plea. A plea to hang a right and
pull into the parking lot. A plea for that "one drink" she'd mention under her breath on occasion. Now he questioned whether seeing the shrink helped at all. So he asked if it had.

Savannah rubbed her temple but her gaze never strayed from the package store, "It'll take more than a couple of trips."

Ennis willed the light to change. If they drove past without a request, he'd chalk it up as a victory. "Georgia's still going to her," he said softly. "Says it's helping her. That the doc seems nice."

"She is," She agreed absently. Her hands clenched into fists in her lap. She knew the window of opportunity shrank with every second, "Ennis."

He heard the apprehension in her voice. She didn't want to ask but her nagging thirst compelled her to. Thankfully, the light turned green. Ennis started the Ram through the intersection at a slow pace,

"What, babe?" He'd give her a chance to fight it out internally before hitting her with a sermon on abstaining. From the corner of his eye, he saw the struggle. As they neared the store, her hands tightened until the knuckles blanched. She stared at the store, "I want to…"

They approached the entrance to the parking lot. Ennis waited – and prayed. It rated as one of the most stressful few seconds of his married life. Keeping her sober when he assumed she had the problem licked.

Savannah's vision followed the store as they neared. Her voice gained more confidence, "I'd like to stop and…" As she spoke, the strength of the request weakened to a whisper, making Ennis grateful her conscience temporarily kicked in.

Ennis kept the truck at a leisure pace. They were nearly safe, nearly past the liquor store now. "Stop and what?" he asked, not hiding the contempt of her thoughts. They both knew what she wanted but he'd make it as hard on her as possible. He'd force her to say the words.

For a second she tensed up, no doubt trying to gather her courage to say them. Then he saw her shoulders slacken and she shook her head, "Nothing. Let's go home."

Ennis released a quiet sigh. The last few minutes sure tested his composure and temperament but it also signified a landmark for her. She'd cleared another hurdle and passed on drinking. He wiped a hand down his face, grateful she fought the urge. "You going back to the doc anytime soon?"

"She said next week – or sooner if I need to."

"Sounds like she's different than the department doc."

"She doesn't push for answers like he does. It doesn't feel like she's analyzing me."

Ennis eased around a corner and headed down the street. In those brief seconds, the tension in his neck and shoulders eased. There were no liquor stores real close to home. No more temptation, at least today.

As he turned down their street, he surveyed the traffic parked along the curb. No cars were parked nearby, nothing to be concerned with – which she would be. One strange car parked within three houses put her on alert for Cole Jordan. Jeffrey might have been safely behind bars but, in her mind, Cole still posed a threat.

Savannah was already checking for cars and people that didn't belong on their street. He tried to ease her anxiety, "I'm glad you're comfortable with her."

"She wants you to attend a session too."

Savannah was looking at him now, gauging his reaction to seeing a shrink, he assumed. He tried not to react, "Whenever she wants me there." He made eye contact, pointedly adding, "And only if you're okay with it."

She nodded, "I am."

He wheeled the truck into the driveway and cut the engine. From the corner of his eye, he saw Savannah recoil at the sight of their house. She retreated into herself every time they returned home. Ennis finally realized the subject needed broaching sooner or later. Dane was right. Savannah wasn't improving and probably wouldn't until the house was a distant memory. Nearly every corner of the place held memories of either Jeffrey or Cole. With Jordan running loose, it wasn't any wonder she always felt vulnerable. "Once you feel like it, we'll discuss selling the house."

She instantly relaxed and tears welled in her eyes. She wiped them away, "Thank you, Ennis. I realize it's a financial burden. We've still got bills for radiation and now the shrink –"

Ennis shushed her, "Don't start worrying again. You'd worry the warts off a frog if you could."

"I'll sell my part of the orchards if I need to. Georgia might buy it. I know there are a few cousins interested in owning part."

He felt his jaw dropping. Thankfully he caught it before she noticed. Considering she dearly loved the orchards outside Augusta, her remark illustrated how important the idea was to her. "Let's take it one day at a time," he said. "We can talk about selling the house – not the orchards – later." The last thing he needed was her dwelling on finances. There'd be plenty of time to discuss and plan.

They climbed out of the truck and Savannah rounded the front. He patiently waited for her new routine to play out – not that he minded the newest habit in her repertoire. It was, as Duke Shelton might call it, endearing.

Once her hand slid into his, she kissed him and they proceeded to the front door. Ennis unlocked the front door and pushed it open. She wouldn't enter without him so he pocketed the key and checked the mailbox while they were there.

It looked like a couple of bills, a few catalogs and a small package. He'd leave it until completing his duties, otherwise Savannah would refuse entry into their own home.

He stepped inside and perused the immediate area. "All clear," he said with a gentle tug on her hand.

Savannah took his lead then hinted, "If you'd let me carry my gun, this wouldn't be necessary."

Ennis nearly laughed at the statement but flinched as his balls reminded him of their close call. At the current time, guns and Savannah equaled disaster, "Your gun is the last thing you need. You nearly shot my nuts off the other night if you remember."

Ashamed, Savannah hung her head and apologized. Ennis felt bad for letting it slip but the image of his balls landing in the neighbor's yard tended to cause a little resentment. "I'm grateful you didn't neuter me but no, no gun for you. Now stay put and I'll check the place out. Lock that door."

Obeying orders, she slid the deadbolt into place and waited while he searched the house for intruders. Once he made the rounds he nodded to her. "Why don't you get comfortable while I get the mail?"

Savannah nodded, "I might call Georgia and talk a few minutes."

Ennis caught the hint of a true smile from his wife. Just the mention of selling the house perked her up more than he thought. He'd study the finances that night and see how feasible the idea was. But for now, the newest bills needed tending to.

Ennis opened the mailbox and scooped everything out. He tossed the catalogs on the dining table and separated the bills. It was the last piece of mail that confused him. The lightweight padded envelope was addressed to her. Ennis didn't recognize the return address but it was local. Using his pocket knife, he opened then tilted the package. An unmarked DVD fell into his hand.

Had she ordered something? He doubted it in the shape she'd been in lately. Neither movies nor TV interested her. Well, he thought, there was only one way to solve the mystery. After switching the TV on, he slid the DVD into the player and pushed the play button.

Electronic snow filled the screen then the frame came into view. Ennis felt his stomach drop. His heart went from elation to cold fear. On the screen: his wife stood naked and spread-eagled with wrists and ankles chained in restraints. Her skin glistened, her hair hung loose and damp from sweat and tears streamed down her face. The only visible wounds were a bandaged calf, bruised cheek, and a deep red welt across her thigh. The only sound was her pained weeping.

Jeffrey Holland stood behind her holding a long, thin cane. He drew back much like a major league hitter ready to hit one out of the park. The instant cane met flesh, a wrenching scream tore from Savannah's lips, her body falling limp in the restraints. She gasped for air, her chest heaving in a laborious effort to fill her lungs. Then, pulling on her wrists, she used the chains to struggle back to her feet.

Like a train wreck, Ennis stood frozen, unable to turn away from the carnage and devastation before him. Someone sent the horrifying video to Savannah to remind her, to make her relive every moment of her suffering. She'd never want him to see this, he thought, she'd be mortified and furious.

On the video, Jeffrey drew back again and Ennis, his hand shaking now, scrambled to turn it off, to erase the image from his mind, to quiet the boiling nausea. His fingers slipped, allowing another crack of the cane and another piercing scream to split the room's silence. Finally, he thumbed the off button just before the cane landed across her lower back.

Ennis prayed Savannah hadn't heard the screams in the bedroom. Ripping the DVD from the player, he watched the bedroom door, listening for any sound. He waited, his heart pounding, his body a storm of fear, dread and sickness.

A soft chuckle floated from behind the door. Ennis released a long tremulous breath. Good, she was on the phone with Georgia. He hurried to the table where he left the envelope. Shoving his hand inside, he pulled out a note. On the paper were four simple words. "See you soon. Cole."

A swell of rage built inside Ennis. He'd never felt hatred in his life but the past few weeks introduced him to it. With Savannah still in the bedroom, he gathered up the note, DVD and envelope. He ripped the note into tiny pieces then unleashed his anger on the DVD, breaking it until only a pile of bits remained. He was still in shock and reeling from the horrifying images and sounds now branded into his brain. He'd never heard her scream in such agony and he'd never forget the sound of it.

Ennis stuffed the envelope and remnants of the note and DVD far into the garbage, burying it under catalogs and other trash. He'd just received the biggest gift in weeks. A smile from his wife. Now the threat returned and she would *not* find out about it. Neither Cole nor Jeffrey would claim Savannah as their victim, not on his watch.

He rifled his jeans pocket for the phone number Georgia gave him. Selling the house still required time to study their finances. If he called right now, it equated a knee-jerk reaction to the DVD. First he needed to provide security for his wife. Physical security. But how? The last week took a hit on his paid vacation. Staying home without pay certainly didn't help circumstances. And installing a security system would cost major big-time bucks.

Well, it couldn't hurt to call the realtor just to see what was available – and what their place was worth. As he dialed the phone, Ennis made a vow to himself and Savannah. If Cole Jordan was stupid enough to show his face, he would not be leaving in handcuffs like Jeffrey had. He would leave in a body bag.

J.L. Lemon lives in Texas surrounded by a loving and supportive family, two adorable and devoted puppies, and hordes of garden gnomes.

Before 2002, J.L. Lemon wrote opinions and product reviews for an online consumer guide. When fellow reviewers cited the author's knack for humor, she decided to return to writing fiction. Along with the standalone title Second Chances, she's published 7 books in the Savannah Stories Series with 2 more in the works.